W9-AAI-856

MURDER IS A MORTAL SIN

Young, worldly, and a little cynical, Father Koesler struggles to serve God and man as both city and Church reel from the uncertain tides of change.

Then the Rosary Murders begin, terrorizing the city, captivating the entire country.

Finally, Father Koesler prepares to hear the most soul-wracking confession of his career. . .

THE ROSARY MURDERS

WILLIAM X. KIENZLE

BANTAM BOOKS
TORONTO · NEW YORK · LONDON

*This low-priced Bantam Book
has been completely reset in a type face
designed for easy reading, and was printed
from new plates. It contains the complete
text of the original hard-cover edition.*
NOT ONE WORD HAS BEEN OMITTED.

THE ROSARY MURDERS

*A Bantam Book / published by arrangement with
Andrews & McMeel, Inc.*

PRINTING HISTORY
*Andrews & McMeel edition published April 1979
3 printings through May 1979
Mystery Guild selection Spring 1979
Literary Guild edition June 1979
Doubleday Book Club edition September 1979
Bantam edition / March 1980
2nd printing
3rd printing*

*Cover photo by Malcolm Pinney,
courtesy of Andrews & McMeel, Inc.*

*All rights reserved.
Copyright © 1979 by William X. Kienzle.
This book may not be reproduced in whole or in part, by
mimeograph or any other means, without permission.
For information address: Andrews & McMeel, Inc.,
6700 Squibb Road, Mission, Kansas 66202.*

ISBN 0-553-13471-X

Published simultaneously in the United States and Canada

*Bantam Books are published by Bantam Books, Inc. Its trade-
mark, consisting of the words "Bantam Books" and the por-
trayal of a bantam, is Registered in U.S. Patent and Trademark
Office and in other countries. Marca Registrada. Bantam
Books, Inc., 666 Fifth Avenue, New York, New York 10019.*

PRINTED IN THE UNITED STATES OF AMERICA

Gratitude for technical advice to Margaret Cronyn, editor of *The Michigan Catholic;* Jim Grace, detective with the Kalamazoo Police Department; and Kim Rezin Knight, R.N.

For Fiona, the sine qua non.

THE ROSARY MURDERS

"Was it an interesting funeral?"

Father Bob Koesler stubbed out his third afterdinner cigarette. Dinners at old St. Ursula's rectory were painfully elongated experiences for Koesler for the simple reason that he tore through his food like a starving European child, while Father Paul Pompilio, pastor at St. Ursula's, toyed with his.

Father Pompilio carefully cut a sliver of meat from his porterhouse, placed the knife beside his plate, transferred the fork from his left hand to his right, and began to swirl the meat in its juice. "Not particularly. You've seen one priest's funeral, you've seen 'em all."

Koesler lit another cigarette. There were a million places he'd rather be, but, for politeness' sake, he always waited until Pompilio finished eating. Which was always a good forty-five minutes after Koesler finished. Which was not helping Koesler's effort to cut down on cigarettes.

"Was Monsignor O'Brien there?"

Pompilio's fork and knife were resting on his plate as he thoughtfully chewed a morsel of steak. "Old O'Brien? It wouldn't have been a valid priest's funeral without O'Brien. He was there, all right, from the first psalm of the Office for the Dead until they wheeled the body out the door. They were great buddies, you know." Pompilio resumed knife and fork and began sawing away at another cut of meat. "Old Father Larry Lord and O'Brien. Funny thing. Before they closed the lid on the casket, O'Brien tried on Lord's glasses—took them right off the old man's face and tried 'em on. Looked around the church, decided his own were better, put the glasses back on Lord, and

I

went back to his pew like nothing happened. It's a good thing O'Brien didn't need teeth."

Koesler's stomach turned. He was glad he'd finished eating. Pompilio built a forkful of mashed potatoes.

"How was the sermon?" Koesler asked, crushing out his fourth afterdinner cigarette. He had tried early on to monopolize dinner conversations on the chance that, with nothing to do but eat, Pompilio would finish sooner. But by actual measured time, Koesler had discovered that it didn't make any difference.

"The arch is out of town, as you know . . ." Pompilio speared his last sliver of meat. ". . . so Bishop Donnelly gave the sermon. Same old Donnelly stuff, very spiritual. Told how Lord had died on Ash Wednesday. How significant that was. Can't see it myself. Good Friday, maybe. But Ash Wednesday just isn't a very significant day to die. By the way . . ." Pompilio shoved aside his well-scoured plate and tinkled the small bell that stood next to it. Sophie, five feet in every direction, entered the room, cleared the table, and served coffee. ". . . why weren't you at the funeral?"

Koesler lit another cigarette. "Couldn't. Had negotiations with the newspaper guild. Contract's up in another couple of months."

Koesler was priest-editor of the diocesan weekly paper. He wasn't exactly assigned to St. Ursula's. He was in residence there, said Mass daily and Sundays, heard confessions, helped out as much as he could. But his primary assignment was at the paper. He sipped his black coffee. "Did anyone say anything about the plug?"

"Plug? What plug?" Pompilio stirred the third spoonful of sugar into his coffee.

"Come on, Pomps," Koesler chuckled. "You know there's a rumor that somebody at St. Mary's Hospital pulled the plug on Lord. Not that anyone, including God, would mind. The poor old guy had no place to go but out."

"Now that you mention it, there was some talk about that rumor at the priests' brunch after the funeral. Say, Bob, if you print any of this," Pompilio was grinning from ear to ear, "you will protect your sources, won't you?"

Koesler grinned back. Of all people on earth, Pompilio would be among those who most wanted to see their names in print. The problem, as usual, was not protecting sources but keeping the whole damn story out of the paper. He remembered just a few weeks back. Tony Vespa, the newly appointed Archdiocesan Delegate for the Laity, had called and asked if the *Detroit Catholic* would consider running an "Action Line" similar to the column in the *Free Press* that solved everybody's problems. He had explained, "Look, Tony, besides the expense of hiring a staff to run a column like that, most of the problems Catholics have with the institution don't have solutions." Tony, after careful consideration, had withdrawn his suggestion.

"Don't worry, Pomps, you'll be well protected. But, go on, did the guys at the luncheon think it really happened?"

There wasn't any question of anything like that appearing in the diocesan paper. Koesler was simply a mystery buff. He read mystery novels like some priests read the Bible. He loved a mystery. And he felt this was as close to a real-life mystery as he was likely to get.

"Disputatur apud peritos." Pompilio didn't know much Latin, but when he tripped over an appropriate phrase like "The experts are in dispute," he liked to throw it in for everyone's amazement. "Some thought yes. Others, no. Jack Battersby made a great point that according to Church teaching, nobody is bound to use extraordinary means to support life, and all those tubes and plugs certainly could be described as extraordinary. Ed Carberry, who, as you know, is still in the thirteenth, the greatest of centuries, argued that God was surely reducing Father Lord's purgatory time with all that added suffering, and to shorten his time of expiration was thwarting God's plan and so, against the Natural Law—or some damn thing—and gravely sinful."

Koesler, now bored, was about to yield to a gigantic distraction.

"However," Pompilio droned on, "Pete Baldwin's sister

is a nurse at St. Mary's. And she told Pete somebody at the hospital definitely detached Lord's respirator system. And that finally put the old man out of his misery."

Koesler, alert to the first bit of genuine news, fought off his distraction. "You mean they actually know the respirator was unplugged?"

"According to Pete's sister, yes."

"Is anybody at the hospital trying to find out who did it?"

"I dunno. I get the idea that if it actually happened— and remember, Father Editor, this is still rumor—nobody at the hospital wants to know."

"Did anyone call the police?"

"I don't think so. If anybody did, there'd have to be an investigation. Pete, who seems to know more about this than I would have given him credit for, says the police couldn't sweep something like this under the rug. If they knew about it, they'd have to investigate, and if they found who did it, there'd be a prosecution. I guess nobody at the hospital wants that. Especially a Catholic hospital with a dead Catholic priest whom nobody cared about anyway."

"I'll bet they don't." For the umpteenth time, Koesler found himself wishing he belonged to a somewhat more legitimate news medium instead of being boss of what was little more than a religious house organ. Nevertheless, he felt drawn to speculate about who might have done it. He pictured a holy nun—one still covered from head to toe with yards and yards of habit—stealthily entering Lord's quiet room, looking every which way to be sure no one was watching, then, with utmost compassion, jerking the plug out of the wall socket. Then, later, in great remorse, confessing her sin. Or maybe it was an agnostic doctor strolling into Lord's room. No one around. He casually lifts his foot and kicks the plug out. Leaves the room. Thinks nothing of it. Never will.

"So the consensus seems to be that Lord's unplugged respirator is gonna be swept under the institutional rug, eh?" Koesler asked, lighting yet another cigarette. He counted the butts in the ashtray. This was his sixth. He shook his head.

"Guess so." Pompilio had finished his coffee. There was the usual residue of undissolved sugar at the bottom of his cup. He gave a little shove to the table. Nothing moved. It was just a signal that the dinner ritual was concluded. "Funny thing, though, about the rosary Lord was holding when he died."

"What's that?"

"It wasn't his."

"Wasn't his?"

"Didn't belong to him. Lord's rosary was mother-of-pearl. It was in the drawer of the table near his bed. The rosary he was holding was an ordinary black one. But I guess a rosary is a rosary is a rosary."

Nelson Kane, city editor of the *Detroit Free Press*, stood looking around his large, rectangular, well-lit city room. As usual, at least whenever he was there, the dozens of reporters seemed to be developing Pulitzer Prize–winning stories. On those rare occasions when Kane wasn't there, feet were propped on desks and typewriters, mobs formed at the coffee machine, after-hours dates were made, and gossip passed. Fortunately for the paper's welfare, Kane was usually there, barking orders and being generally unsatisfied and demanding.

Kane was looking for Joe Cox. Cox had come to the *Free Press* only three months before with an award-winning book under his belt and excellent references. For years, the *Free Press* had had no religion writer as such. Kane learned quickly from experience, and he had experienced a memory full of inaccuracies from past religion specialists. Cox was a staff writer, and a good one, who, among other things was given most of the religious assignments. He handled them well.

Cox came in and had just reached his desk when Kane spotted him.

"Cox!" Kane's practiced tone rose well above the noise of typewriters and ringing phones.

Cox smiled at his master's voice and hurried over to Kane's centrally located desk.

"Did you check that hospital lead?" Kane talked around his never-removed cigar.

"Yup."

"And?"

"And nothing. I talked to just about everyone on the floor Father Lord was on. Nurses, nuns, orderlies, nurses' aides, doctors, interns, even the chaplain. Couldn't get anything from anybody. Not even for nonattribution."

"What did your gut tell you?"

"It happened."

"Goddammit, I know it happened! Are the cops in on this at all?"

"I don't think so. I made the tour of headquarters, real slow, and nobody's movin' on it."

"Whaddya think?"

"Catholic hospital, Catholic priest, they don't wanna admit they got a problem."

"Any more leads?"

"One. There's a nurse I talked to, a . . ." Cox flipped through his small notebook. "a . . . Nancy Baldwin. She just didn't seem too sure of herself."

"How's that?"

"Nobody wanted to talk about no plug in no respirator. But she hesitated. Like she really did want to talk—or already had—to somebody. I thought I'd give her a day or so and get back to her. The story's still there. All locked up in the priests' pasture at Mt. Olivet Cemetery. It won't go away."

"And it won't get so old nobody cares. Not a Catholic priest getting knocked off in a Catholic hospital. That's the closest to an eternal story we got at this goddam paper."

"Right, Nellie."

"Stay on it and keep me informed."

"Right."

Joe Cox, Kane mused, was his kind of reporter. Just as interested in and dedicated to a breaking news story as Kane ever was. With the young legs Kane no longer had.

It was Wednesday, the day the *Detroit Catholic* weekly
newspaper was put together and sent to Brown Printing
for publication. It was also one week, to the day, since
Father Lawrence Lord had died at St. Mary's Hospital.

Father Koesler pondered as he paced back and forth in
his cluttered office at the paper on Forest Avenue close to
downtown Detroit. There had been no mention of the unplugged respirator in any of the local media. There certainly would be no mention of it in the *Detroit Catholic*. It
would be a straight priest's obit, on the bottom of page
one: picture, brief biography, length of service, number of
buildings built, survivors, interment. In Lord's case, there
would be lots of buildings but no survivors. Few besides
priests and other bachelors left no survivors, Koesler
mused.

Maybe there was no unplugged plug. It was, after all,
just a rumor. And the other media, particularly the two
daily papers, had the means to dig out the story if it were
really there. If they had, it would have been the *Detroit
Catholic*'s lot to react and defend the hospital in every way
possible. Koesler had learned long ago that the guys in
the chancery, from the archbishop on down, didn't like
waves. They could live with criticism being aimed at almost anybody or anything, as long as the target was not a
member of the Catholic institution, especially another bishop. They were particularly happy when a controversial
Catholic doctrine, such as abortion, divorce, or birth control, was being defended. On that score, they were often
not happy with the *Detroit Catholic*. However, the archbishop had never suggested that Koesler be removed as edi-

tor. And that, in this day and age, Koesler reflected, was no small virtue.

The tall, thin, blond priest's pacing was interrupted when Irene Casey appeared in the doorway. "The editorial page is done, Father; do you want to look it over before we pack it up? And do you want another cup of coffee? It's going fast."

Dear Irene. She'd been with the paper nearly fifteen years. It wasn't a great deal of money, but it did help get her five kids through an increasingly expensive parochial school system. Irene, technically, was women's editor. But on a publication with the *Catholic*'s small staff, everyone did a little bit of everything.

"No, thanks, Irene, I don't want any more coffee. And, yes, I'd like to see the editorial page. Did you change anything in my editorials?"

"Does the pope change anything in the Bible?"

"It probably hasn't occurred to him."

Koesler was on his way into the editorial office when his phone rang. He backtracked.

"Father Koesler," he said guardedly into the phone. As often as not, he was greeted on the office phone by a hostile voice. He figured he got more calls and letters from Catholic nuts than any other priest in the archdiocese.

"Father, you don't know me. I don't live in St. Ursula's parish, but I go there every Sunday for Mass. I've got a problem, and I wondered if I could talk to you about it?"

"Why me? Father Pompilio is home at the rectory today. Or there must be a priest in a parish near where you live . . ."

"This is a complicated problem, Father. And I . . . well, I like your sermons and the things you write in the paper and I just . . . I'd rather talk with you if you could give me just a few minutes." Her voice was strained and shaky with emotion.

"Well, O.K. then. What's it about?"

"I'd rather not say over the phone, Father. Could I come and see you? I know where your office is, and I drive."

"All right. When do you want to come?"

"Well, this is my day off. I could come this afternoon if that would be convenient with you."

"Two o'clock?"

"That would be fine."

"All right. There's a parking lot next to our building. Use that . . . this is not your Grosse Pointe neighborhood. By the way, can you tell me your name?"

"Nancy Baldwin. I'll see you at two."

Nancy Baldwin. The name rang a bell. Could she be Father Pete Baldwin's sister, the nurse? And, if so, why wouldn't she see Pete instead of him? Koesler was still wondering about that as he entered the editorial office.

Sister Ann Vania, a tall, handsome woman in her middle thirties, was preparing the second graders of St. Alban's parish in Dearborn for their first communion. Sister Ann (she had been known as Sister Paschal before her order decided to return their real names to the sisters as part of post-Conciliar renewal) was religious coordinator at St. Alban's. As such, she was responsible for the religion program for the entire parish. As a professional administrator, she seldom got involved in actual teaching. But second graders and their first communion were a special delight to her, and she would delegate their training to no one.

"Michael, can you tell us the story of the Good Samaritan?"

"Yes, Sister. There was this guy who was goin' somewheres. And some bad guys jumped him and beat him and mugged him and cut him up and . . ."

"That'll be enough of the violence, Michael. Go on with the story."

". . . they wouldn't help him. And then this Summertan . . ."

"Samaritan."

"Yes, Sister . . . Samaritan came by. And the guy thought this Samaritan was his enemy. But the Samaritan helped him."

"Very good, Michael. And do you know what the moral of that story is?"

"No."

Sister Ann sighed and suppressed a giggle. "Does any-anyone? Andrea?"

"The moral is that everybody is our neighbor and that we should love everybody. Even people who want to hurt and kill us."

"Do you think you could love somebody who wanted to hurt and kill you, Andrea?"

"Yes, Sister."

Sister Ann didn't think she could go quite that far her-self. Fortunately, she knew of no one who wanted to hurt or kill her.

It was two o'clock. Father Koesler had been helping proofread for the past four hours, with a break for a sandwich and coffee, and he'd forgotten his appointment. Judy Anderson, the receptionist, bobbed briefly into the editorial room. "Your appointment's here, Father."

Appointment . . . appointment . . . ah, yes, Nancy Bald-win. "O.K., thanks Judy."

As Koesler moved from the editorial room to his adjoin-ing office, he pulled his black suit jacket from the coat rack and slipped it on. Since he was already wearing his clerical collar and vest, he was now in full uniform and ready to face whatever.

He opened the door leading from his office to the recep-tion area, and there was Nancy Baldwin. He recognized her immediately, though he had not hitherto known her name. Ten o'clock Mass on Sundays, toward the middle of the church, left side. Somehow, most regular Massgoers formed the habit of occupying the same place at the same Mass every week.

She was shaking the late winter snow from her imitation fur coat. With her was a small, bundled boy, perhaps five years old.

"Nancy Baldwin, I presume."

"Hello, Father." She smiled.

"Hi, God," said the little boy.

In his twenty years as a priest, Koesler had been called many things. But not until now, "God." He stood staring at the boy, speechless, then glanced at Nancy. "Yours?" he asked.

"Oh no, Father. Billy's my nephew. I'm babysitting today. I'll explain the 'God' bit in a minute. I know this is an imposition, but is there someplace we can leave Billy while we talk?"

"I think I know just the place." He leaned into the editorial room. "Irene . . ." He turned back to Nancy. "Even after five of her own, Irene Casey is still a sucker for little kids."

"Irene, this is Nancy Baldwin and her nephew Billy. Would you please show Billy some of the fun we have putting together a weekly newspaper?"

"I recognize you from your picture in the paper. It's nice meeting you, Mrs. Casey." Nancy extended her hand.

"Pleased to meet you, too, Nancy. Come on, Billy. It's never too early to start a journalism career."

Some people just have a natural way with kids, Koesler thought as Billy trotted off after Irene. If I had invited the kid to come with me, he'd probably have hit the floor kicking and screaming.

"Won't you come into my parlor?" Koesler waved his guest into his office. "May I take your coat?"

Nice trim figure, he thought as he hung up her coat. Carefully pressed pleated skirt, white ruffled blouse under a blue cardigan, small metallic cross on a thin gold chain. Nice legs, nice bottom, small breasts, short wavy hair. He had the intuitive impression she was the proverbial "nice Catholic girl."

"Father, what we talk about, can it be a secret?" She removed a handkerchief from her purse and began winding it through her fingers.

"Sure. If you want to go to confession, that's a very special kind of secret. If you just want to just talk to me, that's a professional secret. In either case, I won't tell anyone whatever it is we'll talk about."

"Oh, good." A brief, nervous smile crossed her lips.

"Are you a nurse at St. Mary's Hospital?"

"How did you know?"

"I won't tell anyone what you tell me. And I can't tell you what somebody else tells me."

"You're just full of secrets, aren't you, Father." There was a trace of bitterness in her voice.

Koesler was angry at himself. This, obviously, was what she had come to discuss, and he had led her into the matter prematurely. He'd been a priest long enough to know that people have their own time to talk about troubling things, and there was no hurrying that time.

"I'm sorry," he said. "Everything in life is not a secret. Your name came up in a conversation about Father Lord's funeral. You were supposed to have said that his death might not have been due to natural causes."

"It must have been my brother, Father Pete." She was slightly flustered. Koesler didn't know if he could recoup the moment and gain her trust. "But I didn't actually say that to Pete. I tried to tell him about Father Lord's death, but he got so excited he scared me and I couldn't. I just couldn't. Sometimes Pete hears what he wants to hear."

"I see. Would you like some coffee?"

"No, Father."

He let things be quiet for a while. She had to have a chance to think it out. She spent perhaps a couple of minutes—it seemed much longer—staring intently at the handkerchief she had tortured through her fingers. Finally, she raised her eyes to Koesler very calmly. Unsure if she were ready to tell her story, he said, "You were going to tell me about why your nephew called me 'God.'"

She laughed. "I never thought it would turn out that way. I live very near my sister and brother-in-law—Billy's their child—and sometimes I take him with me to church on Sunday. To keep him quiet, I tell him that's God up there at the altar and he shouldn't disturb God. Only it's usually you up at the altar. I didn't think he'd put the two thoughts together. But when he saw you here today . . ."

"Gotcha." Talk about Santa Claus and the Easter Bunny! This was wild. But it was all in the interest of peace and quiet in church and, he thought, he'd drink to that.

They seemed to be on friendly terms again. The time appeared to be right.

"Now, would you like to tell me about it?"

"Yes, Father, I would. I've got to tell someone. And I want to tell you. Are you sure this will be between just the two of us?"

"You have my word."

"Well, it really did happen. Someone disconnected Father Lord's respirator. And that's what killed him. It didn't kill him much before he would have died anyway. But it—the lack of a life support system—caused his death."

She paused. Koesler said nothing. Nor did he show any sign of emotion, though he was slightly shocked. He'd learned long ago that when people tell a priest—or, he supposed, a minister or a psychotherapist—something shocking, they knew damn well it was shocking and they needed no response, not even a raised eyebrow, to confirm their conviction.

Assured they both knew what she was saying, and encouraged by his silence, she continued. "I was the one who found him. Just the day before, he'd been moved to this private room from the intensive care unit. The head nurse on the floor—that's me—was supposed to check him regularly. There was no need for a private duty nurse. God, Father, he was practically dead. We all expected him to slip away at any moment. We just tried to make sure he was as comfortable as possible, that he wasn't in any pain. I'll never forget it. I had just come back from the chapel—it was Ash Wednesday and we'd just received the blessed ashes. I went right to Father Lord's room to check on him. Right away, I noticed there was no chest movement. And there was the smell of death in the room. Do you know what I mean, Father?"

Koesler nodded. He couldn't define or even describe it. But long ago he had discovered, for instance, on entering a home where someone had just died, that there was indeed a very special odor of death. Once you experience it, you never forget it.

"I checked for his pulse. There was none. And then I saw the plug hanging loose by his bed. My first impulse was to reconnect it. But that would've been futile. He was gone. If he had been a younger person, I'd have called for emergency equipment. But Father Lord had been hanging on by a very fragile thread. It was just too late for anything." She paused again, this pause clearly indicating she was finished with her story.

"And now, Nancy?"

"And now, Father, I don't know what to do. And I feel just all torn up."

"Does anyone else at the hospital know? I mean, for sure?"

"The only one I know knows for sure is Sister Mildred, the supervisor on my floor. I got her right after I discovered Father was dead, and showed her the disconnected respirator. She didn't know what to do, either. We sort of agreed that someone in the hospital tried to do Father a favor and didn't know he or she was committing a crime. Sister Mildred decided that, all things considered —Father's condition and all—that it would be better to say nothing. She put the plug back in its socket. And that's where things stand right now."

"It's not possible that Father Lord might have made one of those 'living wills' or that some authorized person, like his doctor, might have done this?"

"Not to the best of my knowledge. And I really would have been informed of something like that."

"The police haven't been called, nor have they investigated Father's death, have they?"

"No. They don't ordinarily investigate hospital deaths unless they're called."

Koesler hesitated. He knew what had to be done. And he was pretty sure Nancy knew also. She only wanted, he surmised, to be encouraged. But cautiously.

"Nancy, in effect, you're living a rather crucial lie. The longer it continues, the worse it's going to get, and the worse you're going to feel." Her face brightened slightly and the furrows in her brow smoothed almost imperceptibly. Yes, this was right and she knew it. "Right now, you're aiding and abetting a crime. But I'm quite sure it's not too late. If I were you, I'd go to the police and tell them the whole story. Undoubtedly, it would be good to clear it first with Sister . . . what's her name?"

"Mildred."

". . . Mildred. But no matter how she reacts, I'd go to the police in any case. I'm sure they will not hold it against you. And I can't see them sending a sweet little old nun up the river. But this *is* a crime, and it has to be investigated. Whoever did it, probably, as you suggest, had noble motives. Whoever it is, all things considered, I wouldn't mind being the accused's attorney. It wouldn't take Perry Mason to get him or her off lightly."

It was evident nearly all the tension was gone. Nancy had relaxed the rigid position she'd held throughout the interview. She replaced the now refolded handkerchief in her pocketbook.

"I can't thank you enough, Father. I guess I knew all along what I had to do. I just needed someone to say it."

"You're welcome, Nancy. This is still going to be rough and I'll pray for you. It's going to be a can of worms. But, sometimes it's just necessary to open the can."

"Yes, Father. Oh . . ." She rummaged through her pocketbook. ". . . there's something I wanted to give you." She produced a small black rosary. "This is the rosary Father Lord was holding when he died. It wasn't his. His was a mother-of-pearl rosary. When we prepared his body for the mortician, we sent his rosary with him. He was such a holy man, I kept this—sort of like a relic. I'd like you to have it."

"Thank you, Nancy. I'll prize it." He slipped it into his pants pocket where it clinked against the rosary he always carried. You can never have too many rosaries, he thought, though he was coming close.

He helped Nancy on with her coat. As she buttoned it, she looked into the editorial room. "Come on, Billy, we're leaving." There followed the pitter-patter of little feet.

Koesler accompanied them to the door leading to Forest Avenue.

"Good-bye, Father. And thanks again, more than I can say."

"Good-bye, Nancy. And, good luck, God be with you."

"Goo'bye, God," said the almost forgotten Billy.

"So long, kid." After all, it was in the interest of quiet in church.

Everything was about to hit the fan. Only, Koesler had no notion that this was not the beginning of the end but the end of the beginning.

**FRIDAY
MARCH 4**

St. Mary's Mercy Hospital on Detroit's northwest side was gigantic. Partly due to its location—it was in one of those increasingly rare neighborhoods that had not yet "changed" much, ethnically or racially—and partly due to its isolation—no other comparably large hospital was nearby—St. Mary's was one of the few Detroit hospitals that was not considering consolidation. On the contrary, St. Mary's had just added a new wing.

Mondays through Fridays at least, St. Mary's functioned at full efficiency. Nearly all its beds were always occupied. Nurses, each with her distinctive cap displaying the coded information of her classification and place of graduation, hurried through the hallways, always appearing to be three patients behind, which was usually the case. Orderlies wheeled carts through the halls with an abandon that could cripple a visitor. Patients shuffled through the corridors clutching their hospital gowns at the revelatory rear. Internists, stethoscopes propped in pockets, ambled about as if they owned the place, which they virtually did. And surgeons skulked, head and shoulders bent, as if they had just supervised someone's death, which sometimes they had.

In all of this, St. Mary's was not unlike the public hospitals in Detroit. But St. Mary's was a Catholic hospital and that showed in subtle ways. Morning and evening prayers were broadcast over the hospital intercom. And, most distinctively, there were the nuns patroling the corridors and rooms somewhat more purposefully than any other personnel. The nuns came in various ages and sizes—and various garbs, largely depending on their age. Most of the older sisters still wore the ancient, full habit

16

that so delighted conservative eyes. The younger the nun, the more the habit seemed to diminish. The very youngest sisters wore uniforms not dissimilar to the nurses, with an identifying veil worn off the forehead and, usually, a small crucifix either on a chain or pinned to the uniform.

With the hospital chaplain, the nuns formed something quite recent in Catholic hospital history—the pastoral team. Together they handled much of the spiritual counseling. They comforted the suffering, consoled terminal patients and their relatives, even joined in charismatic prayer. As a pastoral care department, the nuns joined the priest-chaplain in all spiritual activities in the hospital, with the sole exception of dispensing sacraments. That remained in the chaplain's consecrated hands.

It was precisely this—trying to determine whether to anoint one of the patients with the oil of the sick—that was puzzling Father Blaise Donovan, St. Mary's Franciscan chaplain. At one time, this rite had been known by the foreboding title of Extreme Unction. The name alone was able to scare a terminally ill patient from this world to the next. Now, it was more kindly called The Sacrament of the Sick.

At this moment, Father Donovan was trying to determine if he should anoint Mrs. Eulalie Harris, one of St. Mary's few Catholic black patients. The problem was that Mrs. Harris' parish priest had visited her in the hospital, and Father Donovan did not know whether the other priest had anointed her. He did not want to repeat the ritual needlessly.

"When Father Maher visited you, Mrs. Harris, did he anoint you?"

"Ah don't rightly know, Fathah."

"Did he pray over you?"

"Oh, yes, Fathah, he sho' did. Long time."

"Did he do anything else?"

"Oh, yes suh, Fathah, he sho' did."

"What did he do?"

"He greased me."

Marvelous answer. If Father Maher had greased Eulalie Harris, there was no reason why Father Donovan should do it again.

Outside Mrs. Harris' room, a nurse's aide overturned a tray full of breakfast dishes. Startled, an orderly dropped a filled bedpan. Everything was proceeding normally.

Except on the administrative floor. There, everything had indeed become chaotic.

There was no logical reason for the enormous number of police officers roaming St. Mary's administrative floor. In a city like Detroit, with its reputation for being the "murder capital of the world," the death of an old man for whom no one really cared could scarcely be called the crime of the century, even if technically it seemed to be murder. There was only one explanation for all the cops milling about St. Mary's. The Detroit Police Department's massive response was in direct proportion to the splashy publicity the case had received, especially in the *Free Press,* where the story had broken just that morning.

Actually, only a small group of police, a crack team of homicide investigators, was actually doing the work. The others were there to complete the showcase of total involvement. Some of the extras in this drama were drinking coffee in a kind of unannounced competition to see who could drink more. Others were exchanging trade gossip. Others were evaluating passing nurses. Three points for a perky rear, three for firm breasts, two for a trim waist, and three for legs. Few of these headless anatomical studies reached a full eleven.

Earlier, statements had been taken from Sister Mildred and Nurse Baldwin, supervisor and head nurse, respectively, on the floor where Father Lord had died. It had been a trying experience for Detective Sergeant Daniel Fallon, a veteran of twenty years on the force, particularly when he interviewed Sister Mildred. Fallon was the product of twelve years in parochial schools and, like most who shared the experience, he had the unspoken impression that there were men, women, and nuns.

"Sister, how good or bad would you say the security is on your floor?"

"Are you suggesting, young man . . ." Sisters, if they were in the proper frame of mind, no matter what their age, were able to make grown men, no matter what *their* age, feel like little boys again. And Sister Mildred was definitely in the proper frame of mind. Detective Sergeant Fallon felt as if he were back in the fifth grade. ". . . that patients on our floor do not receive proper care?"

"Oh, no, Sister. That's not what I had intended at all."

"Because if you are, you are sadly mistaken. Sadly mistaken. Of all the floors of this hospital, no one gets better care than the patients on fourteen. No one. Read the hospital newspaper, if you will. Most of the published letters of gratitude from former patients are from the souls who spent time on fourteen."

"I understand, Sister," he had flushed. "What I meant was, what's the possibility of an outsider—some unauthorized person—gaining admittance to your floor?"

"Practically nil, young man. Do you think we walk around up here with our eyes closed? Oh, no. The staff of this floor is among the most alert in the entire hospital."

When the interview was concluded, Sister Mildred strode from the room calm, cool, collected, and shaking only at her inner core, where no one could see. Fallon, on the other hand, loosened his tie, mopped his brow, and wondered whether he'd ever get over this thing with nuns.

However, as a result of the statements made by Sister Mildred—when she wasn't launching her own offensive—and Nurse Baldwin, who was nervously cooperative throughout, the police had established the time of death as being between 2:45 P.M. and 3:30 P.M., February twenty-third. At 2:45 P.M., Nurse Baldwin had stated, she had checked Father Lord before leaving for the hospital chapel, and all was well. At 3:30 P.M., she had returned to find him dead and the respirator disconnected.

The police homicide team had determined who among the hospital personnel could not account for their presence in the hospital during the time in question. Even now, those employees were being interrogated.

This would not be a difficult case, Fallon thought, compared with many he'd handled. Unless, of course, it turned out the murder had been committed by someone not on the hospital staff. In that case—and, as a firm believer in Murphy's Law, Fallon sighed—this could be rough. And all those cops jawing their asses off out there would be very busy indeed.

Nelson Kane was experiencing one of his rare moments of near-perfect euphoria. He had propped his feet on his desk, a repose in which he seldom indulged, tilted back in his swivel chair, and was savoring the *Free Press'* early edition page-one headline: "PRIEST MURDERED IN CATHOLIC HOSPITAL." He was reminded of the line from Ben Hecht's "Gaily, Gaily," where an editor yells across a crowded city room at a fledgling copyboy, "Do you know what a sex maniac does? Sells newspapers!" That, he reflected, is a service also performed by Catholic priests who are murdered in Catholic hospitals.

Not only was the *Free Press* story a scoop, but it contained an exclusive interview with Nancy Baldwin, the nurse who had discovered the body. Joe Cox's hunch had paid off. He'd gotten his interview with her just before she'd gone to the police. Since then, the cops had forbidden her to speak to anyone about the case. And they had frightened her enough so that she literally was talking to no one about it.

Kane's reverie lasted only until he sensed that while the cat's feet were on the desk, the mice were being indolent. He stood abruptly and, with that, the city room sprang into action.

At the *Detroit Catholic,* Father Robert Koesler was also staring at the *Free Press* headline. It was strange, he mused, how the media could almost create news. It was true that Father Lord's death was technically murder. It was also true it had happened at a Catholic hospital. But the headline still seemed gross.

The paper's account of events, particularly as Nancy Baldwin had viewed them, was fair enough. But it was anyone's guess how many readers took time to plow all the way through the story. Most conversation would be limited to that screaming headline.

In the recent past, most priests had made news because of their civil rights involvement or antiwar protests. More recently, because they'd decided to leave the priesthood. It was really rare, however, for a priest to be murdered.

In addition, this was an old, tired priest who had been a step away from natural death. True, his life had been taken prematurely. But probably by someone who thought the deed was a kindness.

Koesler's reflection was interrupted by Irene Casey. "May I interrupt you, Father?" Irene always began her interruptions by asking permission. Pulling a chair up to Koesler's desk, she sat opposite him. She handed him a slightly deformed paperback. "I finished this last night," she said.

Accepting the book with a smile, Koesler seemed to weigh it in his hand. It was Thomas Gifford's *The Cavanaugh Quest,* only it was half again as large as it had been when Koesler had lent it to Irene. "Been reading in the bathtub again, eh, Irene?" In the Casey household, one of the few relatively guaranteed retreats, apparently, was the bathroom. Every time Koesler loaned Irene a whodunit, it was returned swollen from the tub's vapors.

She blushed. "Listen, you're lucky to get it back this soon. If I didn't read it in the bathroom, I wouldn't have time to read it anywhere, except maybe here. And you wouldn't want me to read it on company time, would you?"

"Good grief, no. This is a newspaper. You're supposed to write, not read. Did you like it?"

"Uh-huh. It would've been better if you lived in Minneapolis. But it did move at a good pace. But what do we need with Minneapolis murders? We've got our own Catholic murder mystery right here in Detroit."

"I'm painfully aware of that."

"Say, Father, that Baldwin girl in this morning's *Free Press* story. Wasn't she the one who was in here to see you the other day?"

"Yes."

"I thought so. You're famous, even though they didn't mention you in the paper. By the way, have you given any thought to how we're going to handle the story this week?"

"Well, it's still developing, Irene. I wouldn't be surprised if the police find out who did it before Wednesday. But, in the meantime, you might call Father Leo Clark at St. John's Seminary. He's an up-to-date theologian with a special interest in medical-moral ethics. He'll probably give us some good quotes on euthanasia. And I don't think any of the other media would think of contacting him. He'll be our exclusive interview."

"Sounds good. Do you want me to ask Jim Pool to get started on that today?"

"Yeah, sure, why not? The story's not going to change that much in the next few days."

Irene Casey left Koesler's office, and Koesler returned to his ponderous thoughts on news as it is improvised by the news media.

The homicide team was concluding its first day of investigation at St. Mary's Hospital. They had narrowed the probable suspects to five employees who could not satisfactorily account for their presence in the hospital during the time in question. Two practical nurses, two orderlies, and a foreign intern. All had been advised to remain available for further questioning. All had been interrogated, finally, by Sergeant Fallon.

Fallon strongly suspected that one of the orderlies and one of the practical nurses had found a vacant hospital room and had enjoyed a quick roll in bed. Once they realized the alternate consequences of not being able to account for their time, he was sure they would confess to a slight case of lust. Fallon's favorite suspect, at the moment, was the Filipino intern. He had seemed more remote than the others during questioning, and everyone knew that Asians had less respect for life than Americans did.

However, Fallon promised himself, he'd begin bright-eyed and objective first thing tomorrow morning.

St. Ursula's convent was clearly a white elephant. It was the most recent in a pile of old buildings that made up the parish facilities. It had been built only twelve years before to accommodate a maximum of fourteen nuns. That was before the supply of nuns had dwindled to a trickle in the wake of Vatican Council II, before the riot of 1967 had driven the white population—and thus most of the Catholics—out of Detroit, and before the U.S. Supreme Court had denied public monies for parochial schools.

Now, St. Ursula's school had been leased by the public school system and the convent would have been closed entirely, except that two nuns continued to live there. Sister Marie Van Antwerp was on the Mayor's Committee for a New Detroit and Sister Ann Vania was religious coordinator at St. Alban's parish in Dearborn. Both nuns wanted to demonstrate some kind of commitment to the city and so had chosen to live in a core area. Sister Marie was in Washington, D.C. for a five-day seminar on urban planning. That left Sister Ann alone in the rambling building. Her fellow workers in Dearborn had tried to persuade her to stay in the suburb while Sister Marie was gone rather than live alone in the city. But she was unwilling to confirm their prejudices about the city by showing her fear of it. In the deepest recesses of her soul, she did fear the city. But she loved the people who had, in effect, been sentenced to live there. And she refused to abandon them.

It was about 9 P.M. when she returned to St. Ursula's. As she parked in the parish garage that separated the rectory from the convent, she noticed that Father Koesler's car was not there. She was disappointed. She had wanted to talk with him this evening about a lot of things that had been troubling her lately. Chiefly, she was beginning to doubt whether working in the lily-white suburb was what she might do best. She knew the people who lived there could no more help wanting a safe life for their families than most of the white and black people in Detroit could help being trapped by the city. She guessed she just wanted to be assured she was justified, and Father Koesler was good at reassuring. Perhaps she would see him tomorrow.

She had her key ready long before she reached the front door of the convent. She did not want to fumble and dally in the dark of the doorway. She let herself in and made certain the door was locked behind her. Most of the convent was closed off and unheated. Actually, only the two small suites used by Sister Marie and herself on the second floor were in use.

Nevertheless, she went first to the old convent chapel and knelt at the rear. It was, of course, no longer used, but the church furnishings were still there, and she liked to end her day where so many nuns before her had prayed.

Her mind went skeletally over her day. The plans that had been made for this Sunday's parish liturgy, the decision to hire a new guitarist for the Folk Mass, and little Andrea, the first communicant, who was too young to fear anyone who might want to hurt or kill her. What a glorious, untested faith.

Just behind her and to her right, a board squeaked. She spun around, her heart pounding wildly. Nothing. Like all old empty houses, this one had developed its own noises and would speak when it willed. She was a fool, she thought. Of course she should remain in Dearborn when she was alone. There was a fine line between courage and foolishness and, she realized, she had crossed that line with her decision to stay alone at St. Ursula's convent.

Crossing herself, she climbed the steps to the second floor, opened the door to her room, and turned on the light. There was heat, but not much. She turned up the radiator slightly, hung up her coat and hat, and sat in the room's one chair. *The Catechist* magazine had been delivered earlier in the day, and this was her first opportunity to read it. She paged through it perfunctorily but was too distracted to absorb anything.

With a sigh, she decided to take a warm bath and go to bed. She flipped on the bathroom's light switch and turned the water on in the tub. A warming steam filled the room. She returned to the bedroom, laid her nightgown on the bed, turned down the covers, and began to undress. She hung her dress in the closet, and dropped her underthings in the clothes hamper. As she stepped toward the bathroom, a board behind her and to her left squeaked. Again she spun around, heart pounding. Instinctively, she attempted to cover herself. Naked, she felt doubly vulnerable. But, again, nothing. This, she decided, would be her last night alone at St. Ursula's. With that, she stepped into the tub and lowered herself into the welcome hot water.

She didn't see him really. He was a blur she caught in the periphery of her vision. In a single step, he slipped around the side of the bathroom door. Just as suddenly, his hands were on her shoulders. He pushed downward, and her head was under the water. At first, her arms and legs flailed about to gain some leverage but found none. Then her hands went to his wrists, but she could not move his determined grip on her shoulders. Her feet braced against the wall beneath the shower head. She pushed against the wall but succeeded only in raising the lower part of her body out of the water. She could see his face distorted by the water above her as she gasped for air and found only water. The distortion was the last thing she saw. In only a few eternal minutes it was over. Her body slumped in death.

He stood erect and leaned against the wall, exhausted. She had been stronger than he had expected. In a minute, he began completing his plan. He slowly lifted her lifeless body from the tub until she was nearly upright, then, with both hands under her armpits, he slammed her head against a jagged tile on the wall, then let her body slip back into the water. He took a towel from the shelf and dried the upper portions of the bathroom walls and some of the pools of water on the floor. He was wearing gloves so there were no prints to clean.

He looked for a moment at the body. She was a tall woman who scarcely fit into the very normal-sized tub. He reached down and pulled her torso toward the foot of the tub until her head sank once more beneath the water. He was finished. But before leaving, he took a small, common black rosary from his pocket and put it carefully into the dead nun's hand. And then he left through the first-floor window through which he had come in. A very ordinary case of breaking and entering.

SATURDAY, MARCH 5

Saturday morning Mass at St. Ursula's was a simple task. It involved rising about a quarter after seven and arriving at the church about a quarter to eight. Fifteen minutes was usually enough time to try to get rid of distractions and to vest.

In its neighborhood, St. Ursula's was both an anachronism and a sore thumb. Externally, it resembled a little rural Italian *chiesa* and bore no relationship to the squat two-story brick and wood homes that surrounded and occasionally shielded it from nearby commercial Gratiot Avenue. It was as if a small chunk of Italy had been dropped into the middle of industrial Detroit.

St. Ursula's interior was an ecclesiastical joke. Nearly every square inch was covered by a religious symbol, painting, or statue. Crudely painted stars covered the ceiling. A saccharine rendition of the Last Supper covered the front wall. And above each of two doors leading from the sacristy to the church were plump pink angels.

Gossip had it that a couple of Italians had been smuggled into the country some forty years before, at about the same time St. Ursula's was being redecorated. They were given sanctuary—literally if illegally—in St. Ursula's basement. In return for pasta and wine, so the story went, they painted the interior. If the story were true, and the wine and pasta were of poor quality, then those two Italian lads had gotten sweet revenge.

Father Koesler was conducting his usual pre-Mass frustrating search for a long alb. He never could comprehend why parishes insisted on buying the floor-length white garment worn under the other Mass vestments only

26

in small and medium sizes. There *were* tall priests. Besides, short priests were able to adjust a too-long alb, but if the alb were too short, there was nothing for a tall priest to do but look ridiculous.

Finally, he found a long alb. One among so many. Looking ridiculous at Saturday morning Mass was not really a serious problem. Only a faithful few could be expected in attendance. If the regular Saturday morning crew were there, he could expect a total of eight, and the service would consume twenty-five minutes, including a three- to five-minute homily. There was no altar boy this morning—only a minor inconvenience. Koesler put the water and wine cruets on the altar and lit two candles. That's all the practical help he'd have received had there been an altar boy. Servers frequently created more problems than they solved.

He began Mass promptly at eight. He was surprised that there was a congregation of only six. Where were the missing sheep, he wondered. As Mass progressed routinely, he made mental notes to determine for his own satisfaction who the guilty parties might be. There was Mrs. Kraemer, second row right center; Mrs. Sommer, third row right center; Mr. and Mrs. Angelo Trupiano (he was St. Ursula's caretaker, janitor, and Mr. Fixit), mid-church left side; and the two black ladies, Mrs. Jones and Mrs. Hastings, holding down the rear. Funny, he thought, how people always occupied their privately established positions even in a nearly empty church.

Missing, of course, were the two nuns. Sister Marie, he remembered, was off in Washington. But where was Sister Ann? He hadn't heard that she was out of town. He'd always considered her a fairly good friend. She seemed to enjoy talking with him, and he admired her obvious sense of dedication. Perhaps she simply had slept in. Though that was unlike her. Perhaps she was ill. She'd be alone in the convent. He decided he'd check after Mass.

As he was finishing Mass, he recalled Gene Flaherty's spoonerism just after English had been introduced to the Mass. "Go," Flaherty had intoned, "the ass is mended." Reportedly, people at that Mass had later confessed they had never before laughed so hard in church. Koesler had to suppress a grin just in the memory.

He blew out the candles and returned the cruets to their place in the sacristy.

He asked Sophie to hold his breakfast for a few minutes while he checked to see how Sister Ann was.

There was no answer. He let the phone ring a full ten times. He began to be worried. If Sister Ann were ill, there was no one to help her. There was no alternative but to go to the convent. But he had no key. He called Angelo and explained the problem. Angelo would meet him at the convent's front door in five minutes.

Koesler had to wait for Angelo no more than a minute or two, but in that short time he grew more gravely concerned. He tried to contrive reasons for the nun's lack of response to the phone and now the doorbell. Maybe she'd stayed in Dearborn last night. Maybe she's a deep sleeper. But his anxiety was mounting in an uncontrolled way.

Angelo greeted him briefly, sensed his concern and, unlocking the door, said no more. Once inside the convent, the two men began calling. "Sister Ann! Sister Ann!" Angelo began to move through the first floor. Koesler climbed to the second. As he approached her suite, he noticed the door was ajar. Standing to one side, he called her name again. No answer. He pushed the door fully open. He noticed her nightgown lying across the bed. His breathing slowed irregularly. Then he saw it. Knees. He would never forget the sight. Knees sticking up out of the tub. She had to be dead.

Still in the hallway, he called to Angelo. The evident panic in the priest's voice brought Angelo up the stairs two at a time. "The bathroom," said Koesler, pointing.

Angelo preceded Koesler into the small bathroom. It was scarcely large enough to contain the two large men. "Should we . . ." Koesler was part way through the question when, without comment, Angelo grasped the woman's knees. Instinctively, Koesler took her beneath her armpits and together they lifted the heavy, dripping body from the tub and placed it on the bathroom floor. It was as they lifted her that Koesler noticed the small rosary in her hand. As the body hit the floor—a little more firmly than the men had intended, since it was wet and slippery —the rosary fell out of the nun's hand. Though Koesler was nearly numb with shock, the thought occurred to him, "What a crazy place to say the rosary!"

As he straightened up, he noticed the dark indented stain on the wall above the tub. His eyes went to the water in the tub. It, too, had a faint brownish discoloration. He stooped and placed his hand beneath Sister Ann's head. He felt the congealed substance matted in her hair.

"She's dead, Father. Better call the cops," said Angelo, with no particular intonation.

"Yes. Of course," replied Koesler, as he stumbled out of the bathroom. "Better not touch anything," he called over his shoulder as he hurried from the bedroom. Now why did I say that? he thought as he hastened to the rectory. We've already mucked about with a lot of evidence.

Just as Koesler completed his call to the Connor Street Police Station, Father Pompilio stepped into the rectory living room. It was impossible to miss the distress on Koesler's face.

Pompilio put his hand on Koesler's shoulder. "What is it? What's wrong, Bob?"

Koesler recounted as quickly as possible what he'd found in the convent, adding, "Paul, it looks like an accident. Just a horrible accident."

"Oh my God! Oh my God! I've got to get over there." Even as Pompilio left the rectory, sirens could be heard, and the police cars pulled up to the convent.

Koesler leaned back in the overstuffed black leather chair and lit a cigarette. Only then did he notice how badly his hands were shaking. And why not? Sister Ann had been a friend. To discover her nude and dead had been deeply shocking. More fundamentally, Koesler had to admit, he'd always had what he could only describe as a natural revulsion for dead bodies. Anything from a dead bird or mouse to a dead human. On those occasions when he'd been called to anoint someone who was apparently dead, it had required a conscious, determined effort to touch those cold, hard, bluish eyes, ears, nostrils, mouth, and hands. Whenever it happened, the rest of the day or night, depending on when he was called, was shot.

He remembered just a couple of months ago on a Saturday, he was eating lunch alone at St. Ursula's when a call came in that one of the parishioners had been found dead and could a priest come. He was the only priest within shouting distance. So he pocketed his sick-call set and walked the two blocks. A crowd of neighbors and the curious had gathered on the sidewalk in front of the house. He stepped through them and up to the front door. Someone had kicked in the glass. He looked in through the door and noticed the police were talking to someone at the rear of the house. Looking down, he saw that a drapery had been thrown down on the other side of the door, probably, he thought, to cover the broken glass. As he stepped through the door frame, his foot touched the drapery, which he unmistakably sensed, covered not glass but the dead man. In horror, he pulled his leg back through the frame. With that, some idiot child on the street began chanting in glee. "He stepped on the dead guy's face! He stepped on the dead guy's face!" The child was precisely correct. And that experience had ended all further thoughts of lunch and even dinner that day.

But Sister Ann! What a loss. She was giving so much of herself. He felt doubly guilty that he had experienced that same revulsion for her in death that he had with everyone else in the past.

The quiescence, the cigarette, and the cup of coffee Sophie had brought him were beginning to have a soothing effect when suddenly he remembered the rosary. The rosary. He remembered thinking the tub an unlikly place to bring a rosary. But there was something else. Something he could not quite place that bothered him.

Of course. He searched his pants pocket and emerged with two rosaries. One his, the other the one the Baldwin girl had given him. The one Father Lord had been found holding. He could not remember exactly, but it seemed that the rosary he had found in Sister Ann's hand was similar to this one.

He'd better get over to the convent.

As Koesler approached the convent, he realized he must have been lost in deep reverie not to have been aware of all this commotion. The entire neighborhood seemed to have gathered.

The crowd easily deferred to Koesler as he made his way from the rectory. "What is it?" "What happened?" "What's going on, Father?"

He could not pause to speak with any of them. "It's an accident. A bad accident," he murmured as he walked quickly toward the convent.

As he reached the front door, he was nearly knocked over by two white-uniformed men who were exiting. Between them was a stretcher holding what must have been Sister Ann's body, wrapped in a plastic container. He'd seen this sight hundreds of times on television and in the movies. But this was the first time he'd ever seen it in reality.

He shuddered. A person's whole life impersonally packaged in plastic. There was a collective gasp from the crowd. They knew what this was. They just didn't know who it was.

By the time Koesler reached the dead woman's room, the various proceedings were nearly concluded. The most evident figure in the room was Father Paul Pompilio. He was doing his best to make sure he would be in this story. Channels 2 and 7 had sent mobile crews. The Channel 7 group was packing its gear. Channel 2 was still filming. In the center of their klieg lights was Pompilio, talking about what a sad day this was for the Church in Detroit that such a tragic accident could remove so vital a religious figure from our midst. Koesler was fairly sure that when the tapes were edited, Pompilio would not be as prominently featured as he obviously hoped. Looking about the room, Koesler recognized Warren Reston of the *Detroit News*. He was talking with one of the six burly policemen in the room and taking notes. There was one other man, whom Koesler didn't know, standing by the wall near the bed. Koesler guessed he must be a newsman or a plainclothes cop. Koesler approached him.

"Excuse me. Are you a police officer?"

"No. Cox with the *Free Press*. If you want to talk to a

cop, the one to see is the guy standing near the bathroom. He's in charge."

"Thanks." Koesler wove his way through the crowded room. As he did, he noticed the small pool of water where he and Angelo had placed the body. But no rosary.

"Excuse me, officer, did you find a rosary on the floor here?"

The policeman, who had been writing on a small pad, looked up. His eyes swept Koesler, starting with the priest's shoes and ending at his eyes. "You the one who found the body?"

"Yes."

"You shouldn'ta moved it."

"I'm sorry. I know we shouldn't. It was just instinct."

"You shouldn'ta moved it." Sergeant Ross believed repetition was the mother of learning. In his precinct in the heart of Detroit, Ross saws lots of bodies, most of them murdered, some of them drug-related assassinations, some of them the famed family quarrel that ends with a gun. Somebody was always fooling around with evidence. It made police work that much harder. It didn't hurt to repeat warnings. "What's your name, Father?"

"Koesler. Robert W."

"Is that K-e-s-s-l-e-r?" he asked as he wrote.

"K-o-e-s-l-e-r."

"We have a statement from . . ." He flipped three pages back in his note pad. ". . . one Angelo Trupiano. Now I'd like to get yours."

Koesler told him the whole story. As he did, he was peripherally aware that the *Free Press* reporter had moved close enough to listen and was also taking notes.

"Now, what's this about a rosary?"

"It was on the floor when I left here."

"I know. We found it. Mr. . . ." He flipped back again. ". . . Trupiano told us the deceased was holding it. Crazy place for a rosary. The bathtub."

"Where is it now, please?"

"We have it. Evidence."

"Of what?"

"In the deceased's death. The cause of death is not yet determined."

"But it looked to me like an accident. It looked like she slipped getting into the tub, was knocked unconscious, and drowned."

"That may be a fair assessment of the present physical evidence." Ross regarded amateur detectives as being as helpful as bunions. "But we won't know till the autopsy. Until then, everything's evidence."

"Autopsy?"

"Routine. What is your interest in the rosary?"

Koesler told the sergeant about Father Lord and the rosary he'd been found holding, about how he—Koesler —had received it, and that he wasn't sure, but he thought the two rosaries were similar. Throughout the statement, Ross's expression remained unchanged as he jotted notes, But Koesler sensed a heightened interest from the reporter, who had now moved closer to them and was writing furiously.

"Do you have this rosary in your possession at the present time?" Ross asked.

"Yes, I have it right here." Koesler fished out both rosaries, separated Lord's from his and returned his own rosary to his pocket.

Ross took a small white envelope from his pocket, made a notation on it and opened it. "Would you please place it in here? We will advise you as to its whereabouts after the investigation is concluded. You will be available here if we need further information?"

"Yes. At least you can reach me at the rectory. Is that all you want me for, now?"

"Just one more thing." Ross closed his note pad and tucked it and his pencil away in his inside jacket pocket. "If you hadn't come over here to see me, I would have come over to see you."

With that they parted.

But Cox was by no means done.

"Excuse me, Father. Could I get a little more information about this rosary business? Did you say the nurse who gave you the rosary was Nancy Baldwin?"

"Yes, she's a nurse at St. Mary's."

He knew. He *knew*. Small world. Same girl from whom he'd gotten his exclusive story on the Lord murder. Cox had Koesler go over the story again to make certain of every detail. He thanked the priest and hurried from the convent.

As he turned onto Gratiot heading downtown, Cox could hardly contain himself. The TV people had locked themselves into an "accidental death" story. If the nun *had* been murdered, the *News* might discover it in time for Sunday's edition. But he, and he alone of the media, had a possible link between the murder of a priest and a nun. If it were true, he was certain the police would not hand out that kind of information. They'd have to prove it, and they'd want to do it quietly. For him, it was an accessible story that would set this town on its ear.

He propped his press card on the dashboard, locked his car, and walked toward the Wayne County Morgue. Since it didn't matter to the dead nun now, he fervently hoped she'd been murdered.

MONDAY,
MARCH 7

It was fortunate for Koesler that he'd been out of town on Sunday. For on Sunday, the *Free Press* had published Joe Cox's story. "MURDER OF PRIEST AND NUN LINKED," screamed the front-page headline. The bugline read, "Rosary Killer?"

By Saturday evening, Koesler had felt wiped out. He called a Franciscan friend at Duns Scotus monastery, and asked if he'd cover Koesler's Mass schedule at St. Ursula's the next day. He told Pompilio—who was flipping back and forth between Channels 2 and 7 to determine which was giving him better exposure—that he'd be out of town until Sunday night, but that the Franciscan would cover his Masses.

After supper, he drove out I-94 to a small cabin on Lake Huron. He and three of his priest classmates had bought the cabin several years before. It was their retreat. No newspapers or television or magazines. Not even a telephone. There he could be alone. Not only was it still very much winter that far north, he was further assured of solitude, because the other priests would be busy Saturday night and Sunday.

And so he had missed the big *Free Press* story, as well as dozens of phone calls.

Now, on Monday, he had just completed the eight o'clock Mass, after which several disturbed parishioners had given him sketchy details of the *Free Press'* Sunday story. He was now addressing a breakfast of cornflakes, bananas, and milk. There was a batch of phone messages from Sunday, all of which had been taken and recorded by Father Pompilio. They were paper-clipped together under a covering note from Pompilio. "Dear Bastard," the note read, "Here are your Sunday calls. The next time you take a goddam Sunday off, hire a secretary."

Koesler smiled and began shuffling through the messages. Most were from friends and fellow priests. There were a few strange names. One of his two sisters had called; so had Nancy Baldwin (he hadn't seen the *Free Press* story yet, but she must have been in that—two big stories featuring her this week, poor girl). Irene Casey had called. She probably wanted to know how the *Detroit Catholic* was going to handle the story now. Finally, there was a message, marked urgent, from Police Lieutenant Walker Koznicki. That name was familiar, but Koesler couldn't quite place where he'd heard it. Probably in one of the papers. A return call was indicated on the lieutenant's message. That looked pretty official, and Koesler resolved to make that call as soon as he finished breakfast.

He didn't have to wait. "There's a call for you, Father," Sophie was shouting from the kitchen. "It's a Lieutenant Koznicki. Do you want to take it now?"

"It's O.K., Sophie. I'll get it in the living room." He

regretted having to leave the crisp cornflakes. The next time he'd see them, they would undoubtedly be soggy. "Hello, Father Koesler here." He could hear Sophie's extension click off.

"Father, this is Lieutenant Walter Koznicki. I've been reading about you in the paper."

"I haven't read it yet. I was out of town yesterday." Ordinarily, Koesler was given to flip repartee on the phone. But, ordinarily, he didn't talk to police lieutenants about what was probably official business.

"I know you were out of town." Koznicki's tone was that of one who somehow knew where everyone was at all times. "I have, of course, read the *Free Press* story. I also have a copy of the statement you gave Sergeant Ross last Saturday."

There was a pause, which Koesler was determined not to fill.

"Father," Koznicki continued, "there are several bits of information we need that only you can give. I wonder if you'd mind stopping by my office this morning. Say, ten o'clock."

"Gee, Lieutenant, I really ought to get down to the *Detroit Catholic* this morning. There are several things that need my . . ."

"Father," Koznicki interrupted, "it is of utmost importance that I see you at ten." There was a perceptible change in his tone. This was no casual invitation. "I'd be glad to send a car . . ."

Wow, Koesler thought, a bit of overkill.

"No, that won't be necessary, Lieutenant. I'll be there. You're at police headquarters on Beaubien?"

"No, I'm in special temporary offices on the fifth floor of the City-County Building. Simply take the elevator to the fifth floor and ask for me."

"Fine, I'll see you at ten." To hell with the cornflakes. Monday was quickly being ruined.

Nelson Kane was treating Joe Cox to breakfast in the modest eatery on the first floor of the Free Press Building.

Kane, slightly more than six feet tall, was in his midforties and fighting the battle of the bulge. Too many beers with the boys after big stories of the past had given him a paunch. Now that he was being considered for an executive position at the *Free Press,* he was trying to get his act together. Two or three times a week, he walked the six long blocks to the downtown YMCA for a workout. He was letting up on food and beer consumption. Not, however, on straight whiskey. He subscribed, philosophically, to the drinking man's diet.

The trick to conversing with Kane was to wait your chance to get a word in edgewise. Ostensibly, Kane had taken Cox to the coffee shop to congratulate him on his clear scoops, two in a row, the second better than the first. This far into breakfast, Kane had been conducting a nonstop monologue on the riot of '67, for the coverage of which the *Free Press* had won a Pulitzer Prize. If humility is truth, then Kane was being humble. For, in objective reasoning, that Pulitzer was primarily due to Kane's ingenuity, imagination, and dedication. That, in three words, was what Kane admired in Cox. A similar kind of ingenuity, imagination, and dedication. The total connotation of these three words was the only explanation for Cox's latest stories.

Cox, seated across the booth from Kane, was almost dwarfed by him. A graduate of Marquette University's School of Journalism, Cox was the type of person who blended into backgrounds. Perhaps five-foot-seven, sandy-haired, clean-shaven except for a full mustache. His eyes were alert, constantly darting as if there were not enough time to absorb all the details of life.

Kane was putting the "30's" on his account of the riot. He ran a hand through his dark, thinning hair and shifted his everpresent cigar to the left side of his mouth. Something like a typewriter carriage, thought Cox.

"We made that goddam news happen, Joe," Kane was winding down. "I mean, it was one of the most goddam satisfying moments I've ever had."

"Yeah, I remember reading it and thinking at the time it would be a great story to cover."

"Not to regret. These latest two stories of yours are great son-of-a-bitch stories."

"There was an element of luck."

"Luck, hell. Nobody else got 'em."

"Yeah, but the whole thing could've gone down the tube if the nun hadn't been murdered or the coroner hadn't discovered it so quickly."

"I'll give you that. The speed *was* a break."

"Actually, kind of clumsy of whoever did it. The bruises on her shoulders would've been enough, but then when the doc found that she'd been drowned first and then had her head smashed against the wall—there was just no more doubt."

"It's goddam crazy. You'd think with all these cop shows on TV, everybody'd know what you can do with forensics."

"It kinda makes you wonder about the killer. Is he that dumb, or is he trying to tell somebody something?"

"Too early to tell. There's no damn connection between the two murders except those goddam rosaries."

"And right now, that's pretty thin. That's why I had to write such an iffy story. That rosary connection could fall apart fast."

"Right. And everybody's got a piece of the story now. It's gonna be harder than hell to stay ahead of it. Kid, this is our goddam story. We broke it. And we're gonna finish it. You'd better get your ass over to headquarters and find out who's in charge of the investigation."

"Right."

With that, Kane rose abruptly and quickly passed through the foyer into the elevators. Cox was about to leave when he noticed the check on the table. It was left to him to pay for breakfast.

Helen Nowicki, switchboard operator at the Archdiocesan Office of Communications, was wishing they had only one telephone line. Calls were coming in so rapidly she could hardly take the messages. Everyone from the news media to the well-established community of Catholic nuts was calling for information or a statement on the murders from that everpopular anonymous "archdiocesan spokesperson."

Sister Eileen Monahan, trim, pretty, and inefficient, was beside herself. Director of communications for a little less than a year, this was the most serious crisis she'd yet had to face.

Ordinarily, the Office of Communications handed out press releases and tried to keep dirty laundry items out of the news. That the office was not highly regarded by the media was a testimony to its lack of practical purpose. Instead of a help, the office was a hindrance to the news media. Still, it was the only place to get a "statement" when one was expected. Only there was no "statement" available on the two recent murders.

Sister Eileen had been trying through the morning hours to get the desired statement. Three times she'd gone personally from her office in the Gabriel Richard Building across Washington Boulevard to the chancery to try to light a fire under the archbishop and his auxiliary bishops and department heads, who together made up the archdiocesan think tank. Each time, they were, she was informed, "unable to be disturbed" at their meeting.

As the phone in her office rang off the wall, she looked, with unchristian sentiment, at the picture of the think tank members hanging on that wall.

"Men!" she shouted, in terminal frustration.

Koesler exited the elevator on the fifth floor of the City-County Building. He was immediately confronted by a uniformed policeman seated behind a desk opposite the elevators. Koesler asked for Lieutenant Koznicki and was directed to Room 504. He was surprised, on entering 504, which turned out to be a reception room, to find Nancy Baldwin seated on one of the few chairs in the room. He gave his name to the receptionist. He then exchanged brief greetings with Nancy, after which there was an embarrassed silence, almost as if the two were truant children who had been summoned to see the principal.

The receptionist lifted an intercom phone and dialed a single number. In a moment, she spoke into the phone, "They're both here, sir." Hanging up, she looked at Nancy and said, "The lieutenant will see you now." Nancy rose and stepped into the inner office.

Alone now with a receptionist who was busily shuffling papers, there was nothing for Koesler to do but bide his time. He did not like to harbor ethnic thoughts, but he had already reflected on Lieutenant Koznicki's apparently Polish ancestry. He had half-expected to find bowling trophies in abundance, along with a volume of bric-a-brac. Instead, there were only a couple of unmatched pictures on the bare paneled wall. There was no table and no magazines. It occurred to him that this was not Koznicki's permanent office but one that had been set up as an ad hoc base of operations for some specific purpose.

Since there was nothing else to do, he decided he'd give some thought to how the *Detroit Catholic* would handle the two recent murders. He didn't know how long he'd been developing that line of thought when the intercom buzzed. After a moment on the phone, the receptionist asked, "Would you go in now, Father?"

As Koesler stepped into the inner office, the man began rising from behind a massive rectangular desk. He seemed to continue to rise. Koesler was impressed with the size of this burly policeman whose straight black hair started not that far above bushy eyebrows and was neatly trimmed above the ears. As Koesler approached the desk, he was surprised at his first impression. The lieutenant—possibly six-feet-four or -five—was not much taller than he. There were men—John Wayne, he'd heard—who seemed bigger than life. Koznicki was one of those.

The lieutenant took Koesler's outstretched hand and seemed to envelop it in his own.

"Good of you to come so promptly, Father,"

As if I had a choice, thought Koesler.

"You may be wondering about Miss Baldwin's presence here this morning . . ."

Yes, Koesler thought, as he cautiously scanned the room until he located a second door. She must be in another waiting room, he guessed, since she had not returned to the reception area, and there seemed but one door to the office from the hallway.

". . . but the reason for her appearance will be evident soon," Koznicki continued. "Now, Father, according to the statement you gave Sergeant Ross, you were the one who found Sister Ann's body."

"I and Angelo Trupiano."

"Yes. But you were the one to lift her upper torso from the tub."

"Yes." He wondered if he were going to be reprimanded again for moving evidence.

"Now, Father, you stated that as you placed the body on the floor, a small black rosary dropped from the deceased's hand."

"That's correct."

"Can you tell me, Father, how the deceased was holding the rosary?"

"What?"

"There must have been some reason why the rosary hadn't fallen off in the tub, or why it didn't fall as you began to move the body."

"Oh, I see what you mean." Koesler hadn't thought of this before, but, of course, it was a legitimate question. He tried to remember everything in detail. Finally, his memory was able to focus on Sister Ann's wrist as it emerged from the tub. "Yes, yes . . . I remember. The rosary was looped around her wrist and the beads hung through her fingers."

"Would you mind showing me, Father?" Koznicki handed him a small black rosary. Koesler held the crucifix in his right hand so the rosary extended toward the floor. He then inserted his left hand through the rosary's bottom loop, circled the rosary once around his left wrist and dangled the remaining beads between the thumb and index finger of his left hand.

"Sure. That's why the rosary didn't fall off until we dropped her body." He looked self-consciously at Koznicki. "She was wet and slippery. The fall must have jarred the rosary loose from her wrist, and it fell on the floor."

"Very good, Father." Koznicki turned toward the second door and raised his voice. "Miss Baldwin?" Nancy stepped into the office and was directed to take the other chair next to Koesler.

"I am going to tell you both something that may prove of utmost importance," Koznicki said. Both his visitors stiffened slightly. He had their total attention. "You, Miss Baldwin, and you, Father Koesler, have verified that the rosaries found at the scenes of Father Lord's and Sister Ann's deaths were placed on their hands in an identical manner. This is the kind of information that we want to keep to ourselves. It may prove essential should these crimes be duplicated at any time in the future." Both Nancy and Koesler shuddered. Neither had thought about a crime wave. "Too much publicity can be counterproductive to police work," Koznicki continued, "and the news media already have access to a wealth of detail about these murders." He looked significantly at the two. All of them knew who it was that had given the media that wealth of information.

"Now, you may wonder," Koznicki continued, as he leaned back in his oversized leather chair, folding his hands over his ample middle, "why it is I am telling you this specific detail now. It is because we all know how cooperative the two of you have been with the press thus far." He leaned forward. "And under no condition are you to tell anyone of the manner in which the rosaries were found on the two deceased. On the one hand, I'm sure you both want to cooperate with the police in this investigation. On the other, if you tell anyone, *anyone*, I shall," and here he nodded in Father Koesler's direction, "with all due respect, Father, lock you both up and lose the key. Is that clear?"

Both gulped and nodded affirmatively.

"Now, I thank you both for coming. Miss Baldwin, you may leave now. Father Koesler, I wonder if you might stay a few minutes more?"

For one thing, Koesler was fascinated, and for another, he was getting used to Koznicki's commands that were expressed as requests.

Nancy left the office, and Koznicki and Koesler were seated again.

Koznicki had established a solid reputation among the Detroit police as the quintessential cop. He desired no personal publicity and seldom got any. He was meticulous about detail, and his arrests had a high rate of conviction. That he was scrupulous about the constitutional rights of suspects contributed to his conviction record. He was no loner. In a city the size of Detroit with its high murder rate, it was self-defeating to depend either on oneself exclusively or on the breaks. In Koznicki's cases, he used everyone he could, encouraging their cooperation, creating a sense of sharing in an investigation, carefully communicating information that would help others help him in solving homicides.

"Father," Koznicki began once the two men were settled in their chairs, "first, I want you to know that I know a great deal about you. For years, I've been a reader of the *Detroit Catholic,* before you became editor and since. So I know you are at least a mild civil libertarian. Since your involvement in this case last Friday, I've checked on all your previous assignments in the archdiocese, and I've talked to several people about you. And I strongly suspect you are an avid murder mystery novel fan."

Koesler was becoming more and more entranced. He'd never thought his life interesting enough to be the subject of an investigation. The final detail—about the mystery novels—floored him. "How did you know about the murder mysteries?"

"A couple of people I talked to mentioned it. Plus, since you've been in this office, you've been studying the details of the furnishings and memorizing my face. Just like your heroes in the whodunits never miss a detail —and we, in real life, miss more than we find.

"Anyway," he continued, "I want to enlist your help in this case, partly because you are already involved and partly because I think some of your experience may help us."

"Well, I'll be glad to cooperate." Koesler was like a kid again. He couldn't believe he'd really be involved in a real-life murder mystery.

"Fine. Now, I'd like to go over the few facts we have and the assumptions we can make.

"We have here, Father, two murders that appear to be related only in that one was a priest and the other a nun— a relationship that is at best most tenuous—and in that both died with rosaries left on the bodies in an identical manner. We have pretty well established that the rosaries in question did not belong to the deceased persons and that the rosaries are identical. These last two facts, Father, are also among the information we want no one else to know.

"There is no indication any relationship existed between the deceased persons. Our investigation shows that not only were Father Lord and Sister Ann never in the same religious assignment, but there is no evidence they ever met. A fact that argues against the two killings being related.

"However, the rosary link is a strong one, particularly after your and Miss Baldwin's statements this morning, particularly since the killer appears to have ensured, by the secure manner in which he left them, that they would be found. Therefore, a reasonable assumption at this point is that the murders seem to be related. In this assumption, Father, the rosaries become the killer's calling card.

"Now, since the rosaries are the only clue thus far . . . you're following me, Father?"

Koesler, intrigued, nodded.

". . . since the rosaries are the only link, our next assumption is that the murderer has not completed his task."

Koesler found his lips had dried.

"You see, Father, in a case like this, if our assumptions are correct, we are dealing with a psychopath. By no means an idiot but a madman. When someone begins leaving clues deliberately, he begins a dialogue, a communication with the police. He has a goal or a purpose and, at the same time—and almost as much—he wants to be stopped. We can stop him only when we understand the language he uses as he leaves his clues.

"An added assumption, Father, is that the killer is a man. That, only because the weight of Sister Ann, a large woman and already dead, would have been considerable to lift from the tub and still inflict the kind of injury she suffered at the back of her skull. Presumably, the strength of a very strong man would be required.

"One final fact, Father, leads us to a frightening conclusion. That fact is that Sister Ann was not sexually molested. A fact that was reported in the *Detroit News* and not the *Free Press*. Which proves it pays to read everything."

"What," asked Koesler, in an astonished tone, "is so 'frightening' about Sister Ann's *not* being sexually molested? I should think that would be somewhat encouraging. At least the killer doesn't appear to be a complete animal."

"What's frightening, you see, is that Sister Ann, perhaps more than many women, was, with all due respect, a very rapable subject." Koesler's eyes widened. "What I mean, Father, is that Sister Ann was an attractive, fairly young woman. We found her nude but not sexually attacked. That leads us to one of three likely assumptions.

"One, that the killer is a female, which I have already rejected.

"Two, that he is homosexual. It is possible. But, for the moment, I do not accept this as a tenable assumption. Mere nonmolestation would be a fairly weak reason for thinking this. But, more important, homosexuality has nothing to do with the killing of Father Lord. And we are assuming the two murders are connected.

"Third, and this is the assumption I make, that the murderer is so determined to kill that he will not be diverted from his goal even for sexual indulgence. This, in a sense, is unfortunate for us. With that sort of single-minded determination, he is less likely to blunder into a simple human error that would lead us to him more quickly. Frankly, Father, unless we pay close attention to the clues he gives us *and* enjoy good luck, this will prove a most difficult case to close.

"Now, Father, to sum up. We have no leads as to whom the killer might be. We have no idea of his motive. Nor do we know who, if anyone, might be next.

"Not very much. But I want you to know I'll be available to you at any time for any ideas you may have. Here is my card. On it you'll find a number where I can be reached whenever you want to call."

"O.K., Lieutenant." Koesler sensed the meeting was coming to a close, and he felt he had to boil all the questions that filled his mind into one that might synthesize all this newly acquired information. "I'll try to absorb all this. But I just don't know what I possibly could do to help."

"I know I've swamped you with theory, Father . . ." Koznicki smiled for the first time. Actually, it was the first time Koesler had ever seen an on-duty policeman smile. ". . . but it all comes down to this, the same thing all your murder mysteries are looking for: 'Who done it?' What I'd like you to do, at your earliest convenience, is to think about, maybe jot down, the names of people you know or know about who may have a special dislike of or hate priests or nuns. I assure you," he anticipated Koesler's objection, "none you may mention will be considered suspects. They will be what we call leads."

"But in the Church today, especially in Detroit, there must be hundreds of those."

"I know. I read your 'Letters to the Editor.' Start there. Judiciously talk to some of your colleagues. But remember, some of what we discussed today must be kept between us. I know you're good at keeping secrets."

"I've kept some in my time." He knew Koznicki was referring to the confessions he'd heard. It was a subject the laity always fantasized about, inaccurately. He'd been hearing confessions for a couple of decades and could count on the fingers of one hand the number of times he'd heard anything surprising, let alone juicy.

"Father, thank you for stopping by this morning."

"I had a choice?" This time the thought was voiced. And once again, Koesler's hand was lost in Koznicki's.

Koesler put his car in gear and his mind in neutral as he drove up Second Avenue toward his office.

He couldn't get over the fascinating idea that a killer who deliberately leaves clues hopes the police will understand what he's trying to communicate through them so he'll be stopped from doing what he has determined to accomplish. Koznicki was right. The killer was trying to tell them something. But what? What could this killer possibly be trying to communicate by killing an old priest and a very active nun? And what could he possibly be trying to say through the rosaries? Koesler had absolutely no idea. For the first time in his life, it occurred to him to be grateful he was not a cop. He enjoyed outguessing the cops and villains in whodunits, but this was reality, where real lives depended on one's ability to, in effect, understand what was being said without knowing what language was being used.

He entered the *Detroit Catholic* with ruminations swimming through his head. But not for long. Before he could reach his office, both Irene Casey and Jim Pool assailed him with questions about the murders and how the paper was going to handle them.

To add to this confusion, Judy Anderson approached him with the complaint that the switchboard had been unbelievably busy this morning with calls about the murders and repeated calls from media people asking for a statement from the archdiocese.

"Tell them," Koesler said over his shoulder, "to call the communications office."

"That's just it, Father. They keep saying the Office of Communications is telling them to call us."

Shit! he breathed fervently. Just what we needed.

WEDNESDAY, MARCH 9

Lieutenant Walter Koznicki was the tip of an iceberg that had the potential for greater growth.

Most Detroiters resented the title their city had been given—Murder Capital of the World—though they could not argue their city could be a dangerous place to live in or even drive through. But murder in Detroit was not normally a sophisticated crime. That sort of action was reserved unto the suburbs. Like the series of child-molestation murders in nearby Oakland County. Murder in Detroit was senseless, brutal, sudden, unpredictable, quarrel-related, gang-related, drug-related. But Detroit did not kill its priests, ministers, or other religious leaders. On the rare occasion that one of these became a murder victim, it was never a planned, deliberate act but a senseless gesture. Like the hop-headed kid who had killed a retired monsignor, because there were only a few dollars to be ripped off in a core-city rectory. Or the nun in St. Cecelia's convent who died as a victim of random target practice.

Thus, when the deliberate murder of a priest and then a nun became the top stories of the local news media and were even featured in the national press and TV network news, Detroit's black mayor, Maynard Cobb, drew the line. Cobb and Police Chief Frank Tany selected Walt Koznicki to head an elite homicide task force to close this case as quickly as possible. Koznicki was to have as close to carte blanche power as was constitutionally possible. Special offices were set up on the City-County Building's fifth floor to house the task force.

The first person Koznicki selected for his team was Detective Sergeant Ned Harris. Harris, a black, had come up through the ranks, as had Koznicki. At one time, as sergeants, they had been teamed and discovered they were a good match. Both were thorough; both brought in solid cases for prosecution; both kept unblemished records; both had received numerous citations; both shunned publicity as being counterproductive to their work.

Koznicki had entrée to the still strong Detroit Polish community, while Harris was accepted by the evergrowing black population. Where Koznicki tended to be cautious, Harris could create the bold stroke. Where Koznicki tended to rely on his "assumptions," Harris hung loose, always ready to change course with the prevailing wind.

Their first course of action had been to spread the word throughout the entire department that any death of any priest, nun, minister, or religious personality under any circumstances was to be reported to them before any other action was taken. Their team, and their team alone, knew every detail of the two murders under investigation.

But both admitted there were precious few details to be known.

Harris had just entered Koznicki's office. "Fallon just

called from St. Mary's Hospital," he said as he moved to the window overlooking Jefferson Avenue, the Detroit River, and Windsor. "They're not having much luck."

"Damn! I was afraid of that. But it's still our best lead. I'm positive none of the hospital personnel was responsible for Father Lord's death. Somebody from outside killed him, and our best bet is that somebody in the hospital saw him and can identify him."

"That's if your goddam assumption is right."

A faint smile crossed Koznicki's lips. Harris was forever on him about his assumptions. Outside of tips from informants, which both Koznicki and Harris relied on and checked out religiously, Koznicki knew that Harris depended on what he called hunches, which, while they were neither as dependable nor logical as an "assumption," were more viable, if only because they could change from moment to moment.

"You got anything better?" Koznicki asked without looking up from yesterday's *Detroit News* he'd brought with him from home.

"Hell, no. If I had, I'd be arguing with you. It's just that you're basing everything on those rosaries. What if they were a coincidence? What if the two murders aren't related?"

"Then my assumption is incorrect." He said it with a straight face.

"Incorrect! Goddamit, we're on a wild goose chase if you're wrong. We should be investigating two separate killings—unrelated—entirely differently than we're doing now."

"Those rosaries are no coincidence."

"O.K. You're the boss. Unless you're wrong, of course. Then maybe I'm the boss."

"The only way you're going to become boss is if the department goes crazy over affirmative action hiring."

"O.K., Massa." Harris shuffled over to Koznicki's desk. "What yo' wan' yo' nigger to do today?"

"After you get in the watermelon crop, drag your black ass over to St. Mary's and put your expert nose to the case. See if you can smell something Fallon may have missed.

He's good, but it's tough changing the direction of a case you've been investigating. And, by the way, I'm expecting a visit from Joe Cox of the *Free Press* at ten this morning. Know anything about him?"

"Been in town only a few months, I think. Seems to be straight. I trusted him with a few 'not-for-publications' and he sat on 'em. But, 'scuse me now, boss. I gotsa drag my black ass over to the hospital and make you a hero."

As Harris was about to leave, Koznicki called after him, "One more thing. We'll know very shortly if my assumption is correct."

"How's that?"

"There'll be another 'rosary murder.' "

Father Mike Dailey was having a late business breakfast with his parish "team." A parish team was a Detroit answer to a vanishing clergy. St. Gall's parish, on Detroit's far northwest side, had, for most of its fifty years, been staffed by three resident priests. Even now, with its high school closed and a reduced enrollment in its six-grade elementary school, the parish was still active enough to support and perhaps need at least two priests. There just weren't enough to go around. So, St. Gall's, in one of Detroit's few fairly stable white neighborhoods, had one priest—and a team.

Dailey was the pastor, a position that no longer carried the clout it once had. Joining him at breakfast were Sister Dorothy Hoover, religious education coordinator; Sister Elizabeth Martin, in charge of pastoral care for the sick and aged; and Tony Ventimiglio, the parish liturgist.

Ordinarily, their meeting would have been devoted mainly to the preparation of the liturgies for next Sunday, the third Sunday in Lent. But this morning was spent mostly in recovering from last night's parish council meeting.

Dailey, a tall, well-built redhead and former athlete, never had appreciated the purpose of a parish council. As far as he was concerned, parish councils, at least as they functioned in the Archdiocese of Detroit, were an idea whose time never would come. He had once remarked to a few clerical friends at a martini-punctuated luncheon, that if the twelve Apostles had been a parish council, the Crucifixion would have been voted down twelve to one.

"It wouldn't be so bad," said Sister Dorothy, stirring her coffee, "if they knew what they were talking about. But they just go off to their jobs at GM or Ford or the Detroit Bank and wouldn't recognize a book on modern theology if it were tucked between the covers of *Playboy*. I'm getting tired of translating for them. I mean, every time I mention the Sacrament of Reconciliation and get blank stares, I have to say, 'That's what we used to call confession.'"

Sister Elizabeth pushed her chair back from the table. "Don't be so hard on them, Dot. They don't have to know theology. That's *our* job."

"They ought to know something about it, if they're going to meddle in it." Sister Dorothy was building up steam. "How can they disapprove of the new confessional we had built, if they don't know the theology behind it?"

"I think they were upset," said Ventimiglio in a conciliatory tone, "because the cost wasn't in the parish budget."

"What do you mean, not in the budget?" Sister Dorothy was nearly in full stride. "There's $5,000 in the religious education budget for needed repairs and alterations. If the Holy Roman Catholic Church orders it and the Archdiocese of Detroit says 'Do it,' I'd say that's a needed repair and alteration!"

The alteration in question was an outgrowth of Vatican II. The purpose was to offer penitents a more personalized opportunity than the traditional "box" gave. Two weeks ago, the pastoral team at St. Gall's had authorized construction of a small lighted room to the right of where the confessor sat in the confessional. Now those who wanted to go to confession in their accustomed manner could do so by entering the confessional box at the priest's left, while those who wanted to speak face to face with the priest could enter on his right. There was no barrier between priest and penitent in the new facility. Yet priest and penitent, on the left, were still separated by a wall, a small door, and a screen.

"While we're on the subject of confession," said Father
Dailey, lighting his pipe, "the council didn't take too kindly to the new hours for confession."

"Sacrament of Reconciliation," corrected Ventimiglio.

"Sacrament of Reconciliation," repeated Dailey. "By
any other name, they still didn't like it. The ladies and
gentlemen of the council were in a mean mood last
night."

"When was the last time anyone saw them happy?"
snorted Sister Elizabeth.

"When they were blissfully in their pews in church before some damn fool ever thought up the parish council
idea," Dailey answered.

"You weren't actually getting that many people for
confession, were you, Mike?" Sister Elizabeth addressed
Dailey.

"Hell, no. The good old days of wall-to-wall penitents are gone. Four hours for confessions on Saturdays
was three hours too much. I've been catching up on
my reading, but I could be better occupied."

"The thing that steams me," said Sister Dorothy, whose
fuse had definitely been lit, "is that you're actually available for confessions more now than you were before. So,
O.K., there's an hour in the afternoon and an hour in the
evening on Saturdays. But you've got the buzzer system
installed so anytime anyone wants to go to confession,
they can just press the button in church."

"If I'm here."

"Which is most of the time."

With that, an ear-splitting noise only slightly less raucous than that which marks a Red Wing goal jolted the
four of them.

"What in hell was that?" exclaimed Ventimiglio.

"Speaking of the buzzer . . ." Dailey snapped on a
white plastic collar that attached itself to his neck like a
handcuff to a wrist. "I'll get Joe to work on the volume.
There's no use letting the whole neighborhood know some
poor soul wants to be shriven.

"Why don't you go on with the meeting," he added,

throwing a cassock on and beginning to button it, "but don't decide to sell the rectory before I get back. And Dorothy, try to calm down, will you? For all we know, the parish council has bugged this room. And their next meeting will begin with the crucifixion of Sister Dorothy."

He left chuckling. Then, on second thought, he regretted having made the last statement. No one in Detroit made jokes anymore about priests or nuns being killed.

Joe Cox got off the elevator on the fifth floor of the City-County Building. He asked the policeman in the hall where he could find Lieutenant Koznicki. Then, instead of heading for Room 504, he decided to see what else was being housed on the fifth floor. He had a hunch he'd find more cops.

Hunch confirmed. He could not determine the exact number of offices the police had occupied, but it was impressive. Just walking through the hallway, he counted eight uniformed police plus at least four plainclothesmen he recognized. The doors to three offices were open. Two offices were clearly occupied by the police. One evidently was not. Apparently, the police had not commandeered the entire floor, but not far from it. He guessed it was a special homicide task force, and he guessed all were working on the murders of the priest and the nun. It was time to meet Koznicki.

He had seen the big policeman before but never in close proximity. He decided if he were ever to do anything illegal, he'd just as soon not be caught by Koznicki. Being run over by a bulldozer might be a happier experience.

As soon as he was seated, Cox took a notepad and pen from his inside jacket pocket. "Do all the cops on the floor belong to you?"

"Yes." Koznicki did not care for word games or unnecessary conversation that would conclude with information he was willing to give in the beginning.

Cox liked it. He had half-expected a denial, or at

least some stalling. Koznicki, on his part, appreciated Cox's investigation of the floor. It was an indication of the reporter's professionalism. And he'd far rather deal with a professional in any field than some jackass who would foul everything up with his own inadequacies.

"Are they a special homicide task force investigating the murders of the priest and nun?"

"Yes."

"Would you say," Cox was busier shorthanding his questions than Koznicki's answers, "your presence here, instead of at headquarters, is a political move?"

"No, you would say that, not me."

"O.K., fair enough. Let's do it a different way. The fact that you're not at headquarters, won't that hinder your investigation?"

"No, not really. You see, everyone in this city, from the mayor on down, and that should be a partial answer to your previous question, wants a solution to this case. Every once in a while there is a crime that shocks even a city like Detroit, and these murders more than qualify as such a crime. Then, the city—the mayor, the council, the chief of police—takes special steps to have it solved quickly."

"But wouldn't things go more quickly at headquarters?"

"Not necessarily. Real police work is not like Kojak or Columbo on television where one policeman investigates one murder for an hour and solves it. Any real policeman is investigating any number of cases at all times. Some of them are dead ends, sometimes because there's just not enough time to devote to the leads. We are electronically plugged in to headquarters, so we've got that advantage while at the same time being able to devote all our time to this case."

"O.K., these cases are two weeks old for the priest and six days old for the nun. How far along are you?"

"Not far. But you must remember that until the nun was killed, we had no indication that the priest's murder was not an isolated act. So the investigation, up to six days ago, probably was so much wasted time. The previously mentioned dead end. Since the nun's murder, our investigation has taken an entirely different tack. So you might say, logically, that we've been investigating both murders for less than a week."

"Any leads?"

"Nothing that looks good right now. We've been busy with what police work is all about—not unlike your work, Mr. Cox—painstaking investigation that may prove fruitful and may not. We have no idea just now."

"Can you give me any specifics?"

"Certainly." Everything that Koznicki would tell Cox he knew the reporter could and would discover on his own. But the detective wanted to offer shortcuts to the reporter as an act of good faith and to draw Cox into this investigation as an aide. He didn't care who solved the case as long as the murderer was apprehended. "We have teams of police inquiring among the hospital personnel as well as among the neighbors of the convent. It's a common experience that people see more than they readily remember. Somebody got into that hospital, and somebody got into that convent. We strongly suspect it was the same person in both instances. It stretches coincidence too far to think the murderer worked in the hospital *and* lived in the convent neighborhood. So, we assume the murderer was foreign to both the hospital and the convent neighborhood. It is more than likely someone at the hospital and someone in the convent neighborhood saw the one we're looking for. If we ask long enough and repetitively enough, someone will remember. At that point, we'll have turned a very important corner."

"Is that the extent of your progress till now?" Cox was taking notes furiously.

"Well, no. You might say that's our active phase right now."

"You've got a 'passive' phase?"

"Confessors. Each well-publicized case," he looked significantly at Cox as, admittedly, the chief publicist, "draws a number of people who are chronic confessors. They see themselves as the perpetrators of everything. Sick people, generally. They want their names in print or, sometimes, they are so pathological they actually think they've committed the crime in question. But, in each case, we have to check it out."

"How do you know one of your sickies didn't do it?"

"In no instance does anyone but the real murderer know every detail of the crime. Although, in this case," again he looked pointedly at Cox, "the general public does know a great deal more than usual."

For the first time in his short journalistic career, Cox felt a sense of embarrassment. "You mean the rosaries. There was no way I could suppress that. It was the whole story."

"Don't misunderstand me. I don't blame you. Had I been in your shoes, I'd have done the same thing. But, while news of the rosaries does complicate our job, the publicity may eventually prove advantageous. Besides, there are a few details still known only to the police and the murderer."

Cox smiled, knowing the reply he would get to his next question. "What did I miss?"

Koznicki returned the smile and merely leaned back in his chair, again folding his hands across his ample middle. Cox sensed the interview was coming to an end. He had enough material for a respectable continuing story. He would head first to the convent neighborhood, then to the hospital for a little investigating on his own. He shifted forward in his chair. "One last question, Lieutenant."

Koznicki nodded.

"There really isn't much besides the rosaries that ties these two murders together, is there? I mean, this case might fall apart too, no?"

"It might. But, unless I miss my guess, we'll soon know."

"Don't tell me. If you're right, there'll be another rosary murder."

"That's not for publication. But you're very perceptive."

"That's my job," monotoned Cox in his best "Dragnet" imitation; "I'm a reporter."

The two parted with considerable mutual admiration.

Koznicki didn't care who solved the murders as long as they were solved. Cox didn't care who solved the murders as long as he was first to report it.

Father Pompilio had a guest for dinner, so dinner had been delayed half an hour for preprandial drinks. Father Koesler didn't mind that delay in the least. He enjoyed a fresh martini as well as the next man. But it did elongate an already tedious time allocated for a meal. Dinner would be longer tonight not only because of the drinks and Pompilio's meticulous method of food consumption, but because his friend liked to tell stories. And that slowed Pompilio's M.O. even more.

Father Joe Farmer was from Grand Rapids, home of furniture and Gerry Ford and priests who seldom got together. But when they did, they had accumulated lots of stories to tell each other.

Joe and Pomps might have been twins. They did not resemble each other facially, but they were both short, round men who laughed too easily, blissfully cheated at their golf scores, and were simply compatible. They had gone through the seminary in Cincinnati together and had become fast friends. They exchanged visits as often as they could.

"Pomps," Joe was saying as he lit an afterdinner cigar and flooded the room with heavy smoke, "did I tell you the one about the guy who was washed up on a deserted island when he was a little kid?"

Pompilio shook his head, an anticipatory smile crossing his lips as he slid more tartar sauce over his fish. He checked carefully for hidden bones.

"Well," a long cloud of dark smoke came between Pompilio and his fish, "this kid grew up all by himself on this deserted island until, one day, this beautiful girl gets washed ashore. Big, blonde, beautiful, and naked."

Pompilio's smile grew. He found a small bone and deposited same on the edge of his plate.

"So the girl finally finds this guy and says, 'Do you want to make love?' And the guy says, 'I don't know. How do you do it?' So the girl shows him and they make love.

Then the guy looks down at himself and then looks over at the girl kind of disappointed and says, 'You . . . you . . . you broke my clam digger."

"Broke his what?" Pomps asked urgently. "Broke his *what*, Joe?"

"Clam digger! Clam digger!"

It wasn't so much that Pompilio couldn't hear, as it was that Joe Farmer always broke himself up when telling jokes so that it was always a challenge to catch the punch line.

Pompilio dropped knife and fork and threw his head back in uncontrolled laughter. In this he joined the already broken-up Joe Farmer. Koesler smiled. It *was* funny. Funnier than most of the vulgar jokes he'd heard from priests. By no means did all priests tell vulgar jokes. But those who did seemed to have an unlimited supply. Koesler always knew what was coming when a layperson prefaced a joke with, "A priest told me this one . . ." It was going to be vulgar but somehow blessed and singularly approved for mixed company simply because he'd heard it from a priest.

"Whatsa matter, Bob? Don't you get it?" asked Farmer, trying to pull himself together.

"Yeah, yeah, I get it, Joe. Funny. Where'd you hear it?"

"Confirmations at the cathedral. Hank Henning told it. He's got a million of 'em."

"I'll bet." Koesler also would bet all the million were in circulation.

"Well, what's the matter? You didn't seem to appreciate it." Farmer seemed to be getting a bit testy.

"Oh, it's nothing. I guess I've just been too wrapped up in those murders." Koesler had, indeed, been concerned. Since his conversation with Lieutenant Koznicki, he had been thinking of little else. Besides his somewhat personal involvement in both murders—talking with Nancy Baldwin, receiving the incriminating rosary from her, and finding the body of Sister Ann—he'd been trying to comply with Koznicki's invitation to come up with some likely leads. It wasn't that he couldn't think of anyone.

There were too many possibilities if all one looked for were people who seemed to hate priests and nuns. The backwash of Vatican II had left the Catholic clergy and laity alike sharply divided. Where once, so recently, the Catholic Church had presented an incredible unity, now, those who were emotionally involved in the Church had polarized into conservative and liberal camps. Those who had been indifferent were even more indifferent. But Koesler was unable to imagine anyone angry enough to turn to physical violence, let alone murder.

"Yeah," Farmer turned somewhat more serious. It wouldn't last. "That's about all the guys in Grand Rapids can talk about. We're happy, so far, it's happening only in Detroit."

"What about it? Can either of you guys think of anybody who would do something like this?" Koesler lit another cigarette.

Pompilio swished his last piece of fish through the remaining tartar sauce. "I don't know. Somebody who got tossed out of parochial school?"

Farmer chuckled appreciatively. "Or some altar boy who got canned."

Pompilio pushed at the table. As usual, nothing moved. "Seriously, seems like the cops'd be looking for someone who was physically violent."

"Say," said Farmer, examining the long white ash he'd been building at the end of his cigar, "didn't I read in your paper, Bob, about some hothead who pushed a priest down the steps of some Detroit church?"

"That's right," remembered Pompilio, "and there was another guy, sometime back, who—what did he do?— who hit some priest, or—it was Kenny, wasn't it, the auxiliary bishop?—with a protest sign he was carrying? There's a couple of suspects for you."

They had it wrong, but they just might be onto something, Koesler thought with some excitement. It was one and the same man. Harold Langton, leader of the arch-conservative Catholic organization called The Tridentines, after the Council of Trent held in Italy in the sixteenth century. Yes, he had been involved in at least those two acts of violence. And, if Koesler's memory served, Langton insisted that all Tridentines meetings begin and end with a recitation of the rosary. Could this be the tie-in?

He promised himself he'd go through the *Detroit Catholic* files tomorrow and see if he could check out Langton's activities. He was certain he could build a credible case. Then he'd bring it to Koznicki.

"You may just have something there, gentlemen. It's worth thinking about." Koesler stamped out his cigarette vigorously.

"If we're right, will we get our names in the paper?" Pomps was ever alert.

"Sure you will. Headlines," Koesler promised, lighting another cigarette.

"Say, Pomps . . ." The interval of serious discussion ended as Farmer deposited the cigar ash he'd developed in the tray, ". . . did I tell you about George Mayeski at Holy Innocents?"

Pompilio shook his head as the smile began twitching at the corners of his mouth.

"Well, as you know," Farmer warmed to his story, "in Grand Rapids, promotions are made chronologically. You can make book on who's going to be the next pastor. It's the next oldest guy. Well, George didn't know this, and his buddies told him the chancery expects you to apply for the job if you want to be pastor.

"So, every time a parish opened up, George would send in his application. The guys in the chancery were getting a big kick out of this.

"Then, one day, George caught on and got kinda sore about it. The next parish opened up, and George didn't apply for it. The guys at the chancery couldn't figure out why no application from George. So they sent him a letter saying . . . saying . . ." Farmer was beginning to crack up. ". . . saying, 'What was wrong with that parish?' "

"What was wrong with what, Joe? What was wrong with *what?*" Pompilio had lost the punch line again.

Good old irrepressible Joe Farmer.

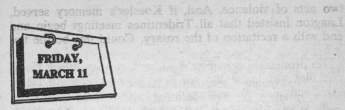

It was another of those Michigan days that couldn't make up its mind whether to be winter or spring. The best that could be said was that it wasn't snowing. But it was bitter cold, with the bite that came from the Detroit River and sliced through the canyons of downtown skyscrapers.

Joe Cox had decided to walk to the *Free Press* from his Lafayette Square high-rise apartment not far from the new Renaissance Center. First, he needed the exercise. Second, he felt good about his story in the morning edition. It was, he felt, a workmanlike job. It broke no new ground in the "Rosary Murder" cases, as they had come to be identified in the news media, but there was no new ground in sight. Instead, Cox's story updated the investigation with solid quotes from Lieutenant Koznicki and an insightful description of the special task force occupying most of the City-County Building's fifth floor.

Cox detoured through the enclave of Greektown with its peculiarly relevant presence in an otherwise nearly abandoned section of downtown. Though most of the restaurants were not open this early in the day, the neighborhood groceries and coffee shops were doing their usual thriving business, and the earthy odors of Greek cuisine permeated the area.

The remaining few city blocks en route to downtown were as drab as Greektown's were invigorating. Here and there in doorways were Detroit's human refuse, some white, more black, all older men with patched, ragged clothing. Some still held the contoured brown paper bags containing wine bottles, the contents of which had been drained as the sleeping potion of the bums.

61

It was mid-morning when Cox reached the *Free Press*. Late for him. But then he *was* feeling good. That feeling lasted until he reached his desk and found the note from Nellie Kane. In Kane's familiar lean prose, it read, "Cox, see me now! Kane." The "now!" was underlined three times. That meant Kane wanted to see him yesterday. Cox felt a mixture of bewilderment and bemusement. He scanned the city room but found no Kane. "Anybody know where Nellie is?" he asked of no one in particular.

"He's at the Y," replied Pat Lennon, who occupied a desk two removed from Kane's. Cox had been aware of Pat from his first day at the *Free Press*. She exuded a quiet but unmistakable sexuality. A full-figured brunette with a sultry voice, her every move sent out signals, particularly when she walked away. Cox had appreciatively received each signal and was waiting only until the appropriate moment to test his theory. "He said to tell *you* specifically," Pat added in a tone of mixed finality and sympathy.

"A bit early for the Y," mused Cox aloud. "Sounds as if he might be a tad upset."

"Slightly more than usual," answered Pat. "If I were you, I wouldn't wait till he comes back."

He did not. Nor did he remove his coat but went right back to the elevators and emerged from the lobby looking for a taxi. He found one on Washington Boulevard and took it the few short blocks to the Y. No use chancing the time a walk down Woodward would take.

Cox was not a member of the Y. But by flashing his press card and dropping the familiar name of Nelson Kane to a series of attendants, he finally was admitted to the members' section. It required many more inquiries of naked, near-naked and towel-draped members to discover Kane's present location—the sauna.

He'd gone this far, he might just as well go all the way. Finding an empty locker, Cox stripped, found an available towel, and followed the signs to the sauna.

No politicians' lair could compare with this steam-filled room, especially when Kane was an occupant. Kane believed an ocean should be wet and a sauna should be hot. So he always sat near the heater, pouring a fairly steady stream of water that was immediately transformed into steam.

Opening the door to the sauna, Cox was greeted by a gush of escaping steam. He stepped in, closed the door, and hoped his eyes would adjust to the pea-soup atmosphere. They wouldn't. "Nellie?" His voice was weak. He felt ridiculous. Like a small child calling out in the dark for Daddy.

"Here." The tone was sepulchral and unmistakably Kane's.

Cox, following the voice, took one step, tripped over a foot and sat heavily on the bench. Fortunately, that section of the bench was unoccupied and, fortunately, he found himself seated next to Kane.

"Take it easy," urged Kane, "you don't want to kill yourself in a sauna. Make a rotten obit."

Cox rubbed his backside. He was sure there'd be a bruise. "I'm wondering why you asked me here."

"I didn't. And I don't know how you got in here."

"Your note said 'Now' and as to how I got in here, I lie a lot."

" 'Now' was earlier this morning when you should've been at work. And if you lie so good, how come you turned in that goddam routine story?"

Cox hadn't been so surprised since he'd had his first wet dream. "Whaddya mean 'routine'? I got the whole thing up to date, all the facts and guesses, the setup of the floor full of cops, and I beat the *News* by a full twelve hours."

"You beat the *News* on a goddam routine story. Where's the witness at the hospital and somebody in the parish neighborhood who saw the murderer?"

"For chrissakes, Nellie, I checked both those leads and got nothing. Most of the time, I was neck and neck with the cops. And the cops didn't get anything either."

"Cox," Kane's voice was soft. He never raised it above the required volume. "The reason we pay you more than the city pays the cops is because we expect you to do a better job. You're not supposed to be 'neck and neck' with the cops. You're supposed to be well out in the lead. And you're not going to get there if you're satisfied with a goddam routine story, if you're late for work, or if you spend this whole sonovabitch day sitting on your ass in a sauna."

Cox pondered the alternatives to a career in journalism.

Kane poured more water on the heater. "And while you're out there in the trenches fighting for *Free Press* superiority, forget this cockamamie theory about a 'rosary killer.' I got a hunch we got two unconnected homicides. As long as the cops keep trying to link 'em, they're not goin' anyplace. Work on 'em as separate murders and crack both of 'em."

Unable to differentiate between the steam pressing in on his body and his own perspiration, Cox felt readier for a nap than work. "You could be wrong," he said, rising to leave.

"The last time was in the big snow of '42. Now get the hell out of here."

Father Robert Koesler had spent most of the previous day trying to track down the file of Harold Langton in the *Detroit Catholic*'s morgue.

Keith Diamond, one of the *Catholic*'s reporters, was the paper's unofficially designated file clerk. While nearly everyone on the staff did a little bit of everything involved in putting a newspaper together, filing was a job universally shunned. Only Diamond took any interest in it, and at those times when his work was caught up, he would do a little filing.

Consensus had it that Diamond's filing technique was a form of job insurance. Diamond alone knew why he filed which items under what. Under ordinary circumstances, Koesler would have asked Diamond to get the file on Langton. But yesterday, Diamond had been at the printer's, supervising the paper's press run. After four to five hours of diligent search. Koesler hoped that he'd found all the records on Langton that the *Detroit Catholic* had. He'd found them filed variously under "C" for conservative (probably), "L" for Langston, "R" for right-wing (probably), and "T" for Tridentines.

Assembling the clippings, Koesler could only conclude

that Langton was a busy young man. His hostile, if not violent, presence had been evident not only in the Detroit area, but all over Michigan. In the Lansing diocese, he had helped a young priest antiwar protester down the cathedral steps with a shove. In the Marquette diocese, he had snatched the sign from the hands of a boycott-nonunion-farm-products marcher and hit him over the head with it. In Detroit, he had almost come to blows with an aggressive nun who had been speaking in behalf of fem lib. Almost everywhere where there was a demonstration or publicized meeting in behalf of a liberal cause, you could always expect Harry Langton and followers.

Langton was by no means the only conservative activist on the scene. But he was the only activist, conservative or liberal, who had exhibited overt violent behavior.

However, there *were* those who were close behind him. One conservative activist, in particular, was forever calling and writing to Koesler about articles in the *Detroit Catholic*. He had even threatened the paper with a libel suit—a threat that was never followed through—and, reportedly, he occasionally carried a gun. But there was no record of his ever having engaged in physical violence.

Actually, the more Koesler considered and researched the incidence of anger and hatred in the Archdiocese of Detroit at Lieutenant Koznicki's suggestion, the more frightening it became.

People of conservative bent had been devastated by all that Vatican II had done to "their" Church. Dogma, the statement of which regularly began with the words, "As the Church has always taught," now held that the Church had never "always taught" anything. Morals that had been measured by inches, ounces, and seconds now seemed to be dissolved in indefinable "situation ethics." And what the modern liturgists had done to the Holy Mass of Trent was sheer blasphemy.

For the liberals, of course, the Church had taken only one small step in what should have been the march of mankind. Canon law, with all its presumptions in favor of the institution, was still in force. The shared responsibility promised by Vatican II was still the impossible dream. The hierarchy was still doing battle with contraception, while the largely Catholic Third World starved. And the storied people of God were the great unwashed.

When one stood in the middle of these great antagonistic forces, a position in which Koesler saw himself, it seemed as if Armageddon could not be far off. Or, as Koesler had thought one day when two news service pictures crossed his desk—one, a man flayed alive by communists; the other, a man burned to death by fascists—it is just as bad to be killed by the left as by the right. Only, at the time, he hadn't considered actual murder. Not in the United States of America.

But two—one priest and one nun—were dead. There were likely to be more. Somebody out there, probably a Catholic, liberal or conservative, with some real or imagined grievance, was actually killing clergy and religious. And Harold Langton was not even a suspect. Only a likely lead. Among that vast army of angry liberal and conservative Catholics, those who could kill probably were legion.

Koesler had made an appointment for four that afternoon with Lieutenant Koznicki to share with the police the dossier on Harold Langton. It might not have been much, but it was the best lead, to date, that Koesler could offer.

As he was inserting the Langton clippings in a folder, Irene Casey approached him with a copy of that week's just-published *Detroit Catholic*. The front page was nearly filled with the combined stories of the murders of Father Lord and Sister Ann, along with commentaries by theologians on the readiness to die and the witness of martyrdom, and a statement of shock and dismay by the Archbishop.

In the lower right-hand corner, the spot at which Irene was pointing a repentant finger, was a single column story, headlined, "Abortion Condemned Again by Holy See." The story's lead began, "To avoid any misconception . . ." Sometimes small blunders like that simply escaped everyone's attention until they appeared in print.

Koesler helplessly raised his eyes to heaven, sighed, and said to no one in particular, "I think they should make a movie about printers' devils to rival *The Exorcist* in horror."

Sergeant Ned Harris knocked perfunctorily but did not wait for an invitation before entering Lieutenant Koznicki's office. "We got a break!" he announced triumphantly.

"It's about time." Koznicki was beginning to think that if they hadn't had *bad* luck on this case, they wouldn't have had any luck at all.

"Fallon broke down the stories of two of the hospital people." Harris was so elated he ignored the chair and began pacing in a tight little rectangle to the right of Koznicki's desk. "The orderly and the practical nurse—you know, the ones Fallon didn't believe from the beginning. He finally got them to admit they were in the sack together the afternoon of the priest's murder. Actually, they hit the bed every time either of them finds an empty room. Horny bastards!" Harris added, admiringly.

"It's nice they're sexually active," Koznicki interrupted, "but where's the break?"

"Oh, yeah," Harris discarded his irrelevance. "Well, after Fallon broke their alibis, they got to be very cooperative. Especially after Fallon agreed to keep their sexual olympic games a secret in return for all the information they could give."

"And . . . ?"

"Well, after they got done havin' a piece of each other, they left the room. But they always leave the scene of assignation cautious, you know." Harris obviously relished this part of the story. He was so pleased with it he began to strut. "They look around, you know, man, to see if there's anyone around to notice they're both comin' out of the same empty room."

Even Koznicki was smiling.

"So," Harris continued, "they both notice this guy dressed in hospital whites, only neither one of them has ever seen this guy before—or since. If he works at the hospital, it's not on that floor."

"How about the time?" Koznicki asked. "Were they able to establish the time?"

"3:12 on the afternoon of February twenty-third."

"3:12?"

"Yup, 3:12. They entered the available room promptly at three, when most of the staff was settled in the chapel, and it always takes them twelve minutes."

"It always takes them twelve minutes?"

"That's right. That's what they said."

Both men were impressed, first, that the two could perform at the drop of an available bed and, second, that they had an inflexible twelve-minute routine.

"That's the damnedest thing I've ever heard!"

"Me too. But by the time they got to that detail they were too scared to lie."

"You're right. Nobody could make up something like that. Well, their timing puts our suspect at the scene at the right time. Where are our lovebirds now?"

"They're with Sundell, the artist. He's getting up a composite. And that reminds me, that's the end of the good news."

"Oh?" Koznicki was too confirmed a believer in Murphy's Law to doubt the existence of bad news in any situation.

"Our witnesses didn't get too good a look at the suspect. But from what they were able to observe, and according to the description they gave Fallon, he's mister average guy. Which means he's not a member of the Pistons or a sideshow midget. And . . ." Harris paused for effect.

"And?" Koznicki responded.

"He's not a member of my esteemed race."

"Caucasian, eh? O.K., that lets him blend in well with the hospital personnel but makes him more easily identifiable in the convent neighborhood."

"If it's the same guy in both cases."

"It's the same guy." Although there was some subtle pressure from a few of his superiors of late, Koznicki was unwilling to abandon his assumptions. There had been ten days between the two murders. Today was only a week after the nun's death. There was time.

"That's not the end of the bad news."

Koznicki leaned forward. "There's more?" Murphy was working overtime today.

"That guy from the *Free Press,* Cox, he's got the story."

"Cox? How?"

"It's one of Fallon's little games. Every time he breaks somebody's alibi, he let's 'em stew a while alone and think about the value of cooperation. Well, once he broke the nurse and superstud, he put them in the reception area just outside the office he was using in the hospital. The cop on guard in the doorway didn't know they were in there, and he let Cox in 'cause Cox said he had an appointment with Fallon."

"Goddam dumb!"

"You know that. I know that. And, believe me, now that cop knows that."

"How did Cox get the story from them?"

"About the same way Fallon did. First convinced them he knew they were witnesses—which he didn't, just a good bluff—then promised not to use the bed bit."

Koznicki was silent for several moments, drumming his fingers on his desk. "Dammit! It's not the story. We'd have given it to the media anyway. Once we get a composite, we'd need them to publicize it. But this case is developing a very nasty habit of leaks. Far too much is getting to the press beyond our control. Our security stinks. And I won't have it! Get word out to the entire team: We'll have a meeting tomorrow morning at nine sharp. We've got to tighten this up."

"Gotcha, Walt. But, after a while, you wanna talk about that twelve-minute drill?"

Koznicki smiled briefly. "Does something to your racial image, don't it? Having a honkie who can perform like that?"

"Could you?" Harris closed the door as he left.

Father Michael Dailey and Sister Dorothy Hoover were seated in the living room of St. Gall's rectory. They had solved all the Church's major problems and now had turned to the field of psychology.

"The trouble with these 'feel good' movements of today," said Dailey, sucking in hard on his pipe several times to keep it lit, "is that you're charged several hundred dollars for a weekend of self-torture just so you can tell somebody what's bothering you. After which, you feel better."

"You mean like Esalen and est and the group-gropes?" said Dorothy, tucking one unshod foot beneath her on the couch.

"Yeah, it happens every time. That's what drives psychiatrists nuts. A patient comes in because he feels guilty or bad and as soon as he's able to tell the doctor what's bothering him, he feels better and doesn't come back. And he leaves the doctor with a $35-a-fifty-minute-hour gap in his schedule."

"Oh, come on," Dorothy waved a cloud of pipe smoke away from her eyes, "it doesn't always work that way."

"Well, no. Not if you've got a really deep neurosis or psychosis. But . . . well, didn't you ever have to make a really difficult or embarrassing confession—excuse me, I mean as part of the Sacrament of Reconciliation?"

Dorothy smiled; she knew she would update even Father Dailey one of these days. But try as she might, she couldn't recall a really difficult confession. "No, I don't think so."

Dailey snorted as he thought of the confessions he'd made and the ones he'd heard. Generally, the only embarrassment in confession was in connection with sexual sins. Little boys masturbated. Strangely, if you could believe them, little girls did not. They didn't get involved in sexual sins until premarital sex or contraception. And then, women always had a way of making their involvement in sex seem like a movie they had watched. As if a wicked man had had his way with them while they passively endured it as a way of preserving courtship or a marriage. And that was only in the good old days. The new morality had taken care of all that. Nowadays, masturbation was natural, premarital sex was necessary, and contraception helped fight the population explosion. Guessing at Dorothy's relative youth and noting her religious vocation. Dailey concluded that perhaps she had never, indeed, had to make a torturous confession.

"Well, then, let me tell you," he said, applying a fresh match to old tobacco, "it can be rough. But if it's a pain-

ful process, there's no describing the feeling of relief that
follows."

With that, a soft, echoing buzz filled the rectory.

"Speaking of the agony of confession, there's some poor
soul now who wants to go through it." Dailey rose and
took a light topcoat from where it lay rumpled over the
back of a chair.

"You got the janitor to fix the buzzer?"

"Yeah. Muffled it and put speakers in every room.
That way, I hear it but it doesn't scare everyone to death.
I'll be back in a few minutes. Wait right here, and I'll tell
you more about the good old days that you missed by being born so recently."

They exchanged smiles as Dailey tapped out his pipe
and left.

It was only a few yards' walk over to the church. Dailey
approached the confessional and noted that the small red
light over the old confessional box was lit. Ah, the plastic
church of today, Dailey thought, as he opened the door
to his compartment of the confessional; you pays your
money and you takes your choice.

Dailey seated himself, bounced a couple of times on
the chair to get comfortable, and slid back the small door
to the penitent's side. While the penitent's box was pitch
dark, the priest was clearly silhouetted by the light from
the open room to his right. Dailey propped his left elbow
on the small shelf under the penitent's window and rested
his head on his left hand. It was the classic pose.

Nothing happened. Not too unusual. With some frequency, penitents were either young and had forgotten
their story, or adults who were too nervous to begin without a little support from the priest.

"May the Lord be on your lips and in your heart,"
intoned Dailey, "so that you may rightly and sincerely
confess your sins." With that, his right hand traced the
sign of the cross in the air.

It was a small sound, not unlike a popping champagne
cork. But the bullet crashed through Dailey's head, scram-
bling much of his brain in its wake, and embedded itself
in the wall. Dailey fell from his chair like a puppet

whose strings had been cut. He lay on the floor of the confessional room with blood beginning to ooze from his mouth, nose, and the bullet holes in either side of his head. All was quiet in the empty church but for the involuntary sounds old buildings make.

The man stood and detached the silencer from his revolver and tucked both in inside coat pockets. Emerging from the penitent's box, he entered the larger confessional room where Dailey's inert body lay, the eyes open in an eternal look of surprise. Removing a small black rosary from his coat pocket, the man bent down and carefully wound the beads around Dailey's left wrist, then guided the opening strand of beads and the crucifix between the dead priest's thumb and index finger. Then he left.

In the rectory, Sister Dorothy had been reading the latest copy of the *Detroit Catholic*. She was startled when she realized that she had finished the entire paper and Father Dailey had not yet returned. This was a long time for one confession. Perhaps there had been more than one penitent. She didn't know why she felt so uneasy. Maybe it was the *Catholic*'s front-page story on the murders of Father Lord and Sister Ann. It couldn't hurt to just go over to the church and check.

Later, she remembered screaming. Many, many times. She remembered fighting off nausea. She remembered struggling not to faint. She remembered somehow making her way back to the rectory and calling the police. Then she allowed herself to be human. She did faint.

Even though it was late afternoon with the attendant problems of rush-hour traffic, Sergeant Ned Harris decided to take the Lodge Freeway from downtown out to the far northwest side. He had both the flasher and siren on, something he seldom did. But he was in a hurry.

Seated next to him was Lieutenant Koznicki. Neither man had said anything since leaving the underground garage ten minutes ago. Both were harboring private thoughts in anticipation of what they would find in St. Gall's church. Koznicki broke the silence.

"Damn!" He picked up his car phone, waited a few seconds, then asked the operator to patch him through to his secretary. Another few moments of waiting and he asked her to call Father Koesler and postpone their meeting.

"What was that all about?" asked Harris, as he ran the blue Plymouth over the curb and rode the shoulder of the freeway.

"I just remembered, I had an appointment with Father Koesler, the editor of the *Detroit Catholic*."

"What's he got?"

"A lead, I think."

Harris shook his head and grinned. "You'd take a lead from the devil himself."

"Frequently have."

They drove a few more minutes in silence, while Harris expertly slalomed through the maze of crawling cars and trucks. Again Koznicki broke the silence.

"Do you remember how many phone calls we got this past week on the death of nuns and priests and the like?"

Harris thought a moment. "Four, I think. The Lutheran pastor, the old priest at the seminary, and two—no, three —nuns. How many's that make?"

"Five."

"Like I said, five."

"I can't believe this order is working so well. So far, we've been informed first on every single death. And somebody from our team has been on the scene early enough to check out every one of them. Murphy's Law must be working on somebody else. And that's fine with me."

"Looks like you got a gusher on this one."

"Yeah."

"If this is another rosary murder, you got a convert."

"Good to have you aboard."

Harris flipped off the siren and light, turned off Wyoming and parked at the driveway entrance to St. Gall's. For a rainy Friday afternoon, there was a considerable crowd gathered outside the church. A cluster of neighbors was at the inner core, with passersby adding to the crowd by the minute, and there were enough cops around to control a parade.

Koznicki and Harris left the car and walked toward the church. They were an impressive pair. Despite Koznicki's enormous bulk, he walked with an unexpected lithe grace. Almost like an elephant who'd gone to ballet school. Harris, several inches shorter than Koznicki, was, nevertheless, a six-footer. Brown-skinned, clean-shaven, with close-cropped hair, he was impeccably dressed, his trim, athletic body reminding one of a cat ready to spring.

The two men passed through the crowd as easily as the Israelites through the Red Sea. Koznicki was pleased to see Sergeant Fred Ross, who had been borrowed from Connor Station for Koznicki's special squad, in charge of the crowd. Ross was dependably professional, and his police procedure was letter perfect.

"It's clean, Lieutenant," said Ross, as Koznicki passed him. "No one's touched the body."

Koznicki nodded and proceeded into the church. Inside, it was more like a train depot than a place of worship. People, mostly uniformed police, were everywhere. And everyone seemed to be talking. Some civilians were being interviewed by the police; some of the police were being interviewed by reporters; some of the police were taking in the dimensions of the church; others were examining the confessional. Flashbulbs were popping incessantly, giving the scene an even more surreal quality. Detective Sergeant Dan Fallon, who had hurried over from St. Mary's Hospital and had been among the first to arrive, was making sure no one approached the body.

Koznicki and Harris spent a quiet moment just looking down at the late Father Dailey. By now, the blood had formed a halo around his head, the darkened red contrasting with the priest's gray-flecked carroty hair.

Both Koznicki and Harris squatted beside the body.

Koznicki looked up at Fallon. "Have they photographed this?" he asked, pointing to the priest's hand holding the rosary. Fallon nodded. "From every angle?" Again Fallon nodded. Koznicki lifted the priest's arm, and with a handkerchief he had taken from his pocket, carefully unwound the rosary from the dead man's wrist. He then en-

closed the rosary in the handkerchief and put both in his
pocket.

Both Koznicki and Harris stood. "Wrap it up," Koznicki told Fallon.

Back in the car, Harris started the motor, but before
putting it in gear, he turned to Koznicki and said, "I
believe."

SATURDAY,
MARCH 12

There was no way of missing the added member of
the eight o'clock Mass congregation. Lieutenant Walter
Koznicki took up a good part of the first pew left side.
Father Koesler noticed him immediately on entering from
the sacristy. Not only was Koznicki a very visible addition to the usual small group who attended daily Mass;
the lieutenant would have stood out like a bull moose at
an SRO Midnight Mass. Koesler could not help but wonder why Koznicki had come. But reasons would have to
wait for ritual.

At the Prayer of the Faithful, Koesler led a petition for
the happy repose of the soul of Father Dailey. As he did
so, he took particular note of Koznicki. But the policeman seemed without special reaction. He merely responded with the rest, "Lord, hear our prayer." When
Koznicki received communion, Koesler's final question
about his religious persuasion was answered. He had presumed that the policeman's Polish name indicated Catholicism. It didn't work with all Irish or even all Italians, but,
almost invariably, to be Polish was to be Catholic.

As soon as he had removed his Mass vestments, Koesler hurriedly left the sacristy. As he'd expected, Koznicki, seated all over the front pew, was waiting for
him.

"Welcome to St. Ursula's, Lieutenant."

"Thank you. You've heard, obviously, about Father Dailey."

"Yes, last night on the radio and TV. I'm sorry."

"So am I."

"Was he really . . . ?"

"Yes. He was another victim of our friend who leaves rosaries. The black rosary, identical to the first two, was wrapped around Father Dailey's wrist just as you and Miss Baldwin have described."

"Poor Mike. From the reports, it seemed it was a quick death."

"Instantaneous."

There seemed to be nothing further to discuss about the murder. In addition, it always seemed awkward holding a conversation in church. Koesler beckoned Koznicki to follow him. "Won't you have a little breakfast with me? And you can tell me what brings you here today."

Koznicki quieted Sophie's surprise at having a guest for breakfast by requesting just toast and coffee.

"When my secretary told me she was unable to contact you in time yesterday and that you had come all the way downtown for our appointment, I decided I owed you a visit."

Koesler noted that his breakfast companion ate his toast unbuttered. Dry toast and coffee! There must be some meal during the day when that bulk gets filled, he thought, but said only, as he waved an empty spoon in reply to Koznicki's quasi-apologetic statement, "Oh, that's all right; couldn't be helped."

"I wonder," Koznicki rubbed the thumb and index finger of both hands over his plate, gently distributing crumbs, "if you have the material you were talking about that we would have discussed at our meeting yesterday."

"Yes, sure. I brought it home with me. Just a minute and I'll get it."

Koznicki looked about the rectory dining room. Strange to hear a place like a rectory referred to as "home." Since Koesler worked at an office, it was not true in his case, but, for most priests, a rectory was half home and half business, and neither one did any priest own. He was trying to think of people who lived where they worked and simply waited for customers to come. No advertising. No sales pitch. He had thought of no one but priests and, perhaps some ministers, when Koesler returned with a manila folder.

"Here, this should help." Koesler opened the folder and spread the clippings before Koznicki. "It may not be everything on Harold Langton, but it's all I could find. However, I think these clippings are indicative of something."

"Yes. For one thing," Koznicki had arranged the clippings so that their datelines corresponded with their geographic locations in the state, "our friend Langton gets around a good deal."

"And at times he is violent."

"And, at times he is violent," Koznicki echoed. "I've been vaguely aware of Mr. Langton, mostly from items in the papers. I haven't met the man. I'd have no reason to. He hasn't murdered anyone—that we know of."

Koesler did not miss the point, but he was concerned about what would happen to Langton. This was the first time since childhood that Kocsler had considered himself a stool pigeon. "What will happen now?"

"To Langton?"

"Yes."

"We'll do some quiet investigating, probably call him in, ask a few questions. With all due respect, Father, is your conscience bothering you?"

Koesler smiled self-consciously. "Yes, a little bit."

"I can understand that, Father. You're thinking of yourself as an 'informer' with regard to Mr. Langton. You shouldn't. Mr. Langton probably would have surfaced rather early in our investigation. You've just saved us some time. And remember, right now he is not a suspect. He is a lead. One of the better leads, I might add."

"That surprises me." Koesler poured a second cup of coffee for himself and another for his guest. "I mean that Langton would be such a good lead. I mean, you've got the composite picture from those hospital witnesses."

"You saw the picture?"

"Last night on the local TV news."

"Did it remind you of anyone?"

Koesler thought a moment. "Now that you mention it, no."

Koznicki smiled. "That's the way it goes, pretty much, with composites. Look at it this way, Father." Koznicki shifted in his chair as Sophie quickly cleared away the breakfast dishes. "We have a picture of someone who was described to our artist by two people who saw the suspect briefly. It did not remind *you* of anyone. It will not remind most who see it of anyone. Some will misidentify it. Rarely does such a lead result in an arrest."

"I hadn't thought about it that way. But now that I remember the composite drawings I've seen in papers and magazines, they hardly ever look like a real human being." Koesler was anxious not to take too much of Koznicki's time, but the policeman showed no sign of haste.

"In addition, Father, the description we have is from two hospital employees who were unable to identify a man who may, indeed, work at the hospital. He may simply have been out of his designated station at that time. In that case, he would really be in the wrong place at the wrong time."

"You're checking on whether or not he's an employee?" Koesler had not yet decided whether he preferred the always-resolved challenge of mystery novels or the danger of real murders that might never be solved. But, like it or not, he was thoroughly caught up in the Rosary Murders.

"Of course, Father, we are checking into that even now." Koznicki sensed the priest's fascination and wished to encourage it. Police regularly depend on every conceivable source of help. "So you see, Father, with our case as open as it is, your suggestion of Mr. Langton as a lead is most appreciated. Our investigation may clear him entirely. If so, it is to his benefit. It not, we may have closed our case."

Inasmuch as Koznicki gave no indication of wishing to leave, Father Koesler invited the policeman into the living room, where they could continue their discussion more comfortably. Koznicki swiftly appraised the rectory living room. Large color TV, an adjoining office space, a series of tasteless pictures on the walls, and several pieces of overstuffed leather-covered furniture, not one piece of which matched any other. Typical of a series of male occupants in search of decorless comfort.

"You were saying, Lieutenant, something about closing the case. Did you mean that in terms of catching the murderer or does that imply you think there may be more murders?"

"Both." Koznicki settled himself in a too-soft armchair. "If we catch the culprit now, there will, of course, be no more of those murders. However, I do not believe our murderer is finished.

"For instance, Father, consider the Oakland County killer. He murders young boys and instead of discarding the bodies carelessly or trying to conceal them, he arranges them carefully. Particularly by his method of disposing of his victim's bodies, he is communicating something to the police that may help them stop him.

"Or take that special series of murders in New York City. The primary victims are young brunette women, each of whom was shot with a .45-caliber pistol. The murderer sends notes to the police and news media signing himself 'Sam's Creation.' So, he's known as 'Son of Sam.' He, too, communicates to help the police catch him. Otherwise, no communication would take place.

"Now, our murderer is very subtle. So far, the rosaries he leaves behind are the only clue that definitely joins the murders. Yet, it is almost accidental that we've found them. He will not help us very much. Think, Father, what have we so far?"

"Three murder victims, two priests, one nun."

Koesler had been paying rapt attention. He was glad to rejoin the conversation. "One murder on a Wednesday, two on Fridays. Ten days between victims one and two, one week between two and three."

"Tell me then, Father, do you see any pattern at all besides the rosaries?"

Koesler needed no time for this answer. "No, I certainly don't."

"Well, then," said Koznicki, rising, "if the killer continues with his careful planning or we do not get very lucky, there will be more murders, *and* a pattern may emerge more clearly. As disconnected as everything seems so far, I am certain the killer is telling us something we simply do not yet understand. If he should finish whatever it is he's planned, we should by then understand what he's been trying to tell us. But, by then, of course, we will have been too late."

"Like the medical examiner," Koesler added.

"Exactly. The one who discovers everything when it's too late to do anything. So, Father," Koznicki slipped his coat on and took his hat, "there's something more for you to do."

"What's that?"

"Think about it. Just think about it. Something may click. You like solving puzzles."

With that and a word of thanks for breakfast, Koznicki departed. As Koesler shut the door, it occurred to him that if he thought about this long enough, he'd probably move to New York, where it was safe.

Father Dailey's death had been discovered too late for any significant coverage in the Saturday *Free Press*. It was one of those stories that fit radio and television perfectly.

Ordinarily, Joe Cox would not have come into the *Free Press* on a Saturday. But today he was working on an article about the priest's murder for the Sunday editions.

The story almost wrote itself. Facts of the killing; time, place, caliber of gun. Details of the victim's life—most of these facts Cox had culled from the *Detroit Catholic*'s morgue. Connection with the other "Rosary Murders." Statements from the police, city officials, members of Dailey's "team," and remarks from parishioners.

Once again, Cox picked up the composite picture of the supposed killer that had been released by the AP Friday. He could think of thirty or forty people who resembled the indefinite line drawing—including his former wife.

Actually, he had picked up the drawing several times as a better excuse for studying Pat Lennon, who was also working on a story. Although her desk was two removed from Cox's, this Saturday there was no one occupying those desks. Cox simply was not sure of Pat Lennon. She exuded sensuality in her walk, the way she stood, always with her weight on one or the other foot, her husky voice, her full figure. If you've got it, her attitude seemed to imply, flaunt it. Yet, in several months of working in the same office, she had never exchanged more than a few words with Cox.

He thought of whistling or humming a chorus of "Some Enchanted Evening," but dismissed that as too uncool. He also considered tapping out a Morse Code message on his typewriter but quickly discarded that. His article completed, he decided to linger, type a letter or two and, if desperate, try the repetitious "The quick brown fox . . ." He was determined to stay until she was through with her work and see what, if anything, might develop.

At the moment she was smiling. And, Cox thought, the smile made her particularly appetizing.

Pat Lennon was doing a story on Michigan State Police patrolling the Detroit freeway system. The state police had taken over this job almost a year ago. Because of budget and manpower cuts, both the Detroit Police and the Wayne County Sheriff's Department had been forced to cut back the number of cars they could put on the freeways. It had not taken long for Detroit's dedicated looters to take advantage of the opportunity. As a result, motorists were fearful of driving on Detroit freeways, and cars that had to be abandoned there soon became carrion for criminal vultures. But soon after the state police took over patrolling, the message went out through Detroit's petty crime community that the freeways were no longer safe for looting. Now, nearly a year later, the freeways were among the safest places in the metropolitan area.

Pat was smiling as she completed her article for tomorrow's paper. She was typing out an anecdote one of the state troopers had given her during an interview. A motorist had told the trooper the story just after the state police had assumed responsibility for the freeways. The motorist had been driving his pickup truck on the Lodge Expressway near Woodward, when the engine began to ping. He pulled off onto the shoulder, opened the hood, and began looking among the maze of wires and innards for the source of the trouble. Suddenly, he got the impression his truck was moving. Walking around to the rear of the truck, he saw two black men jacking up the back bumper. They looked slightly startled when they saw him, but one of them hurriedly explained, "It's O.K., you can have the engine; all's we wants is the tires!"

Pat finished typing the story, giggled audibly, wrote a concluding paragraph to the article, and was done.

As she whipped the paper out of the carriage, her eyes met Cox's intently for a moment. She said, simply, "Let's."

Dropping their copy in the copy editor's basket, the two walked off together into the sunset.

TUESDAY, MARCH 15

One of Detroit's living legends was Mother Mary Honora. Ten years before, at the age of sixty, she had decided to end a forty-two-year career as a parochial school teacher. At an age when most people anticipate a proximate retirement, she had begun a fresh vocation of social activism. As a member of the Immaculate Heart of Mary order, she had taught a goodly number of Catholics throughout the state of Michigan, many of whom were now prominent clergymen, nuns, politicians, and business and labor leaders. She preferred the title "Sister," but so many Detroiters remembered her in a series of Mother Superior roles that everyone continued calling her "Mother."

She lived in a small mansion in what had once been an extremely wealthy section of Detroit near the cathedral. Most of the stately old homes still stood; some were occupied by families of some means, mostly black professionals. Some were owned by a few of the major pimps and drug dealers. A few were a sort of revolving door for fairly bizarre cults. Prophet Jones had lived in the neighborhood. So had Sweet Daddy Grace. It was an area in Detroit's north central section that couldn't quite make up its mind what it was going to become. The neighborhood had barely escaped being a victim of the 1967 riots.

Mother Mary had moved into a house her IHM order had purchased for her. Two other IHM sisters, both slightly older than Mother Mary, had moved in with her, both because they admired her and to escape being put on a religious shelf. The two cooked, kept house, and generally made themselves useful dispensing food, medicine, and clothing that Mother Mary scrounged from every possible source. Together, they were as sweet and lovable as the two sisters in *Arsenic and Old Lace,* without the arsenic.

Mother Mary had known little of the special problems of the poorest urban section of a city like Detroit. But she brought a generous heart and a willingness to learn and help. Just after moving into their Arden Park home, there had been a learning experience that still embarrassed the three nuns, although Mother Mary could laugh about it now. The one room they had been most eager to complete was their makeshift chapel. They had converted what had been a good-sized den in the front of the house into an attractive place for worship. Several priest friends agreed to take turns saying Mass there.

After the first Mass in their prized chapel, the nuns wanted to show everyone that Christ in the Eucharist had taken residence in their neighborhood. So the good nuns had placed a large red vigil candle in the chapel's front window. One of their more sympathetic neighbors discreetly told the nuns the next morning what a red light in the front window would more likely signify in that or any adjacent neighborhood. The nuns agreed there were more effective ways of getting their message across and hastily removed the light.

Since that and other similar early blunders, Mother Mary, if not her two companions, had grown streetwise. She did not seek publicity, but it was a rare month when Mother Mary did not appear in one or more of the local news media. At times her copy was so appealing

she appeared in the national media too. There was, for
instance, the time the city council wanted to destroy some
very livable houses in the name of urban renewal. To
make their point, in the face of determined opposition
led by Mother Mary, the city fathers had a wrecking crew
go through the homes destroying bathroom facilities. That
evening, viewers of Detroit television news watched as
Mother Mary presented a toilet seat to the members of
the common council. Then there was the time Mother
Mary's picture appeared on the front pages of both the
News and the *Free Press,* as well as on all three television
channels. Clad in full IHM habit, there she was, a member of a picket line around Detroit's Playboy Club, along
with some of the bunnies. It wasn't that she was in favor
of bunnydom; she simply agreed with their demand for
better wages.

Today, she was bundled against the biting chill in her
great blue coat over her habit. Sister Anita had insisted
she wear her heavy overcoat. "This is the time of year,"
Sister Anita had warned, as she supervised Mother Mary's
departure, "when Detroiters come down with pneumonia.
They think it's got to be spring when it's really still
winter. We old ducks should have better sense. Besides,
maybe you'll encourage some of our neighbors to bundle
up if they see you sensibly dressed."

Mother Mary's thick round frame shook with laughter
at the memory. Nothing else the nuns had done seemed
to influence the lives of this overgrown ghetto. After ten
years, there was still every bit as much crime, drug dealing, and murder as there had been when the nuns moved
in. But if nothing else had been accomplished, the nuns
had come to be accepted and loved by the poor, black
and white, for whom they had been able to provide some
of life's necessities.

As she walked briskly along Rosa Parks Boulevard,
nearly every passerby greeted her with a cheery word.
"Hi, Mothah Mary. How you do-un?" She returned each
greeting, occasionally halting to speak with one whose personal crisis she knew to be particularly precarious.

She no longer needed to beg for food or clothing.
Everyone from the Teamsters to city and state politicians

to suburban parishes saw to it that Mother's Arden Park home was well stocked regularly. From time to time, downtown businesses sponsored fund-raising events for her mission.

Today's journey was to neighborhood branches of the large supermarket chains. It was common for them to rip off the poorer sections. Sometimes fresh hamburger was wrapped around stale meat. As long as it looked good, the poor would buy it. And when they learned that they'd been duped, they had no way of protesting. More often than not, prices were higher in poorer urban sections than in suburbia. Ghetto residents either didn't have the transportation to shop elsewhere or didn't even understand comparison shopping.

Mother Mary entered the first supermarket on her list and began recording prices of various items on her ledger, while the manager, familiar with this routine, could only sigh. Later, she would check her list against those gathered by some of her friends in suburban stores.

As she was leaving the market, she remembered an item she'd forgotten to check. Returning to the checkout counter, she asked a very attractive black cashier, "Dear, how much is your ground round today?"

The girl glanced at a list attached to the cash register. "Dollah, thir'-sic' cen'."

Mother Mary looked at her with a mixture of kindness and concern. "Dear," she said, "if you had said, 'One dollar, thirty-six cents,' you'd have the world in your pocket." She left behind her a puzzled but slightly more thoughtful young woman.

Few people, black or white, walked through Mother Mary's neighborhood, day or night, without an awareness of the danger of those streets. No one, black or white, was as safe as was Mother Mary. Even the drug-dulled hopheads of the neighborhood, who could kill without any reason, would not think of harming Mother Mary for fear of the certain and terrifying retribution that would be visited upon them. Mother Mary was uniquely protected in an enclave of crime, drug abuse, and murder.

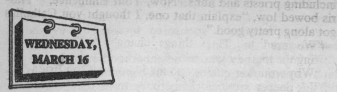

"How did the interview with young Langton go?"

Lieutenant Koznicki was balancing precariously on one foot while struggling to remove a boot from the other foot. It was snowing, one of those days Detroiters hoped would be the last snow of the season. Koznicki had arrived at his temporary office a little late this morning, after delivering some clothes to the cleaners and two of his children to school, and fighting slippery pavements and weather-congested traffic.

"Zilch," replied Sergeant Harris. "He had solid alibis for two of the three murders."

"Two for three?" Koznicki was wrestling with the other boot.

"Yeah. He couldn't come up with anyone to substantiate his whereabouts March fourth, when the nun was killed. But when we're lookin' for one guy who killed three times, two for three ain't bad." There was a glint in Harris' eye as he stared fixedly at Koznicki's feet. From the first time they had met, Harris had been fascinated by Koznicki's feet. He had never seen larger feet. Somehow, they were not inappropriate when considered as a part of the rest of Koznicki's huge body. But, Harris thought, isolated, they belonged in the *Guinness Book of Records*.

"Fallon did the interrogation," Harris continued. "I just went along for the ride. Funny though, if Langton hadn't been busy on the twenty-third and the eleventh, he'd be prime contender for the role of guilty party. That guy's got a lot of hate goin' for him. Along the way, we discovered he doesn't like blacks, Jews, and communists. But way up at the top of his list is Catholics, including priests and nuns. 'Now, Your Eminence,' " Harris bowed low, "explain that one. I thought you Catholics got along pretty good."

"We used to. Then things changed." Koznicki was sorting the mail on his desk.

"Why would anyone get so mad about fish on Friday?"

"It's deeper than that."

"Or 'domino go friskum'?" Harris insisted.

"It's deeper than that. But it's past the understanding of a Baptist."

"A good detective would have known that, despite my racial persuasion, I couldn't be Baptist. No Baptist dresses this good. I'm Presbyterian. By their threads ye shall know them."

"Harris, I'll bet your mama wishes you'd grown up to be a good man. Like Joe Louis or Sammy Davis."

"That's right; I'm the white sheep in my family."

The conversation drifted off as Koznicki became more involved with his mail. Harris, coffee cup in hand, wandered to the window to contemplate the comparative peace of Windsor. "Beats headquarters," he said.

"What?"

"The view—it beats the sights and smells of Gratiot and Beaubien."

"Right. But I'll be glad to get back there."

"Because by then we'll have caught our man?"

"Right. But you know, Ned," Koznicki was wagging a letter he'd just finished reading, "that inane conversation we just had reminds me that most of our guys who aren't Catholic don't realize how much things have changed for Catholics in the past ten years or so. And our killer may be motivated by something so different from anything we're used to, we could miss a vital clue."

"What do you want to do, make being Catholic a requisite for membership on this task force?"

"Get serious."

"Well," said Harris, opening the door, "let's go over to Control and see."

The two men walked briskly along the fifth-floor corridor toward the floor's largest room, which had been specially outfitted and termed the Control Room. There could be doubt in no one's mind that this was no ordinary floor of an office building. Police were virtually everywhere. Even plainclothes police, when seen together in large numbers, could be unmistakably recognized as cops.

Inside Control, about twenty policemen and -women were answering recurringly ringing phones. The walls were nearly covered with charts, pictures, and bulletin boards. Pertinent data were prominently displayed. Names of the victims, along with their photos, coroner's pictures, their biographies, dates and places of death; in short, everything that had been discovered, including mistakes and misjudgments, was displayed in the room, which was off-limits to everyone but task force members. It was also a testament to Koznicki's thoroughness. Too many cases he'd worked on had been filled with needlessly wasted time due to repeated mistakes and identical false leads. He didn't mind honest mistakes. He considered repeated mistakes to be dishonest.

Koznicki was also aware that most of the police work in cases like this was "busy work." With so little to go on, the killer's almost nonestablished method of operation, police work at this stage was mostly an exercise in wheel spinning. But it was vital to check every genuine lead carefully and to pool knowledge. It was always possible, even after examining the facts over and over again, that the team would discover a new dimension in something they had considered many times before. Koznicki hung to the belief that someone would break the coded language the killer was using by purposely leaving clues, chief among which was those ordinary black rosaries.

Harris and Koznicki separated and mingled with the men and women on duty. From their conversations, the two discovered that most of the task force had been amazed at the kinds of calls they'd been receiving. Most had considered their amazement at the nature of those calls a private experience and were surprised to learn that nearly everyone had had the same kinds of calls. Most had never heard of many of the liberal and conservative Catholic organizations that had sprung up over

the past few years. Several such organizations had been
mentioned, either as an identification for the caller or as
a lead to be investigated.

Some team members wondered that all the murder
victims hadn't been Detroit bishops; everyone seemed to
hate them. To a person, not one non-Catholic on the
team understood what was going on. Even some of the
less involved Catholics were not fully plugged in.

Koznicki determined that at the earliest opportunity,
he'd have Father Koesler come in and talk to the task
force. Koznicki knew the priest was very familiar with
the topic the force needed to learn: why and how a
goodly number of Catholics hate one another.

Father Fred Palmer was forty-seven years old, going
on seventy. To say he was fat, good-natured, and lazy
would be an exaggeration. That he was fat was a biological
verity. That he was good-natured was a matter of common consent. But that he was lazy was simply unfair
and untrue. However, he was extraordinarily inept.

He was the only member of his seminary class who
was still an associate pastor. A very few of his classmates, like Bob Koesler, had special jobs in the archdiocese. The rest were pastors.

Father Palmer was reflecting on this very fact this
morning, as he drove down Telegraph Road from St.
Helen's, the suburban parish to which he was assigned,
toward Vic Tanny's health club in Dearborn.

When he had been ordained twenty-two years before,
the road to pastorship had been entirely chronological.
Depending on the life span and health of one's senior
clergymen, the average wait was between twenty and
twenty-three years before one could expect to become a
pastor. However, in the past decade, roughly, several
things had happened to upset the pattern. Pastoral appointments were no longer being made in chronological
order, priests were leaving and retiring in unprecedented
numbers, and the seminaries were nearly empty. Why,
hell, Palmer thought, as he stopped for a red light at
Joy Road, just a few weeks ago, some young punk who'd

been out only six years had been named pastor of a prestigious Farmington parish.

That he was not yet a pastor was a matter of mild shame to him, a source of peripheral embarrassment to his family, and a rare example of good judgment on the chancery's part. If he had gone into the business world, it's likely he would not have made it into middle management. In the priesthood, even as a perennial assistant, he was successful in one of the few professions that did not demand achievement for continued employment.

Wednesday was Palmer's regular day off. Today, as he did each week, he was headed toward a workout at the health club he'd joined three years previously.

He had presided over a thoroughly undistinguished Mass at eight o'clock, followed by a breakfast of bacon, eggs, and waffles. Not an unusual breakfast for Palmer. Besides, he'd reflected while pushing his third waffle through a sea of butter and syrup, today he'd work it off at the club.

Palmer guided his Oldsmobile from Michigan Avenue into Tanny's parking lot, got his gear from the trunk, and hurried in through the unlit foyer.

"Hi, Billy." Palmer could never remember the young man's last name. In fact, remembering names was among the many things at which Palmer was inept.

"Mornin', Father." Bill Turner had joined the Tanny staff a little more than a year ago. He had taken an immediate liking to Father Palmer and had not given up trying to motivate the pudgy priest to be serious about a health program. Invariably, Palmer would toss off a mixture of jokes and excuses and manage to forestall reformation for another week.

Turner followed Father Palmer into the locker room. "What's your program today, Father?"

"Same as usual, Billy; weights, board, pool, sauna, whirlpool."

"Sounds good. But, if I know you, you'll leave your game in the locker room."

"Come on, now, Billy. Don't be so hard on the poor old parish priest." Palmer was removing his right support stocking. It was his final article of clothing. The resultant sight required an act of faith.

"Do me a favor, Father. Stand up."

Palmer, whose initial reaction invariably was obedience, rose. Gravity claimed layers of fat as the priest's trunk took on the configuration of a many-tiered layer cake.

"Now, don't bend over, Father, just look down. Can you see your feet?"

"Are you supposed to?"

"You're going to find this hard to believe, but, yes, you are . . . if you were in any kind of shape at all."

"Oh, well, blessed am I who cannot see but still believe I have feet."

"C'mon, Father, get serious. Your diet is garbage, and you smoke and drink."

"Yes. But I'm still celibate." Palmer had to admit that, unlike most of the others who gave him unsolicited advice and admonitions, Turner practiced what he preached. To lose weight, the young man would have had to carve flesh from his bones.

"O.K., Father. But try to be serious about your exercise today. Remember," Turner randomly selected one of the layers of Palmer's belly and patted it, "this could be the death of you."

Palmer pulled on his sweat togs and bounced into the exercise area. He selected a twenty-pound barbell for either hand and waggled them around for about ten minutes. Then, with the peculiar short rapid steps common to obese persons, he waddled to the slantboard, carefully fixed his feet into the straps and tried several times to raise his torso. Sweat flowing through the folds of his body, he decided that was enough violent activity for this day.

Changing to his swim trunks, Palmer padded to the pool, dropped heavily into the cool water, took a few strokes, rolled to his back and floated for a while. Then to the sauna, where he was lubricated by a combination of the steam and his own perspiration. A few moments in the whirlpool and, he felt, he'd paid his dues toward health.

He showered, dressed, packed his gear and, before

leaving, looked down. He still could not see his feet. Another day, perhaps. At the front door, he once again encountered Billy Turner.

"How'd it go, Father?"

"Not bad. I think I made some progress," he lied.

"How about joining me at our health food bar, Father?"

"No, thanks, Billy. I think I'll drop in at the Holiday up the street. I feel a yen for a beer, 'burger, and fries."

"Remember, Father," Turner again familiarly patted the priest's black-garbed stomach, "this could kill you."

Palmer affectionately waved at the young man and worked himself and his gear through the door. I wonder, the priest thought, if it's possible to have a *mens sana* without the *corpore sano*. It seemed workable to him.

FRIDAY,
MARCH 18

It was one of those days in the *Free Press* city room when TGIF was in the air. Bright and crisp, the glorious weather promised a quick transition to spring. It had been a demanding week for many of the reporters, with several major local stories either breaking or developing. But now the weekend was near, and most of the news-people would get a break.

Joe Cox had spent the better part of this morning alternating between the phone, his notepad, and the type-writer. He was only a couple of paragraphs short of completing another story on the continued patrolling of the metropolitan freeways by the state police. There was a lot of union pressure for this duty to be resumed by a combination of city police and county sheriff's deputies. Political influence on the question was about equally divided. There was little doubt that public opinion heavily favored the continued presence of the state force. During the almost one-year program of state patrol, citizen confidence in expressway protection had grown solid. There was still time for heavy lobbying before the state legislature and the governor would undoubtedly come to some sort of compromise.

Cox had completed his calls and gathered quotes that nicely balanced the story. Now, as the article was all but completed, Cox's gaze wandered over to Nelson Kane's desk. The city editor was busily scanning copy. Cox thought of the rumors he'd heard going around the city room. There was no doubt in anyone's mind that Kane was about to move up the executive ladder. Kane himself expected it. He felt he deserved the promotion. He'd worked through the organizational level from near the bottom rung to near the top of the heap. There was no doubt in his mind that he could handle greater responsibilities, make weightier decisions, be more instrumental in setting directions for this already influential publication.

But that was not the direction some of the rumors were taking.

The most persistent rumors had it that some of the Knight-Ridder hierarchy wanted Kane up and out. According to this school, the anti-Kane group thought Kane represented an outdated type of journalism. Sex and violence, this group held, sold everything from refrigerators to newspapers.

Kane, of course, recognized the market value of sex and violence. He simply believed other things also interested readers and sold newspapers. Things like pictures of kids and animals, an occasional upbeat human interest angle and, as he had often insisted, tabernacle veils in the folds of which people saw the face of Christ and, of course, weeping statues of saints.

His opponents would be little interested in any of these unless those essential two elements could be insinuated into the story. For instance, kids who hid in trees and sniped at their neighbors. Or statues with obscene messages painted on them.

To an outsider, these might appear to be minor ideological differences. To those directly involved, it was a struggle that would end with Kane victorious and the *Free Press*' present policies intact, or Kane either out of the organization or on a useless titled shelf and *Free Press* policies subtly but radically changing.

Cox was caught looking at Kane's head raised from the copy he was reading, and their eyes met. Kane beckoned Cox. The reporter sighed as he approached the editor's desk. Three more paragraphs and he would have been able to wrap it up for the day.

"Joe . . ." Kane's voice was so low Cox could barely hear him and decided to try to read lips as an auxiliary aid to understanding. ". . . you know I don't give a goddam who sleeps with whom around here. But I do care about starting work somewhere near on time. You and Lennon are making it pretty obvious. Not only have you both been coming in late but late together. From now on, I don't care if you come in at the same second as long as you're both on time. Got it?"

"Got it." Cox did not blush. Cox could not remember ever having blushed. But he did raise one eyebrow. It was an admission of mild surprise that anyone would notice or care about two consenting adults. He had to admit they had been coming in late regularly. That was because Pat Lennon was entirely open to as much sex as possible each morning, and Cox's schedule wasn't programmed for that sort of frosting. Until he had met Pat, Cox would have been unwilling to admit anyone was more interested in sex than he was. Now, he was nearly convinced he should abdicate.

"How're things coming with the Rosary Murders?" Kane's voice was raised to its usual soft growl.

"It's simmering. The cops are busy following leads. But I'm almost positive they haven't uncovered anything new. Of course, they've got more than they're giving us. This guy is leaving some kind of a calling card, and it's got something to do with the rosary. That much I got from Koznicki . . ."

"Koznicki told you that?"

"No. It's what he refused to say. He was really open about just about everything else I asked."

"Any chance you can get it?"

"I think I could get it if I could get into the room they call Control on the fifth floor. But I've tried everything. That task force Koznicki's assembled . . . I know it's a cliché word, but the only way to describe it is 'crack.' And they've got no dummies on the door." Cox paused a moment. "Nellie, if I could get it, would we use it?"

It was Kane's turn to pause and then smile. "No, we gotta let the cops have their little secrets if they're gonna stay employed. But, remember, we want to at least be in on the solution of this thing if we don't crack it ourselves. So it would be good to know what they know. Hell, Joe, we don't want to see any more murders than the cops do. But it's a delicate balance. Stay on it."

"O.K. I'm going to see Koznicki Monday and check out any good leads they may have gotten."

Leaving Kane to finish looking over the freeway story, Cox reflected on how generally satisfying it was to work for a guy like that. There were few enough ethics or principles left in the news business. What few were left, Kane seemed to have. He wondered what might happen if Kane came out the loser in the current power struggle. It might just mean that Cox might be forced into job hunting. He cared too much about the profession of journalism to be drawn into a shlocky performance.

A rather promising day had developed into a brooding early evening. Clouds coaxed the sun into early obscurity. The humidity was high, and the wind spanked obsolescent street lights and made them shiver and sway, casting eerie shadows of bare tree limbs across the old and stately homes. It might better have been Halloween than the threshold of spring. But Michiganders knew this too would pass. As the popular local expression had it, if you don't like the weather, just wait a minute and it'll change.

Residents of Arden Park had either retreated into their homes for the night or were headed for weekend parties. The three nuns who lived at No. 25 had just begun eating their evening meal. Sister Mary Grace had spent a good part of the afternoon preparing a simple but savory fish dinner.

In her forty-three years as a nun, Sister Mary Grace had performed a potpourri of jobs, just about whatever her superiors had asked of her. In her first couple of decades as a religious, she had taught school. Later, when postgraduate degrees became both demanded and common, she had been directed into more domestic work. By now, she was the equivalent of a master chef, able to turn quite ordinary fare into near gourmet meals. Hers was an uncluttered life. Whatever she did, she did to the best of her ability and demanded no more of herself.

Sister Anita and Mother Mary had already complimented Sister Mary Grace on the meal, even though they had just begun it. Anticipating a satisfying dinner from Sister Mary Grace was the safest bet in town.

The casual passerby might have presumed this was far too large a home for three old ladies. What the casual passerby could not know was that the three nuns not only observed canonical poverty as one of their three vows, but they were frugal to the point of being genuinely poor. Outside of the one small front room they'd converted into a chapel, the other enormous street-side rooms were usually stocked with food, clothing and medicine that were dispensed liberally on designated days. When these rooms were not in use, they were shut off—without heat—from the rest of the house.

The sisters ate in what had been the servants' dining area adjacent to the large kitchen. Ususally, they ate in silence. On the one hand, they felt they had said and heard just about everything by this stage in their lives and, on the other, they were wise enough to know that silence is a positive virtue and one ought to have good reason for breaking it. The occasional exception was Sister Anita, who sometimes babbled a bit.

"I see they've just about completed the new Renaissance Center downtown," Sister Anita threw the line out like a center jump ball. It was certain Sister Mary Grace would not contest it.

"Yes, they have," replied Mother Mary, retrieving the conversational ball. "I saw it the other day. Looks like a concrete fortress. I didn't get close enough to see if they've got a moat around it, but I wouldn't be surprised."

Sister Mary Grace left the table to get some homemade rolls that were toasting in the oven.

"Oh, dear, do you really think it's that bad?" Sister Anita thought it so bad she rested her fork on her plate and pondered the possibility of a mistake that gigantic. "I thought this was supposed to be a fresh start for downtown Detroit."

"A fresh start like the Tower of Babel." Mother Mary delicately balanced a forkful of peas. "It may get a few more people in from the suburbs for a brief visit. Somebody even told me that Ford's may move some of their office workers in from Dearborn. But it's not going to do anything about the real problem. No, my dears, if there is one thing I grow more convinced of the longer I live, it is the words of our Blessed Savior, 'The poor you will have with you always.'"

At the reassuring Biblical words, Sister Anita resumed her fork and pried apart a small morsel of fish. Sister Mary Grace threw open the napkin covering the rolls; a soft puff of smoke rose like a Native American's signal, and the unique aroma of fresh-baked dough filled the small room.

The doorbell rang.

"I'll get it, dears." Mother Mary, who always answered the doorbell, gave a determined shove against her chair and it skidded noisily over a few floor tiles. "It's probably someone who knows we don't have office hours."

"Oh, Mary." Sister Anita fluttered her napkin. "I forgot. We're all out of meal tickets. What if it's somebody or a family who needs food?"

"Then I'll just bring them back here."

Sister Mary Grace was so startled she dropped her knife. It clattered against the butter dish. She had no talent for multiplying loaves and fish. Especially halfway through a meal.

"Don't anyone get upset . . ." If Mother Mary had

been any wider she would've had to exit the kitchen door sideways. ". . . I'll handle it," she said, quieting Sister Mary Grace's fears.

Mother Mary waddled through the long hallways, floorboards creaking madly on either side as much from their age as from her weight. The thought crossed her mind that this was an unusually patient caller. The bell had not sounded again since its first ring. That was out of the ordinary.

She reached the door, then hesitated. She knew no conscious fear, but one couldn't be too careful. There were, after all, the other two nuns to consider. She turned on the porch light and peered studiously through the semi-opaque door glass. The caller appeared to be a man of medium height, wearing a hat, and with his coat collar pulled up.

She unlocked the door and opened it. "Yes?" she said, her eyes fighting the shadows. "May I help you?"

The man took a step closer. Her eyes widened in recognition. She was about to smile, but something in his quick movement toward her changed the forming smile into a small gasp of surprise and fear. His left hand covered her mouth as, simultaneously, he thrust his right hand from tight at his side. She didn't actually see the long broad knife. She caught only a reflection of light from its shining surface. In one powerful movement, it pierced her several layers of clothing, entered her side, brushed by a rib and lodged just beneath her heart. He twisted the knife; it tore through arteries, and blood gushed through the wound.

It was all so fast she felt little pain. No more than if she had received an injection. What pain there was was swallowed by shock. She staggered backward a step and then a half, stumbled and fell heavily on her back.

The man knelt quickly at her side, careful to avoid the blood that had already saturated her clothing, and was beginning to seep onto the tiled floor. Taking a plain black rosary from his pocket, he wrapped it around her left wrist and trailed the beads between her thumb and index finger. He closed the door behind him, removed his gloves, and walked quickly into the darkness.

With her right hand, Mother Mary felt the wound, the knife still in it. She held the hand above her face, saw it covered with red. With her bloodied index finger, she traced some letters on the floor at her right side. Her finger stopped moving. The blood continued to pump from her chest. She began a silent prayer for forgiveness for her assailant. Her eyes stared at the ceiling but saw nothing.

It was one of those times when everything worked in favor of a police investigation. Sister Anita had grown impatient when Mother Mary did not return to the dinner table. Anita was the one who found the body, and she had called Sister Mary Grace. They knew that even together they could not have moved Mother Mary's huge bulk, even heavier in death. So Anita called the police.

The first officers to respond noticed the rosary immediately and began the string of calls that would summon at least the key members of Koznicki's special task force.

Within the first quarter hour, Sergeant Fred Ross, who had been having dinner with his family, was on the scene. In full uniform, within a few moments he had everything organized. As soon as enough members of the task force arrived, which was only a matter of minutes, Ross ordered the house cordoned off. A small crowd had gathered on the sidewalk. They were mostly from Second Avenue; a few had been shopping on Woodward. Porch lights were on in most of the homes on Arden Park, but the residents were behind curtains, gawking at the growing number of police cars with their rotating flashing lights. It was not the typical scene one saw on TV or in the movies. Everything was too quiet. No sirens, no noise at all. The assembled crowd was waiting for someone to tell them what had happened. What was going on was efficient, brisk police work that required no explanations.

Detective Sergeant Dan Fallon had been about to begin his regular Friday night poker game when he was reached. He had been next on the team after Ross to arrive, in the same rumpled brown suit he'd been in all day. Ross had been mostly occupied with getting statements from the two nuns. Both Sisters had been confused and nervous. But under Fallon's calm, sympathetic questioning they were able to remember more details than they had first thought they could. Meanwhile, Ross was guarding the body like a mother hen.

Lieutenant Koznicki had not been difficult to locate. His children had known where he was—at a dinner party in Grosse Pointe Farms—and the phone number. As soon as he was notified, he made arrangements to have his wife driven home after the party, and he then left immediately for Arden Park.

By far the most difficult member of the team to locate had been Sergeant Harris. He'd gone to a discotheque in northwest Detroit, and when finally reached by phone, there had been a good deal of shouting on both ends of the line just to be heard above the noise before he could understand the message. The last of the core group to arrive, he came up the walk just in time to meet the solitary and solemn figure of a priest, who was slowly descending the porch steps, having just given Mother Mary the last rites of the Church.

They made an odd-looking tableau as they stood around the dead woman's body: Ross in uniform, Fallon in extremely plain clothes, Koznicki in a tuxedo, and Harris in black velvet trousers, a ruffled shirt, and a shrieking orange jacket.

"God, Walt . . ." Harris found himself shuddering. ". . . why would he hit Mother Mary?"

"Why would he hit any of them?"

"Yeah, but Mother Mary! Even her enemies liked her."

"The shit is gonna hit the fan on this one," said Ross reflectively.

There was no doubt all of them were stunned, just as everyone else would be once the news got out. For a moment, each was lost in his own thoughts.

Koznicki broke the silence. "It's our first real break."

"Yeah . . ." Fallon removed his hat and scratched his head with the same hand. "But what does it mean?"

" 'R-O-B'—robber? Do you think?" asked Harris, rhetorically.

"Not 'robber,' I think," said Koznicki. "By the time she traced those three letters on the floor, she had been stabbed. She was dying and she probably knew it. I think we can safely assume that, because she did, indeed, die before she finished writing whatever she was trying to tell us. There was no point in telling us the person who killed her was a thief. If he were a thief, we'd know soon enough by what he stole.

"No, Mother Mary either knew or thought she knew her assailant. And she tried to tell us his name. This may just be the break we've been waiting for."

Koznicki was evidently exhilarated, and it was contagious. They all felt his elation.

"Well, what do you wanna do with this one?" asked Fallon, scratching his head and replacing his hat with the same hand—the habit reversed. "Do you wanna keep this one from the media?"

"By no means," answered Koznicki. "No, this is something our killer didn't count on. His first mistake. Until now, everything has gone his way. I want him to know he made a mistake. It's sure to shake his confidence and maybe cause another mistake. Meanwhile, we're going to make the most of these three letters."

"Yeah, but the shit is gonna hit the fan after this one," said Ross, repeating himself.

"You're right, Fred," said Koznicki, "and if we're not careful, we'll overreact to the public pressure. We've got to make sure nobody on the team panics. At this point, it's just as easy for us to make that fatal mistake as it is for the killer. We've got to continue with solid, methodical police work. I'm counting on you, Fred, to check right through the rank and file of our team, no matter how much flak comes from this murder. We've got to bring in a good solid case, and we're not going to do it if we react to pressure by panicking or trying to cut corners."

"Yessir, Lieutenant." Ross, Koznicki knew, would be the last to panic under almost any pressure. It was no idle commission.

"Dan, Fred, wrap this up, will you?" It had been a long day. Koznicki wanted to get home, get some sleep, and start fresh tomorrow, armed with their new clue. "Fred, spread the word to the team to be in early as possible. Dan, handle the media tonight. Be sure they have the 'R-O-B' evidence clearly. I don't want our killer confused by any inaccuracies of the press."

Fallon and Ross nodded. Koznicki and Harris retrieved the topcoats they had deposited on a nearby chair. They stopped to repeat a few consoling words to the two nuns who were still in a combined state of confusion and loss.

As they walked toward their cars, Koznicki paused and fingered Harris' jacket. "Nice threads," he said, smiling.

"Thanks," Harris replied, and added, "Congratulations."

"On what?"

"Learning more of the vernacular. I'm gonna make a cool dude outta you yet."

SATURDAY
MARCH 19

For some reason, Father Koesler wasn't as shocked as he thought he should be. He'd been sitting in the rectory living room with Father Pompilio when word of Mother Mary's murder had been broadcast on the eleven o'clock TV news. Of course, the news had that sudden breathtaking impact any unexpected cataclysmic announcement has. But Pompilio and most of the people Koesler had talked to today were especially and particularly disturbed that the victim was Mother Mary.

To Koesler, each and every one of the recent murders had been equally tragic and senseless. Since he had been unable to determine any rhyme or reason to these killings, he presumed the murderer was selecting his victims more or less at random. The target, as far as Koesler was concerned, might have been any priest or nun who was available and vulnerable at the time the killer decided to strike. And that made just about any priest or nun appropriate, because just about all of them were both available and vulnerable anytime. Last night, it happened to be Mother Mary.

Just now, duty called. And Koesler was trying to get comfortable for a Saturday afternoon shriving session in the confessional St. Ursula's parish provided. Thinking of homicidal maniacs reminded him of the maniacs who designed confessionals. It was still cold enough to turn the heat on in church, and heat was the special torture feature of St. Ursula's confessionals.

At St. Ursula's, heat moved by large blowers descended from the ceiling. It was neither an effective nor a comfortable system in the body of the church, but it was torture in the confessional. In "the box" it was either freezing or steaming at any given moment. If it was cold when you arrived, you bundled up, pulled your coat collar up around your neck, and shivered. When it got cold enough, the blower would activate, and heat would pour down, forcing a general unbundling. When it got sufficiently hot, the blower would shut down, and cold would begin creeping up from the floor, forcing a general rebundling. The process continued through early spring.

Koesler recalled an assigned confessional in another parish. It was the only one he'd ever experienced that had no window or any other means of ventilation. In summer, it was a steambath. Once, a salesperson had asked if he was interested in an air conditioner for the confessional. Was he! However, when the appliance had been installed, there was no room for Koesler's long legs. And when it was turned on, it made so much noise Koesler couldn't have heard the penitent if he or she were shouting, let alone whispering.

Today, he'd brought his dog-eared copy of *The First Deadly Sin* with him. Penitents were so few and far between these days, he always brought something along to read. He'd selected *The First Deadly Sin* because it had been several years since he'd first read it. But more because the fictional murderer's M.O. in some ways resembled that of Detroit's very real Rosary Murderer. He hoped rereading the novel might give him some clue as to some method of discovering the identity of Detroit's killer.

It was cold in the church, nearing that magic degree that would call forth heat. Koesler, trying to stay warm, tugged his coat collar tightly. He was still trying for some measure of comfort when the afternoon's first penitent arrived. Koesler flipped off the overhead light, slid shut the small door to his left, and leaned over to the open door on his right. All was in near total darkness. "All right," he whispered, letting the penitent know he was listening.

"Oh . . . Bless me, Father, for I have sinned. My last confession was four and a half weeks ago."

Koesler recognized the voice immediately. He had no idea who the man was. Nor was he likely to be able to identify him in ordinary conversation. But the whisper, the delivery, the borderline scrupulosity he couldn't miss in this setting.

"I had evil thoughts five or six times, more or less. I argued with my wife unnecessarily four or five times, more or less . . ."

Here was the classic product of a Catholicism that was passing away in the wake of the Second Vatican Council. This was the way Koesler himself had been raised and trained. An obsession with numbers, times, kinds, and a protective qualifying clause thrown in just in case a human error might be misinterpreted by God. Koesler didn't know if the penitent would say it this time, but he recalled the time this gentleman had confessed doing something "once, more or less," and Koesler's subsequent pondering about the sinfulness of something done less than once.

". . . I punished the children excessively six or seven times, more or less. I took some inexpensive things from work three or four times, more or less. I am sorry for these and all the sins of my past life, especially for disobedience."

His concluding formula was an indication of how long this man had been glued to this manner of confessing. He couldn't have "disobeyed" in the past several decades. This is the way he had confessed in childhood. He would take it with him to his grave.

There was a time in his early days as a priest when Koesler had tried to introduce such people to spiritual adulthood. Generally, he had succeeded only in driving them into deeper scrupulosity.

He gave this penitent what he knew the man wanted, a few panacean words of encouragement, a simple, easily fulfilled penance of five Our Fathers and five Hail Marys, and absolution. The man would leave the confessional, kneel in the church, and recite the Lord's Prayer and the Hail Mary six times each—one extra to ensure having at least the prescribed five—and then leave, vaguely relieved.

While Koesler had been engaged in this first confession of the afternoon, the heat had gone on. With the departure of the first penitent, and no one waiting in the other confessional, the priest turned on the light, loosened his clothing, and recommenced skimming through *The First Deadly Sin*.

His perusal of the novel was interrupted by penitents only a half-dozen more times in the hour and a half he spent in the box. He had concluded there didn't seem to be many similarities between the fictional killer and Detroit's real murderer of priests and nuns. However, he was more than ever convinced that, just as in the novel, the real murderer was picking his victims haphazardly.

It was nearing five-thirty when the afternoon's final penitent arrived. By the soft thunk of knees on the kneeler, Koesler correctly assumed his customer to be young.

"The last time I was to confession, I promised to be nicer to my sister. I did pretty good. This time, I'm going to try to cooperate better with my Dad."

The new breed, mused Koesler. No times, kinds, numbers. Probably no scrupulosity or obsessive-compulsive behavior in *his* future.

"O.K., sonny. Try real hard. And for your penance, say five Hail Marys."

"I don't know five Hail Marys, Father."

Koesler paused as he was about to begin absolution. The boy clearly was grammatically correct. But no one had ever done this to Koesler.

"Do you know *one* Hail Mary, sonny?"

"Yes, Father."

"Well, will you say that one Hail Mary five times?"

Brightly, "Yes, Father."

Back in the rectory, Koesler made himself a bracing Manhattan and lit a cigarette. He was trying to decide whether that kid was a sincere if premature grammarian or a technical smartass.

SUNDAY
MARCH 20

Over the years, the Top of the Flame had remained one of Detroit's better dining places. The restaurant's name was based on its being located on the top floor of the Michigan Consolidated Gas Building. It boasted a magnificent view of the Detroit River and the riverfronts of both Detroit and Windsor.

Over the years, each Sunday evening, with rare exception, three Detroit priests faithfully dined at the Top of the Flame.

Monsignor Al Thomas held his age, fifty-seven, very well. His full head of hair was sleek and black, partly the work of nature and partly the gift of a bottle of hair dye. At five-feet-nine (he claimed five-feet-eleven), he fought a constant battle with baby fat. At the moment, the outcome was in doubt. Thomas had spent nearly all of his priestly career as a member of the Archdiocesan Matrimonial Court, technically called the Tribunal. For the past seven years, he had been head of the Tribunal, and he ran a tight court.

Father Edward Killian's thinning hair was silver. Still slender and athletic, his six-foot-four frame looked good in the clerical black suit. Killian was part of a new phenomenon in the Catholic Church, a pastor who had purposely reduced his status to that of an associate pastor. He had worked himself up through the ranks to become pastor of a stylish suburban parish, only to resign that post to become the associate at St. Olaf's parish on Detroit's far east side.

Completing the troika was Father William O'Shea, a small, bald, peculiar-looking man, whose skin seemed always to carry a kind of greenish hue. He was pastor of St. Perpetua's parish in Sterling Heights, an affluent far suburb.

As always, the threesome, classmates thirty-two years ordained, had met before dinner, this time at Killian's rectory, for drinks. They were now feeling little pain as they settled in for an undemanding evening of good food, good drink, and good bitching. Sunday dinner at the Flame was their way of rewarding themselves at the end of a working weekend.

Their drink orders were typical of their personalities. Thomas' was a double-dry martini, O'Shea's a draft beer, and Killian's a bourbon on the rocks—in keeping with his drinking man's diet.

"Oh, God!" Thomas moaned.

"What is it? What's the matter, Al?" Startled, O'Shea had turned even greener.

"The people at the next table. They're talking Catholic talk, can't you hear them?"

"Catholic talk?" Killian stopped in mid-stir of his bourbon.

"Yes, Catholic talk. Somebody at that table is talking about Mass this morning and what a lovely homily so-and-so gave."

"So what?" Killian resumed stirring.

"You'll see! With a table full of Catholics sitting next to one with three priests, eventually they're going to talk to us."

"What's so bad about that?" Killian asked.

"What's so bad about it!? We talk to Catholics for a living. This is our night off. We deserve a few hours to ourselves. We've paid our dues."

"Oh, c'mon, Al," Killian laughed. "It may not even happen. If it bothers you so much, next time we'll wear our civvies."

"No," O'Shea corrected. "We'll be here in our clericals. And Al will order the same damn pork chop dinner he always does."

"What's the matter with that? It's the best pork chop dinner in town and inexpensive, too."

"You, Father Thomas, are a victim of routine." O'Shea thought he might order another beer. "Which reminds me, I'll bet that Rosary Murderer depends on the routines of his targets when he's going to kill one of them."

"Rosary Murder, Rosary Murder," Thomas huffed, "that's all we talked about at Ed's place. Can't we talk about something else for a change?"

"That's all *anybody's* talking about," said O'Shea.

"True," said Killian, "but Al's got a point. Why should we spend the whole evening on the Rosary Murderer? Not when we've got all the problems of Holy Mother Church to solve."

"Like when am I going to get an assistant," complained O'Shea.

"An associate." Thomas smiled smugly.

"Probably never," said Killian. "That's something we're running out of. The new endangered species."

"How's it feel being a member of that seeshies?" Thomas' speech was beginning to slur slightly. He needed food.

"A hell of a lot better than I did being a pastor. Who needs that kind of grief?" Killian pushed the garlic toast toward Thomas, knowing from experience his classmate would level off once he got something in his stomach. "Morning-to-night meetings. Parish councils, commissions, school boards, vicariates. Same money whether you're on the top or bottom. But in the trenches you can do priest work. You oughta try it, Bill."

"Or not get in the rat race at all," said Thomas, who barely remembered what parish life was like. "Whaddya say to another drink?"

"Why don't we wait till the food gets here? It should be just a few minutes," Killian urged.

"That reminds me." O'Shea looked up brightly. "Did you guys ever hear the one about the pastor who threw a big party for a bunch of his classmates? They musta put away three cases of booze. Next morning, the housekeeper was dumping out all the empty bottles when the garbage man comes up and says, 'A lot of dead soldiers there, lady.' And she says, 'Yes, but isn't it consoling that there was a priest with each one right to the end?'"

Thomas and Killian laughed appreciatively. Thomas, in fact, laughed so hard he began to cough violently. Killian pounded him sharply on the back several times.

"Easy," Thomas protested, "I'm O.K. You trying to sever my spine?"

"No." Killian was genuinely concerned. "But I am worried about you. You drink too much, and you've got a weight problem. You know that, don't you?"

"What d'ya want me to do? Run my ass off every day like you?"

"You belong to the DAC. They've got a gym. You could do it. Work up to a few miles a day, but slowly."

"This comes," Thomas was speaking to O'Shea, but pointing to Killian, "from the author of 'Are You Jogging With Me, Jesus?'"

"You oughta get serious, Al," Killian said. "Booze and that weight could be the death of you."

The elderly purple-haired lady at the adjoining table turned in her chair and tapped Thomas on the shoulder. "Excuse me, Father, but are you a Catholic priest?"

"Oh, God!" Thomas moaned, sotto voce.

"I beg your pardon?" she mumbled.

"He prays a lot," said O'Shea, enjoying Thomas' anguish at being afflicted with the laity.

"Well, you can't be too careful these days. It's hard to tell your genuine Catholic priests from your ordinary ministers. And then, there are your deacons." Clearly she was winding up for a long conversation.

At this moment, the waitress approached Thomas. "I'm sorry, Father, but the chef says we are out of the pork chop dinner."

"Oh," the purple-haired lady said, fluttering her hands as one who knows the answer to a mystery, "I must have gotten the last pork chop dinner."

"Oh, God!" Thomas was in genuine distress.

MONDAY, MARCH 21

Lieutenant Koznicki and Sergeant Harris had invested in a midmorning coffee break. Actually, Koznicki had called Control and asked Harris to bring some coffee.

"The news media now own the corridors of this floor," said Harris, as he carefully placed one of the coffee-filled paper cups on the corner of Koznicki's desk.

"How's the Control Room?"

"Secure." Harris balanced his cup on the windowsill. "God! Those media guys really latched on to that 'R-O-B.' The *News* even reproduced it in red. I think there's as much speculation about what it means going on in the media as there is in Control."

"Good." Koznicki was signing the latest of numerous requisition slips his secretary had prepared. "I like having all that cheap police work done for me."

"But what pleases you most is that our killer finally made a mistake."

"You betcha. Until now, he's been in the driver's seat. Speaking his own language, telling us only what he wants

us to know. And, on top of that, we haven't broken
his code. Then it happens. Something he didn't count
on. He was undoubtedly aware that Mother Mary knew
him. He never thought she'd live long enough to leave an
identification. It's just possible this break has confused
him. And if this assumption is correct, the mistakes may
multiply. And thereby hangs arrest."

"We still don't know what the 'R-O-B' stands for."

"What's your guess?" Koznicki knew Harris was as
much at home with a guess as *he* was with a firmer
assumption.

"I'd say it was a first name," said Harris, retrieving
his cup, and sipping a bit of the steaming coffee. "Robert
or Robin."

"You reveal your nonparochial background."

"Walt, I do that with my entire lifestyle. How is it,
in this specific instance the astute detective would know
I was not a product of Catholic education? Except for
my periodic craving for watermelon, that is."

"If you had gone to parochial school, and if you were
old enough to have had the old-style nun, like Mother
Mary was, you'd know that the nuns always called pupils
by their last names."

"You've gotta be puttin' me on. You mean when you
were in the first grade, some nun called you Koznicki?"

"Worse. *Mister* Koznicki."

"Why?"

"I don't know. Questions weren't encouraged." Koznicki sipped a bit of the still hot coffee, careful to keep
his mustache uninvolved. "But you can see how important
it is not to make a first name an odds-on favorite for
'R-O-B.' It could just as easily, and more than likely,
be a surname. Roberts, Robertson, Robinson, Robb . . ."

"Good point, Walt. I'd better make sure everybody in
Control understands this." Harris started to leave but
was stopped by Koznicki's question:

"How are they following the 'R-O-B' lead now?"

"I've got Ross on it. He's assembling about twenty-
five of our people. They're going to track down as many
records as they can find of kids Mother Mary taught,

and find all the variables of R-O-B. It's cutting a helluva lot of people out of our team, and it's going to take a helluva lot of time."

"That's pretty nitty-gritty work." Koznicki dropped the now empty cup in his wastebasket. "Tell Ross to hold on that. I'll get the chief to special detail some more personnel pro tem just for this job. Searching records takes no special skills. After they find all the Robs, we'll have to start checking them out. And I want *our* team to be free to check out all the other leads that are coming in over the transom. With Ross in charge, the new people will be kept thorough."

"Think the chief will give us some more on such short notice?"

"At this point, the chief will give us his mother and father if we've got a hot lead."

"You're probably right." Harris hesitated. "By the way, Walt, what's your guess on the next one?"

"How do I know? So far, he's hit on a Wednesday and three Fridays. But he's alternated priests and nuns. If I had to make an assumption, it would be Wednesday, the day after tomorrow. And it would be a priest."

"I wouldn't cover that bet."

"Then it must be an extremely improbable wager. You'll bet on anything. Now get out of here."

"O.K., Boss. But . . ." as he was closing the door behind him, "I'll be back in precisely twelve minutes."

Twelve minutes? What the hell did he mean by that? Oh, yes. Koznicki smiled.

TUESDAY,
MARCH 22

St. Camillus Hospital was one of Detroit's oldest private health-care facilities. On East Grand Boulevard where the Boulevard makes a sharp ninety-degree turn, it had once denoted one of Detroit's extremities. Now it was well within the city limits.

It seemed longer ago than it actually was that this had been one of Detroit's stylish sections. Now, it was an area marked by housing decay, heavy drug traffic, and high crime. Periodically, city officials gave public thanks to the Religious Sisters of Mercy for hanging in there. Which, while a vague morale booster for some of the staff, did not make their difficult job any easier.

Sister Marie Magdala Connors was quite young to be administrator of such a complex facility as a major hospital. Just thirty-five, she was an impressive woman. Tall, almost six feet, dark-complexioned, with Titian hair and almond-shaped brown eyes, this immensely talented woman would have—were things as they once had been—been condemned by her relative youth to an innocuous existence in the relentless system of seniority. However, with the present paucity of religious sisters, her credentials had been allowed to surface.

As administrator of St. Camillus, Sister Marie worried, mostly. She worried about the patients and the neighborhood. The two were related. Elective surgery was not high on St. Camillus' priorities. Rather, many of the patients were the neighborhood's victims. ODs of every age. Old black men who had been using street drugs before the white community knew they were for anything but purely medicinal purposes. Poor young kids, black and white, whose brains were being scrambled by their habitual escape from reality. Pregnant women whose unborn babies were already addicted. The victims of drug violence—shootings, knifings, assaults—for drug dealing was the king of organized crime in that neighborhood. Finally, the end product of poverty—the malnourished, the undernourished, the beneficiaries of a heritage of discrimination, unemployment, and hopelessness.

At the beginning and end of her worries was money. The majority of the patients were very poor, and many were either underinsured or without insurance entirely. And there were precious few health-care corners she could cut. As a result of financial pressures, there was a very real possibility that St. Camillus Hospital might be forced to close.

This was the least demanding moment of Sister Marie's day. It was nighttime, and visiting hours were over. The halls were quiet after the hubbub and confusion of visitors. In a few minutes, Sister Marie would go to her large office on the main floor, turn on the public address system, and lead night prayers. But, for the moment, she wanted to wander through the halls assuring herself all was well.

As she turned the corner leading to the psychiatric ward, she stopped, startled, and gave a strangled squeal. She hadn't expected to encounter anyone. But here was the aged and ageless Sister Bonaventure, clad from head to toe in her traditional white habit, pushing her aluminum walker ahead of her. In the dim and otherwise empty corridor, she had at first appeared to be a ghost.

"What's the matter, Magdala?" Sister Bonaventure chuckled; "don't tell me you let old ladies scare you."

"I didn't expect to see you." Sister Marie blushed slightly. In her job and in this neighborhood, fear was a luxury. She had grown to believe she should be above the demands of human emotion. "What are you doing here, anyway? No one except authorized personnel is supposed to be in this corridor unless the security guard informs me."

"Don't worry, dear. I won't disturb anybody on this corridor any more than they're already disturbed. And, besides, the security guard isn't at his desk."

Oh, Lord! If there was anything they needed in that neighborhood, it was tight security. The security firm they'd hired was not the best, admittedly. It was also not the most expensive. It was all they could afford. But she would have to locate that guard and impress him with his responsibilities, as only she could. And, of course, notify his superiors in the morning.

She was also troubled, as she had been many times in the past, that Sister Bonaventure might think she was not wanted in the hospital. Quite the contrary was true. Now in her late eighties, Bonaventure had never stopped learning and developing, the only formula for avoiding senility. She brought both warmth and rare wisdom to the patients.

"Bonnie," Sister Marie touched the old nun's arm gently; "I'm only worried for your safety. Hospitals can be dangerous places, especially if, like yourself, you can't move quickly, or signal for help, and the staff is reduced as it is at night."

"Pshaw, Magdala! Who'd want to bother hurting a sweet little old lady like me? Why, it'd be like shooting fish in a barrel."

"Bonnie, where do you think that expression came from in the first place? There are some people who will shoot fish in a barrel."

"Oh, very well. If it'll make you stop screeching in the hallways, I'll go park my bones away for the night. But if you're going to shove me out of here, the least you can do is complete my mission of mercy."

"Glad to, Bonnie; into what private affair were you about to meddle?"

"Don't be bold with me, young lady. You may be my superior for the moment, but don't forget, I'll be in heaven long before you know half of what I've forgotten."

"All right, Your Beatitude," Sister Marie laughed. Sister Bonaventure was always able to make her laugh. Even in the darkest moments. "What shall I do next?"

"I promised I would pray with Mrs. Washington tonight."

"Where is she?"

"259-D."

"All right. Now you get off to bed." She watched as Sister Bonaventure slowly made her way down the corridor.

Room 259 was no trouble to find. The room was dark, but she found Bed D at the left window. "Mrs. Washington?"

"Yes. Who are you?"

"Sister Marie Magdala. Sister Bonaventure wasn't able to come tonight. She asked me to pray with you. Will that be all right?"

There was a moment of silence. "Well . . . O.K. You sure you know how to do it?"

"Probably not as well as Sister Bonaventure. But I'll do my best."

"Well, O.K." Obviously, Mrs. Washington was unsure. But willing to chance it.

"Father in heaven . . ." Sister Marie had learned only relatively recently to pray without reliance on formal ritual. "Hear us, your children. We ask you for health, to give us your healing hand and make us well."

"Amen!" Mrs. Washington was entering into the spirit of it. These antiphonal interruptions had once been greatly distracting to Sister Marie. Early on, she had taken great breaths and delivered paragraphs of prayer without hesitation. But she had learned the value of this shared prayer to those whose tradition it was.

"Jesus, you knew suffering."

"Amen! Believe it."

"Come to us! Console us! Strengthen us! Let us see the value you found in suffering, and then heal our bodies and souls!"

"Say it, Sister!"

"We pray, too, for our loved ones who suffer because we suffer. Be with us and them this night."

"Amen, Lord Jesus!"

"We ask this with faith that you hear us. Amen."

"Amen! Amen! Amen!"

"Was that all right, Mrs. Washington?"

"That was jes' fine, Sister. Thank you."

From the light in the hallway, Sister Marie detected a tear on Mrs. Washington's face. She touched it with her finger. The old black woman took the nun's hand and they held each other tightly for a moment.

"Good night, Mrs. Washington."

"Good night, Sister. And thank you."

Sister Marie headed for her office and night prayers, which she broadcast to the hospital. She worried again over the special vulnerability of Sister Bonaventure. She thought, with a touch of bitterness, that the events of the past several weeks in Detroit proved that nuns and priests do occasionally get killed like fish in a barrel.

**WEDNESDAY,
MARCH 23**

For a day off, today was having inauspicious beginnings for Father Fred Palmer. He had not slept well. For the past several hours before rising, he had felt uneasy. It was a vague feeling, but unsettling enough to allow him only intermittent napping.

He nicked himself several times while shaving. He had more trouble than usual zipping his pants. Could that before-bed beer and popcorn have made that much difference?

There was no altar boy for his seven-thirty Mass. And none of the fifteen-or-so people in church had come forward to help. As a result, he found himself sweating profusely as he finished Mass just a few minutes before eight.

Breakfast was in keeping with the rest of the morning. Father Thaddeus Winiarski, pastor of St. Helen's, had picked this morning to berate and beleaguer his associate.

"Father, look at you!" Winiarski was wagging a spoon in Palmer's direction. "To say you are overweight is not to say enough, to understate. You are FAT, Father! And this is hurting your career. Others who are thinner are moving ahead of you into pastorates. Don't you want to be a pastor, Father? Of course you do. Doesn't everyone? Isn't that enough for you not to eat so much?"

Palmer speared a three-tiered chunk of pancakes and swirled it into the pleasant blend of butter and syrup that had gathered at one side of his plate. The gravitational pull of an unbalanced table always provided a warm repository on the plate wherein to slosh food through substances such as gravy or melted butter.

This was not the first sermon on self-improvement that had been preached to Palmer. Sometimes, he was able to retreat all the way back to the childish defense mechanism of denial and convince himself it wasn't happening. Today, too many things had gone wrong, and most mechanisms were unavailable. He was absorbing but not willingly.

"And don't think, Father, that just because you go over by that health clinic, spa, whatever, once a week that you are being changed. I don't know what you are doing over there. But whatever you are doing, it is not doing much of anything for you." Winiarski was stirring his coffee in rhythmical figure eights, occasionally resting the spoon against the side of the cup to wag a finger at Palmer.

Palmer stabbed an entire link of sausage, saturated it in the butter-syrup mixture, and plopped it in his mouth.

"What can your good parents think of all of this, Father? Oh, I forgot, your good father is dead, Lord rest his soul. But then, what of your good mother? She knows well that the others of your classmates have become pastors. How it must wound her mother's heart, Father, to see you like this!"

If it were possible for Father Fred Palmer to assert himself, this would have been the moment of self-assertion. However, it was impossible. Winiarski was reaching him. Not to the point that he would speak. But the diatribe was increasing his general feeling of discomfort.

"Why, Father, when the bishop was here for confirmations, he mentioned—it was when he was cleaning the consecrated oil off his fingers—that you could have a better future in the Church, that it was not too late, that you could change. He also mentioned that it would be no small feather in my cap if I could effect some change for the better."

So that was it! Palmer had been puzzled at the special fervor of this lecture. There were strings attached. With special glee, he pierced another triple-tiered glob of pancakes, along with a piece of sausage, dunked the combination over and over again, and dumped the whole super-caloric mess in his mouth.

"Think about it!" Winiarski was mercifully abrupt in today's peroration. The balding, moderately sized priest plodded determinedly from the dining room, his hands clenched skaterwise behind his back.

Palmer finished his breakfast shortly after Winiarski's final admonition. He climbed the stairs to his room, puffing all the way. He found white socks and an athletic supporter, both freshly laundered, and dropped them into the floppy black bag that contained tennis shoes and sweat clothes that were nearing their monthly wash cycle. The atmosphere around the bag was always a bit gamy.

Palmer was nearly three-quarters of the way toward Vic Tanny's, when he suddenly decided he was too depressed to go through his regular Wednesday routine. The truth behind Winiarski's diatribe was really reaching him. He was on a treadmill going nowhere. A pastorate these days was a simple achievement. In the old days, it had been quite possible to live one's entire priesthood without becoming a pastor. But nowadays, men with the oil of ordination still wet were being named pastors. When he was forced to think of it, it was depressing.

On a whim, he turned onto Edward Hines Parkway. He decided to drive out to St. John's Seminary in Plymouth and get one of the students to play racquetball with him. Uusally, seminarians were respectful enough not to single out any of Palmer's many weaknesses for sarcastic comment.

Hines Parkway, an elongated tree-lined stretch of park, protected the path of the winding Rouge River. Signs of spring were unmistakable in this peaceful setting.

As was his habit while driving, Palmer, in one gesture, removed the rosary that always hung from the radio's volume switch and, in the same motion, turned on the radio. He habitually recited the rosary while driving and, not to waste time, listened to the radio simultaneously. As with most Detroiters, Palmer's radio dial never left station WJR, Michigan's most popular clear-channel station.

Palmer was halfway through the third Glorious Mystery—the Descent of the Holy Spirit on the Apostles —and thinking that in a few more weeks, the familiar voice of Ernie Harwell would be describing Tiger baseball games on this same station.

The pain was sharp and uncompromising. It hit in his left arm and shot like a bolt of lightning across his chest. Only one thought occurred to him, this can't be happening to me. It was a thought clouded by his life's last moment of panic. His right arm jerked to his chest. His body lurched forward. His head slammed into the steering wheel with such force that his forehead was cut and began to bleed profusely. The car drifted slowly from the roadway. It crossed some thirty yards of turf before hitting the large oak that blocked any further movement.

It was only a matter of minutes before a Dearborn Heights police officer, patrolling the parkway, spotted Palmer's car. It was not an unusual sight; the parkway was the site of many accidents, usually caused by speeding or reckless or drunk driving.

The policeman noticed that both front doors of the car were unlocked. He opened the door on the passenger's side, reached in and turned off the ignition. He then circled the car and opened the driver's door. He noted the victim was wearing a black suit. A little unusual. Probing through the layers of fat around the man's neck, he checked for the presence of a pulse, and found the Roman collar. A priest. Instinctively, he checked the dead man's hands. The left hand was hanging lifeless and empty. The right hand was pinned between the body and the steering wheel. Dangling from the hand was a rosary.

Never had this policeman called in so quickly.

The clue left by the dying Mother Mary was having the electrifying effect Lieutenant Koznicki had predicted. Previously, Koznicki's special task force had been receiving many tips every day. Since the revelation of Mother Mary's painfully drawn 'R-O-B,' the number of tips had more than doubled. The news media were alternately referring to the murderer as the Rosary Killer and, simply, Rob. Koznicki's team had all it could do to sift the tips, check nearly every one, and pay greater attention to the more likely.

Koznicki was in Control, wandering about, glancing at notes as they were made by the officers handling the phones and talking to other officers between calls.

He was engaged in one such conversation when he was summoned to the phone. It was Patrolman Andy Bologna, the special dispatcher Koznicki had selected for his team. Not long on the force, Bologna had the kind of unflappable nerves needed by air traffic controllers.

"Lieutenant." Bologna's emotionless voice was precise. "We have a probable in Dearborn Heights, a priest on Edward Hines Drive near Telegraph."

"Do we have anyone in the vicinity?"

"Sergeant Ross, sir. He's in Wayne."

"Has he been notified?"

"Affirmative. He's on his way."

"So am I. I'll be in Sergeant Harris' car."

Harris was between Koznicki and the door. He could tell by what was for Koznicki a rapid pace that something serious had happened. He joined Koznicki, who, with a touch of controlled excitement, said, "We've got a probable, a priest, in Dearborn Heights."

As they exited the room, they noticed Warren Reston of the *News* in the hallway.

"Anything up, Lieutenant?"

Koznicki told him of the report; Reston was out the door only a few steps behind the two detectives.

In the car, Harris turned to Koznicki. "I've gotta hand it to you, Walt."

"What?"

"You called it. You said the next one would be a priest, and you called the day—today."

"So I did." Koznicki hadn't been thinking about his prediction. "Maybe now you'll have a little respect for me."

Sergeant Fred Ross was the third person at the scene. Corporal William Nickerson had discovered the body. Dearborn Heights Police Chief Paul Markham had arrived just moments before Ross. Whatever had happened, accident or crime, had happened in the jurisdiction of Dearborn Heights. Ross was in the delicate position of requesting the cooperation of a neighbor force.

They had not moved the body. For that Ross was grateful. The three now stood looking through the open car door at the dead priest, as flashes from the police photographer's camera signaled that the scene was being captured for future reference.

Markham spoke: "It's in the wrong hand, isn't it?"

"Yes, sir," said Ross, adding, "and it's the wrong kind of rosary." The rosary, clearly seen hanging from the lifeless hand crushed against the steering wheel, had large, translucent beads.

"There's just one more thing." Ross turned to Nickerson. "If you would help me lift the body . . ."

Nickerson crawled into the front side from the passenger side, and grasped Palmer's right shoulder. Ross, from the driver's side, took firm hold of the left shoulder.

"Slow and careful," Ross warned.

Little by little, the two officers moved the body away from the steering wheel. Ross watched as the limp right hand appeared. The rosary hung loosely in the priest's fingers, and, as the hand was exposed, the rosary clinked to the floor.

The phone in Harris' car rang. Koznicki answered.

"We have a negative on the Dearborn Heights run, Lieutenant." It was Andy Bologna.

"Was it Ross's report?"

"Yessir."

"Patch me through to him."

"Yessir."

In a few seconds, Ross was on the line. "Lieutenant?" Strange how similarly flat both Ross and Bologna's voices were.

"What did you find?"

"Large rosary with clear beads held in right hand, not wrapped around wrist. Priest was overweight. Skin had discolored shortly after death. Looks like the Dearborn Heights Police have a heart failure."

"O.K., Fred."

"One more thing, Lieutenant."

"Yes?"

"The media are going to be here. That guy from the *News* just arrived. How do you want us to handle it?"

"Who's 'us'?"

"Chief Markham and Corporal Nickerson of Dearborn Heights."

"Give them everything but the specific details of the clue."

"Tell them why we know it's not the perpetrator without telling them exactly how the perpetrator leaves his rosaries?"

"That's right, Fred."

"Right, Lieutenant. Ten-four."

"Good-bye, Fred."

Harris had already turned the car and was heading back to the city. He glanced at Koznicki. "Why did you do that, Walt? If they've got a heart attack, they don't have to tell anything."

"This is an excellent opportunity to communicate with the killer. Until now, we haven't had a chance to tell him we understand his calling card. This is one message he's sending that we are getting, and I want him to know that."

"O.K. Good move. But you know what? You don't have the right day, you don't have a murdered priest, and you don't have my respect."

"I wanted your love."

THURSDAY,
MARCH 24

The "Rob Murders" had become a source of shock to the nation and a special tragedy to the Archdiocese of Detroit. Weekly, they had been featured in the national media. If one could look at their news value alone, they had proven a fertile second-day story for the *Detroit Catholic*. As usual, the weekly could not compete with the frequency of the dailies, nor the slick competence of the national magazines. But the relatively small Catholic paper had performed perhaps better in this crisis than it had in its more than one-hundred-year history. And Father Robert Koesler thought he knew why.

"We've never gotten anywhere close to this kind of cooperation before," he was telling Irene Casey. It was the comparatively slow day in the *Detroit Catholic*'s week. This week's issue was published and mailed, and the paper's small staff was regrouping for the coming week.

"I'm not sure I know what you mean, Father." They were standing at the rear of the large editorial office, the kitchen, as the staff referred to the area. Hot plates, dishes, and a large coffee urn mingled with bound copies of the *Detroit Catholic*, recent copies of Detroit's two daily papers, and large bunches of galley proofs.

"I didn't think you would, Irene. With you, everybody cooperates. It's not so with the rest of us."

"You can say that again." Jim Pool turned from the urn with his coffee and joined them. "Actually, Irene, you just think everybody is cooperating because you don't mind making twenty calls just to find out that the pastor is away on a well-deserved vacation."

"Now, wait a minute!" Mrs. Casey was using a tone frequently and effectively used on her many children.

"He doesn't mean anything derogatory, Irene." Koesler was searching for an ashtray for the cigarette he'd just lit. "But you'll have to admit the kind of statements, comments, and just general cooperation we've been getting lately from everyone from the Archbishop to priests and nuns in parishes is unprecedented—at least in my time at the paper."

"Well, maybe it's improved a bit." Casey did not yield a point lightly.

"The funny thing is," added Pool, "I'll bet the guys at the dailies think they're the only ones who can get nothing out of the Catholic Church, retroactively. They don't know that's just how the Church is."

"My guess is . . ." Koesler had found an ashtray filled with wadded paper, which Casey surreptitiously emptied and replaced near him, ". . . that these murders of priests and nuns have revived that old ghetto mentality that was a part of being Catholic before John Kennedy became president."

"That was before my time." Pool grinned behind his beard.

"Sometimes, James," Koesler crushed out his cigarette and refilled his cup, "I get the impression that everything was before your time. But there was a time, and not that long ago, when American bishops actually could deliver a 'Catholic' vote. When Joe McCarthy was a hero simply because he happened to be a Catholic who became politically famous.

"You've got to be kidding—not McCarthy!" Pool sometimes physically resembled a miniature Karl Marx; ideologically, there was probably little difference between them.

"Oh, no!" Casey hastily added. "Father's right. Most of the people who still believe in Joe McCarthy are Catholics."

"Well, anyway," said Pool, "thanks to all the new cooperation, I think we've done a damn good job with a really tough story, for a weekly."

As Pool made the statement, it reminded Koesler of a remark that had been made to him several months earlier. Koesler had been having lunch at the Detroit Press Club when Nelson Kane of the *Free Press* had come over to his table. As the priest rose to shake hands, Kane had remarked, "I just wanted to tell you, Bob, that you're doin' a helluva job at the *Detroit Catholic,* all things considered."

Koesler had said nothing in return. Indeed, he was still trying to decide whether the statement had been a compliment or an insult. In the absence of any clear indication to the contrary, he leaned toward accepting it as a compliment. That road led to a happier psyche.

The *Detroit News,* the old gray lady, was usually about as somber inside as it was outside. But today, there was, for the *News,* almost a festive air about the city room. For the first time in the string of Rosary Murders, the *News* had scored a clear scoop on the *Free Press.* It was enough to lift the spirits of the most entrenched conservative. Warren Reston was the man of the hour. As he strode through the long city room toward his desk, heady comments were hurled from staffers and copyboys alike.

"Damn good job, Warren!"

"Way to go, Reston!"

"Congratulations, Mr. Reston!"

"Hit 'em again, Babe!"

It was a nice feeling. But Reston was no cub. He'd been around long enough to know that man does not live by one scoop alone.

At the same time, he felt he'd made a slight break-through. Sometimes a big breaking story like this could get away from you, and you could never quite catch up with it. On top of that, this kid at the *Free Press* was good. He lacked experience. But he showed a natural feel for news reporting. Reston knew he'd have to rely on every bit of skill he'd built up to stay ahead of that young man.

Beating the *Free Press* on the Palmer false alarm was, perhaps, just the break he needed to get back in step with this story. From experience, he knew that any change in the situation would be subtle at first. But if he could just build momentum, he'd be getting the tips from the police to which he'd grown accustomed in the past. Most of them now were going to Cox at the *Free Press*.

At the moment, things were looking up, and he felt elated. He anticipated this afternoon's press conference with renewed confidence.

Joe Cox could scarcely bring himself to go into work this morning. He'd spent all of yesterday tracking down leads—all of them going nowhere. If he'd been anywhere in the vicinity of the City-County Building . . . well, life was filled with ifs.

But he knew well how covetous Nelson Kane felt about the Rosary Murders. He was not eager to encounter Kane under these circumstances.

So he was surprised when he got to his desk to be met by a benevolent Nelson Kane.

"You probably feel bad about yesterday." Kane stood jangling coins in his pants pocket.

"Yeah."

"Well, don't. It was no goof-off. You were doing what you should've been doing. God! I know what it's like going down an unending series of blind alleys. But that's what this business is all about. Only an absolute idiot thinks you win 'em all.

"Besides, this wasn't all that big. Just a priest who happens to be holding a rosary when he dies. The coroner confirmed it was a heart attack. Probably more important to the police than us. The *News* blew it all out of size 'cause they had a beat on the story.

"Don't let this get to you. You're doing it the way you should. A thing like this, it could drive you to showboating. We didn't get as far as we have on this story by showboating. What I want from you is solid investigative reporting. Just like you've been doing.

"Are you going to the press conference this afternoon?"

"There's no way out of it. I don't think much'll happen. But it's a base that's gotta be touched."

"O.K. But keep me informed on what you find and what directions you're going in."

"Sure. And, Nellie, thanks."

Cox felt as if he'd been absolved. Suddenly, the story appeared as fresh and inviting as it had been before Warren Reston had gotten on the scoreboard.

The press conference, of the variety termed "major," mainly because of the caliber of the participants, was scheduled for two in the afternoon at the Detroit Institute of Arts auditorium. The location had been selected because it was an easily accessible section of the central city, with adequate parking facilities, and it was large enough to contain the impressive numbers of media and police personnel expected to attend.

On hand to speak and answer questions were Detroit Mayor Maynard Cobb, Detroit Chief of Police Frank Tany, and Dr. Fritz Heinsohn, a psychiatrist who, in addition to having a lucrative private practice, was on retainer with the police department as its consulting therapist.

Easily the most interesting of the three was Maynard

Cobb, Detroit's black mayor. If Cobb had been white, he could have been typecast as Gaylord Ravenel, king of the riverboat gamblers. Moderate-sized, trim, light-complexioned, graying at the temples, Cobb seemed to have a perpetual smile playing at the corners of his mouth—as if he were enjoying a private joke to which he would give no one else privy.

Cobb had grown up in a notoriously tough section of Detroit known as The Black Bottom. He'd worked on Ford's assembly line, been involved in the infancy of the labor unions, fought for his college degree, and experienced racial prejudice from every imaginable source, from industry to the union hierarchy. Even with his outstanding credentials, he probably would not have been elected mayor had not the black population of Detroit grown to equal that of the everdiminishing white electorate.

Cobb was at ease with Detroit. It was his city. And, as an almost purely political animal, he was at home with the white as with the black communities. Throughout this, his first term as mayor, he had made a declining homicide rate one of his top priorities. He was determined to erase Detroit's image as "Murder Capital of the World." The Rosary Murders were counterproductive.

Police Chief Frank Tany was a holdover from the previous administration. Balding, portly, and moderately tall, he preferred conservative business suits to a uniform. His suits always had a homey, slept-in appearance. He was a career cop who had advanced on merit-based promotions from the rank and file. He eschewed politics and was generally respected by the police and public alike.

Dr. Fritz Heinsohn belonged to the Transactional Analysis school of psychiatry—currently. No form of therapeutic approach seemed to escape Heinsohn's attention and participation. He was probably the best known psychiatrist in the Detroit area, if only because he was forever appearing in the local media. He offered opinions, character sketches, and probable motivation only in cases of major crime. Not infrequently, he made appeals through the news media for malfeasors to contact him. He would, he averred, care for them, cure them, and render them happy to surrender to authorities. There was no record that any of the accused ever bothered to get in touch with him. But it was an assured grandstand play that never failed to get media exposure for the doctor.

Today, he was clad in one of the many mod outfits he had been affecting lately, a Bill Blass creation with multicolored silk shirt, open at the throat.

Members of all the major local news media—TV, radio and print—were present. Local stringers for *Time* and *Newsweek* were joined by several out-of-town representatives. Filling out the auditorium were plainclothes and uniformed police, including Lieutenant Koznicki and Sergeant Harris.

It was now thirty-five minutes into the press conference. Cobb, Tany, and Heinsohn had given their prepared statements. Cobb had effectively insisted on the city's complete commitment to end these murders and apprehend the guilty party. Tany had presented a skeletal outline of the crimes and some of the leads being followed by the police. He had told those reporters who had been closely following the case little new. Heinsohn had waxed eloquent on the personality type responsible for this sort of serial crime.

The TV people were packing their gear as the Q and A session began. An uncoordinated kind of order prevailed as one reporter after another rose, identified himself or herself and directed a question to one or another of the speakers.

"Emery, *Newsweek*. Mr. Mayor, what has this investigation done to your budget?"

"It hasn't helped. Most of the extra money has gone for overtime for *po*lice work." As a carry-over from his early days, Cobb still placed the accent on the first syllable of the word. "But money is not our prime concern. Protection for some of the finest people who live in this city *is*."

"Sylls, *New York Times*." A kind of sacred hush descended on the auditorium, indicative of the awe that a representative of the "newspaper of record" would actually be in Detroit. "That leads to the question of whether the police are doing all they can. Does the force need to be beefed up for this investigation?"

"I'll let Chief Tany handle that one."

Tany made his distracted way to the mike as if he'd forgotten where he was. "It's not a matter of numbers so much as quality. We've got our very best officers on this one. And, yes, whatever they need, they get."

"Reston, *Detroit News*. Dr. Heinsohn, can you add anything to what you've previously told us of the killer's psychological profile?"

Heinsohn arrived at the mike shooting his ruffled cuffs. "From the pattern, I'd say a definite schizosociopath. Of course, the most compelling element in this series of murders is the vocation of the victims—priests and nuns. I think, when he's found, it will turn out that our killer had a most peculiar relationship with his parents, especially his mother. My theory is that he comes from a broken home and is at least a latent homosexual. The victims represent not only religion—usually associated with the mother, but also with authority—thus the parental conflict. Also, I think it's clear he's selecting his victims at random. There is not even a vague connection or relationship among any of them. All they have in common is that they represent religion and authority. This lack of relationship is a further indication that the killer is striking out blindly at his mother. And, you will find, his homosexual preference springs from this aversion-attraction relationship with his maternal parent.

"It's also my theory that the man desperately wants to stop this aberrant behavior. He has struck out at his mother frequently enough. Now he wants to find some exit. But he's afraid of the consequences. I'd like him to know, through you ladies and gentlemen of the press, that I am available to act as intermediary. All he need do is contact me—"

"Oh, God!" Harris' tone was heavy with disgust. "Here we go on a trip down ego lane. Whaddya say we blow, Walt?"

"That's the best thing I've heard this afternoon."

The size of Harris and Koznicki made their exit a matter of public record. They were followed, shortly, first by individuals, then by small groups of police. Then the media began to leave.

Heinsohn was so consumed with his appeal to the killer that he did not notice the exodus until it had become a veritable stampede. At that point, he huffed angrily to an abrupt conclusion.

Mayor Cobb and Chief Tany left the stage. No one thanked the press for attending. For their part, the press thanked no one. It was an ungrateful exchange.

It was no great wonder that the Koznicki kids were big. Wanda, the lieutenant's wife, was a large woman. Her five-feet-ten inches accompanied a heavy bone structure. Neither fat nor hefty, however, she was a rather attractive woman. Her black hair was heavily streaked with patches of white. Her eyes, framed with lines of concern and laughter, were soft. The kind that were ready to cry with you.

The Koznickis had finished dinner. Their five children, each formally excused, had left the table. Koznicki and his wife were sitting silently. Koznicki fingered his coffee cup and stared into space. Wanda broke the silence.

"Pressure getting bad, Walt?"

"What?" Koznicki, started from his reverie, looked across at his wife. "Oh, no. The pressure's there, as it always is in a case like this. And there are the special problems we've talked about before.

"No. It's just that I got the oddest feeling yesterday when that priest died in Dearborn Heights. I've never had a feeling like it. I've been trying to figure it out ever since."

"Oh?"

"I felt anger. I was angry."

"Why?"

"That's what's been puzzling me. The only reason I can think of is that I was angry because we had a probable Rosary Murder victim, and he was out of my jurisdiction. We've had four murders in this series, and each has been within the corporate limits of the city of Detroit. My people have investigated each one. All the assumptions made and theories acted on have been mine."

"But, dear, the killer doesn't have to confine himself to Detroit. For one thing, if he's got a grudge against the Archdiocese of Detroit, why, good grief, the Archdiocese is . . ." She was searching for a size.

"Six counties, one hundred and three cities and townships, total population of more than four and a half million."

"My goodness, you've been doing your homework. I just meant it's big."

"I know. And, at this point, anything could happen. He may be finished. He may kill someone who is neither priest nor nun. He may kill outside the city of Detroit, and that would involve so many other jurisdictions it might as well take me right out of the case."

"Would that be so bad? I mean, this is one of the toughest cases you've ever worked on. I've felt your frustration with it. Would it be so bad if the buck didn't stop at you any more?"

"I don't know if I can explain it. It's sort of like a . . ." He searched for the word he wanted. ". . . an extrasensory perception. I've never felt like this on any other case. It's as if the killer is trying to communicate with me. That *part*, at least, of the reason why the killings have not taken place outside the city is because this game of communication is meant to go on between him and me. I can't explain it, and I certainly can't prove it. But I feel it. And that, I think, is why I felt so resentful yesterday when a priest who appeared to be his victim died outside Detroit. It was as if what I had assumed to be reality turned out not to be real."

After a moment of silence, his wife poured them both a second cup of coffee.

"Do you understand what I'm talking about?" Koznicki stirred his coffee in a preoccupied manner.

"Of course, dear. Any mother knows ESP. It's what tells her to call her children before they're hurt. To anticipate a problem no one else expects. Things like that."

"The thing that disturbs me most is that I understand so little of what he's trying to tell me."

"You will, dear."

"And the frustrating thing about it all is that I won't even know if any of this is true unless we get him and get him alive."

"Is there some special problem with taking him alive?"

"Well, that's one of the messages I seem to be getting."

"What?"

"That he doesn't intend to be taken alive."

FRIDAY,
MARCH 25

The alarm clock had barely begun to sound when the firm hand of Father Ed Killian snuffed it. Six A.M. and all's well, he thought. He was quick to answer his first demand of the day. Just as he was generally prompt and disciplined in performing all the duties called for by his vocation.

The soft way was not for Ed Killian. Someone had given him a clock radio several Christmases ago. He had used it as a clock, sometimes as a radio, but never as a clock radio. No way for a man to get up in the morning. Music or some idiot talking about farm prices.

Killian threw back the covers, stepped briskly to the open window, and began his deep breathing exercises. Foggy day. Sure sign of spring.

God! How many parishes had he been assigned to now? This was his fifth. At their roots they were all alike. People. Churchgoers and sliders. Very few anywhere near happily married, most couples together because everyone expected them to be. A couple of sadomasochistic nuts who were forever trying to involve the parish priest in their sick games.

He slipped out of his pajamas and into his jogging togs, wrapped a towel around his neck and noiselessly left the rectory. No need disturbing the pastor, who was actually younger than Killian. A fact that was no embarrassment whatever to Killian.

He can have it, Killian thought, as he began his exercise with a moderate, steady pace. It was the most wonderful vocation in the world until those young jackasses came along with their bright new words. Renewal, ecumenism, charismatics, folk liturgies, guitar masses, shared responsibility, parish councils. Hell! It's just people. A few high spots. A lot of disappointments. When they were down they used to come to confession. Now, Hell! They go to some group-grope led by some hairy hippie young priest. Spends all his time making up happy-time liturgies. Wouldn't know how to say a breviary if you put one in his hand. Doesn't know how to relate to one person who's in need. Got to have a *community*. No such thing as an individual person any more.

Unconsciously, Killian had picked up his pace in keeping with the tempo of his thoughts. Now, aware that he was moving slightly too rapidly, he slowed.

Wasn't worth thinking about all that was wrong with the Church anyway. Just get angry. He had made his own cocoon and he was relatively safe and happy within it. Outside of doing his job and staying as far away as possible from the machinery of the new Church, he was just living for retirement, which was by no means just around the bend. As a young priest, he had never thought he would ever retire. You were supposed to die in harness. But then he never would have thought he'd resign a pastorship, either.

Not many of St. Olaf's parishioners were up yet. Normally, those who did rise this early and who lived near the rectory could see the priest as he jogged by. And they could set their watches by him as he passed. It was always the same, every weekday.

Because of the fog, no one could see him today. They could hear the soles of his shoes hitting the sidewalk in measured paces. If they had wanted to set their clocks, they could have. It was twenty-two minutes after six.

Killian turned onto the pathway that surrounded St. Olaf's playground. No homes close by here. Shrubs and trees that bordered a large field. The grass had just about decided it was time to turn green.

The priest would take two turns around the playground and head back for a bracing shower. People who didn't start their days in this vigorous way didn't know what they were missing. He slowed his pace a little. He'd wait for the second time around to turn it on.

Sweat was beginning to pour from his body. He used the ends of the towel around his neck to dry his eyes. As he looked up, trying to refocus, he thought he saw a figure approaching on the pathway. Which was strange; he seldom encountered anyone on the path, especially this early. He felt a sense of foreboding. For a second, he had an impulse to turn and race back to the rectory, but he dismissed that immediately. As he neared the walker, he was able to make out a few details of the man. Moderate height, heavy head of hair. What did they call that kind of haircut? Shaped. Trench coat, hands in pockets, probably feels the cold, ought to get out and run mornings.

The path was quite narrow. The walker stepped slightly off the path to allow the priest space to continue his exercise. As they came even, the walker said clearly, "Mornin' Father." The priest merely grunted. But, as they passed, the man's right hand emerged from his coat pocket, bearing a shiny black gun.

Partly due to his apprehension, the priest caught the movement out of the corner of his eye. In mid-stride, he began to turn, but the stranger's gesture was one smooth continuing movement. He pulled the trigger as the revolver reached the level of the priest's head at a point just behind the priest's right ear.

It was a small, popping noise. Not enough to draw anyone's attention. Inside the priest's head, the bullet exploded, driving bone, tissue, veins in crazed directions.

His hand snapped to his head as his body pitched sideways onto the soft turf. He groaned once and was dead.

Quickly, the stranger knelt at the priest's side, looped a small black rosary around the priest's left wrist, guided the beads between the thumb and index finger, removed his gloves and walked swiftly down the path, disappearing in the fog.

Detective Sergeant Dan Fallon had been the first of the special task force at the scene of the latest murder. He was just entering the inner office of Room 504 of the City-County Building. In the room were Lieutenant Koznicki and Sergeant Harris. Koznicki was the first to speak.

"Another one confirmed, Dan?"

"Yes, sir. Luckily, I was less than a mile away when the call came. We were able to get things moving faster than any of the others."

"Who found the body?" Koznicki had selected a pen and begun taking notes.

"Kids. On their way to school. Pretty big shock for 'em. They knew who it was right off. I guess the priest was a jogging nut. They thought he'd fainted. Then they saw the blood. The only good part about it, it scared them enough so they didn't touch anything. They told some nun at the school and she called. A black-and-white got there in time to keep everyone back. The rosary was wrapped just right around the deceased's left hand. Far as we could see, a single entry just behind the right ear, and one hell of an exit. Must've been hollow-nosed."

Harris had briefly left the room and now returned with a cup of coffee, which he handed to the seated Fallon.

"What's the situation now?" Koznicki leaned back, pencil still in hand.

"The medical examiner's got the body, and ballistics got the bullet." Fallon blew across the steaming contents of the paper cup. "Both will call as soon as they complete their work."

"Anything else at the scene?" Koznicki expected little. If the killer had made another slip such as he had with Mother Mary, Koznicki knew it would have been mentioned at the top of the report.

"Not really. The ground was soft enough to leave footprints. Trouble is, there were too many prints to identify the killer's. It was tough on the kids who found him. A doctor was called; he treated them for shock."

"Whaddya think, Ned?" Koznicki turned to Harris.

"Interesting that he used a gun." Harris turned back from the window. He'd been absently watching the traffic on Jefferson. "It's the first time he's used the same method of homicide twice."

"That's right." Koznicki leaned forward. "First, he pulled the plug on the old priest, then drowning, a revolver, a knife, now a gun again."

"Unless," Harris added, "he used a different gun from the first time."

The phone rang. Koznicki picked up the receiver with his left hand, the pencil ready in his right.

"Koznicki . . . yes . . . I've got that. You're sure it was the same . . . what about the difference in . . . I see . . . O.K., thanks."

"Ballistics?" Harris asked.

"Right. It was the same gun in both killings. He used regular ammo on Father Dailey, and hollow-nose on Father Killian. But in both cases it was the same .38-caliber revolver."

"Why the difference in ammo?" Fallon dropped the empty cup in the wastebasket.

"I'd love to find him and ask him," said Harris.

"Unless . . . unless . . ." Koznicki drew one finger over his mustache. "Unless that incident with Mother Mary has frightened him enough to make him change his M.O."

"How's that?" asked Harris.

"There's no indication this guy has ever killed before. We've had nothing like this set of circumstances in any other series of homicides, ever. The first three times he kills, everything goes exactly as he's planned it. With our experience, we know the odds against that happening.

"His fourth murder, however, something very significant happens that is outside his planning. His victim lives long enough to give at least a partial identification. He learns the hard way that murderers make mistakes, and he knows a mistake could end his plans before they're completed. So he switches to a bullet that is much more likely to inflict a mortal wound."

"Not bad, Walt." Harris' enthusiasm returned. "And it gives us another lead."

"What's that?" asked Fallon.

"Stores that sell ammo. Thirty-eight hollow-noses aren't all that common. He may have had to stock up on a considerable supply. In any case, it could be one of our better leads."

"Right you are," said Koznicki, who had already begun writing the order.

Fallon leaned forward. "But Ross has got just about everybody who's free checking on the 'Robs' who were students of that nun."

"Don't worry." Koznicki handed the written order to Harris. "It's about time we added to our staff, and this is a good reason for doing so. By the way, how's that 'Rob' search coming?"

"Slow," answered Fallon. "It's proved that the old nun taught a helluva lot of Roberts, Robins, Robinsons, and so forth. They've got just about all the available names from her past. They're starting to check out each one now. It's slow, but Ross is making sure it's thorough."

"Good," said Koznicki. "I'm sure one of 'em is our man."

"Only problem is," sighed Harris, "do we have time to find him?"

When Nelson Kane learned that the priest's body had been found by a group of school children, he decided, as much on a hunch as any rational reason, to send a female reporter along to help cover the story. Again, on a whim, as much as anything else, he assigned Pat Lennon to accompany Joe Cox.

As they left the city room together, they were escorted out by discreetly raised eyebrows. Perhaps all the world loves a lover, but it was an acknowledged fact that all the *Free Press* was intrigued by and gossiped about who was sleeping with whom. And the Cox-Lennon liaison was the best bit of gossip going. However, whatever could have been surreptitiously said about them was literally innocuous. Cox and Lennon couldn't have cared less what anyone said or thought about their affair. If free spirits had not already been invented, Cox and Lennon would have held the patent jointly.

Kane's hunch had been prescient. Lennon was the only reporter allowed to speak with the children. She had talked to them in the St. Olaf School infirmary just before they were released to their parents to return home.

"How'd it go with the kids?" Cox turned the *Free Press'* Plymouth onto Jefferson for the long ride back to the paper.

"Zilch! I had a distinct coup with very little grace."

"Huh?"

"I was the only one who got in to see them, but I got almost nothing. I still don't know why the cop let me into the infirmary. He must think women won't hurt kids or even scare them. I know Reston was sore as hell."

"That's Reston's problem. He who lives on his reputation will die by it."

"But, once inside, nothing. The kids were still too shook up to be very coherent. After all, they're only in grade school. They just happened to be on their way to school. They just happened to be the first to see the body. For each and every one of them, this was the first dead body they'd seen outside a funeral home. Nobody remembered even seeing the rosary."

"Well . . ." Cox was having trouble maneuvering through the sluggish midday traffic. "You can always use their shock as your lead."

"That occurred to me, smartass."

"That's right. I forgot you were good at more than one thing."

Lennon gave a short, piercing whoop. "I'm grateful to know your opinion of my homework, sir. I haven't written my review of your performance last night yet."

"I didn't know you were going to write it. *Free Press* readers are in for a treat."

"If they don't fall asleep. I did."

They rode in silence, smug that they lived well together.

"What did you get?" Lennon crossed her shapely legs. Cox chanced a glance.

"The story."

"I know that, dummy. What is it?"

In a flat, emotionless, Dragnet fashion, Cox recounted what had happened, pausing only occasionally to editorialize. As when he told of Killian's penchant for jogging every morning. "You see?" He swiveled, and wagged an index finger at Lennon. "If he had begun each morning with a screw for exercise, instead of running all over the neighborhood, he'd be a healthy and, I might say, a considerably happier man now."

As he finished his narration, Lennon slowly shook his head. "The trouble with you, lover, is that you don't understand what priests and nuns mean to Catholics."

"How would you know? Were you ever a Catholic?"

"I AM a Catholic."

Not many things surprised Cox, but that did. "Whaddya mean? You never go to church."

"That's just what I mean. You don't understand. There's no way I can stop being a Catholic. Even if I don't go to church any more. I've got this indelible mark—"

"What mark? Where? I've never seen one, and I've looked."

"On my soul, idiot! That's what you get when you're baptized."

"No shit! If it's on your soul, it's not only indelible, it's also invisible, right?"

"Right."

"Then you can't see it. So how do you know you've got it?"

"How do I know? How do I *know?* The Bible told me so!"

Done with that word game, they were again silent for a short while.

"So what does this latest murder do to all the current theories going around?" Lennon recrossed her legs. Again Cox glanced appreciatively.

"Well, it shoots hell out of one of my pet theories," Cox answered. "This one's an anachronism."

"A what?"

"The first priest's plug was pulled in mid- to late afternoon. The first nun was killed in the late evening. Then there's a priest in the afternoon and another nun in the evening. This priest was killed too early to fit in my theory. He's out of his proper time. An anachronism."

"That sounds like a pretty flimsy theory in the first place."

"Sweetie, there are so few solid things to go on in this case, after a while you go for anything that seems to make any sense at all—no matter how far-fetched."

They were stopped for a light at the corner of Jefferson and Cadillac, not far from her apartment. Pat noticed that all ten of Cox's fingers were drumming on the steering wheel. "How would you like," she began in her sultriest voice, "to stop off for a quick one before we face the remaining hazards of the day?"

"Good Lord!" He tried unsuccessfully to mask an unmistakable tone of relief and anticipation. "You are insatiable!"

Sister Marie Magdala Connors felt proprietary about St. Camillus Hospital, and she was aware of her covetous feelings. But her reason was simple: virtually no one else cared. Most officials, both civic and religious, treated St. Camillus like an orphan. From time to time, the hospital was patted on its figurative head and thanked for staying in the core city. As a private hospital, there was no earthly reason for continuing this discouraging and financially unrewarding service. Heavenly reasons were all that could explain this singular determination to prolong this terminal fiscal illness. That also explained the hands-off policies of both ecclesiastical hierarchy and city government. St. Camillus was a bottomless pit, a money-eating monster, all expenses and almost no income.

St. Camillus, or more specifically, the poor who made up almost all the hospital's patients, needed not only health care, but acceptance and love. Sister Marie was intent on delivering these rare inner-city gifts as long as humanly possible.

Evening visiting hours were nearly over. Sister Marie decided to visit emergency. Friday nights were surpassed only by Saturday nights in the number of victims of drug overdoses, guns, knives, hated, jealousies, and organized crime. Tonight was typical.

Emergency was organized chaos.

Every admitting cubicle and stall was occupied. The hallways were filled with stretchers, gurneys, and wheelchairs, each with its groaning, bleeding, or otherwise suffering cargo.

Doctor Savage, in charge tonight, made a quick evaluation of each patient as soon as possible, and they were filtered through the admitting routine with a speed dependent on need.

Sister Lilla, a small, nervous young nun in a modified white habit, hurried over to Sister Marie.

"Marie," she said breathlessly, "do you know where the chaplain is?"

"Father Schuck? I have no idea. Have you tried calling?"

"Everywhere. I can't find him. And he hasn't even contacted his answering service. Several of the sick down here have asked for a priest, and a few of the more seriously injured should be anointed. But where IS the man?"

Yes, where is he? Sister Marie remembered the good old days when prime qualifications for Catholic hospital chaplains were senility and having been placed solidly on the diocesan shelf. There had been a lot wrong with that system. The problems centered on the conflict of senility and what should have been a demanding job. But one thing you could always count on: when you needed those old men, they were always around.

The new breed of chaplain was a much younger man, especially trained for a hospital ministry. However, unlike his ancient predecessor, he tended not to consider his hospital as a round-the-clock responsibility. People were supposed to die during office hours. Thus, there were frequent and unexpected emergencies during which he simply could not be found.

The more things change, mused Sister Marie the more they stay the same—sometimes. She was roused from her reverie by the voice of Sister Lilla.

"If only *we* could anoint. The people would accept it. And *we* are here."

"Yes, we're here, but we *can't* anoint. People tell us their troubles and their sins, but we can't absolve. It's not fair. It doesn't even make any sense. Well, Lilla—" Sister Marie touched the other nun light on the arm, "do the best you can."

Sister Marie made a hurried tour of the emergency area, speaking briefly with those who were able to converse. Some ugly bullet wounds tonight and some horribly vacant-eyed drug addicts. One pregnant white woman in rags, who must certainly be passing her addiction on to her unborn.

Visiting hours had been over for nearly half an hour. Sister Marie wandered through the corridors of the first two floors, checking to see if all were bedding down, and peripherally keeping an eye out for Sister Bonaventure.

Marie worried about Bonnie. She could topple over of her own weight anytime, and it might be hours, or even days, depending on where she fell, before she'd be found. There was always the possibility someone would do her some mischief. Bonnie was a sweet old lady. But muggers were disinterested in the endearing charms of their victims.

A casual search revealed no Sister Bonaventure loose. Besides, there were only a few minutes before she was scheduled to lead night prayers. Hospital routine being a hallowed tradition, it would be disturbing to patients and personnel alike if she were late.

As she turned down the corridor leading to her office, she glanced at the large, white electric clock on the wall. Thirty seconds before nine. Just enough time, she knew from experience.

As she neared her office, she was aware of something odd. Her office was dark. She usually left the light on until after night prayers, when she would lock up and go to her room. She was certain she had left the light on earlier. Perhaps someone had left something for her and automatically turned out the light when leaving the room. Still, she felt a bit uneasy.

Her hand groped against the inside wall for a moment before locating the familiar switch. She turned on the overhead light and cautiously looked about the room before entering. All seemed as she had left it. She checked her wristwatch. Ten seconds to nine. She walked to her desk, pulled the intercom mike close, picked up the prayer card, flicked the switch on, and began.

"In the name of the Father and of the Son and of the Holy Spirit. Blessed be the holy and undivided Trinity, now and forever. Amen."

There was no nonsense about St. Camillus Hospital's prayer. It was a Catholic hospital, and by jingo the prayers were Catholic.

"I give you thanks, O my God, through Jesus Christ, for all you have given me throughout my life, and particularly for preserving me this day . . ." Sister Marie read the familiar prayer while her eyes darted about the desk searching for something that might have been left for her and would explain the light's being turned off. "Hail Mary, full of Grace, the Lord is with Thee . . ." She could find nothing. All looked familiar. "Now and at the hour of our death. Amen."

There had been a time when words like "death" were never mentioned in the hospital. But a new attitude toward the acceptance and productive use of the inevitable was encouraged. She thought this a good development, as twice more she repeated the "Hail Mary" response. "Holy Mary, Mother of God, pray for us sinners, now and at the hour of our death." But she continued to wonder who had turned off the office light.

"I offer up to you, my God, the rest I am going to take . . ."

Behind her, a closet door that had been left ajar slowly swung open.

". . . in union with the rest which Jesus Christ took while on earth, and with His death and burial . . ."

The man stepped noiselessly from the closet. On his hands were leather gloves. His right hand held a pistol bearing the grotesque addition of a silencer.

". . . and my awakening on the morrow in union with His awakening and with His glorious resurrection."

The man steadily approached her, his eyes riveted to the back of her head, wary that she might suddenly turn.

"May our evening prayer ascend to you, O Lord. And may your mercy descend upon us."

There was something in the room. She sensed it. She could not recognize the presence.

"In the name of the Father and of the Son and of the Holy Spirit. Amen."

She flicked the mike's switch off and he fired. The gun was no more than a few inches from her head, which almost exploded from the impact. Her body pitched forward on the desk as if she had been pole-axed.

In the next few seconds, the stranger detached the silencer, pocketed both it and the revolver, looped a black rosary around the nun's left wrist, strung the beads between her thumb and index finger, removed his gloves, stepped to the door, glanced down the empty corridor, and hurried out of the hospital unobserved.

MONDAY,
MARCH 28

Lieutenant Walter Koznicki and Detective Sergeant Ned Harris strode briskly down the fifth-floor corridor of the City-County Building. Both were solitarily obsessed with their common problem. If they had not been convinced of it earlier, there was little doubt now in their minds: the Rosary Murders seemed beyond their control. Last Friday, for the first time in his killing spree, the faceless Rob had murdered not one, but two of Detroit's religious community on the same day. He had become bold almost to the point of recklessness. The crack team Koznicki had assembled had to admit they were little closer to cracking the case than when they had started. Additionally, they were surprised and discouraged that the murderer had altered his method of operation by killing two people in one day. It was a fairly dependable rule of thumb that when a consistent method of operation was present in a series of crimes, odds of apprehending the perpetrator increased.

So, it was with a mixture of distraction, frustration, concern, and discouraged determination that the two officers traveled toward Koznicki's office.

Tall, imposing, broad-shouldered, white and black, easily carrying their considerable authority, they were like the lead blockers of a football team's suicide squad. The crowd of reporters, photographers, police, the curious, and the legal staff assigned to Koznicki's team parted before the two advancing detectives as generously as if they had been running against the Little Sisters of the Poor.

The sole exception to this pattern of deference was the *News*'s venerable crime reporter, whose star was steadily setting in the east. Warren Reston abruptly stepped into Harris' path and said, loudly enough to be obstreperously offensive, "What about it, gang, have you had enough? About ready to call in the Feds?"

It was within the realm of possibility that Harris neither heard nor saw him. The crowd at that particular juncture of the corridor was especially heavy. In any case, Reston got no response. Instead, he was sent reeling back toward the wall as Harris, in effect, walked right through him. In a lame effort to relieve a badly bruised ego, Reston said, to no one in particular, "There go Batman and Robin. Only they've lost their mystic power."

On entering his office, Koznicki went directly to the chair behind his desk. Harris sat across from him. Neither said anything for several moments. Koznicki broke the silence.

"Did you run into Reston on purpose?"

"Yeah."

"Damn good shot!"

Another few minutes passed in silence.

"How's the team doing?" Koznicki swung his ample bulk back in his chair, his hands folded in their accustomed spot across his stomach.

"Plodding and discouraged. So far, they've uncovered

some eight hundred variations of 'Rob' in Mother Mary's background. Some of those, by the way, went on to become priests. Have you given any thought to Rob's being a priest?"

"I haven't excluded anyone."

"You know, it would explain a lot if the murderer were a priest. He'd be more familiar with the comings and goings of nuns and priests. And, of course, his access to that group would surpass that of anyone else, wouldn't it?"

"Yes." Koznicki leaned forward and began toying with his pen. "The thought has crossed my mind. But if it's not a priest, whoever it is has done his homework very carefully. Everyone is accustomed to think of priests and nuns as being the most accessible people imaginable."

"Well, that's true, isn't it?" Harris shifted in his chair. "You want a priest, you go to a rectory. You want a nun, you go to a convent." Harris was quietly proud of what he considered to be his growing "Catholic" vocabulary. Prior to this case, his knowledge of things Catholic had been comparable to his fluency in Chinese.

"It used to be more true a few years ago than it is today," Koznicki corrected. "Now, it's really rare to find just the priest you're looking for in the rectory you'd expect to find him in. And the same goes for the nuns and their convents."

"They're out being relevant." Harris smiled contentedly. He may not have been very alert to things religious, but he did read the papers. He'd seen the pictures of priests and nuns in marches and protests for all manner of causes, from peace to Farah workers.

"Something like that," Koznicki conceded. "But in this new, at best, chancey availability, when it's very difficult to bump into just the priest or nun you want, consider how amazingly available Rob's victims have been."

"You mean you don't buy Fritz Heinsohn's educated diagnosis that the killer's victims are haphazardly selected?" When Harris was being facetious he simply couldn't hide it.

Koznicki treated Harris' question with eloquent silence. And then continued:

"Take the victims in order: Father Lord, totally vulnerable, yet the killer selects a perfect time when the hospital staff is at its minimum.

"Sister Ann, alone in a large convent. Even if her companion had been home, the killer's plan was so careful, it wouldn't have been disturbed even by that eventuality.

"Father Dailey had just arranged it so that he could be called to an empty church. He, himself, set himself up as a perfect target.

"Mother Mary, more mobile than either of her two elderly companions. She always answered the door. Another perfect target.

"Father Killian always jogged every morning. So precisely paced that people could set their clocks by his passage. The exact time he would be at the empty field would be completely predictable. Nature even cooperated with a heavy fog.

"Sister Marie always led night prayers from her empty and solitary office at precisely the same time each evening in a minimum-security hospital facility.

"Outstandingly good planning, wouldn't you say?"

"If he's not a priest, how does he do it?"

"It's not that hard, Ned. You're adding a special mystique to this because the victims are priests and nuns. Good surveillance on the part of anyone who was intelligent and determined would uncover their patterns of behavior and their schedules. So that's it. Rob is intelligent and determined. It doesn't really matter whether he's a priest. The questions are: Is he done now, or not? Will he strike again? If so, where? When? And at whom?

"And the prime question, of course: Who is Rob? I know it's tempting with all this pressure to try for shortcuts—like following a hunch that the killer is a priest—but it's most important now to continue solid police work. So, I'm leaving it in your hands that those on our team who are investigating the Rob clue continue professionally and not depend on any special breaks."

"Right, Walt." Harris rose to leave, then hesitated.

"One thing, Walt: Brainard and Schommer, the two guys from Tactical Services Division that you just added to our team—"

"Yes?"

"Well, they just don't seem to fit. I mean, those guys have guns where other people carry spare change. What did you ask for them for?"

"Took a page from your book, Ned, and played a hunch. Rob seems determined to use a .38 for his weapon. It's pretty clear he's using a silencer. In the latest two murders, others surely would've heard the sound of gunfire if there had been any sound. I've just got a hunch that if we're lucky enough to bump into Rob, he's going to be armed, dangerous, and with nothing to lose. If that happens, I want a couple on our side who fire first and then think of questions. A lot of us may stay a lot healthier."

"Hey, Walt, I got a piece and I know how to use it." Harris' hand went under his jacket, half-removing his revolver from its holster.

"Don't draw on me, Tonto." Koznicki rose from his chair. "It's just a hunch. Humor me."

"O.K., Massa." Harris left for Control. It was clear he was at least slightly offended. Koznicki was convinced of two things: Harris would recover, and the team needed some heavy artillery.

One goddam thing that hadn't changed over the years: getting people to turn out for Forty-Hours Devotions was still as hard as pulling hens' teeth.

Father Ed Sklarski was letting his stream of consciousness reasoning have its head, as was his wont.

Sklarski, pastor of St. Robert's parish, in the Detroit suburb of Inkster, was driving his new silver, four-door Olds 98 up Inkster Road toward the Cherry Hill package liquor store.

It hasn't changed one damn bit since I was ordained thirty-six years ago, he thought. People just won't go to church unless there's a law on the books. Those imbeciles who want to fool around with the Sunday Mass obligation don't realize what a can of worms they're playing with. Take that away and you can kiss the Catholic Church good-bye. You'd think they'd have learned from Confession. Call it the Sacrament of Reconciliation, pooh-pooh the penance and fear—now nobody comes any more. Nothing wrong with fear. The beginning of wisdom. That was someplace in the Bible.

But Forty Hours! How in hell were you supposed to get people out for a devotion that didn't even propose to ask for anything? You couldn't. Maybe that was the answer. Make it Forty Hours of Perpetual Help.

He smiled at the solution's insanity.

Every parish has to have Forty Hours once a year, and every parish has the same formula. Start with one of the Sunday Masses. Give it a big kickoff. Then, figure some Band-Aid way of getting at least a couple of people to volunteer keeping the Blessed Sacrament company through the rest of Sunday, Monday, and Tuesday. Then the big closing Tuesday evening.

The Tuesday closing ceremonies had its own well-tested formula for success. Make sure two or three grammar school classes have to attend. That brings in the parents. Then there are always a few dependables in every parish who'll be there. And, for the icing on the cake, I invite my classmates and clerical golfing partners and friends and, voilà, good old St. Robert's is full.

Sklarski guided his 98 onto Cherry Hill and pulled into the liquor store's parking lot. Adam Sierminski, proprietor, knew it was Forty Hours time at St. Robert's, and had been expecting Father Sklarski. In fact, had Sklarski not come in today to load up stores for his clerical friends, Sierminski would have canceled his ad in St. Robert's parish bulletin.

"Good afternoon, Father. Forty Hours time again."

"Yes, Adam. It's a good thing Forty Hours is only an annual event; I don't think St. Robert's could afford more than one a year."

Sierminski chuckled but said nothing. He was always afraid one of his clergymen customers would ask for a special discount. And he was always surprised that none of them did.

"I did not see you over by church these past few days, Adam."

"No, Father." He lied broadly. "Not been feeling well, and what with the work here in the store . . . but we do plan on being there for the closing tomorrow."

"That is good, Adam. Usually there are so few of the parishioners at the closing, it is easy to tell who will be among the sheep and who among the goats on the last day."

"Say, Father, have you been reading about these killings of the poor priests and nuns?" Sierminski was eager to change the subject, since he had no intention of attending the Forty Hours closing.

"Who could help it? The work of some damn fool kid, if you ask me." Juvenile delinquency was Sklarski's universal goat for all the world's problems. "But I must hurry along, Adam; I have much to do before tomorrow's closing."

Sierminski stepped back to allow the priest's girth behind the counter. Sklarski struggled through the narrow aisle, making his selections. Sierminski knew what they'd be. It was always the same. Two gallons each of Cutty Sark, Canadian Club, and Beefeaters Gin, several quarts of sweet and dry Vermouth, and a haphazard potpourri of Tia Maria, B and B, and other afterdinner liqueurs. Then several fifths of Jack Daniels for the priest's private stock. What was generally lacking in gourmet selection was more than balanced by quantity.

"Charge this to the parish account, Adam."

Easy come, easy go, thought Sierminski.

"See you at the closing, Adam."

"Yes, indeed, Father." Sierminski breathed a quick prayer that a standing-room-only crowd would show, so Sklarski would be unable to sort out the goats from the sheep.

It's a good thing, thought Sklarski, easing his bulk into the supportive padding of his 98, that I sent Mrs. Dearing down to the Broadway Market this morning for the jumbo shrimp. Ordinarily, I wouldn't send anyone into downtown Detroit. But Mrs. Dearing is a tough old bag. Anyone tries to mug her will know he's been in a fight. When I get back to the rectory, I'll have to check with Mrs. Bullingin. I'm sure she's taken care of the ladies of the Altar Society serving the dinner. But it never hurts to check. God! Another name for Forty Hours is trouble.

"Goddam it, Frank, there's an election coming up in a few months!"

Detroit's dapper mayor, Maynard Cobb, leaned forward in his oversized executive chair, smoke steaming from his nostrils. He seemed to Police Chief Frank Tany as nothing less than an enraged bull about to charge.

"And, as I begin a campaign for reelection," the mayor continued, "there is some jackass maniac out there wasting Detroit priests and nuns." Cobb tapped white ash from his Antonio y Cleopatra small cigar into the gigantic executive ashtray on his desk.

"We're doing all we can, Mr. Mayor." Tany stood directly in front of the mayor's huge desk. As usual, they were a study in sartorial contrast. Cobb wore a stunning vested gray suit that nicely set off the gray temples of his black, wavy hair. Tany once again looked as if he'd slept in his navy blue suit that had been slightly too large for him to begin with.

"It's no longer a case of 'all you can do,' Frank. It's no longer a case of all *anybody* can do. It's a case of catching this mother and putting these killings behind us. Frank, 'Rob, the Rosary Murderer' made the covers of both *Time* and *Newsweek* this week. That kind of publicity can kill me politically. Our plans were that Detroit would get national coverage for the opening of the Renaissance Center, not for killing its clergy!"

Tany shifted his weight to his right side. He always tried to stand during meetings with Cobb in an attempt to make them as brief as possible. He admired Cobb's political savvy, but the mayor was a complete political animal with unerring skills for survival. None of these qualities was any part of Tany's marrow. He was a cop who had worked hard and, admittedly, had been in a series of right places at the right times. He held the respect and loyalty of his department at a most difficult time in Detroit's history. The city was slowly passing from a white to a black majority. He had originated affirmative action hiring and promotion policies aimed at achieving at least an approximate racial balance on the force. And he stood at an awkward center between a black mayor and a police department that had little love for that mayor.

The mayor drew deeply on his cigar. "Frank, are you sure this lieutenant—what's his name? . . ."

"Koznicki."

"Koznicki . . . is the best you've got in homicide?"

"He's the best anybody's got."

Cobb was never sure if Tany were leveling with him or being blindly defensive of his department. "Then why hasn't he got this case solved?"

"I know the public is impatient . . ." Tany tactfully chose to exclude Cobb from an impatience the mayor obviously shared. ". . . but this case is different, I dare say, from anything this city has ever experienced."

"Different?" Cobb brightened. If it were different enough, perhaps the very difference could be an argument against his opponents. Something he could sell the voters.

"Yes, different." Tany saw no political advantage here. Only that this type of case was traditionally the toughest nut of all to crack. "The kinds of homicide we're used to dealing with in Detroit happen in family arguments where one or another person has a deadly weapon, usually a cheap gun. Or it's the result of organized crime, where it's a clear assassination. Or it's some punk who's seen it over and over again on TV and wants the thrill. In all, either the killer is an amateur and makes countless mistakes, or it's a professional who has a clear motive. The police work is clear: discover the mistakes, or work from the motive back to the perpetrator.

"With this present series of murders, Mr. Mayor, not

only do we not know who is committing them, much more importantly, we don't know why."

'Don't know why,' thought the mayor, a smile crossing his mind. Perhaps he could amplify that "Why" into political gold.

"This is like a novel, Mr. Mayor," Tany continued. "Except that in a novel, you know, if you read far enough you'll find out who done it. Unfortunately, this is real life. We may never know."

It was enough. Cobb had some additional ammunition for the political wars. The fact that the motive was unknown could be used as an explanation for the lack of progress. It was an excuse that had not yet been used, and possibly an excuse the press and the public just might buy.

"This lieutenant—what's his name again?" Cobb stubbed out his cigar.

"Koznicki."

"Koznicki. Does he have everything we can give him?"

"He has everything he asks for. I'd stake my job on his ability."

"You have." Cobb pivoted his chair toward the wall, indicating the interview was over. "Maybe we both have."

TUESDAY,
MARCH 29

Of all institutions to be found in a modern American city, probably the clearest anachronism is a monastery of Discalced Carmelite nuns. Yet, there are sixty-three Carmelite monasteries sprinkled throughout the United States, and one of them is located in the outskirts of Detroit.

The Monastery of Mary, Mother of Divine Charity, is

tucked unpretentiously off Wyoming Avenue in an isolated corner of the Marygrove College campus.

Not much of substance has happened to the Discalced Carmelites since Saint Theresa of Avila removed their ornate boots in 1562 A.D. They lead a life of such stark simplicity that the average complex American would find them incredible. They seldom speak, never frivolously. They are sparing vegetarians. They pray specified prayers at specified hours. They are encouraged to follow their famed foundress into flights of mystic contemplation. They have almost no contact with the world in which they have placed themselves as uninvited visitors.

The Monastery of Mary, Mother of Divine Charity, housed nine professed nuns, one novice, in training to become a professed nun, one postulant, in training to become a novice, and one extern nun, in contact with society to the extent of receiving visitors and dispensing food to the deserving poor as well as to the bums of Wyoming Avenue who came to them in varying degrees of need.

The nuns of the Monastery of Mary, Mother of Divine Charity, were permitted, if not encouraged, to read the *Detroit Catholic,* under the misbelief that it constituted "spiritual reading." To be sure, there were sections of the *Detroit Catholic* that could qualify as spiritual reading. But, as a whole, it was not intended as competition with Theresa of Avila, John of the Cross, Thomas Merton, or even Andrew Greeley.

In any case, it was because they had read about them in the *Detroit Catholic* that the small Discalced community of Detroit knew about the Rosary Murders. They knew little of the more lurid details of the killings, however, nor were they aware of the speculative stories appearing in the local and national press. But the past four issues of the *Detroit Catholic* had set some sort of record for being read by a greater percentage of Detroit Carmelites than any other issue in the paper's history. It proved to be as fascinating a story to these otherworldly people as it was to their very worldly brothers and sisters beyond the cloister.

Four of the Carmelites were sitting in the sun room, appropriately named this day as the rays of an early spring sun streamed warmly through the tinted glass that shielded the nuns from the frequently unseeming sights of Wyoming Avenue. It was "recreation" period, during which they were allowed to speak while they engaged in "recreational" sewing. Three of them were working on exquisitely embroidered Mass vestments. The fourth was mending her black veil that should have been discarded long ago.

"What do you suppose it all can mean?" Sister Margaret Mary of the Holy Martyrs asked of no one in particular.

"Trust Providence," urged Sister Theresa of Jesus and Mary. "God writes straight with crooked lines."

"How can God have anything to do with the murders of all those priests and nuns?" asked Sister Mary Elizabeth of the Holy Face.

"Not a sparrow falls to the earth without Our Father in heaven knowing it," quoted Sister Theresa, who was the convent's resident curmudgeon and Biblicist. "You can be sure these six good and holy men and women have not gone to their eternal reward without God's Holy Providence being involved."

"Well, it doesn't make much sense to me," said Sister Mary Elizabeth. A postulant in her early twenties, she had doubts about everything, including her vocation. "I can understand why a man can murder someone, but I can't understand how God is involved."

"It's the problem of evil, child," said Mother Agnes Ann of the Infant Jesus. The prioress of the Detroit monastery was in her well-wrinkled eighties and had virtually mastered the art of aging gracefully. "No one's been able to solve it. God permits evil because He has given us free will to choose between good and evil. Someone out there has chosen evil and with it the death of those consecrated men and women."

"Meanwhile," said Sister Margaret Mary, who was the convent's cook, and perhaps the warmest personality of all, "we must pray for the poor man who's doing these terrible deeds."

"Pray for him?" asked a somewhat astonished Sister Mary Elizabeth.

"Pray for his apprehension," stated Sister Theresa flatly.

"And for his conversion," added Mother Agnes Ann.

"Father Brown would have caught him by now," said Sister Margaret Mary mischievously.

"Father Brown?" Sister Mary Elizabeth looked from one nun to the other, bewildered. She was unaware of any archidiocesan police force. "Who's Father Brown?"

"Father Brown was an invention of G. K. Chesterton, dear. He's fictional. Sister Margaret Mary, you shouldn't go on like that!"

Sister Margaret Mary buried her cherubic, peasant-like face in the vestment she was embroidering.

"When he is apprehended," said Sister Theresa, returning to the objective of her prayer, "he should be executed!"

"Sister!" exclaimed Sister Margaret Mary. "What a perfectly dreadful thing to say! You above all should know that God desires not the death of a sinner, but that he be converted and live." By no means did she spend all her time with her nose in a cookbook. She had, indeed, absorbed the Gospel message as well as anyone and better than many. God, after all, had been duly thanked by Jesus Christ that He had revealed the message to "little ones."

"That's the very point," said Sister Theresa.

"Ouch!" exclaimed Sister Mary Elizabeth, who, on sticking herself with a needle, had rejected several exclamations she had left behind in her life in "the world."

"Did you hurt yourself, dear?" Mother Agnes Ann leaned toward the young postulant with evident concern.

"It's nothing." But it would have been if I'd said what came to mind, Sister Mary Elizabeth thought.

"Go on, Sister," prodded Sister Margaret Mary. "You were about to explain how execution fits in with God's plan for salvation."

"Exactly!" Sister Theresa proceeded. "I've thought it all through. You see, if a man like the one who is guilty of these murders is given a long sentence—say, life in prison—he will think of all the time he has to be converted before he dies, and he may never be converted at all. Whereas, if he knows he will be executed in a short time, he will be converted immediately."

"I suppose that makes sense. I just don't understand it." Sister Margaret Mary said a short, silent prayer of thanksgiving that Sister Theresa had never become a judge.

After a brief silence, Sister Mary Elizabeth stopped embroidering and said, "I must confess, for the first time since I've been in this monastery, I feel guilty."

"Why is that?" asked Sister Margaret Mary.

"Well, I've always thought this was the greatest sacrifice—to leave the world so completely. But now I wonder. All the priests and nuns in Detroit seem to be in danger from this killer—except us. We are the only protected ones."

"Sister," said Mother Agnes Ann, touching the young woman's shoulder lightly, "each person's cross is just big enough for him or her. God sees to that. For most, the cross awaits out there in the world. For the moment, at least, yours is here in this cloister. We waste our time wondering whether we could carry another's cross. We have all we can do to take up our own, daily, and follow him."

Another name for Forty Hours is boredom, thought Father Robert Koesler, as he sipped his 7-Up. His drink bore enough apparent resemblance to gin to forestall any objection that he was not taking his imbibing seriously enough. It surely was not that Koesler did not appreciate a drink now and again. It was his experience, however, that when the clerical gang got together, there was usually a little too much drinking. He simply had a better time observing the results than participating in the libations. It was extremely rare that anyone ever got falling-down drunk when the boys gathered at the drinking hole. But tongues and collars loosened, voices became raucous, and everything seemed somewhat funnier than it actually was.

It was now almost midnight. Forty Hours had closed,

solemnly, almost four hours earlier. Ten priests remained of the original thirty-four clergy guests of St. Robert's parish. They were gathered in the rectory basement. Heads of numerous dead animals stared sightlessly from the light tan, paneled walls. In the basement's southwest corner was a large display case, containing most of the rifles that had been used to kill the animals. Opposite the gun case was a large, circular poker table, whereon a game had been going nonstop since the last of the candles had been extinguished in the church.

In the basement's northeast corner, walls had been constructed, separating a ten-by-twenty-foot room from the rest of the basement. The room had been lovingly christened "the bomb shelter," presumably because that's where people went to get bombed. It had a wet bar and a closet filled with enough wine, liquor, and beer to supply the initial thirst of a small army.

Koesler was standing near the bar in the bomb shelter. The location was comparable to Grand Central Station, in that if one stood there long enough, nearly every priest in the Archdiocese of Detroit would eventually pass by.

The conversation, most of the evening, had, quite naturally, been about the Rosary Murders. The topic was winding down now, mostly because several conversers were no longer able to keep some of the crimes' statistics clear.

"I don't care what anybody says; as far as I'm concerned, it's a black guy." Monsignor Jasper Max was standing, as was everyone else in the shelter.

Koesler dropped another ice cube into his already diluted 7-Up. "Why's that, Monsignor?"

"Because all the murders have been committed in Detroit. Black guys just blend into the landscape in the city, but they stand out like sore thumbs in the suburbs." Max was a huge, sixty-seven-year-old whose self-image exceeded reality. A former jock, he was still a prodigious swimmer. He had spent a large part of his early ministry in the inner city. But as it had turned black, he had maneuvered a series of suburban assignments. Now, he was nearing retirement. "That's why all the murders have been in the city, 'cause the guy wouldn't dare try it in the suburbs." Max splashed a little more bourbon into his glass.

"There are black people in the suburbs, Monsignor." Father Harold Steele, whose strikingly handsome face was framed by a heavy head of hair and a shaggy gray beard, resembled Moses. His parish marked the spot where the 1967 Detroit riot had begun.

"Domestics, maybe. Here and there a homeowner. But not many," Max allowed.

"Have any of you noticed anything peculiar about the wakes and funerals of the victims?" asked Father Alfred Dalton. It wasn't a perfectly segued question, but at that hour and in their condition it made little difference.

"They're too frequent," Koesler responded soberly.

"They're depressing," added Max.

"No, no," said Dalton, addressing his own question, "I mean all the police who are always at both the wakes and the funerals."

"How can you tell?" asked Max.

"How can you miss them?" Dalton returned. "They don't fit in with anyone else. They have these bulges under their coats. They're usually pretty big. And, what I consider most significant, they don't participate." Dalton's straight, stocky body was topped by a bald, bullet-shaped head. A navy veteran, he considered himself an expert on nearly everything.

"Maybe they got caught," observed Steele.

"Caught?" asked a startled Dalton.

"Yeah. Didn't you ever notice how, when you get to a mortuary to lead the rosary, a lot of the mourners get out before you start? A couple of weeks ago, I went into the Dingle Funeral Home, sort of pulled up my coat collar to cover the Roman collar, and I just knelt down and started." He grinned, reminiscently. "I trapped everybody. You should've seen the looks I got afterward."

The story got a collective laugh.

"Put it on the roof!" The words were fired like cannon shots, followed by Father Ed Sklarski's explosive laughter.

The four who were standing at the bar turned toward

Sklarski, who had just delivered the punch line to Father Kevin Scanlon, with whom he'd been talking near the doorway.

"Put it on the roof?" inquired Koesler.

"I was just explaining," explained Sklarski, "to Scanlon here how you justify parish expenses you don't want the chancery to know about. Put it on the roof. I don't know one guy at the chancery who'd be willing to climb up on the roof to find out whether you'd spent anything on it."

"Not bad," noted Steele. "Another way is just to have an inner-city parish. They don't want to know what you're doing. And you haven't got any money for them to be interested in. The other day, a bunch of us had a meeting with the archbishop. At one point, he said 'Gentlemen, if you're running street-front churches, don't tell me.'"

The conversational road turned toward Church politics, a perennial favorite.

Pleased with himself at having caused the conversational switch and thus prolonging the evening, Sklarski decided to visit the boys in back.

As he left the shelter, Sklarski was smiling. St. Robert's Forty Hours had been a success, by and large.

Attendance had been spotty during the three days' daytime hours, but it had been excellent for the closing tonight. The children who were forced to attend had apparently done a marvelous job selling their parents on coming along. When the priests talked about St. Robert's Forty Hours closing, and they would, they'd have to admit it was a good crowd. Goodly number of priests, too. Sklarski was proud that St. Robert's featured the best food and drink on the Forty Hours circuit. Mrs. Bullingin and her Ladies of the Altar Society were largely responsible for that. Largely? He grinned at the unintended pun. They *were* pretty big.

Damn! His stream of consciousness carried him on. When he had publicly thanked the ladies for their marvelously prepared dinner, and the priest guests were wildly applauding and whistling, the ladies were simply crowded around the doorway of the kitchen, too shy to come all the way out into the gym, and so Mrs. Bullingin had never gotten out of the kitchen at all. From experience, he knew he would not hear about *that*. Mrs. Bullingin would erect a wall of silence for the next couple of weeks. If only he had thought to insist on a parting of the ladies so that Mrs. Bullingin could've emerged for her special share of the accolades!

Well, sufficient for that over the next couple of weeks. He wasn't going to let that spoil the afterglow.

Sklarski's eyes strained to pierce the halo of smoke that hovered over the poker table.

"Five-card draw. Jacks or better to open. Ante two bucks." Father Darin O'Day intoned the game's description as if it were a flat form of Gregorian chant. O'Day resembled a bald and paunchy Robert Taylor, the late screen actor.

"The trouble with you, O'Day, is you got no imagination." Father Donald Curley. Tall, overweight, bald, hard of hearing, with bad eyesight; he was organized religion's response to Don Rickles.

"You mean because he hasn't named five wild cards?" asked Father Joe Marek.

"Exactly," said Curley.

There was no response from O'Day. Nor was any expected.

"Got any extraordinary ministers at St. Henry's yet, Pat?" asked Sklarski. The question, as everyone knew, was loaded. Father Patrick McNiff, who resembled Carroll O'Connor physically and Archie Bunker ideologically, clearly would be the last to allow the laity to distribute Communion.

"No, and we ain't gonna have any!" McNiff carefully arranged his five cards.

"Why not?" asked Marek, a slightly built inner-city pastor whose parish bordered on Steele's.

McNiff tapped his cards on the table and peered myopically through thick glasses at his confrere. "Ain't gonna have no married man who's been foolin' with his wife handlin' my Communion!"

"Make up your mind, McNiff," demanded Curley, "is it good or bad?"

"What?"

"Marriage!"

"Good, I guess. So what?"

"He could always wash his hands."

"That ain't the point."

"McNiff, you belong in the Old Testament!"

"I can open," said Father Felix Lasko, delightedly. Laski taught Latin at the local high school seminary, where the students had long ago dubbed him "Bubbles." He wore a smile most of the time for no apparent reason. Seated, his feet barely touched the floor. When he became excited, his feet wiggled. Thus, he was not a particularly effective poker player. His four opponents could hear a steady clatter of rhythm coming from beneath Lasko's chair. Each decided he would not stay in this pot unless he had an exceptional hand.

"Cards?" asked dealer O'Day.

"Can I get anybody something from the bar?" Sklarski was ever the solicitous host.

McNiff flipped three of his cards onto the discard pile. "I'd like another beer," he said flatly.

Curley discarded one of his cards. "McNiff, when are you gonna lose some weight?"

"What makes you think I have to?"

Curley reached over, grabbed two handfuls of fat that bulged over McNiff's abdomen, pulled the mass forward and placed it on the poker table. "Anybody got a knife and fork? I didn't have any dessert."

McNiff sat back, the fat falling back in place. "Keep your hands to yourself. You some kind of weirdo?"

"You really should, Pat," said Marek. "You're inviting a heart attack. Don't forget what happened to Fred Palmer."

O'Day's fist hit the table with a thud. His index finger snapped at Lasko.

"Oh-oh, is it my turn?" Lasko looked bewildered.

"Bet," O'Day's voice was emotionless.

"Oh," said Lasko, his toes beating furiously against the tile floor. "Oh, I think I'll just bet thirty dollars." Ordinarily, Lasko considered a five-dollar bet a risk that approached sinfulness.

One by one, the others threw their cards in.

"Doesn't anybody want to see what I've got?" asked Lasko, plaintively.

"No," said Curley, "that's why you're still celibate."

Sklarski left to get McNiff's beer.

The group in the bomb shelter had thinned. Only Koesler, Steele, and Max remained. Why, Sklarski wondered, hadn't Dalton or Scanlon said good-bye? Or had they? He couldn't remember.

"Dalton and Scanlon gone?" he asked.

"Yes," answered Max, topping off his bourbon on the rocks. "Dalton drove Scanlon home. Had a bit too much to drink. You'll find an extra car in your driveway tomorrow."

"I'll have the janitor drive it over to Scanlon's."

"I'm afraid you're mistaken, Monsignor. It was Scanlon who drove Dalton home."

"Oh, whatever."

Koesler turned to Steele and resumed the conversation that had been interrupted by Sklarski's entrance. "How've you managed to hang in there all these years?"

"You've got to be programmed for failure, I think," answered Steele. "You try something, watch it fail, try something else, watch it fail—"

"But it must be depressing." Max was quite depressed just by participating in this conversation.

"On the contrary," said Steele, "it's just the opposite of depressing. It's exciting. The core city is one of the few remaining places where a priest is really needed and truly appreciated. Suburbanites can and do pay professionals for what they need and want. The inner city is where the good old days have never gone away. That's why it's hard to understand why these murders are taking place in the city."

"Why?" asked Max. "After all, it's Detroit that's known as Murder City, not Dearborn."

"Oh, well, we all know some hophead can waste us anytime for a few bucks that will keep him in dope a little while longer. We simply have to live with that. But these are premeditated murders. None of us can figure out why."

"Maybe it's over," guessed Koesler. "Maybe there won't be any more."

"I'll drink to that," said Max.

Sklarski popped open another can of Coors, especially imported for the occasion, and returned to the table.

Curley, the new dealer, was shuffling cards endlessly. "Seven-card stud, the last two down. One-eyed Jacks, deuces, and eights are wild."

"Is this poker or a memory game?" grumbled O'Day.

"What's wild? What's wild?" Lasko's feet drummed against the floor.

Sklarski thumped the Coors down in front of McNiff.

"I thought you were going to go easy on the calories, Pat," said Marek.

McNiff adjusted the currency before him. "I won't eat any more peanuts."

"McNiff," said Curley, "you belong in the Old Testament with a muzzle on."

A fist hit the table, the index finger snapping at Curley. "Deal!" O'Day suggested.

WEDNESDAY,
MARCH 30

Attendance at St. Ursula's Wednesday evening Lenten Devotions was holding up pretty well, Father Koesler reflected, as he joined Father Pompilio and Father Farmer for dinner. Each Wednesday evening so far there had been about a hundred parishioners present. This despite the fact that Farmer was preaching the series.

Koesler guessed that Farmer had written these sermons some thirty years before, shortly after he'd been ordained, and he had not performed even minor alterations on them in the meantime. Not only was the theology pre-

Conciliar, it was even bad for its time. But the sermons did display a good measure of hell fire and brimstone. Perhaps that explained the steady crowd of acceptable numbers. Koesler certainly got enough letters to the editor complaining about the lack of good old-fashioned hell fire and brimstone sermons. Undoubtedly, the writers were serious. At least a core of critical Catholics would turn out if you tried to scare them to death. Thunder and lightning never had been Koesler's style, and he wasn't about to begin now.

Last Wednesday, Farmer had even pulled the old "mountain of solid steel" out of his bag. Koesler had heard the performance as he waited in the wings to help with confessions after Devotions.

"My friends in Christ," Farmer had intoned, "imagine, if you will, a mountain made of solid steel, taller than the tallest mountain in the world. Now, my friends in Christ, imagine that once every thousand years, a small bird flies by that mountain and just brushes it with its wing. My friends in Christ, when that bird has that mountain worn down level with the ground . . ." Pregnant pause. Triumphantly, ". . . eternity will not . . ." His voice rising, ". . . even have *BEGUN!*"

Impressive, especially since Farmer had prefaced all this with a vivid, if fanciful, description of hell. It was enough to drive a sinner to sobriety, if a sinner were motivated best by fear.

Koesler, as he took his seat at the dinner table, wondered how Farmer would scare the customers tonight. He noted that Sophie had treated a standing rib roast with the respect due such a magnificent cut of meat. Its pink center gave way to darker hues and, finally, a charcoal-textured exterior. Pompilio ordinarily provided a good if quite ordinary table. But when guests were expected, he made certain Sophie had enough to buy the very best.

Pompilio crossed himself. "Bless us, O Lord, and these thy gifts which we are about to receive from Thy bounty, through Christ, Our Lord."

"Amen!" thundered Farmer, as he whipped his napkin across his lap.

"Say, Bob . . ." As the canonically appointed "Father"

of this canonical family, Pompilio began slicing the roast. ". . . wait till you see what Joe here brought me today."

"I can hardly wait," said Koesler.

Neither could Farmer. He reached down at the side of his chair and produced a cylindrical instrument with a glass covering at one end and open at the other. Pompilio and Farmer, shameless gadgeteers, were forever giving each other strange gadgets.

"Guess what it is," said Farmer, brightly.

"Damned if I know." Koesler examined the new plaything with a casual interest as he held his plate out for a slice of roast.

"I couldn't get it either." Pompilio shared in Farmer's childlike delight both over the gadget itself and the fact that no one could guess what it was.

"It's for fishin'," exulted Farmer, as he leaned over the side of an imaginary boat and submerged the cylinder, glass-covered end first, in an imaginary body of water. "You look through this and see if there are any fish around."

"What'll they think of next?" Koesler observed juice ooze from the roast as he cut into it. Rectory living, he mused, had its compensations.

Pompilio carefully carved a small corner from his slice of roast, laid his knife down and began tapping the meat in its juice. "Say, Joe, did I tell you they're thinking of opening a porno movie house on Gratiot near Harper?"

"That's in this parish, ain't it?"

"Damn right! And so, consequently, you know what follows a new porno movie house." Pompilio laid his fork down and began slowly chewing his piece of meat. chronicled, dabbing juice from his chin.

"Dirty book stores, massage parlors, perverts," Father Koesler stabbed a selection from the mixed vegetables. "And there goes the old neighborhood, eh?"

"It ain't Grosse Pointe," said Pompilio, his hands raised in a gesture of helplessness, "but it's all we got. . . ."

"You know, there's a sweet, little old lady, no, the embodiment of a sweet, little old lady," Koesler corrected himself; "trim little figure, purple hair, who comes down to my office faithfully once each year. She always carries this large brown leather briefcase, which she opens in my office, and dumps dozens of pornographic magazines on my desk. Then she says, 'Have you seen these?' "

"And you take the Fifth Amendment," laughed Farmer.

"Something like that. No two of these magazines are alike. I don't know where she gets them all. I think she gets her highs at Morality in Media meetings. And I've often thought that if she ever had a car accident, say, and the police found that briefcase in her car, they'd think they'd caught Detroit's top smut peddler."

"Or a sweet little old hooker," added Pompilio.

"That reminds me, Pomps," Farmer said, helping himself to a second portion of potatoes, "have you heard the one about the little old lady who killed her husband? Beat him to death. You, Bob?"

Pompilio and Koesler shook their heads negatively.

Farmer continued, "The cops came, took the bloody body away, and asked her, 'Lady, why did you do it?' She says, 'Because he called me a two-bit hooker.' Cop says, 'What did you hit him with?' She says—" Farmer began to break up. "She says . . . she says, 'A sack full of quarters!' "

As usual, Pompilio couldn't discern the punch line. "A sackful of what, Joe, a sackful of *what?*"

"Quarters," supplied Koesler, since Farmer was too convulsed to reply. All three laughed.

Koesler speared another slice of roast. "So, is that what you're going to preach on tonight, Joe? Sex?"

"Hell, no. I preached on that two weeks ago. You must've missed it."

"I'm afraid I did. Now, let's see," said Koesler, "sex two weeks ago. That explains why you talked on hell and eternity last week. And, if you talked on hell and eternity last week, this week it must be . . . judgment!"

"Now you've got it." Farmer was almost finished with dinner.

Pompilio, nearly halfway through his first slice of roast, rested his knife and fork across his plate, and mused, "I once had a lady for instructions who was fascinated by the idea of the general judgment. She couldn't figure out how, if everyone who had ever lived was going to be there, how everyone would be able to see and hear what was going on. So I told her we'd just have to let God handle the audio and video since the whole thing was His idea in the first place."

"So, Joe," returned Koesler, lighting his first afterdinner cigarette, "you gonna scare hell out of 'em tonight?"

"You betcha."

"Sock it to 'em, Joe!"

Pompilio, carving another small portion out of his slice of roast, looked up at Koesler. "You are going to help us with confessions after devotions, aren't you, Bob?"

Koesler could think of no good reason for helping with confessions. There never were enough penitents around to call for the multiple available confessors of days of yore, at least until Good Friday. However, it was small enough an effort to help pay for his room and board at St. Ursula's. "Sure. I'll be there. But I'm afraid I'll have to skip Joe's sermon. I know how the judgment scene comes out. I read the book."

Father Koesler thought he had allowed Joe Farmer plenty of time to have finished his sermon on the Last Judgment. But when he arrived at the passageway linking rectory to church, Farmer was still droning on. Koesler had to endure the sheep and the goats, the shame and the blame, the regret and the irreversibility. He waited in the passageway, smoking cigarettes, his mind flitting from editorials he must write, to sermons he must give, to the Rosary Murders that were never far from his consciousness.

Farmer finally wound down. He was followed by Benediction. At the final strains of the everpopular "Holy God, We Praise Thy Name," Koesler adjusted the black cape he was wearing over his cassock and entered the church.

Good crowd. Maybe a hundred. Maybe a few more. As he walked to the rear of the church toward his confessional, he noted that a goodly number of people were, mostly from habit, leaving before the service had been officially ended. He was suddenly surrounded by a dozen or so parishioners intent on but one thing—exiting. Koesler had that odd thought that reoccurred whenever he was in a position such as this. If he just stood still, he would be floored and trampled to death.

But he moved along briskly with the crowd. He spotted Nancy Baldwin among those still standing and singing the closing hymn.

He winked at her. She smiled and nodded back.

He took a deep breath and entered his confessional. It was getting harder and harder to man the confessional because less and less was happening there. Perhaps this was a phase the Church was going through.

He flipped both light switches. This turned on the small green exterior light immediately beneath his nameplate on the door, as well as the naked bulb in his compartment. He gathered his cape and sat down, checking the sliding doors on either side to make sure they were open. From the ample pocket in his cape, he pulled *The Second Deadly Sin,* Lawrence Sanders' new murder mystery. Koesler had enjoyed *The First Deadly Sin* immensely and had been anticipating the new novel.

He heard the curtain move at the confessional to his left. He flicked off the interior light, closing the sliding door to his right, and leaned toward the left panel. It was a teenage boy who had looked at dirty pictures, read dirty books, had dirty thoughts, said dirty words, and had been scared by Joe Farmer. Five Our Fathers and five Hail Marys later, all would be purified.

The boy shuffled out of the confessional, and Koesler relit the interior and resumed reading. He was determined not to read beyond one chapter. If no one else were coming to confession by then, to hell with it, he'd take his murder mystery to the comfort of his room.

The curtain rustled to his right. He extinguished the light, closed the small door to his left, and assumed the more naturally comfortable position, leaning against the right wall.

Silence.

"It's all right. I'm here. You can go ahead," Koesler whispered, the side of his face nearly pressing against the wire screen.

Silence.

Koesler thought he detected a slight sound. A kind of muffled sob.

There it was again, more clearly. Whoever was in the confessional was crying bitterly but softly.

Koesler silently cursed the walls. This was one of those times when a human needed a human shoulder and found only unyielding plasterboard.

As gently as he could, Koesler whispered, "Take your time. There's no hurry. Just begin when you feel better."

There followed another prolonged silence, broken by irregular restrained sobs. Finally, a man's choked whisper. "I . . . I'm the one . . ."

A wave of presentiment engulfed Koesler. The man could have been anyone. But Koesler felt the beginnings of an icy chill that had nothing to do with the thermostat. "You're the one? You're the one what? Take your time. There's no hurry."

Another silence, during which subtle sounds indicated the penitent was settling down, getting a semblance of self-control.

"I'm the killer . . ." Another silence.

Koesler had to test his presentiment. "Of the priests and nuns?"

"Yes."

Koesler's mind was racing. He was confused. Could this be a part of the killer's regular procedure? Does he talk to his victims before killing them? God! Am I next? If a shot came, it would be point-blank. Koesler tried to lean aside and away from the screen. But . . . he'd better try getting the man to talk. And to do so, he'd have to talk to him. And to talk to him—one couldn't shout in the confessional—he'd have to lean close to the screen.

He closed his eyes—the very action was a prayer—and put his mouth to the partition. "Why are you doing this?"

A long silence.

"Incest."

This wasn't making any sense. Could the unknown penitent be insane? Koesler's thought pulled up short. Silly; of course he'd have to be—wasn't anyone who committed a series of murders like this insane?

There was no longer any sound in the church. The two of them were undoubtedly alone. Koesler tried to calculate the danger, but it was impossible. He could only continue and see if he could make some sense of it.

"Incest? How could incest have anything to do with the mur—the killing of priests and nuns?" He tried to pick his words carefully.

"Years ago . . ." The quiet voice took on a tone of bitterness. ". . . many years ago, I was committing incest with my daughter. It went on for years. I told myself it was all right. I told my daughter somehow it was all right. She was fifteen. She was a good girl. We both knew it was wrong. We needed help. I told her to go to one of the nuns in her school. I went to the parish priest in confession."

There was a pause.

"What happened?" Koesler whispered.

"The nun told her her father wouldn't do a thing like that, that there must be something wrong with her to think foul thoughts like that and to spread lies about her own father. The priest was indifferent. He gave me a mechanical penance and dismissed me. I pleaded; I begged him for help, some kind of help . . . he told me to pray, and he shut the door."

Silence.

"Then . . . ?"

"We went back to it. Miserably. More out of habit than anything else. It was joyless. Cheap."

Silence. Koesler's mind was in disarray.

His jumbled thoughts were brought sharply back to stark reality by the man's next words.

"Then, one day, my daughter committed suicide." And then, in a monotone that was at the same time triumphant and defeated, "I have planned revenge ever since."

Koesler was now perspiring heavily. "Why are you telling me this?"

"I had to tell somebody. Somebody who couldn't tell anybody else."

"But would you like to make this a valid confession? We can do that if you'd like."

A seemingly indecisive silence. Then:

"Oh, God! Oh, God! I can't! I can't! I can't! I'm NOT DONE YET!"

The final three words were shrieked with such intensity that Koesler recoiled against the opposite wall of the confessional. It was as if a diabolic power had been unleashed on the other side of that thin partition.

The man swept past the confessional's curtain, stumbled several times and ran sobbing from the church.

Koesler sat for a few moments, his heart racing, his mind in a shambles. The words taking shape before him were, "Satan entered Judas and he left them. And it was night!"

Koesler made his way back to the rectory slowly, thoughtfully. He did not even hear Angelo's salutation as the janitor began locking the church.

Pompilio and Farmer were seated before a blaring TV set in the rectory's living room.

"Say, Bob," said Pompilio, as Koesler entered, "you should of heard Joe tonight. He was terrific."

"What? Oh. Well, maybe next time."

Farmer studied Koesler who was standing motionless just inside the living-room door. "What in the world happened to you? You're as white as a ghost."

"Is anything wrong, Bob?" asked Pompilio, with some concern.

"What? Oh, no. I guess I just need a drink." Koesler crossed the room to the liquor cabinet. He dropped a couple of ice cubes in a cocktail glass and was about to fill it with Scotch when he thought better of it. He needed a clear mind now. He poured in a finger of Scotch and filled the remainder of the glass with water. "I think I'll go up to my room. There's nothing wrong, Pomps. I'm just tired, I guess."

Koesler climbed the stairs accompanied by the awesome thought that he, alone, had knowingly talked to the killer. He, alone, knew the killer's motive. He, alone, could be sure the series of murders was not complete. And he was tortured by the question, could he tell anyone?

His instinctive inclination was to call Lieutenant Koznicki, immediately. On the other, and heavier, side of that coin was the storied seal of the confessional. Hundreds of novels, scores of movies had anchored their plots on that seal. Should protecting the seal cost a priest his life, or another innocent life, no reason was sufficient, no cause important enough to violate that seal.

Although, he thought, there certainly were extenuating circumstances in this case, he was filled with doubts he knew he'd have to resolve.

He could call another priest. Maybe Leo Clark, the moral theology prof at the seminary. But, no matter whom he called, the answer would be no more than an opinion that could be mistaken.

His dilemma ranked as the most serious problem he'd ever encountered.

He'd have to solve it himself. If a mistake were to be made, he'd rather shoulder the blame himself—even if it had to be for all eternity.

Koesler stood before the bookshelf that held his old theology textbooks. Many were the times, particularly when moving from one rectory to another, he'd been tempted to leave them behind. Nostalgia had always won. And now he was glad. Much of the thinking on moral theology had changed in the years since he'd been a student. But he was certain he could depend on the principles governing the seal of the confessional, even those found in a book published over twenty-five years ago.

He found it. Noldin's *Summa Theologiae Moralis, De Sacramentis*. He leafed through the index until he found "De poenitentia"—on penance—and located "de obligatione sigilli"—on the obligation of the seal. He found page 419 at the same time that he found his Latin had deteriorated. But he plowed through the text with a dedication born of practical necessity.

His study revealed three pertinent conclusions: the inviolable seal applied only to a "sacramental" confession, meaning that the person revealed his sins with the intention of being forgiven; a judgment was required as to the elusive intention of the penitent; and, finally, the text was flooded with warnings about protecting the seal in the face of any doubt.

The reasoning was clear enough. People told priests the

secret evils of their lives. Secrets frequently shared with no other human. Penitents needed the assurance that what they confessed would never be revealed. Thus, under NO condition could the secrets of the confessional escape it. Human nature being what it is, the seal must have been violated at some time in history, but Koesler was unaware of any specific violation. He was sure the unblemished image, at least, of well-kept confessional secrets encouraged the continued confidence of penitents.

He was also growing more certain that what he had heard tonight fell under the seal. True, the killer had said he had come because he "had to tell someone." And he had fled before absolution was even offered, however conditionally. But how could Koesler be sure the killer had not at least entered the confessional with the intention of being forgiven. There was no way of being sure. And the textbook was insistent on "tutior pars"—favoring the seal when there was a hint of a question.

Sort of like—Koesler mused—baseball's rule of thumb. In case of a tie, the decision is in favor of the runner . . . in case of a doubt, the decision is in favor of the would-be confessor.

Yet he was so eager—so anxious—to share his unique information with the police. He might be able to save the lives of other priests and nuns, literally. But how? If what he had learned was protected by the seal, it meant that he was bound to make certain that no specific sin could be attributed to a specific person. What, he thought, if he told Koznicki that the murderer had confessed to him, revealed the motive, and said that there would be more killings?

But what, he reflected further, playing devil's advocate, if the police were able to determine the identity of his penitent? There had probably been other people still in the church when the man had entered the confessional. What if one of them knew the identity of the man he or she had seen entering the confessional? Or could describe him so accurately it would eventually lead to his arrest? Koesler wouldn't be able to keep Koznicki, or any halfway worthwhile policeman, from doing his job—questioning churchgoers—in an attempt to do his sworn duty.

But what of *his* sworn duty?

He must remain silent.

He would have to guard even his own reactions to any future involvement in this case. It would be a violation of the seal if he even inadvertently let slip anything he'd learned in the confessional, if he let his knowledge gained in the confessional play any part in identifying the killer.

Someone once said that it wasn't so hard to do right; what was hard was to know what was right to do.

For one who wanted to do what was right, Koesler's was a pretty helpless feeling.

THURSDAY,
MARCH 31

Most people perceive sexual promiscuity as a vice. To Joe Cox, it was a life-style. Since his first sexual experience in high school, he had held to the simple formula that girls were nice, and sex was fun. It was a philosophy that proved inimical to stability. Cox had tried marriage once. It had been a barren and doomed experience that left him a determined bachelor but an active heterosexual. As he had once explained to a friend, "There are any number of women in this world with round heels. I am a man with round toes."

While his availability to these round-heeled women was virtually undiscriminating, he tended toward the brief encounter. When it came to extended affairs, Cox was an epicure. He cared little for women with underdeveloped bodies or undeveloped brains. Nor could he tolerate candidates for a weight farm. He favored women with full-formed curves and lively minds. On the rare occasion that he chanced upon one who measured up in both categories, he would prolong the relationship until the shadow of an altar crossed his path. Then he was gone.

Cox had been living with Pat Lennon for almost two weeks. She, also a victim of a marital disaster, seemed as determined as he to avoid repeating history. So far, the enjoyment of their relationship had been mutual. At times, they dined at The Old Place, out Jefferson Avenue. At others, they dropped in for the authentic German cuisine of nearby Schweizer's. Most often, they shopped for gourmet food among the aromatic odors of the Broadway Market, and for the Rolls Royce of meats at Ye Olde Butcher Shop, a friendly, Babylonian-owned market near the Lafayette Towers, where Lennon rented an apartment not far from where Cox lived. It was, of course, expensive renting two apartments when they were living in only one. But neither was sure yet how long their relationship would last.

Since Nelson Kane's warning, Cox and Lennon had been scrupulously punctual about arriving for work. The punctuality had seriously cut into their morning lovemaking, thus throwing into question the saying that all the world loves a lover. The *Free Press* management had never considered making allowances for love time in its union contracts.

In certain ways, newspapers were the antithesis of the assembly line. In other ways, there were definite similarities. The machines that handled wire-service copy kept up a fairly steady chatter through the day. Copy editors, whose job it was to read that copy, were presented with an assembly line procession of news. Reporters, staff writers and columnists, on the other hand, worked very hard when they worked, which was by no means all the time.

This morning, for example, Joe Cox had started work diligently. He began by transcribing notes he'd taken at a press conference the day before. Next, he began a series of phone calls. He was currently working on two stories. The Rosary Murders consumed much of his time. But he was also following leads on a possible story involving Detroit's mayor and the city's burgeoning drug traffic. Allegedly, some commercial property the mayor owned was being used as a center for cutting and marketing imported drugs. The trouble with a story like that was that after weeks of following leads, sometimes taking dangerous chances, there frequently was no truth to the allegations. Or there was a story so weak it wasn't worth publishing. The appreciated element in a story like the Rosary Murders was the given reality of the story. Not only were people being killed, but the reporter who stayed close to the story and perhaps got lucky might contribute something to the crime's solution. Of such circumstances are Pulitzer Prizes made.

At the moment, Cox was between busy periods. For the past twenty minutes, he had been sitting at his desk waiting for the birth of a fresh idea and the return of several phone calls. In his idle mind, a distinctly unprofessional idea was forming. He remembered something he'd seen on the building's fifth floor the previous day.

Cox maneuvered his chair a few degrees to the left so he could see Pat. She was gazing into space, tapping her front teeth with the eraser end of a pencil. She appeared to be in a state of inactive boredom similar to his own. He rose, and, in the noisy activity of the city room, crossed unnoticed to her desk. He bent and whispered in her ear.

"You've got to be out of your mind!" she said, but not loudly enough for anyone to overhear.

Cox whispered again. He stood for a moment while Pat seemed to be considering what he said. Then he bent over and whispered again.

Finally, she shrugged, smiled, and, a few minutes after his departure via elevator, followed in the same direction.

It was about fifteen minutes after the exit of Cox that Nelson Kane stood and scanned the vast rectangular expanse of the city room, unable to locate his reporter.

"Cox!" he bellowed, as if his voice could reach what his eyes couldn't see.

"Anybody know where Cox is?" Kane addressed those in the periphery of his desk. He received a series of shrugs and negatively shaken heads. "Goddammit!" Kane continued, to no one in particular, "I'm gonna get some leg irons for that guy and chain him to his desk." Kane kicked his own desk, hurting his toe and further intensifying his frustration level.

He lumbered toward the elevators, limping slightly as he

favored his injured toe. "Probably in the goddam coffee shop," he muttered. At the elevators, Kane met Larry Delaney, the *Free Press* theater critic, who'd been watching Kane's approach.

"Hurt yourself?" Delaney asked.

"It's nothing. Old war wound acting up," Kane lied for no reason. "You haven't seen Joe Cox, have you?"

"Matter of fact, I have. He was getting off the elevator at the fifth floor as I got on."

"Thanks." What the hell is he doing on the fifth floor, Kane wondered. I'm gonna burn his ass when I find him. He boarded the elevator, noticed the fifth-floor button had already been pushed, and settled back to futile fuming.

As he limped through the fifth floor, Kane alternated between asking, "Anybody seen Joe Cox?" and breathing *sotto voce* curses. Adding to his frustration was the fact that he was forced to ask for information from fifth-floor denizens—movie critics, record reviewers, columnists—people the news-oriented Kane considered the effete prima donnas of journalism.

Finally, Kane found someone who thought she knew Cox's whereabouts. "I think you'll find him in that empty office at the end of the hall," said TV writer Beverly Peters, with a trace of conspiratorial enjoyment in her tone.

Kane did not bother knocking. The absence of a nameplate clearly indicated this was a vacant office.

That was only partially correct, as Kane discovered when he opened the door. In that no one had been assigned the office and it contained only a desk and a chair, it was vacant. However, literally, it was not unoccupied.

Pat Lennon reclined on the desk. Joe Cox was leaning over her. They were having intercourse. Kane thought he might be having a heart attack.

Lennon let out a small shriek. Cox's lower jaw dropped. Kane coughed and said, "Cox . . . I want to see you . . . when you're . . . uh . . . done!"

Kane slammed the door determinedly. He shook his head, whistled softly, and murmured, "Good God! We've got an X-rated staff!"

Inside the room, Cox was indeed done. The interruption had destroyed the mood. He cursed his luck as he hitched up his trousers and remarked, "It's nice to be needed, but why in hell did Kane pick this moment to need me?"

Pat Lennon, arrant libber though she was, was clearly embarrassed. As she pulled down her skirt and smoothed the wrinkles, her jumbled thoughts tumbled out. "I never should've let you talk me into the damn-fool scheme. I feel like a little girl who got caught doing something naughty. Honestly, this is ridiculous! If Nellie Kane were my father confessor, he'd give me about ten rosaries for this!"

Cox, his fly half-zipped, stood stock still and looked intently at Lennon. The gears in his mind came unmeshed. "What did you say?" he demanded.

"That this is ridiculous. This is another fine mess you've gotten us into, Ollie!"

"No, about the rosaries."

"Oh, that. Only that if Nellie Kane were my father confessor, he'd probably give me a bunch of rosaries for my penance."

Cox still had not continued the zippering process. "What does that mean?"

"What does it mean? Oh, I forgot. You're not a Catholic."

"And you are."

"We've been through that. It's just that when a Catholic goes to confession, the priest gives a penance to say, a sort of punishment for the sins. The worse the sin, the heavier the penance. Usually, it's just a few Our Fathers and Hail Marys. If the sins are really miserable, the penance escalates. Sometimes into a rosary or more."

"But why a rosary?" Cox's hand on his zipper still had not moved.

"Because it takes so long to say it." Lennon sighed; she was tiring of this subject. "There are five decades, with one large bead and ten little beads in each decade. You say an Our Father on each of the big beads, and a Hail Mary on each of the little ones. That's a total of five Our Fathers and fifty Hail Marys. That takes a lot of time . . . what is this, anyway, a catechesis?"

Cox said nothing.

"Aren't you going to zip yourself up?"

Cox did nothing.

"Joe! Joe! Kane wants to see you, remember? Joe! . . . oh, what the hell!"

Lennon left the immobile Cox, who was utterly lost in thought.

After waiting almost fifteen minutes for the return of Cox and Lennon to the city room, Kane considered a revisit to the scene of the assignation. At that moment, Lennon, her face flushed by what Kane considered appropriate shame, slid as unobtrusively as possible into her chair. Another fifteen minutes passed without a sign of Cox. Kane's impatience was near choleric. Then, he noticed the reporter approaching in a very distracted manner through the maze of desks.

"Cox." Kane spat out the words through tight lips, just loudly enough for his reporter to hear. "That was the most unprofessional behavior I've ever seen at a newspaper. The *Free Press* is not paying you for your ability to screw!"

Kane hesitated as he noticed that Cox, his right hand toying with his mustache, was lost in his own thoughts.

"What the hell is going on?" raged Kane. "You're in trouble up to your ass, and you're not even paying attention to me!"

"Nellie . . ." Kane was aware of a trace of singular excitement in Cox's voice. ". . . what do you know about the rosary?"

"Whaddo I know about the rosary? What is this, a Bible quiz?"

"Did you know that priests sometimes made people say the rosary when they went to confession?"

"Yeah, I know that."

"And did you know they call that 'a penance'?"

"Yeah, yeah . . . so?" Kane was almost snarling.

"Nellie, that's *it*. I just went back in the morgue and reread a piece I did before Lent. It said that Catholics used to have to fast and abstain every day during Lent. But for the past few years, they're supposed to do penance just on Ash Wednesday and all the Fridays of Lent. That's got to be it. The Rosary Murderer has killed a priest and/or a nun on Ash Wednesday and on the last four Fridays. He leaves a rosary with each victim to connect what he's doing with the special days of penance during Lent."

Kane pondered for several moments, his mind exploring the possibilities. "O.K.; supposing this makes sense . . . whatsit mean?"

"Nellie . . . if I'm right, the killer's going to hit tomorrow and again next Friday—Good Friday, the last Friday of Lent. And then he'll be done."

"Holy hell," Kane breathed, now sharing Cox's barely bridled intensity. "I think you may just have something. We can protect our rears if we attribute the theory to 'an informed source' and write in some disclaimers. We've got plenty of time to get this into the first edition this evening. If we write that the killer strikes tomorrow, and he does, we're prophets. If we run it, and he doesn't hit—maybe because we've scared him off—we've got to have disclaimer language to cover us. So be careful how you write it."

Cox, now thoroughly enthused, was halfway to his desk when Kane called him back. "Listen, get an interview with the cops. Get a reaction to your story. God! I'd hate to be in their shoes!"

Cox shrugged and left, reflecting on the fickle finger of fate. Just a few minutes ago, he'd found his own figurative shoes unpleasantly tight.

Lennon, who had been surreptitiously observing the animated exchange between Kane and her irrepressible lover, was puzzled. She had expected Kane to deliver an uninterrupted monologue. Instead, she could see that Cox had done most of the talking. She'd expected Cox to slump back to his desk, evidencing some sort of punishment. Instead, he was furiously dialing on the phone, obviously hot on a story. Evidently, Dame Fortune was working overtime in Cox's corner. As far as Pat was concerned at that moment, Cox could move in with the dame.

The scene in Lieutenant Walter Koznicki's office resembled a tableau. Sergeant Fred Ross stood stiffly near the door. Detective Sergeant Dan Fallon stood near the window, shifting his weight from one foot to the other. Detective Sergeant Ned Harris sat at one side of the large desk. Behind the desk, Koznicki leaned back in his chair, hands linked as usual across his stomach. Across from him sat Joe Cox. No one moved. No one said anything.

Cox had just explained his theory, connecting the rosaries left behind by the Rosary Murderer with the days of special penance for Catholics during Lent. For several moments, the police officers had been absorbing the tale.

"The *Free Press* intends to print this story?" Koznicki broke the silence.

"In tomorrow's issue," Cox answered, "the first edition of which will be on the streets tonight."

"Do you anticipate the local TV and radio stations will pick up the story?" Koznicki asked.

"Absolutely!" said Cox. "We'll make sure their news departments get an early copy. It's copyrighted, so they'll have to mention the source. Sells papers."

After a slight pause, Koznicki looked from one to another of his men, then said, "Mr. Cox, I assume you want some reaction from us to this theory of yours?"

"Yes," said Cox. "The story's incomplete as it stands. It doesn't make either you or us look very competent without a police reaction. It doesn't make much sense to tell our readers we have reason to believe the Rosary Murderer is going to kill some priest or nun tomorrow, without telling them what the police intend doing to stop him."

"Very well, Mr. Cox." Koznicki rose and gestured toward the door. "We'd like a little time to think about this. Would you wait in the outer office? We won't be long."

The reporter nodded. Ross opened and closed the door at Cox's departure.

Koznicki resumed his chair. "Well, men, what do you think?"

"Makes sense to me," said Fallon. Unconsciously following a police pecking order, he seated himself in the chair vacated by Cox, while Ross moved to the window position where Fallon had been standing.

"I see a hole in this theory," said Harris, who was looking at a small, plastic calendar he had taken from his wallet. "Cox claims these special penance days are Ash

Wednesday and all the Fridays of Lent. Then what about February twenty-fifth, the first Friday in Lent? No priest or nun murdered that day."

"Hell, Ned," said Fallon, "it doesn't have to hang together like a goddam novel."

Koznicki leaned forward. "There may be an explanation for that open date. We've already theorized that the killer has been operating at two levels. On the one hand, he had a carefully made plan that he intends to complete. On the other, he wants to be stopped. Obviously, he'd rather kill than be stopped—otherwise, he'd stop himself. So, he's afraid to give us too much help.

"For instance, in his first four murders, he used different weapons. He also made at least a slight effort to make his first two killings appear to be accidental deaths. No reason for this except to confuse us and make it more difficult for us to establish his M.O. He felt he needed breathing room, especially in the beginning. If he had killed his second victim on February twenty-fifth, it would've been just two days after his first murder and would have gotten us on his trail a good ten days earlier than we began to connect this case.

"And yet, gentlemen, there can be little doubt that he's been carefully leaving these rosaries, identically placed on his victims, as clues to something. At the moment, I can see no better explanation than Cox's. And, after all, even with this interpretation, the killer is not telling us very much—only the days of his crimes."

"He's telling us something else, Lieutenant," said Fallon. "If we don't get him before tomorrow, one, maybe two more people will be hit. And if we don't get him before next week—Good Friday—we may never get him."

"So, O.K." Harris scratched his head. "How do we respond?"

"Is surveillance possible?" asked Fallon. "How many priests and nuns do we have to protect?"

"I've got some figures on that," said Ross, paging through his notebook, "but I've learned they don't tend to be too accurate. If you're talking about the whole Archdiocese of Detroit, you're talking 868 priests and 3,550 nuns—333 parishes in six counties."

Harris gave a long low whistle.

"If you're talking metropolitan Detroit, there's 132 Catholic parishes, 292 priests, and God knows how many nuns."

Koznicki shook his head. "You said something about those figures being inaccurate, Fred?"

"Well," said Ross, "you'd think an organization like a diocese would keep better records, but I was surprised. There's a good deal of moving about. Priests and nuns leave, and they're not recorded immediately. The biggest problem is the residences. Some priests don't live in the rectories, and lots of nuns don't live in convents. Sometimes they've got more than one residence, and a good part of the time the diocese doesn't know where they are."

"How can we try and protect people if we can't find them?" asked Fallon.

"We can't," acknowledged Koznicki, "but we've got to do our best for the ones we can locate. I wouldn't even suggest this if we weren't dealing with just one day, but tomorrow we're going to put our best efforts into protecting a lot of innocent citizens and the possible apprehension of a murderer.

"Dan, get some help and contact the law enforcement departments in all the communities that are within the diocese's boundaries but outside metropolitan Detroit—including the county sheriffs. Tell them what we've learned and how we're reacting, and urge them to provide as much protection as possible tomorrow.

"Fred, get all our people in Control. They're to leave whatever they're working on and get on this. Get a list of all the rectories, convents, and known residences of priests and nuns. Call every one of them, warn them about tomorrow, and tell them we intend to provide protection. I want a police officer—just as far as we can do it—to be with every priest and nun in Detroit all day tomorrow. Let me know, as soon as you can, how many additional personnel you'll need, and I'll get them.

"Ned, give a statement on the plan to Cox.

"If any of you need me and I'm not here, I'll be with the commissioner. Let's go!"

Flashing on the screens of the majority of Detroit-area TV sets was the serious, concerned face of Bill Bonds, anchorperson of WXYZ-TV's 11 P.M. news.

"Good evening. At the top of tonight's news: Detroit-area priests and nuns warned to look out for the Rosary Murderer tomorrow."

There were a few other teaser headlines, as well as a word on sports and tomorrow's weather. Then the station cut away for commercial messages. When the news returned, it was Bonds again, with the lead item.

"A copyrighted story in tomorrow's *Detroit Free Press* says that there's been a break in the mystery that has shrouded the infamous Rosary Murders. The paper, quoting an 'anonymous reliable source,' claims there is a connection between the rosaries left at the scene of each of the murders and the days of special penance observed by Catholics during Lent. The Rosary Murderer has struck on Ash Wednesday and four of the five Fridays in Lent, days of required penance for Catholics. The Rosary is frequently used as a prayer of penance. If this theory is correct, the Rosary Murderer should strike again tomorrow, and finally, next week, on Good Friday.

"Commenting on police reaction to this theory is Detective Sergeant Ned Harris, of the Detroit Police Department's special task force investigating the Rosary Murders."

Appearing on the screen was a head-and-shoulders shot of the black officer, in a taped interview.

"We have enlisted the aid of all law enforcement agencies in the six counties that make up the Archdiocese of Detroit. Along with these agencies, the Detroit Police and Wayne County Sheriff's deputies intend to provide maximum protection for the priests and nuns of this area tomorrow. We urge all of them to exercise special caution in their activities tomorrow, and to notify the police if they become aware of the slightest occurrence that is out of the ordinary."

The policeman's image was replaced on the screen by Bonds. "In other news on the local scene . . ."

All the local TV and radio stations carried the story.

Among the sets that were not turned on for the eleven

o'clock news was the Panasonic owned by a man who had retired earlier, after carefully checking his .38-caliber pistol.

FRIDAY,
APRIL 1

The alarm clock sounded at seven o'clock. After a few seconds of strident ringing, it was turned off by Father Harold Steele. He raised his head from the pillow, running his hand through his heavy beard and his thick, graying head of hair. He peered through the window, testing the day. The pastor of St. Enda's parish, he was also sole occupant of its rambling rectory that had once housed as many as four priests, and a housekeeper, with room to spare.

St. Enda's, on Rosa Parks Boulevard near West Grand, was just a block east of the blind pig where the 1967 riots had begun. The neighborhood was a prototype of black ghettos, where drug abuse mingled with a pervasive atmosphere of hopelessness.

With it all, Steele's style of ministry had been fairly effective. Far more effective, indeed, than had he attempted to offer his black community the official Church's moral interpretations now being rejected by even white Catholics. Long before Pope Paul had divided the Church with his encyclical on birth control, Steele's determined silence on the matter had solved the problem for St. Enda's parishioners.

Similarly, he respected his parishioners' conscience decisions on marriage validity. He was determined to keep it simple and deliver the message of love as it had come from Jesus Christ without a top-heavy layer of man-made laws.

The lack of interest in his parish on the part of anyone who had clerical power or influence ensured his continued success in his life of ecclesiastical "crime." So, Steele was content to stay where he was, and no one at the chancery had any intention of asking him to move.

Steele showered, dressed, took his small, gold-plated pyx from a drawer and went to the church through the hallway that connected church and rectory. He would begin the day by bringing communion to some of the shut-ins of the parish, as he did each Friday.

He removed four consecrated hosts from the tabernacle, placed them in the pyx, and left to get his car.

He was slightly surprised to find a Detroit Police Department patrol car parked in front of the rectory, its uniformed driver standing leaning against the front fender.

"Mornin', Father." The tall, slender young black officer smiled engagingly at the priest.

"Mornin', officer. Anything I can do for you?"

"Just the opposite, Father. I'm doin' for you today."

"Huh?"

"You didn't hear the news? They're expecting some trouble from that Rosary Murderer today. I'm going to be with you as much as possible all day. Just for safety's sake. Name's Ray Mills."

"Oh, yes; I got a phone call yesterday. Guess I forgot all about it . . . good to know you, Ray." They shook hands. "Mine's Harold Steele."

"I know, Father. Where you headed?"

"Communion calls to some shut-ins. I was just going to get my car."

"Get in, Father." Mills opened the passenger door of the black-and-white. "I'll take you. Just give me the addresses."

They settled in the car, as Steele reflected on this unusual procedure. "Is everybody getting this kind of protection today?"

"Just about. There's at least one officer assigned to every rectory and convent. Since you're alone, you got a personal bodyguard for the day."

Steele was confused. The Rosary Murders had, of course, been very much on his mind. But he had never seriously considered himself a possible target.

It took only a few moments to reach the first home on

the list. Both the officer and the priest approached the front steps of the house. Steele turned to Mills. "I'm sorry, but you can't go in with me. I'm going to be hearing confessions."

"Wait a minute, Father. I've got orders to be with you today like a shadow."

"Those may be your orders. But my orders are to protect the secrecy of confession. And in the small flat these people live in, there's no way to get you out of earshot."

Still undecided, Mills protested, "Well, let me at least go in ahead of you and check things out."

"Officer, I appreciate your concern, but my shut-ins are just poor old people. We try to make sure they never get a visitor without being informed ahead of time that someone's coming. They're expecting me. If someone in uniform like you came in, you'd only scare them.

"Oh, come, Ray . . . they're just old, ill people. They're not going to hurt me."

Mills hesitated. Finally, he nodded. "O.K., Father. But I'll be right here."

Mrs. Jessie Smith opened the door for Steele. She and her husband were in their seventies and seldom left their deteriorating home. Members of St. Enda's Christian Service Commission called on them from time to time and shopped for them, as well as for other shut-ins in the parish.

Steele heard the confessions—innocent self-accusations —and gave the two communion.

Back in the car, he reflected that it had been a long time since he'd traveled with anyone within his parish. It had been almost seven years since he'd last had an assistant priest. But he remembered that young man well. The beginning of Father Bob Hastings' tour of duty at St. Enda's had marked the most peculiar sick call Steele had ever participated in.

It had begun with a hospital call Hastings received near midnight. A woman was dying and wanted a priest. The problem was, Hastings didn't know where the hospital was. He woke Steele, who drove him to the hospital. Steele had dozed in the car until Hastings returned and announced that the dying woman did indeed want to confess, but spoke only Polish. Together, they had driven to St. Florian's, where they had roused a sleepy Father Robleski. The three then returned to the hospital only to discover that the dying woman was a Polish National Catholic, not a member of the Roman Catholic Church. It had taken three priests two hours to accomplish nothing.

Steele was smiling at the recollection when they arrived at the second house on his route, located on West Grand Boulevard. Mills again leaned against the fender of his car, as Steele mounted the front steps of Bessie Gates's house.

One of the few whites left in the area, old Mrs. Gates was seriously crippled and never left her home. On Fridays when she expected Steele, she would unlock the front door and struggle back to the living room, where she would wait patiently for the priest's arrival.

Steele entered through the unlocked front door and stepped into the living room. Mrs. Gates was seated in her straight-back chair. Rather, she had been tied into it. Her head hung down on her chest, and Father Steele could see she'd been gagged. But everything happened too quickly. Intent on the woman's inert figure, he hadn't noticed the man who stepped in back of him from behind the front door.

Steele's first thought was that poor Mrs. Gates had been robbed. He was to have no other thought; the hollow-nosed bullet crashed through his brain at point-blank range. His body pitched forward, falling across Mrs. Gates's seated figure and rolling onto the floor.

The effect of the silencer, together with traffic sounds, had made it impossible to hear the gunshot outside the house. Mills remained waiting at the car.

The man separated the gun and the silencer, tucking both back into his coat pocket. He produced a small black rosary, wrapped it securely around the priest's left wrist, stringing the beads between the dead man's thumb and forefinger.

He turned to leave, when, for the first time, through the curtained window, he noticed the police car and the officer leaning against it. He retraced his steps, exited through the rear door, hurried down the alley, and disappeared from sight.

Mills became concerned. It had been fifteen minutes since the priest had entered the old house. He decided to investigate. He knocked at the front door, opened it, and called in, "Father? Father Steele?"

No answer.

Drawing his revolver, Mills cautiously entered the house. The scene that greeted him would be etched forever in his mind.

He rushed to the black-clad figure on the floor, bent to look at the priest's left wrist, saw the telltale rosary, and exclaimed, "Oh, my God!" Then: "My ass is in a sling!"

It was the only thought that came to mind.

The scene on West Grand was what one would expect when life's routine is upset by the presence of a dozen or so police cars, their blue and red lights flashing like neon signs. Clusters of neighbors and curious passersby formed around the perimeter of official vehicles. Rumors, most of them wildly inaccurate, spread from group to group. The prevailing consensus was that there had been a drug bust and that several mobsters had been slain in a brief but lethal shootout.

Inside the modest house, with its plethora of religious pictures, statues and bric-a-brac, Sergeant Harris had pretty well lost the characteristic cool for which he was famous, at least among members of the force.

It had been *his* face on TV screens, *his* voice on radio yesterday, promising police protection for Detroit priests and nuns. A protection promised for only one day. That day had barely begun and the Rosary Murderer had already hit a Detroit priest.

Harris was clearly embarrassed, both for himself and for his close friend and immediate superior, Walter Koznicki, who was waiting at the commissioner's office for word from Harris. Hell, he was embarrassed for the entire department that had proved itself incapable of protecting an isolated and identified group of people for just one lousy day. He felt a combination of impatience and fury as he paced quickly back and forth.

"Goddammit," he said more loudly than necessary. And then, "Shit! This wasn't one of those priests we weren't supposed to be able to find, somebody lost in the shuffle. Dammit, this was one we had a fix on. This was one of the so-called easy ones. In a parish all by himself. We could give him one-on-one protection. Damn!"

No one responded to what was, in effect, a statement of irrefutable fact.

"Who was the officer assigned here?" Harris asked in a grim tone.

"Patrolman Raymond Mills," Detective Sergeant Fallon replied.

"How long's he been on the force?"

"Seven years."

"Where is he?"

"Ross has him in the kitchen."

Harris nodded. Nothing he could say to the unfortunate officer would be any worse than he was now hearing from Sergeant Fred Ross.

The technicians had completed their work, and the bodies of both the priest and the old woman were being placed on stretchers to be taken to the morgue.

Harris turned to Fallon. "Well, what's his story?"

Fallon recounted the events, from the meeting of the priest and policeman almost two hours before, to the time when the officer found the priest's body.

"Was he dead when Mills found him?"

"Yeah. Point-blank at the rear of the skull. Probably dead before he hit the floor."

"How 'bout the old lady?"

"Bound, gagged, and dead. No physical evidence of wounds or signs of any kind of scuffle. Probably a heart attack."

"Damn," Harris breathed, as he continued pacing, "an eyewitness. You say the priest told Mills not to go in with him?"

"Insisted that he stay out. Told him he was going to hear confessions."

"Why didn't Mills at least insist on going in first to see that everything was all right inside?"

Fallon shrugged and held his palms upward in a gesture of frustration. "He *did*. The priest told him that that would just scare the old people. Finally, he figured that a series of old, sick people wouldn't hurt anybody. However, he did admit that if he had it to do over . . ." Fallon's voice trailed.

"Damn!" It was becoming Harris' favorite expletive. "How in hell can you protect these people! Anybody can have access to them just about anytime. And a lot of what they do can't be heard or seen by anybody else. They're harder to guard than the president. I'm beginning to believe that anyone who wants to take out a priest or nun has got himself a piece of cake."

"Yeah. It's a revelation, ain't it." Fallon paused. "Only one thing: I don't think the media or the public will believe it."

"No . . . you're right. They'll probably blame it on us." Harris glanced out the front window. Through the faded lace curtains, he could see the police line cordoning off the house, and beyond that, the reporters and TV cameras. "Dan, go out and talk to the boys and girls of the press. Try to stress the vulnerable position of the clergy and religious. Maybe they can convince some priests and nuns that we're not trying to get in on confessional secrets. Maybe they'll let us protect them better.

"I'm going to call Walt."

As Fallon left the house, Harris began dialing the commissioner's office. He had been somewhat calmed by talking the thing out with Fallon. It was a process that Koznicki had yet to go through.

In a sense, the marked police car was an incongruity parked in the semicircular driveway of the Monastery of Mary, Mother of Divine Charity. Inside the monastery, it was the sixteenth century revisited. Inside the police car could be found all the twentieth-century gadgetry contemporary technology had produced to help modern police perform their complicated work.

Assigned to guard the monastery's nearly invisible inhabitants was officer Dietrich Bernhard, a first-generation American whose parents had escaped Nazi Germany.

Bernhard had been on the Detroit Police force little more than a year. Proud of his profession, he was methodically correct in the performance of his duties. Earlier that afternoon, he'd been called by Patrolman Andy Bologna, as had everyone assigned to guard priests and nuns, and informed of what had happened at the Gates home. He was told to take every imaginable precaution, as it was within the realm of possibility that the murderer would act again this day.

After the call, he had rearranged his schedule slightly. He rang the monastery's front doorbell and was admitted by the extern sister, the only sister he or anyone else was allowed to see without special permission from the Mother Prioress. The extern had been frightened ever since this morning, when he had told her, in no uncertain terms, the fatal possibilities of this day.

Now, he told her that he would enter with any visitor she might have that day. As long as he accompanied the visitor, she had nothing to fear. If, *for any reason,* he did not appear at the door with a visitor, she was not, *under any circumstances,* to let *anyone* in. If he was not in the vicinity of the front door, it would be only because he was checking the rear of the building, and he would return in a few moments.

Once again, he had frightened the nun. But, he reasoned, he'd rather have her frightened than dead.

From that time on, every fifteen minutes on the quarter-hour, he would leave his patrol car and circle the monastery on foot, checking the security of the windows and rear door. At all other times, he was in his car, his eyes riveted on the building's front door.

Twice, visitors came. One, a well-dressed matron; the other, a panhandler. He supervised the panhandler's handout and limited the matron's visit, which he also supervised, to ten minutes.

This rigid routine was being carefully registered by a man in a car parked half a block north of the monastery. He was dressed in a telephone repairperson's uniform and had been parked in various locations on Wyoming for four hours, always in sight of the monastery and its uniformed guardian.

After he had left the Gates home, and after he had caught his breath, the man had picked up the latest edition of the *Free Press* and read the details of the theory that had almost gotten him caught.

After reading the story, his mind had whirled. So they had finally gotten the message—or at least part of it. What if priest and cop had entered the house together? Either he would have killed two or he would have gone down from a police bullet. What if there had been only one exit from the house? What if the cop had come in sooner? It was almost as if Providence were protecting him. His very success this morning against odds with which he had not reckoned buoyed his confidence.

Everything about his plan had gone like clockwork. Especially since he'd abandoned that part of the plan that called for a different weapon for each killing. That had been bizarre anyway. And when Mother Mary had lived long enough to scribble part of his name, going for a certain fatal shot was the only thing that made sense.

He was sorry about the old lady; he hadn't meant to hurt her—just keep her quiet long enough to get the priest within range. She couldn't have given the police any information about him that would've told them any more than they already knew. Too bad about her.

Well, she was in heaven now, that was for sure—no need to bother his head about her. He had more pressing things on his mind.

For hours, the solitary watcher had marveled at Bernhard's precise fidelity to the routine the policeman had composed. In that routine, concluded the watcher, lay his only possibility of success.

He watched as the panhandler approached the monastery's front door. He watched as the two men entered the building together. So that's it: no one gets in without big brother.

He smiled as he saw the matron approach. As the front door opened, and the matron entered with her police escort, the man pulled a rectangular toolbox from the passenger's side of the front seat, left the car, hurried the few steps to the monastery, and slipped to the rear of the building where a high brick wall separated the monastery from the Marygrove College grounds. There, out of sight of anyone, he pressed his face tightly to the wall and was thus able to peer between the latticed bricks and the ivy that clung to them.

From this position, for the next forty-five minutes, he timed his meticulous policeman. Superb: every fifteen minutes, he would appear at the rear of the building, and in thirty seconds he would disappear around the building's north side.

Immediately following the four-forty-five patrol, the man swung himself and his box over the brick wall. He hurried to the monastery's rear door and rang the bell. In a few moments, a well-rounded, smiling nun opened the door, her index finger covering her mouth. The smile indicated she was friendly; the finger indicated she wasn't going to talk.

"Sister," he began, "I'm here to work on the phone."

Still smiling, she shook her head negatively.

"I know there's nothing wrong with it," he continued. "They're getting some new phones at the college, and we have to change the numbers on some of the neighboring exchanges. Yours is one."

Smiling broadly, she nodded and beckoned him to follow her into the kitchen, where she had been preparing dinner. She pointed to the phone on the wall and turned from him to continue her work.

Unknown to him, and for the first time in his career as a murderer, fate was about to play a disastrous trick on him. For, as Officer Bernhard returned to the front of the building, he found another visitor—a visitor who had just arrived and was irked that he had been refused entry. Dr. Edward Bailey, a psychiatrist, was Sister Margaret Mary's brother. A regular visitor, he could not grasp why he had not been ushered in without question, as he always had been. Bernhard, after checking the doctor's identity, told the extern nun it would be all right to summon Sister Margaret Mary and began explaining to Bailey the reason for these unusual precautions.

Meanwhile, in the kitchen, the man attired as a telephone repairman had toyed with the phone for a few moments, then reached into his toolbox and removed a pistol already equipped with its silencer. He slipped quickly and quietly behind the nun, who was busily tearing lettuce leaves and dropping them into a large bowl for the evening's salad. He brought the revolver up to the rear of her bonneted head and fired. Her round body pitched forward across the sturdy wooden block table, sending assorted vegetables and the large salad bowl skittering over the floor. The man removed a small black rosary from his pocket, and circled it on the nun's left wrist, running its beads between her thumb and index finger.

At this precise moment, the extern nun appeared at the kitchen door.

She screamed several times with no inhibition whatever. For a split second, the man was immobilized, his hand still resting on the rosary he had so carefully arranged. Then he turned and fled through the rear door.

Down the hallway, Bernhard had wasted not a split second. Reacting instantaneously at the sound of the first scream, he had bounded down the hall, cursed at the door that had automatically locked behind the nun, kicked it open, took in the bloody scene at one glance, and raced for the open rear door.

As he reached the door, Bernhard saw the fleeing man about to disappear over the wall. "Hold it!" he shouted, raising his service revolver to eye level. The two men fired almost simultaneously, Bernhard only an infinite second after the other. Blood spurted from the man's thigh. Bernhard was struck in his left shoulder, the bullet's force spinning him to the ground.

With a strength that came partly from duty and partly from fury, the officer pulled himself to his feet and staggered to the wall. With his last ounce of determination, he dragged himself halfway over the barrier.

The last sight he saw before passing out was a figure in a telephone repairperson's uniform, limping badly, but now out of further harm's way.

SATURDAY,
APRIL 2

Young Dietrich Bernhard, "Fritz" to his friends on and off the force, periodically regained consciousness. He did not have a choice of states. If he had, he would have preferred the unconscious one. For one, his shoulder ached with sharp, burning pain. For another, he had two extremely embarrassing memories that kept whirring through his mind. One, the body of the nun—one of those he'd been assigned to protect—sprawled across what had appeared to be a meat block, blood gushing from her head; the other, the view of the murderer limping along the brick wall toward freedom.

What Officer Bernhard could not know was that he'd been made a media hero.

In the more than five weeks this series of killings had gone on, Bernhard had come closest to getting the killer. And in his heroic action, he had placed his life in jeopardy—indeed, nearly lost it. The murderer's bullet had exploded inside his left shoulder. Internal injuries were extensive. A fragment of the bullet had barely missed his heart. His name and official police photo were featured in national as well as local newspapers and on network and local TV.

Bernhard lay in the intensive care unit of St. Mary's Hospital, the emergency facility nearest to the scene of the shooting. His wife had been waiting in the hospital corridor most of the night and on into the morning. Periodically, she went to the window of the ICU and peered in at him helplessly but hopefully. She was the only civilian permitted to get even that close by the policeman who stood guard at the doorway. Bernhard's condition was listed as serious but stable.

It was now nine in the morning. By prearrangement, Lieutenant Koznicki and Sergeant Harris had just arrived at the hospital. They introduced themselves to Mrs. Bernhard, offered encouragement, asked a few questions about her husband's condition, and joined the parade of hospital personnel who had fruitlessly urged her to go home and get some rest. They greeted the officer on guard, looked in at Bernhard's inert form, and sat in the adjacent waiting room.

"We lost two more," said Koznicki, as he tried to shift his bulk into a comfortable position in the small chair.

"That's the *bad* news," said Harris, stretching his long legs and crossing them at the ankles.

"Yeah, and it's bad enough to pretty well cover any good news."

"O.K., Walt." Harris rubbed his eyes with the heels of his hands. "I know how you feel. Hell, I feel as bad as you do. But don't forget, we got a wounded killer now. If he tries to get that bullet out of his leg, we'll get a report on it. If he tries to live with it, it'll probably kill him. Odds are strong that Bernhard will recover, and he'll be able to give us the best description of the guy we've had so far."

"I know, Ned." Koznicki shook his head. "Our man's in more trouble than he's had to this point. But there are four priests and four nuns dead, and he's been leaving a path for us to follow, and we've stumbled pretty badly on that path. Our best assumption so far—and it was given to us—was that he was going to hit yesterday. We defensed the situation, but he *still* got around us."

Harris stood, thrust his hands into his pockets, and began to pace. "I never gave it any thought until this case, but priests and nuns must be the most difficult group of people in the world to protect. I s'pose ministers might fall into the same category, but at least they usually have a family around to insulate 'em a little. Priests and nuns are alone a lot, sort of sitting ducks.

"But even given that, the amount of planning this guy's done amazes me. That nun—the second victim, what was her name? Ann, he got her at the rare time she'd be alone in that convent. Then there's the jogger.

Got him at the most deserted point of his run. That's careful planning. But the priest yesterday takes the cake. Inside one of the homes he always stopped at on Fridays. This is one killer who's done his homework."

"There's one problem with that line of reasoning." Koznicki shifted again in discomfort. "Granted, the Catholic clergy and religious are perhaps the most vulnerable group there is, the killer is not necessarily using their vulnerability."

"He's not?"

"No. And nothing indicates that better than his latest victim. He got her, yes, but she was a Carmelite, a cloistered nun. You see, Carmelites give up a lot, as far as we're concerned. By our standards, they give up just about everything in the world. Literally. But, as they give up the world, they also grow physically apart from the world. Their very way of life protects them from the world. They're almost invulnerable from any worldly harm short of a nuclear bomb. The very last place I would've expected our man to try to hit would be a Carmelite convent.

"So what does that do to our theory that he's methodically executing the most vulnerable group in the world?"

"Sort of shoots holes in it, I guess . . ." Harris' voice drifted off as he noticed an extremely attractive nurse approaching. Ever an appreciator of feminine beauty, an almost beatific smile began to form as she stopped and looked up at him.

"Excuse me," she said, "but is one of you Lieutenant Koznicki."

"Koznicki certainly isn't my name." The tall, black officer aimed his most engaging smile at her.

The kid never quits, thought Koznicki, with a shake of his head. "I'm Lieutenant Koznicki."

"There's a call for you, Lieutenant. You can take it at the nurses' station."

Koznicki followed her but quickly returned. "Come on," he said to Harris, "we've found a guy who thinks he saw the killer and may be able to identify him."

"Hot damn," exclaimed Harris, "the good guys are winning!"

The pain was intense, but no more than he deserved, he thought. All the evil that had befallen him since his daughter's suicide he had accepted as just punishment for his sins with her. And much had happened since Edna's death. After her suicide, he had lapsed into a state of depression from which he scarcely ever escaped.

Mary left him. That was only natural. He had not been able to bring himself to tell his wife why their daughter had taken her own life. Nor had he been able to offer his wife any comfort or support in her grief. So filled with self-hate and remorse was he, he could offer no one anything. After nearly a year of experiencing a relationship that deteriorated by the day, Mary had simply packed up and left. Except that his meals were no longer prepared for him or his laundry done for him, he was insensitive to her absence.

He had barely held on to his job at the insurance firm. His sales had dropped to the point where he was merely servicing his old clients. He made no new contacts. His employment was not terminated, partly because the manager felt sorry for him, and partly because he had once been the quintessential salesperson, and the manager hung on to the hope that his erstwhile star might recover a talent for sales that was all too rare.

Now, in his underwear, he sat in the bedroom of his small east-side bungalow, changing the dressing that covered the wound in his right thigh.

After being shot yesterday, he had found an alley behind a row of stores that fronted on Wyoming. With two small slats and a piece of wire from a crate that had been discarded in the alley, he had made a tourniquet and managed to halt the bleeding. A plastic raincoat he'd packed in the pocket of his jacket covered his legs to knee-length. Near shock at that point, he had needed his every reserve of emotional and physical strength to reach a nearby drugstore, get some medical supplies, make it to his car, and drive all the way home. At that, he was fortunate that the scene around the convent area had been chaotic. No one paid any attention to him as he left.

It was an ugly wound, though it had pretty well

stopped bleeding. Fortunately for him, the bullet had struck in the fleshy rear part of his thigh and passed completely through his leg.

Once again, he poured iodine into the openings on either side of his leg. He ground his teeth and groaned at the burning sensation. He would have cried aloud but for the neighbors and the certainty that his suffering was further punishment for his sins. He fixed the gauze strips and began wrapping his thigh tightly with an Ace bandage.

He felt oddly ambivalent about having been wounded. When he had begun planning his revenge, he had been well aware that he might be apprehended, wounded, or even killed somewhere along the line. Of these alternatives, he thought he preferred death. Though whether he lived or died made little difference to him.

Maybe, he thought, I should never have begun playing these games. Maybe I should just have gotten my revenge in some haphazard way.

But they played their games with us, with Edna and me, that priest and that nun. If either of them had taken either of us seriously, they could have helped us or sent us to someone who could have helped. It was our last chance. It was Edna's last chance. Now, that beautiful young life is gone. And there's not a single legal way of bringing those pious frauds to justice.

No, what I've done is right, he concluded, as he completed the medical work on himself. It's right in every way. They're being punished after their own medieval fashion of penance. God knows, I've spent enough time planning my revenge. I've given the police more help than they deserve. And now, finally, they seem to be beginning to understand.

It all comes down to this final week. It's their last chance to stop me. But if I had a last dollar, I'd bet it that they can't stop me.

His thick lips, normally turned down at the corners, tensed into a thin straight line. His narrow, dull brown eyes squeezed shut as he struggled to a standing position. The pain was nearly unbearable. But he must force his badly wounded leg to remain mobile. He would need it for at least one more week.

The two impressively large men strode through the City-County Building's fifth-floor corridor. Lieutenant Koznicki and Sergeant Harris nodded perfunctorily at fellow officers who passed them in the hall. A scattering of media people had positioned themselves at various locations in the corridor. Word had spread that there had been a new development in the case, so questions trailed after the detectives as they passed quickly through toward Koznicki's office.

"Anything new, Lieutenant?" "Got a new lead?" "Got a suspect?"

Koznicki plowed ahead silently, lost in his own thoughts. It was Harris, who, without breaking stride, kept answering, "We'll have a conference for you soon's we can."

Detective Dan Fallon was emerging from Control just as the two passed. He quickly joined them and, speaking through the side of his mouth as quietly as he could and still be heard by them, said, "Good news and bad news."

"Oh?" Koznicki continued his brisk pace.

"The good news is we got a druggist who claims he saw the killer yesterday. Sold him some medicine and dressings. The bad news is the killer isn't wearing Bernhard's slug. We found the bullet embedded in the wall back of the monastery. Ballistics confirms it's from Bernhard's revolver. We also got our man's blood type, A negative, kind of rare.

"The good news is waiting in your office."

With that, the three reached Koznicki's office. In the waiting room, a small, nervous, balding man with a Hitlerian mustache sat fingering the brim of his hat. Standing protectively next to him was Sergeant Ross. It was as if the little man were a member of an endangered species that Ross was determined to preserve.

"Mr. Irving Morris." Ross grasped the shoulder of the man's coat and almost lifted him to his feet while making the introductions.

"This is Lieutenant Koznicki, Detective Sergeant Harris, and Detective Sergeant Fallon."

Koznicki smiled disarmingly and gestured toward his inner office. "Good to meet you, Mr. Morris. Won't you step in here?"

After seating their nervous guest at one side of Koznicki's desk, the men positioned themselves in a circle around the desk.

"I understand you have some information for us, Mr. Morris." Koznicki leaned forward, his massive hands joined, his forearms resting on the desk.

"Well," began Morris, still nervously fingering the brim of his hat, "I think so."

"Mr. Morris," interjected Fallon, "owns a small pharmacy on the corner of Wyoming and McNichols, just a couple of blocks from the monastery."

"I see," said Koznicki, looking intently at the small man sitting opposite him. He waited patiently for Morris to continue.

"Well, it was a little after five yesterday afternoon— maybe closer to five-thirty. Anyway, I was behind the pharmaceutical counter—that's where we keep the drugs and prepare prescriptions—when this guy came in. The first thing I noticed about him, he was sweating a lot."

"That was odd?" asked Harris.

"It wasn't that hot. Besides, this was a real sweat I'm talking about. He looked like he was about to go into shock.

"Well, he started to ask me if I had something for a deep cut. Then he stopped himself and just bought some iodine, some gauze, and a couple of Ace bandages."

"You consider that very strange, Mr. Morris?"

"No . . . well, yes . . . I mean, it was something else I noticed. The guy was wearing a raincoat, even though it wasn't raining. But I could see he'd been bleeding. Where the raincoat stopped, at about his knees, his leg, his trouser leg, was covered with fresh blood. Same for his shoe.

"Then I heard on TV and read in the paper where this guy who killed the nun had been shot. Well, I added it all up. The shooting about five, just down the block, the condition of this guy, the blood, and I figured this could be him . . . this could be the guy."

"Now, Mr. Morris . . ." Koznicki leaned even closer to the fidgeting witness, ". . . this is important, and I want you to think about this question before you answer it. Which leg was bleeding?"

Morris leaned back in the chair and concentrated so intently that he stopped toying with his hat brim. His eyes closed. His forehead furrowed; he grimaced as if trying to call up a vision.

After a few moments, he opened his eyes and looked directly into Koznicki's own. "The right?" he asked, hopefully.

"Are you sure?" returned Koznicki.

Another pause.

"Yes. I'm sure."

Smiles appeared on the faces of the officers.

Koznicki leaned back. "Very good, Mr. Morris. That's the one detail we did not release. Officer Bernhard, the policeman who was wounded, was able to give that information to Sergeant Ross here, in the ambulance. After that, Officer Bernhard lost consciousness. No one but the officers of this special detail knew which of the killer's legs had been hit."

He turned to Ross. "Fred, send Sundell in, please."

Bill Sundell was the police artist requested by and assigned to Koznicki's special task force. Solidly built, five-feet-seven, blond, Sundell's open Nordic face ordinarily wore a bland expression. As he entered Koznicki's office, Sundell looked inquiringly at Morris, who now appeared inordinately pleased with himself. Something like a poor student who hadn't expected to pass but somehow had gotten one hundred percent on the exam.

"We've got a live one for you, Bill." Koznicki got up, moved to one side of his desk, and motioned Sundell to take the large chair he'd vacated.

As Sundell arranged his equipment and artist's supplies, nearly covering the desk's large surface, Koznicki verbally sketched Morris' involvement in the case.

As Koznicki completed his narration, Sundell looked at Morris, smiled broadly, and commented, "I think the police made you up."

Bewilderment replaced Morris' smug look. "Oh, no, I'm for real," he protested.

"I know you're for real, Mr. Morris." Sundell laughed. "I meant that the police were so desperate for a witness like you that if you hadn't happened, they'd have had to invent you."

Morris relaxed slightly, but his prior confidence did not return.

"So . . ." Sundell busily arranged his equipment. ". . . you saw the suspect up close for several minutes, eh, Mr. Morris?"

Morris nodded. "Yes."

"O.K. Now, I'd like you to close your eyes for as long as it takes you to remember the man's face clearly. When you've got a clear picture, I want you to open your eyes and look at something."

Morris obediently closed his eyes in contemplation. When he opened them, Sundell showed him a series of outlines of faces. Every imaginable outline was presented—full, fat, thin, joweled, oval, oblong, rounded. Morris selected the oval outline.

One by one, the other appropriate facial features were culled by Morris. As the features were selected, Sundell drew them on a series of large white sheets of paper, altering and moderating them at Morris' direction.

Many police departments used plastic overlays to build up a picture of a suspect; Koznicki preferred the old-fashioned method. He felt that more nuances could be transmitted through the hands of a sensitive artist.

Finally, Morris was satisfied with a drawing he claimed was an accurate resemblance of the suspect. Sundell leaned back, ripped the approved sheet from his pad and spread it across the desk as the officers gathered around eagerly.

They saw an oval face topped by a heavy head of dark hair. Morris had described the hair as disheveled, but Sundell had taken into account the probable recent violent activity, and smoothed it into what it probably looked like when freshly combed.

The hair was parted on the left, covered the top tip of the ear and would have touched the shirt collar at the nape. The chin was small, firm, not dimpled, with a determined set to it. The ears were quite ordinary, neither especially large nor small. The lips were rather full. Morris had initially insisted on more thinness to the lips, but had finally agreed with Sundell that the suspect's pain might have drawn his lips taut, particularly since Morris had noticed that when the suspect spoke, his lips had seemed fuller. The nose was small with a pug quality to it. Most impressive were the eyes. Under full eyebrows, the dark eyes were intent, sinister, obsessed.

In the final analysis, they all knew it was only a drawing. And, like a candid photo, a drawing could show only one expression, could suggest only in a static fashion features that changed constantly.

Odds that this drawing would enable someone out there to make a positive identification were not good. But it was one of the best clues they had so far, and they, of course, were determined to play those odds, no matter how small.

Koznicki handed the drawing to Fallon. "Dan, have repros made and get them to all the media. I want our man to comprehend some of the dimensions of his mistake yesterday. I want him to hear on the radio that we've got his picture. I want him to see that picture on TV and in the papers. I want him to panic just a little bit more. Even if no one can identify him from that picture, I want him to wonder about it. I want to distract him enough to make one more large blunder. And then, dammit, we've got him!"

As Fallon left with the drawing, Koznicki turned to Morris. "Now, Mr. Morris, I want you to know how grateful we are that you volunteered this information. One final favor. I'd like you to go to a special room we've set up on this floor for press conferences. Sergeant Harris will do most of the talking at first, but then the reporters will want to ask you some questions. It's perfectly all right to tell them everything you know. And then, after that, you may go."

Morris, whose eye level was somewhere between Koznicki's belt and chest, looked up with some excited anticipation. "Will I get my picture in the paper?"

Koznicki smiled down at him. He felt almost like patting the small man's head. "And on TV."

Morris began fingering his hat brim once more. Suddenly, he stopped, and with a look of intense worry, addressed Koznicki again. "This guy . . ." He looked from side to side nervously. ". . . this guy—when he finds out I'm the one who told you all this, will he come after me? I mean, I'm just a little guy owns a drug store. And, in that neighborhood, he could kill me anytime he wants."

Koznicki turned Morris to the door. As Harris took the little man's arm to lead him from the office, Koznicki gave the druggist a reassuring pat on the back, saying, "Mr. Morris, I'm not sure who our man wants next. But I can assure you, it isn't you."

With that, Morris was whisked from the room, wondering whether he wasn't in this thing over his short head.

He would have been sure he was, had he heard the order telephoned by Koznicki immediately after his departure. "Dan, have a couple of the boys keep an eye on Morris—just in case."

Koznicki was definitely a belt-and-suspenders man.

SUNDAY,
APRIL 3

Father Robert Koesler was in the living room of St. Ursula's rectory. He was seated in an overstuffed chair, smoking a cigarette. He had just officiated at the noon Palm Sunday Mass. In half an hour, he would return to the church for baptisms. For the moment, he was left alone with his thoughts.

As usual, he was thinking about the Rosary Murders. The bizarre string of killings had had a pervasive effect on the entire city. But nowhere was the awareness more pronounced than in the Catholic churches. The danger seemed to be in thinking and speaking about them too much. There was a Gospel message in them, of course. But the Gospel message was far more broad than the violence of murder. And the entire Gospel must be preached.

One by-product of the killings was the fact that more people seemed to be going to church since the murders had begun a little over a month before. At first, the increase in numbers going to confession on Saturdays and attending Mass on Sundays seemed attributable to its being Lent. But there were too many to be explained away by this penitential season. Koesler had conducted an informal poll of metropolitan priests. All had experienced an otherwise inexplicable influx of sinners.

Koesler smiled. Strange how people get religion when something upsets the normal flow of life. He remembered the Cuban crisis. On a Thursday evening, President Jack Kennedy had announced a blockade of Cuba. The ensuing Saturday night confessions were more numerous than those of Christmas and Easter combined. Everyone who could remotely be considered Catholic came to Mass that Sunday. Then, as Dean Rusk put it, "We're eyeball to eyeball, and I think the other fellow just blinked."

And as the Soviet vessels turned away from Cuba and returned to Russia, normal religious indifference returned to America.

Attendance at Masses this morning had been slightly more than even standing-room-only. At the 10 A.M. and noon Masses, people were even standing on the outside steps of the church. Fortunately, the weather was decent. Koesler guessed the crowd was due to a combination of uneasiness over the killings, and the fact that it was Palm Sunday.

And that was another puzzle. Koesler's stream of consciousness led him on. It was easy to understand why Christmas and Easter drew larger than ordinary crowds of worshippers. Those two days were well promoted by commercial interests as well as by the ordinarily less successful efforts of religions. But Palm Sunday, and—now that he thought of it—Ash Wednesday, always drew uncommonly large numbers. He wondered if the answer could possibly be that those were the only two feasts when the Church gave something tangible. Ash Wednesday, blessed ashes to wear on one's forehead; Palm Sunday, a blessed frond to hang in one's house. Perhaps the Church should begin giving blessed dishes on ordinary Sundays.

At this point, as his rationality was beginning to unravel, the phone rang. Since he was the only one in, Koesler answered it.

"St. Ursula's," he identified.

There was a moment's hesitation. "Is this Father Robert Koesler?"

"Yes, it is."

"This is Lieutenant Walter Koznicki, Father. I didn't expect you to answer the phone."

"Nobody else here. What can I do for you, Lieutenant? I've got to go baptize some babies in a few minutes." He added the latter, aware how insistent the lieutenant could be. When the lieutenant wanted a body in front of him, he got it.

"This won't take but a moment, Father. I have an appointment with your archbishop tomorrow morning at nine. I was wondering if you would mind accompanying me."

"Tomorrow at nine? Yes, I believe I can make it. But why do you want me there?"

"Several reasons. If nothing else, what we speak of may require some communication with the priests and religious of the archdiocese. And communication is at least your avocation."

"I'm not trying to get out of this, Lieutenant—but we do have a communications office."

"Our experience with that office has not been—uh—productive."

"I understand. If you'd called them they'd probably tell you to call us."

"Indeed."

"But, tell me, Lieutenant. If I had hesitated, would you have told me you'd send a car for me?" He could hear Koznicki's answering chuckle.

"You are perceptive, Father. But I'm sure you would not refuse your archbishop's invitation."

"You mean he knows I'm coming?"

"The appointment was made for both of us."

"I'll see you tomorrow, Lieutenant." He hung up, shaking his head. It was reassuring to know the police department was efficient.

Koesler checked his watch and noted he had only a few minutes till baptism time. He picked up the certificates that had been completed the day before by the parish secretary. There were only two babies to be baptized. Wonder of wonders.

Koesler could remember when, even into the 'sixties, there were regularly as many as twenty babies for Sunday baptisms. Then came Vatican II, and the laity began solving their own personal problems. Gone were questions about birth control. And gone was the hitherto common sight of pregnant women in church.

As he made his way over to the church, he considered the present position of the Church's hierarchy. He said aloud to no one, "There go my people. I must hurry and catch up with them, for I am their leader."

"What I'd like to know," Joe Cox called in from the kitchen, "is why in hell we had to go to church this morning?"

Pat Lennon was stretched out in the reclining chair in the apartment's living room. She had just begun reading the thick Sunday issue of the *Free Press*. "Because everybody goes to church on Palm Sunday."

"Not if you're a lax Episcopalian. We go only at Christmas and Easter. How was I to know that by living with a lax Catholic, I'd get another day of church thrown in?"

Cox was rinsing and shredding raw spinach leaves.

Sundays, by mutual agreement, were his turn to make brunch. Invariably, it was a multi-ingredient salad. Between them, the day was known as super salad Sunday.

"And, while we're at it, what about your sales pitch that we'd hear Koesler preach? He said the Mass, but he didn't preach."

"How am I supposed to remember they don't preach on Palm Sunday because they read a long Gospel? God! I go to church only three or four times year. How's a person supposed to keep track that way?"

"Can't you remember back to when you were a good Catholic?" Cox began rinsing and shredding romaine.

"I'm trying to forget the good old days. They're too painful. And quit picking on me; if you went to church more often, you'd have known the connection between rosaries and penance a long time ago."

Cox decided to add iceberg lettuce to today's super salad. "Not in the Episcopalian church, I wouldn't have. We got rid of things like rosaries ages ago. Besides," he grinned, "I like the way I learned about it from you better."

Lennon reddened slightly. The memory of being discovered in that vacant office still embarrassed her. "Let's not get into that again, love. The next time you feel amorous at work, I don't care what you do, as long as it's not with me."

"I can't help it," Cox protested, "sometimes I just feel so horny I could deflower a chicken."

"I don't care. If you tried that twice at work with a chicken, the second time even she would tell you to cluck off."

There was a long silence that told her he was laughing. "How long must I play straight man for you?"

"Others may think you're straight, but we who know you well know you're kinky."

"Stop, already, or I won't let you write sidebars to my feature story." Cox began chopping carrots. "What, by the way, was so important about my hearing Koesler preach? Or was that just one of your maidenly ploys to get me to church?"

"No. He's good, they tell me. Besides, I thought you'd like to hear a sermon from the guy who first plugged you into the Rosary Murders."

"I guess I do owe him. That was a bigger break than Mrs. Cox ever thought her baby boy would get."

"This is a great story you've got in today on the Rosary Murders."

"Where'd they put it?"

"Page one, where else?"

"Where are you?"

"The jump page."

"Where'd they put that?"

"Page eleven."

"They could've put it on two."

"That's another definition of fat chance. Too many ads on page two. And this is a long story. You must think you're getting paid by the word."

Cox smiled. "Then they didn't cut it."

"If they did, it should've been a book."

Lennon turned from the paper and gazed out the broad expanse of window that covered the entire length of the apartment's living room. It was a breathtaking sight on this clear, sunny, springish day. To the right was a jutting corner of the new Renaissance Center. The rest of the view was an uncluttered panorama of Windsor and Detroit's east side. On a clear day, she thought, you could see Mount Clemens. But who wants to?

"What are the cops going to do now?" she asked.

Cox was slicing a cucumber. "Whatever they do, they're not going to panic. Not as long as Koznicki's in charge."

Lennon smiled as she continued to contemplate, from her aerie, Belle Isle, that gem of a recreation island in the middle of the Detroit River. "You've really become Koznicki's fair-haired boy, haven't you?"

Cox's face had a serious look as he quartered a piece of green pepper. "No, not really. I figured him for a straight shooter. I've honored his embargoes. I've told him what I know. Maybe I've told him more than I would've another cop. But it's worked both ways. He's made sure I got a few breaks, too. But he hasn't let me in on any of his bottom-line secrets. I didn't expect him to."

"Secrets?"

"I don't even know how many there are in this case. But I know there are some things about this killer's M.O. that the cops use to verify each successive murder—so they won't get thrown off the track if someone else tries to pass himself off as the Rosary Killer. That's how they were able to determine right off that Father Palmer, that priest who died of a heart attack, wasn't one of his victims. Yeah, Koznicki's task force has kept its secrets well."

"But what are they going to do?"

"My guess is they'll continue with the investigation the way they have from the beginning. They might just get lucky and crack it that way. But, come next Friday, I'll bet they cover the priests and nuns like a blanket. According to my theory—"

"*Our* theory. I gave you the clue."

"And may you continue to give me clues in the very same fashion. Anyway, according to *our* theory, this Friday should be the murderer's final day to kill."

"Think it'll go off?"

"I don't know. Probably it'll all come down to luck. This latest nun he killed on Friday—that was unadulterated luck from every angle. It was luck that brought the visitor to see the nun at just the right moment. That luck brought the cop into the convent. And sheer luck that the killer was able to get away."

"How 'bout that composite picture they made from the druggist's description?"

"Look like anybody you know?"

She picked up the paper again, turned back to the front page, and looked intently at the reproduction of the drawing. "No," she admitted.

"They never do." His words seemed mumbled.

"Hey," she called, "are you getting choked up over this?"

"No. I'm slicing an onion."

She rose from the chair, walked quietly to the kitchen door, and peered around the corner. Cox was no more than a foot from her. "How's the salad coming?" she asked.

"I'd say . . . ten minutes and counting."

"Can you put it on hold? I was just thinking how rotten it was that I'm horizontal and you're vertical!"

He frowned at her. as he wiped his hands. "Very well . . ." He laughed, unable to continue the charade. ". . . if you insist."

He scooped her up and carried her down the hall toward the bedroom. The super salad was put on hold. For a while, it was completely forgotten.

MONDAY,
APRIL 4

It was 8:30 A.M. as Father Robert Koesler backed his car out of the garage adjoining St. Ursula's rectory. It would take approximately twenty minutes to drive downtown. He was sure he could find a vacancy in one of the many parking lots and reach the chancery building within another ten minutes. Still, he knew he was cutting it close. He turned from Georgia onto Gratiot and was able to maneuver quickly into the fast lane of traffic. As usual, when driving these familiar streets, his mind was wandering.

Meetings between him and the archbishop were extremely rare. Koesler remembered the time he had been called downtown about a dozen years ago. It was unusual for the archbishop to summon one of his many priests for a personal interview. Usually, it meant either being called on the carpet for some misdeed or a special sort of assignment.

An ordinary assignment from one parish to another, back in those days, was accomplished through a simple form letter, which routinely began, "For the care of souls,

I have it in mind to assign you to . . ." There followed the identification of where the priest would be spending his next five years—approximately.

Koesler, at that time, was not aware of having done anything bad enough to be summoned to the chancery. It must, he had thought, be a special assignment. Even so, he had been stunned when the archbishop's opening words were, "Father Koesler, I have it in mind to give you a special assignment. You will be the editor of the *Detroit Catholic*."

So astonished had he been by this announcement that Koesler, even now, could not remember what the archbishop had gone on to tell him about the archdiocesan newspaper. He recalled only the archbishop's concluding words. "If you have no serious objection, we will consider this assignment to be final."

Koesler, at the time, could think of no serious objection other than that he didn't want the assignment. And that, he concluded without verbalizing it, would not have been considered by the archbishop a serious objection.

Thus, with no journalistic experience whatever, Father Robert Koesler had assumed what the *Free Press*, in a front-page article on the appointment, had described as an "influential" position. Koesler came to learn the position was short on influence but long on controversy.

His reverie was interrupted as he neared downtown and had to concentrate on the intricate series of one-way streets that added to the difficulty of downtown driving. He found a parking spot a block from the chancery. As he entered the building, he was overwhelmed by the unmistakable figure of Lieutenant Walter Koznicki pacing the ground-floor corridor.

"Ah, Father Koesler . . . how good of you to come," Koznicki greeted him warmly.

"Not at all." Koesler smiled as he shook Koznicki's hand. "I consider this a command performance, literally. I don't know why I feel like apologizing . . ." He glanced at his watch. ". . . we've got two minutes to spare. But, sorry I'm on time."

"Shall we?" Koznicki gestured toward the elevator at the end of the corridor.

They stepped into the elevator. It was operated by a fragile elderly gentleman, probably a retiree, thought Koesler, and, from what little the diocese paid him, well able to stay within the maximum allowed by his social security.

The man was reading last week's *Detroit Catholic*. He looked up as the two entered the elevator. He knew neither. "Floor?" he asked. "Two," answered Koesler.

He looked at them again. "Names?"

"Father Robert Koesler and Lieutenant Walter Koznicki." Koesler unsnapped the top of his black raincoat, revealing the Roman collar he thought might reassure the operator.

As the elevator began an extremely slow ascent, Koznicki noticed a small index card taped to the elevator's front wall, directly in front of the operator. His name and that of his priest companion were the third and fourth on the list typed thereon. The archbishop's appointments for the day, he thought. If one's name isn't on the list, one doesn't get off on the second floor. Good security, he concluded.

A conclusion that was reinforced when they emerged from the elevator and entered the deeply carpeted reception area. There was but one door in view, obviously leading to a staircase. The presence of a panic bar indicated that the door was locked from the other side.

The two men hung their coats and hats inside a sliding cylinder that, when closed, preserved the decor of dark brown paneling.

The reception area was long, narrow, and tastefully decorated. One wall displayed two coats of arms—one the archbishop's, the other the pope's. A secretary was seated at her desk in the far right corner of the reception area. She smiled and nodded when Koesler gave her his and Koznicki's names.

At precisely nine, a door out of view of the reception area opened. A few muffled words could be heard. A rotund, balding priest appeared and hurried toward the closet area, smiling nervously at no one in particular. Koesler watched with amusement. If was Father Ron Peterson. Putting two and two together, Koesler guessed that Peterson had just been assigned to a new pastorate. Judging from his unaccustomed ebullient state, Peterson probably had been moved from his down-at-the-heels Ferndale parish to one of the more affluent suburbs.

"Good morning, Father," said Koznicki, a touch of old-world reverence in his voice.

"Oh . . . uh . . . yes, yes, of course . . ." Peterson was too happy to focus on even this giant of a man.

"Hi, Ron," said Koesler, smiling. "Got yourself a plum, eh?"

"Oh . . . uh . . . yes . . . Bob, isn't it? But . . . but . . ." Peterson's incoherence was at least partially due to the fact that the archbishop, as was usual in pastoral assignments, had impressed him with the necessity of keeping the move a secret until the official announcement. And Koesler appeared to know already.

". . . but how did you know?"

"The *Detroit Catholic* sees all, knows all, tells all."

Peterson, more flustered by the moment, fumbled his raincoat several times before stumbling into the elevator that had stopped half an inch above floor level.

"An improved assignment?" asked Koznicki, eyeing Koesler with renewed interest. "But how did you know?"

"Lucky guess. Peterson follows the party line exclusively. It would be extremely unlikely he'd ever be called on the carpet. He's usually a dour man. Fits well into Ferndale, in fact. The only thing the archbishop could do to make him that happy would be to send him off to some place like Rochester where the rich people live. But, as you see, the bluff worked. Now, he's afraid if the news gets out before the archbishop releases it, the archbishop will take the parish away from him. The anxiety will be good for Peterson . . . keep him balanced."

A tremor of amusement played at Koznicki's lips. "Did you ever consider police work?"

"Frequently. But it's too late. Now, I just read whodunits."

On that note, a door opened, and Archbishop Mark Boyle came around the corner of the reception room and walked briskly toward the two men. He was slightly taller than Koesler, yet not nearly as tall or large as Koznicki. A shade portly, he carried his weight well, the combined result of good food and a penchant for walking at least a mile every day. His face was heavily lined, but handsome; his eyes intensely blue. Though his thinning hair was gray, his bushy eyebrows were still sooty black, a combination typical of the aging Celt. The only visible trappings of office that distinguished his black-suited appearance were a patch of vivid red beneath the front of his Roman collar, and a single strand of the silver chain that held his pectoral cross.

He smiled perfunctorily at the priest and greeted him simply. "Father Koesler."

"Archbishop."

"Lieutenant Koznicki . . . it's good to meet you at long last."

"Excellency." Koznicki fell to his right knee, grasped Boyle's extended hand, and kissed the archbishop's ring.

The gesture startled both Koesler and the archbishop. No one kissed a bishop's ring any more. At least not the Archbishop of Detroit's ring. Boyle had conducted a quiet campaign against the medieval practice since shortly after his arrival in Detroit. In the beginning, as people would start to genuflect, the archbishop would raise his hand slightly, indicating that a simple handshake was a sufficient gesture. That led to many aborted genuflections that resembled half-curtsies. Gradually, nearly everyone had gotten the word that ring-kissing was not de rigueur in Detroit. Obviously, Lieutenant Koznicki was not among those who had gotten that word. And there was no way Boyle could prevent Koznicki's enormous bulk from completing his reverential act.

"Won't you come in?" Boyle led the small procession around the corner of the reception area and into his office.

Koznicki swept the room with a glance. The wall shelves were filled with books, mostly reference works. To the left was a large, neatly kept desk with a large padded chair behind it, and two straight-back chairs in front. Just inside the office door were four comfortable-looking swivel chairs, placed around a large circular coffee table. Three large windows revealed a once elegant but now increasingly tacky Washington Boulevard.

Koznicki surmised the desk area was Boyle's work space and for clergymen who were in some sort of trouble with the institution, while the coffee table was for less formal visiting. He was correct, as Koesler could testify, having occupied each of the areas at different times.

At Boyle's direction, they seated themselves at the coffee table. Koznicki sat at the edge of his chair. It was as if a condor had perched on the small swing of a birdcage.

"It was kind of you to give us this time, Your Excellency," Koznicki opened.

"Not at all." Boyle's rectangular face was solemn; his eyes pierced Koznicki's. "I assume you wish to speak about the series of murders of our priests and nuns."

"Precisely," said Koznicki. "I'm sure you know that, according to our best information, the killer will strike again and, we believe, for the final time this coming Friday."

"Yes, I know."

"My purpose in coming here, Excellency, is to discover to what extent the archdiocese is willing and able to cooperate with our local law enforcement agencies to prevent any further fatalities."

"Of course, Lieutenant, we will do everything in our power to cooperate with you."

"We have good reason to expect the next murder—or murders—to be committed within the corporate limits of the city of Detroit, as have the previous eight. One of the things that has worked in the killer's favor and against our being able to stop him is the incredible vulnerability of priests and nuns. There is no other group as available to the public. This vulnerability will be especially intensified, I fear, for priests on Good Friday." Boyle nodded his understanding. "So, Excellency, I must begin by asking how willing you are to curtail public services within the city this Friday?"

"Cancel Good Friday?" Koesler made no attempt to disguise his amazement.

Boyle glanced at Koesler, a trace of slight amusement

passing over his face. Still somewhat amused, the archbishop returned his attention to Koznicki.

"Oh, no, my dear Lieutenant. There can be no question but that we will conduct the full services and sacraments of Holy Week, including Good Friday, just as we do each year. I could not ask any less of the priests, nor would they give any less.

"While we are addressing this point, Lieutenant, it might be helpful if I pointed out—and this is not in any way meant to disparage any other priests—that the priests who minister within the city are among the most dedicated of all. Their voluntary commitment to the city —and this is, indeed, what it is, a commitment—is a sign of their dedication. I am certain that to suggest that any of them respond with abject fear to this threat is not realistic."

"I was sure that would be your reaction, Excellency. However, it was an alternative that had to be explored."

"Is there any other way we can cooperate with you, Lieutenant?"

"There is one other way. According to the killer's method of operation, he must be close to his victim when he strikes. As you know, a rosary has been left at the scene of each murder. The rosaries are left in such a way that the killer must be literally at his victim's side." Koesler reflected that this fact was another in the long line of secrets he had to keep. "We have no reason to believe this most determined murderer will change his method of operation even now, when, I believe, we are so close to apprehending him. And his determination to be close to his victims when he strikes can be of advantage to us in helping us protect the intended victim.

"We attempted to protect the priests and nuns of this city last Friday. That we failed is largely due to a lack of total cooperation on the part of the clergy and religious. Not just in the cases of the two who were killed —almost all our officers reported a rather cavalier attitude from those they were assigned to protect.

"Excellency, bravery is one thing, foolishness is another. Of all the cases of premeditated murder in my experience, this killer stands alone in his preparation and planning. His next victim could be any nun or priest in this city, including, with all due respect, yourself, Excellency. However, I am certain that if every priest and every nun follows our orders and observes the precautions suggested by the police, not only will there possibly be no next victim, but we stand a very good chance of apprehending the killer.

"We will provide protection to all the clergy and religious in the archdiocese but especially in the city of Detroit. They must cooperate with us—blindly, if I may be so blunt."

Koznicki sat back in his chair. Koesler was motionless. The archbishop toyed with his ring. For several moments there was silence. Finally, Boyle spoke:

"There is something you must understand, Lieutenant; something I perceive you have already observed. Priests and nuns today, particularly those who minister in the core city, are not prone to blind obedience, as they once were."

Koesler reflected on the number of times Boyle had patiently explained that he wished the *Detroit Catholic* to be free of controversy. In a pre-Vatican II era, that wish would have had the force of law. However, considerable controversy was a matter of simple reality. Koesler felt that any newspaper, if it were an honest media effort, should reflect reality. It was, Koesler believed, Boyle's greatest virtue that the prelate was able to tolerate opposition, that he did not demand a blind obedience whose time had passed. The priest hoped, for everyone's sake, that Koznicki would understand and believe what the archbishop was saying. For it was true.

"Nevertheless, Excellency," Koznicki remonstrated, "I think it is vital, literally, for you, in your capacity as Archbishop of Detroit, to issue as strongly worded a statement as possible, urging, if not commanding, that all the clergy and religious of the archdiocese cooperate *fully* with the police assigned to protect them."

"Excuse me, Lieutenant," Koesler interjected, "but may I pose a hypothetical situation?" Ringing in his ears, as it had so many times in the past few days, was the shrieked asseveration of the tormented man who had occupied the other side of the confessional—the man protected by the seal of that confessional—the seal that made a mute of Koesler: *"I'm NOT DONE YET!"*

Koznicki and the archbishop were looking at Koesler attentively. The priest spoke. "Even if our cooperation were complete, do you think you'd be able to stop hi—to stop the killer?" He forced himself to think of the man impersonally, objectively, as he would any other faceless penitent.

"Well, Father, it is possible that news of this blanket protection *might* deter him from acting. He would have to realize that his chance of success would be minimal with this massive police presence. But, frankly, I believe he would try to act anyway."

". . . NOT DONE YET!"

"His plans have been carefully, though not rigidly made. He has demonstrated that there are very few elements of his method of operation that he is not willing to change.

"Finally, killers such as this are almost always extremely determined people."

". . . YET!"

"And I have never experienced any murderer more determined than this one. No matter what we do, I anticipate he will try to strike. If we are well prepared, and *if we have total cooperation,* I believe we will stop him and perhaps even apprehend him."

Koznicki was aware he was repeating himself; yet he felt he had to impress the archbishop with the rightness of his cause.

He had.

"Very well, Lieutenant," said Boyle. "The cooperation you need will begin with me. What would you suggest?"

"A press release and a press conference. We want maximum coverage. Not only do we want to inform the clergy and religious, I want to make sure the killer hears about this."

"I'll compose a statement now," said Boyle, as he turned to the priest. "Father Koesler, would you be able to contact the proper news people? You can notify my appointments secretary as to the time of the conference."

"Certainly, Archbishop."

Boyle stood, as did his visitors.

Koznicki took the archbishop's extended hand, genuflected, and kissed the ring. There was no point in trying to stop him.

"Thank you, Excellency, for your time and cooperation," said Koznicki, "my people will take it from here."

As Koznicki and Koesler left the elevator, the priest said, "You know, Lieutenant, Lefty Gomez once attributed his pitching success to good morning prayers and a fast outfield."

"Oh?" noted Koznicki, not breaking stride.

"I was just thinking. What we've got going for us is good police work and a bunch of potential victims who pray a lot."

"I doubt we could succeed without both."

"Protect me, Lieutenant."

"Pray for me, Father."

They parted at the Washington Boulevard entrance.

Mayor Maynard Cobb sat behind his oversized executive desk, his mouth twitching in conflicting emotions of amusement and annoyance. "Why is it, Frank, that every time I ask to see Lieutenant Koznicki, I get you?"

Police Commissioner Frank Tany stood in front of the mayor's desk. He had not attempted to be seated, nor had he been invited to sit.

"It works out better this way, Mr. Mayor. This is the way we've been handling relations between the executive branch and the department these three years of your term." Tany shifted his pear-shaped bulk to the right. "It would blast the chain of command all to hell if we were to get individual officers in here to see you. Besides, Lieutenant Koznicki is doing everything possible to conclude this case. It wouldn't do any good. In fact, it would be disastrous to try to replace him."

Cobb smiled disarmingly. "Frank, don't jump to conclusions. I got no notion to bump Koznicki. What do we have left? Less than a week? *If what I read in the papers is correct.*" He emphasized his last few words, clearly intimating that there had, at least in his view, been less than an open line of communication between the police and the mayor's office. Neither the intimation nor the attempted intimidation escaped Tany's attention.

"Mr. Mayor, the department is aware that the welfare of the entire city is your responsibility. I try to keep you informed of major developments in this case. But we know you can't be as obsessed with this one case as we are."

"One case! One case!" Maynard Cobb's fist struck the desk top. "My entire political career may hinge on this 'one case'! The election campaign is getting closer by the week. I just might be back on the line at Ford's because some goddam nut is out there killing priests and nuns. This is the third week we've been on the front page of every paper from New York to L.A., and we've already been on the covers of *Time* and *Newsweek*. This is considerably more than 'one case'! This is my career we're talkin' about."

Tany hesitated, trying to choose his words carefully. "What can I tell you, Mr. Mayor, that we haven't already gone over? Not every murder is solved. Not every series of murders is solved. Short of some very lucky breaks, we've got to follow routine procedures."

"Lucky breaks!" Cobb stood up behind his desk. Rare for him. "What do you call the info that the man hits on Fridays? Or the guy who gave you the eyewitness description of the killer? To me, those seem like pretty damn lucky breaks!"

Tany had never encountered the mayor in such a distraught state. But then, Tany had never been present at one of the many times when Cobb had fought with his back to the wall against overwhelming odds.

"Those may prove to be lucky breaks." Tany again shifted weight. "We may not know except in hindsight— if we ever get hindsight. This Friday business is no more than a theory. It looks good now. But how will it look if he strikes tomorrow, or if he never strikes again?

"And as far as the eyewitness, there is a strong probability the man he saw is the killer. Evidence is actually no more than circumstantial. As to the composite drawing the police artist made, composite drawings are notoriously poor at eliciting a positive identification."

Cobb experienced a feeling of helplessness welling within him. His shoulders sagged almost imperceptibly. "So, where does that leave us?" he asked more quietly, as he slumped back into his chair.

"As I started to explain earlier, Mr. Mayor, we'd be up shit's creek without a paddle if Lieutenant Koznicki had staked everything on those showy breaks that the news media love so much. But he hasn't. Not that he's overlooked them. But he's continued and even increased the routine investigation. Like just about everything else in life, Mr. Mayor, that's the way things get done. Not by waiting for and depending on a lucky break."

Cobb's politically sensitive mind began to uncover another silver lining.

"Actually," Tany continued, "the task force is doing rather well with its routine investigation. For instance, they're certain that old nun who was stabbed knew the killer and partially identified him by scrawling the letters 'R-O-B' before she died. By the hour, they're narrowing the list of people she knew who could qualify in any way with those letters.

"And this is only one of many routine investigations that are continuing. Whatever the outcome of this investigation, Mr. Mayor, you can be sure of this. No police department in the country could be doing more."

By the time Tany had finished, Cobb had determined his course of action during the campaign for reelection. If the killer was apprehended, and at this point, Cobb virtually discounted this possibility, he would claim it was the result of superior police work in close cooperation with his administration, which, in turn, had worked hand-in-glove with the police.

In the more likely outcome that the killer would not be caught; that, indeed, he would successfully kill again, this, too, would be in spite of superior police work. What was the phrase Tany had used? Cobb had liked it. Yes: No police department in the country could have done more. Throw it out there as a gauntlet. He was sure no other department would challenge the statement, partly from esprit de corps and partly because it probably would be true.

By the time he returned his gaze to Tany, Cobb had regained his composure. He smoothed his trim mustache, removed a cigar from the box on his desk, and began elaborate preparations to light it.

"O.K., Frank," he said, as he snapped off the tapered end of the cigar, "I just wanted to be sure we were doing everything we could." Cobb pivoted his swivel chair to the wall, dismissing Tany. "And, Frank, tell that lieutenant—Koznicki—that I wish him luck—sincerely."

"Thank you, Mr. Mayor."

Tany exited, thinking of that "routine investigation" and the number of men and women of the department who had spent countless hours of overtime on this case, who had voluntarily made this case part of their lives.

Whatever would happen, he was enormously proud of them.

WEDNESDAY,
APRIL 6

Officers David Brainard and Thomas Schommer occupied adjacent desks in the special task force's Control room. Members of the Tactical Services Department, Detroit's version of SWAT, neither of them was happy with his assignment to the task force. A desk job, particularly the tedium of an investigation, was not what they had bargained for when they had joined the police department fresh from Vietnam.

Members of the TSD were taught a jargon that helped them explain their singular work to others. They were an "interventionary" department, used in cases of particular "danger or stress." They had the "capability" of entering a building with "blocked accesses," the "capability" of using "special weapons," and were "capable of chemical munitions delivery."

In reality, the TSD more nearly resembled a paramilitary force with the capability of using almost every weapon imaginable and an inclination to do so. Even the name, Tactical Services Department, was a euphemism. It hardly suggested the mayhem that was inherent in such a force.

Generally, the self-image of TSD members was far from that of a patrolman directing traffic. It was even far from that of an officer in a mobile unit, for whom a call to resolve a "family dispute" could easily be fraught with danger.

TSD officers were geared for danger and violence almost exclusively. There were occasional stretches of time when they were rarely called upon. But when they were called, they could be quite positive there would be plenty of action.

So, when Brainard and Schommer had been tapped for duty on the task force, they first had been surprised, then disappointed. Since joining this special unit, they had been favorably impressed with the thoroughness and professionalism of the force. Also on the positive side was their enduring self-discipline. It ensured that their work was thorough and painstaking, even if unenthusiastic.

However, they sorely missed the excitement and constant threat of imminent danger that they were accustomed to in their own department—one of the few divisions that had successfully resisted the inclusion of women.

One of the hardest facts for Brainard and Schommer to swallow was that a woman was in charge of this Control Room.

There was no denying that Lieutenant Marjorie Washington was qualified in leadership. She had been in systems management at General Motors before joining the police department. And, like all women filling jobs formerly the exclusive domain of men, she was several times better than any male counterpart, simply because she had to be. Asking machos like Brainard and Schommer to accept direction from a female was, indeed, asking much. Only their devotion to discipline and the fact that this tour of duty was temporary had softened the blow.

This morning's work had begun with a briefing by Lieutenant Washington. The petite, middle-aged black woman with serious gray eyes and firm, no-nonsense mouth, was at this moment continuing her briefing. The subject was the method of operation to be used the coming Friday in providing protection to all Detroit-area priests and nuns. Almost everyone on this special task force would be a part of this duty, and many of them would brief the additional police personnel who would be added to the task force for that one day.

Lieutenant Washington had spoken at length about the department's double failure at providing protection the previous Friday. The one failure she attributed to the officer's decision not to follow what he knew was sound police procedure. He knew it was potentially dangerous to allow his subject to enter private homes alone and without reconnaissance. But, because the subject had insisted, the officer had permitted him to go unprotected into a private home; thus the ensuing homicide.

The other failure was the result, she stressed, not so much of poor but of incomplete procedure. That officer had done an excellent job of setting up surveillance and establishing a sound perimeter of protection. However, he had failed to communicate his orders *personally* to all in the house, because the subjects were cloistered women. That failure cost one of those women her life.

"Learning from these cases," Lieutenant Washington said, "we will stress two things: first, insist on sound police procedures. No matter what objection the subject may raise, sound procedure is to be carried out at all times.

"Second, be thorough. Note every item on the check list you'll be given. Make certain that each and every one of your subjects—and this is even more important if you have been assigned more than one subject—is aware of every detail of how you will work together.

"The tired old motto, better safe than sorry, is a weak way of paraphrasing what I've said.

"There are two further items I want to call to your attention and emphasize. You all know that in each previous murder, the killer has wrapped a small black rosary around the victim's left wrist. It is heavily probable that he will not change his M.O., even now.

"Your subjects, therefore, will be in greatest danger when others can have close access to them. For instance, if your subject is a priest, rehearse with him the procedure that has him leaning forward when he opens the confessional slide door, so that he is out of a line of fire. He is not to sit upright until he is certain the person is an authentic penitent making a legitimate confession.

"Finally, the killer's M.O. clearly indicates that he has carefully cased the routines and habits of his victims and has planned his attacks to take full advantage of these routines. You must be equally prepared. Go over every detail of your subject's schedule for Friday. Learn his or her routine activities. Familiarize yourself with Good Friday services he or she will either conduct or attend. Above all, win your subject's confidence so that he or she will promptly inform you if any of them notices anything out of the ordinary.

"Now, are there any questions? Karnego?"

A tall, well-groomed, uniformed policewoman stood. "About those cloistered places. I think there are some for men as well as women. How are they going to be covered?"

"O.K. By prior agreement, each and every such establishment within the city of Detroit will permit the presence of at least one officer, depending on the number of subjects in the establishment, for the entire day. A man for the males, and a woman for the females, of course."

A ripple of laughter passed through the room. Brainard leaned close to Schommer and said, "I ain't never seen a nun who turned me on."

"You haven't looked lately, Dave," Schommer replied.

Washington waited until the laughter and comments subsided. Then she asked, "Any more questions? Papkin?"

A rather portly, middle-aged uniformed policeman stood. "The nuns I remember from school . . . they . . .

they . . ." He searched for a diplomatic term. ". . . they had it their way." The audience broke up. Even the normally staid Lieutenant Washington grinned and shook her head knowingly. "I mean," Papkin continued as the noise subsided, "I can't remember an argument I ever won with a one of them. Matter of fact, now that I think of it, I don't remember ever having enough nerve to argue. I mean, how do you turn that around for one day?"

There was still a small measure of snickering.

"O.K.," said Washington. "Seriously, that's liable to be one of your major problems. And it's not just the nuns who may resist your protection. As we learned Friday, the priests can be stubborn as well. The best I can tell you is to think how you'd feel if your subject gets his or her own way and becomes the next victim. You think about that long enough, and you'll keep a tight rein no matter what it takes.

"Any more questions?"

No hand was raised. "O.K., you've got your assignments. Let's get crackin'!"

There was modified chaos in the room as some officers resumed their work routine and others began preparing to leave.

Brainard and Schommer separated stacks of papers. Some they put in their desks. Others they stuffed into briefcases.

"Where you going?" asked Brainard.

"A briefing at the twelfth precinct. You?"

"Brief the thirteenth. It ain't much, but at least it gets us outta this room."

"Yeah, I was beginning to be a launching pad for spider webs. God, it'll be good to get back to the action when this is over."

"Won't be long now. Hang in there, pardner."

Brainard folded his computer readout sheet of possible suspects. The next name he would have checked out, had he had time for one more call, was that of Robert Jamison.

It had been a long, tiring day for Father Robert Koesler. Besides putting the April seventh issue of the *Detroit*

Catholic to bed, he'd gotten a call just before noon from Patrolman Lou Jackson. The officer said he'd been assigned to be with Koesler throughout Good Friday and asked for an appointment that afternoon.

Koesler explained how very busy he was. The officer was insistent. Koesler gave up and made an appointment with him for two.

They met in the lobby of the paper. Koesler's first impression was that Jackson could play linebacker for the Detroit Lions. From within that massive black body, a row of gleaming white teeth smiled at the priest. Well, thought Koesler, if you have to be protected, why not by the Colossus of Rhodes?

Yet, though no one else could know it, Koesler believed himself to be the least likely potential victim in the archdiocese. If he'd wanted to kill me, he thought, he surely would've done it in the confessional. I'm the only one who's safe.

It was almost like being vaccinated.

Koesler's afternoon alternated between trips to the editorial room to read page proofs and returns to his office, where sat officer Jackson, pen poised over notebook. The afternoon was otherwise filled with countless, "Now, where was I—" questions, as the policeman gradually extracted in minute detail everything Koesler thought he would be doing or would happen to him from midnight to midnight of Good Friday.

During the protracted interview, Koesler reflected that if every Detroit priest was going to have a cop babysitter, and he assumed they were, Good Friday would at least be a day of unprecedented good behavior on the part of Detroit's clergy.

Then, there was Joe Farmer, the unsilent guest at every Wednesday evening dinner. Pomps with his molasses-slow method of eating, and Joe with his tired, if slightly risqué, jokes.

Dinner had been followed by Lenten services featuring Joe's borrowed-from-St.-Alphonsus sermon, "Jesus Died for Your Sins." It was heavy in blood and gore, with graphic detail. Koesler wondered whether, in either delivering or absorbing a sermon like that, it helped to be either a sadist or a machochist.

Pompilio, Farmer and Koesler were now seated in the rectory living room. Farmer, as was his wont, had, upon entering the room, immediately flipped on the TV. At the moment, he was telling a series of rather stale jokes. The combination of TV noise and Farmer's habit of breaking himself up at his own punch lines forced Pompilio into a series of antiphonal questions.

Farmer: "Did you hear the one about the lady who kept coming to church in low-cut dresses. Plenty of decolletage!" He gestured to indicate just how plenty. "Most of the guys were paying more attention to her than to the sermon. So, one Sunday, the pastor is waiting for her outside church. When she comes up, sure enough, lots of chest." Another gesture to indicate just how lots. "So the pastor says, 'Sorry, but you can't come in here like that.' She says, 'What do you mean I can't come in here? I've got a divine right.' He says, 'You've got . . .'" Semi-strangled laughter from Farmer. "'. . . you've got . . .'" Laughter coming almost in gasps. "'. . . you've got a great left, too, but you still can't come in here!'"

Pompilio: "Got a great what, Joe? Got a great *what?*"

Bored and bone-tired, Koesler paged through the *TV Guide* to ascertain what program they were barely watching. It was "Eight is Enough." He stubbed out a cigarette and swished Scotch-on-the-rocks around in his glass. "Eight is Enough." His mind began to wander. Four priests and four nuns murdered. Yes, eight is enough. Maybe the special police protection would prevent any more murders. Maybe not. The thought of the killings, several of the victims Koesler's close friends, depressed him. The mental battle over whether the Seal of the Confessional applied to the killer's admission and avowal had been fought and refought, always with the same conclusion. Each successive agonizing conflict had racked him.

His eye drifted down the TV listings. He found nothing that interested him until he noted a late-night showing of "The List of Adrian Messenger." Years before, he'd seen the movie. Still earlier, he'd read the book. He could scarcely remember the plot. He did recall the film's special feature had been the cameo appearances of lots of disguised stars. And he remembered George C. Scott's preoccupation with a list of names. That's how he'd solved the murders, wasn't it . . . ?

He sipped the diluted Scotch. Lists. Solved the murders. Certainly the police must have every conceivable kind of list for the Rosary Murders. Everything from manual to computer listings. Their lists hadn't solved the crimes. Could it be possible the police had looked at their lists so long they were not seeing clearly?

Could it be possible they wouldn't know what they were looking for—even if they saw it? Maybe if he tried his luck with some lists . . .

He was about to dismiss this line of thought, when he considered the alternative: sitting here with a partially watched TV program and Joe Farmer's humor.

Not much of a choice.

Careful to take his drink with him, Koesler excused himself and climbed the stairs to his room.

Not willing to rely entirely on memory, he pulled out back issues of the *Detroit Catholic,* where facts and commentary on each murder could be found. Similar information could be found in any other periodical, local or national, but, being the editor, copies of the *Catholic* were right at hand.

Logic led him to begin by listing the names of the victims in the order of their deaths.

Father Lawrence Lord

Sister Ann Vania

Remembering that she had had another religious name, he added, "Paschal."

Father Michael Dailey

Mother Mary Honora

Father Edward Killian

Sister Marie Magdala Connors

Father Harold Steele

Sister Margaret Mary of the Holy Martyrs

He lit a cigarette, exhaled the smoke through his nostrils, sipped his Scotch, and looked at the list, waiting for an inspiration that might be divine intervention.

Nothing came. He tried listing the manner of deaths.

Life-support system disconnected

Drowning

Shot—.38 caliber gun

Stabbed

Shot—.38-caliber gun, hollow-nosed bullet

Shot—.38-caliber gun, hollow-nosed bullet

Shot—.38 caliber gun, hollow-nosed bullet

Shot—.38-caliber gun, hollow-nosed bullet

Nothing.

Obviously, the killer had alternated between priests and nuns. There was no point in making a list that read, priest-nun-priest-nun, etc.

He decided to try listing the institutions where the victims had been killed.

St. Mary's Hospital

St. Ursula's convent

St. Gall's

IHM House

St. Olaf's

St. Camillus Hospital

Bessie Gate's home, St. Enda's parish

Monastery of Mary, Mother of Divine Charity

Two hospitals, two convents, a monastery, three parishes. There might have been some pattern here, but if there were, he couldn't see it.

He considered that freshening his drink might freshen his mind or put him to sleep. Either eventuality seemed desirable.

Back down in the living room, he dropped an ice cube in his glass and added Scotch. Pompilio and Farmer were convulsed over Joe's latest attempt at humor.

"How're things going, Bob?" asked Pompilio, totally unaware of what Koesler was up to.

"Slow," answered Koesler, giving his listings project an undeserved speed.

Back in his room, he sat studying his lists. He tried a geographical inventory.

Central city

Near-east-side

Far northwest

Central city
Far east-side
Near-east-side
Core city
Northwest
Zilch.

He pushed his chair back from the small desk, closed his eyes and let the data tumble about in his mind.

Suddenly, his eyes opened, slitted for a moment, then closed again. After a few moments, he reopened his eyes, pulled close to the desk, and restudied the lists. He grabbed a pencil and began to underline words, occasionally shaking his head as if his system were not working. He stopped, stared at the total of his efforts, then suddenly returned underlining certain words, decisively.

When he had completed his task, a sense of exhilaration almost overcame him. He looked at his work with a mixture of incredulity and certainty. After another moment's thought, he picked up his copy of *The Catholic Directory and Guide for the Archdiocese of Detroit* and began to page furiously through it.

Wanda Koznicki was knitting, mostly just to keep her hands busy. Her gaze kept darting to her husband seated across from her in their home's compact den. He was not reading the newspaper that lay open on his lap. Brahms' Third Symphony, one of their favorites, was playing on the stereo. Walter Koznicki was lost either in that or in thought.

"What is it, Walt?" She paused in her knitting.

"Oh." He seemed startled. "It's just this case." He didn't have to tell her which case. "If all our assumptions prove to be true, the killer may strike for the final time just two days from now. There are times when I just feel helpless."

"But not hopeless . . . you've done everything you can."

"We've done everything we can, and we've lost four priests and four nuns. What if we lose one or more on Friday? What if we never apprehend the killer?"

"Walt . . ." She put her knitting in its bag. ". . . it's

not like you to be this way. Your record is excellent; you're admired by your peers. But you haven't solved every case you've ever handled. Everyone understands that not every murder is solved."

"This one has been different, though, from the beginning. You know I've felt all along that the killer has been trying to communicate—with me, personally—and I haven't been able to break his code, to understand the clues he's deliberately leaving.

"Or . . . is there really a code . . . or do I just want to believe there is, to make myself believe that there is some message being sent?

"And even if there is, who knows what might be making sense to a deranged mind?—The clue could be something—anything—that would never occur to the ordinary normal person, even . . ." He grimaced. ". . . even to those of us who are not unused to dealing with what some call weirdos.

"When—if—we do catch this guy, the whole thing . . . well, none of it might make any sense to us even then."

It was natural that Wanda would share his feeling of helplessness, as they had shared nearly everything in the course of their long marriage.

"How about that latest composite?" she asked, trying to introduce something positive. "Has that brought in any new leads?"

"More than we can handle all at once. Our people are checking them around the clock. But, so far, our investigation hasn't produced enough solid leads or evidence for us to be able to take much initiative. We're still on the defensive, still reacting to this guy's moves, rather than attacking him.

"We know he's a male caucasian, about five-feet-nine or -ten . . ." He was reciting the clues for the umpteenth time just to give himself a feeling of something's having been accomplished. "Probably in his late thirties or early forties. We have a fairly good idea of his facial features, but those, of course, can be disguised easily enough. We have good reason to suspect that, for some reason, he has selected days designated for special penance for Catholics to kill a series of priests and nuns. And we know he's been wounded, probably causing a definite limp.

"Not much, considering the length of time we've been on this," he concluded.

"But, Walt, you're going to provide protection for all the priests and nuns on Friday. If you're right about Friday, and I just feel in my bones you are, that should either frighten him off, or you should get him."

"Dear, the easiest thing to do these days is to kill somebody. No one in the world is given better protection than the President of the United States. Not only was Kennedy assassinated, but had someone not involved in security not intervened, Ford would have been shot in San Francisco.

"Our best hope is that the killer doesn't abandon his need to be close enough to his victim to leave the rosary. But, no matter what they say about the vocation shortage, there are so many priests and nuns in Detroit, it's nearly impossible to provide quality security for all of them. We're spread pretty thin. Actually, short of learning the killer's identity, if there were only some way of knowing who his intended victim is, it would strengthen our chances immeasurably."

The phone rang. Wanda answered it.

"It's for you, dear."

He placed the newspaper on the coffee table, crossed the room, and took the phone. "This is Lieutenant Koznicki," he said.

"Sorry to bother you so late in the evening, Lieutenant," the voice said. "This is Father Koesler."

"No bother, Father; I told you you could call me here at any time."

"Lieutenant, I find this hard to believe, myself. And maybe I'm wrong . . . but I don't think so."

"What is it, Father?"

"I think I can tell you who the remaining intended victims of the Rosary Murderer are."

Koznicki's adrenalin began pumping.

"Where are you, Father?"

"In my room, at St. Ursula's."

"Don't move. Stay where you are. We'll be right over."

He hung up and turned to Wanda. "If I were positive what a *deus ex machina* is, I would say I'd just experienced one."

The three men were seated in Koesler's room on the rectory's second floor.

Koesler was as excited as a schoolboy who knows an answer and is about to thrill his teacher with it.

Ned Harris was skeptical that anything helpful to police work could come from a rectory.

Walt Koznicki was hoping against hope that the priest had come up with what he'd claimed to have discovered.

Koesler lit a cigarette. The two detectives silently noted that the priest's hands were trembling. Whatever he'd found clearly had shaken him.

"I think," Koesler began, "I'd better tell you this, not in the chronological order in which it came to me, but in a way that may make more sense."

The two officers nodded tersely. Each was determined not to interrupt but to hear the priest out.

"First," Koesler began, "let's consider the theory, pretty well established, I take it, that the Rosary Murderer has selected days of special penance, at least as far as Catholics are concerned, on which to commit his murders. I think it's fairly generally known that Catholics used to be bound, by Church law, not to eat meat on all Fridays of the year, and also to fast, or eat less than usual, every day but Sundays during Lent."

Koznicki knew these laws well, having grown up with them. Harris was vaguely aware of them.

"After the Second Vatican Council," Koesler resumed what he believed was a necessary ground-preparing catechesis, "only Ash Wednesday and the Fridays of Lent remained as days of special penance for Catholics.

"But we must keep in mind that penance can mean other things besides dietary observance. Penance also refers to the Sacrament of Penance, or, as it's more popularly known, confession. Not only do we have the Sacrament of Penance, but the task that is assigned to the penitent by the priest after confession, usually the recitation of certain prayers, is also called a penance. Now, gentlemen, I ask you, what is the most traditionally common penance ever assigned?"

"Check," said Harris, who had never been to confession, let alone been assigned a penance.

Koznicki thought carefully over his years of going regularly to confession. "I'd say a certain number of Our Fathers and Hail Marys."

"Exactly," said Koesler, triumphantly. "Since the confessor doesn't know who the penitent is, and since all Catholics are presumed to know at least the Our Father —the Lord's Prayer—and the Hail Mary, these prayers have become, by far, the most common form of assigned penance.

"Now . . ." Koesler looked at Koznicki, ". . . would you hazard a guess at how many Our Fathers and Hail Marys make up the average penance?"

Again Koznicki thought of the hundreds of times, since boyhood, he'd knelt after confession and counted off those familiar prayers on his fingers. "I'm no expert," he allowed, "but I'd say five each."

"Precisely." Koesler was nearly beside himself. His reasoning was being ratified. "As one who has not only been reciting penances, but assigning them for most of my life, I can testify that not only are Catholics most familiar with a penance of five Our Fathers and five Hail Marys, but most Catholics would count off the prayers on the fingers of one hand, alternating them . . . one Our Father and one Hail Mary per finger."

Koznicki nodded and smiled at the memory.

"Now," Koesler continued, "I think it safe to assume that if our man has selected days of penance on which to kill priests and nuns, it is also safe to assume that he is not only familiar with this all-too-common prayer penance but that he intends a connection to be inferred."

Silence. The "I knew it!" button clicked in Koznicki's mind. His feelings, his assumptions—his ESP—had been right all along!

After a few moments, Harris whistled softly. "Five Our Fathers and five Hail Marys said alternately. Five priests and five nuns. A priest and a nun and a priest and a nun—"

"That's it!" said Koesler. "Four priests and four nuns so far. That means that on Good Friday, he intends to murder one more priest, then one more nun, and the time and the task he has set for himself will be completed."

"But . . . why?" Harris asked.

"I'm afraid I can't help you there," said Koesler, all too aware of the irony of that statement but fully satisfied that he had been able to reach his conclusions and solve the riddle without using any of the knowledge gained in the confessional.

"Remarkable," commented Koznicki. "But, on the phone, Father, you said you could name the intended next victims."

"That's right," said Koesler. "And this, oddly, is where I began. Once this came to me, what I've already explained simply fell into place.

"Remember," he asked, looking at Koznicki, "how you once told me that the reason this killer was leaving clues was that he was almost as hopeful of being stopped as he was determined to kill? You told me the secret to understanding all these clues was something like breaking a code. Once you break the code, you understand what the message is."

"I remember," Koznicki replied quietly.

"Well," Koesler said, "I think I've broken the code. Would you gentlemen mind coming over here to my desk?"

Koesler was quite certain he had, indeed, broken the code, but he was eager to have his theory verified by these two experts. He turned his chair to the desk. Koznicki stood at his right, Harris at his left.

"Now," Koesler said, "please note that I have written the full names of the eight victims in the order in which they were killed."

The list was more than familiar to the two officers.

"Now, note the names I have underlined," Koesler directed.

The two silently read: "Lord-Vania-Dailey-Honora-Killian-Magdala-Steele-Martyrs."

There was a prolonged silence. Obviously, the names did nothing for them.

"I couldn't find any connection between these names, myself," said Koesler, "until I sat here this evening, looking at them over and over again. Then, reciting them repeatedly, a connection began to form among just a few of them. There was a familiar ring to those few. Specifically, 'Lord, Honora, Killian and Steele.' They reminded me of words from . . ." He paused. ". . . the Ten Commandments."

"The Ten Commandments!" said an astonished Harris. Koznicki, an odd look on his face, kept silent.

"Yes," Koesler continued. "Bear with me. Take the first name, Lord, and the first commandment: 'I am the *Lord,* thy God; thou shalt not have strange Gods before me.' Now, the fourth name, Honora, and the fourth commandment: *'Honor* thy Father and thy Mother.' The fifth name, Killian, and the fifth commandment: 'Thou shalt not *kill.'* The seventh name—" The intensity in his voice was evident as the tempo of his speech accelerated, "Steele, and the seventh commandment: 'Thou shalt not *steal.'* "

"Damn!" Harris said fervently. Then, "Oh, excuse me, Father. But . . ." The excitement in his voice overrode the pro forma apology. "What about the others?"

"They don't fit as perfectly as the four I've just mentioned. But IF the killer's code is the Ten Commandments, and IF he has isolated just Detroit priests and nuns whose names suggest commandments, the others fit admirably.

"Let's take them one by one. The second name, *Vania,* the second commandment: 'Thou shalt not take the name of the Lord, thy God, in vain.' The third name, Dailey, the third commandment: 'Remember, keep Holy the Sabbath *day.'* The sixth name, Magdala, the sixth commandment: 'Thou shalt not commit *adultery.'* Here, I think he met his greatest challenge: no one is named 'adultery,' but Mary Magdalene was known as the adulteress.

"Finally, the eighth name, Martyrs, the eighth commandment: 'Thou shalt not bear false *witness.'* Again a problem. But nicely handled, because 'martyr,' in Greek and as used in the Church means *witness*."

Koesler leaned back. He was suddenly close to exhaustion.

There was an extended silence. The other two resumed their chairs.

"I don't know what to say," Koznicki finally said, "but I do believe you have it, Father."

Harris wore a puzzled look. "There's something wrong here," he said, finally, "and I don't know quite what it is. But, adultery—a subject I've always found interesting—isn't that the seventh, not the sixth commandment?"

"Ah," Koesler answered, "a point well taken. For reasons not germane to this issue, there is a different numerology for Protestants and Catholics. But, trust me, Catholics understand adultery as the sixth.

"No, the numerology the killer has used is Catholic, as is his understanding of penance and his predilection for priests and nuns."

"All right, then, the final clue, the rosary?" asked Harris.

"I hadn't thought about that until now," Koesler replied. "But now that I do think about it, it fits perfectly. Again, at least in the recent past, assuming that most Catholics not only knew the rosary, but usually carried one, priests regularly assigned the saying of the rosary as a penance after confession. Especially . . ." He glanced at Harris, ". . . to mortal sinners like adulterers.

"It's also, now that I think of that, a symbol of death, since most Catholics have a rosary intertwined in their fingers when their bodies lie in state after death."

"And," picked up Koznicki, "it was handy as the one visible clue that linked the series of murders together." He turned back to Koesler, "But, Father, the next victim?"

"Yes," Koesler said, almost tiredly. "After figuring all this out, I consulted our archdiocesan directory, knowing at least what I was looking for.

"The ninth commandment: 'Thou shalt not covet thy *neighbor*'s wife.' The ninth victim: Father Ted Neighbors.

"Ted is a classmate of mine. He's pastor of St. William of Thierry, the next parish over.

"For the tenth victim, we have considerably more of a problem. The tenth commandment, Catholic version," he said, inclining his head in Harris' direction, "is, 'Thou shalt not covet thy neighbor's *goods*.'

"Before calling you, Lieutenant, I called the vicar for religious. The key word, I believe is 'goods,' and there are many variations of the word among Detroit nuns. For instance, there are several Sister Bonaventures—the 'Bona,' of course, being Latin for 'good.' However, the vicar had one even more likely listing—a Sister Roberta Goode."

"All right," Koznicki said, "we can check into that. But if we can stop the killer before he reaches this Father Neighbors, we've got him. Would you call this Father Neighbors right now . . . don't tell him what it's about, but ask him to see us first thing tomorrow morning? No use depriving him of sleep tonight."

Koznicki stood up.

"I don't know how to thank you, Father. We needed a miracle, and you've handed it to me."

"That's all right," Koesler said. "I told you the killer was picking on people who prayed a lot."

Ted Neighbors would sleep well that night. Bob Koesler would not. His euphoric high had drained him, but the overexhaustion it left in its wake was not conducive to sleep.

Especially when, like the moans of Marley's ghost, the sobs of an obsessed killer gave his confessor no peace.

THURSDAY, APRIL 7

Father Robert Koesler gazed abstractedly through the car window as Lieutenant Walter Koznicki drove the few blocks of Gratiot that separated St. Ursula's from St. William of Thierry parish. The familiar sights of Mt. Olivet cemetery, the Detroit City Airport, and Connor Street Police Station flicked by as Koesler tried to think of a gentle way of breaking the news to Ted Neighbors.

In the past, Koesler had had to break the news of their impending death to a variety of people. Even though each was terminally ill, it was never easy to be the bearer of that news. And now, how on earth, he wondered, do you tell a healthy man in the prime of his life, and a friend, at that, that he might be killed the following day?

He had not resolved the question when they U-turned the island on Outer Drive and parked in front of St. William's rectory.

As he and Koznicki began the long walk toward the rectory, the lieutenant said, "Father, do you see that man sitting in the car that's parked just ahead of mine . . . and the one parked on the side street?"

Koesler turned and noted both cars. "Yes."

"Police. There's another at the rear of the rectory. They've been here since shortly after we spoke with you last night."

Koesler shook his head. "You don't take any chances, do you?"

"Not when we're this close." Koznicki rang the doorbell. "At this moment, Sergeant Harris and Lieutenant Washington are with your vicar for religious, checking the list of Detroit nuns whose names have any relationship to the word 'good.' "

At that, the door opened. Father Ted Neighbors was dressed in a red-and-white sport shirt, black trousers, and red-and-white tennis shoes. "Bob," he said, extending his hand to Koesler, "good to see you, but what brings you here at this hour?"

"Hi, Ted." Koesler took Neighbors' hand and nodded toward his companion. "I'd like you to meet Lieutenant Koznicki. He's with the Detroit Police Department."

"Hello, Lieutenant." Neighbors searched his mind vainly for a memory of some crime he'd committed and forgotten.

"Pleased to meet you, Father. Is there somewhere we can talk privately?"

As Neighbors led them into his office at the corner of the building, Koznicki made a snap appraisal of the priest. Bald on top, with a fringe of gray set off by muttonchop sideburns; strong rectangular face with aquiline nose and firm chin; bifocals with gold metal frames; about five-feet-eight or -nine, medium build; loose-fitting trousers made him look as if he'd recently lost weight.

"Cigar?" Neighbors shoved a box of Van Dams in the direction of his guests. Both demurred; Koesler lit a cigarette.

"Well, gentlemen," Neighbors continued, as he unwrapped and prepared to light a cigar, "what can I do for you?"

"Father," said Koznicki, "we have reason to believe you are the next intended victim of the Rosary Murderer."

That, thought Koesler, was one way of doing it. Then, noting that Neighbors' motion had been frozen with the flame of a burning match nearing his fingers, Koesler further reflected, it's also one way of getting somebody's attention.

The match burned Neighbors' finger. He shook it out. Otherwise he didn't move. Finally, he lowered the hand holding the match but continued to sit bolt upright, the unlit cigar still in his mouth. The thought occurred to Koesler that Neighbors might suffer a cardiac arrest and not to be around tomorrow to be an intended victim.

"It's only natural that you find this news shocking, Father." Koznicki's tone was solicitous. "But, look at it this way. You would have been next on the killer's list whether or not you or we knew about it. This way, as you'll see, is much better."

"But . . . why me? How can you be sure it's me?"

Good Lord, thought Koesler. He's going through a denial phase just like the terminally ill. It must be an element of dying whether you're dying or not.

"Our means of knowing this are a little too complicated to explain, Father. Suffice it to say we know.

"Now, I must ask for your cooperation. There is no way we can keep you here. If you wish to leave the parish, the city, for all of tomorrow, the killer may miss his opportunity.

"On the other hand, if you stay, and if you cooperate with us, I believe you'll be perfectly safe, and we stand a very good chance of apprehending the killer."

Neighbors felt like running. With every fiber of his being, he felt like running. But he couldn't, and he knew it. His usual ebullient spirits were dampened.

He exhaled and looked at Koznicki. "What do you want me to do?"

"Actually, Father, you need not do anything differently than you would have if we hadn't come to see you this morning.

"A police officer visited you yesterday, didn't he?"

"Yes . . . I don't remember his name."

"Paul Mahoney. But that's unimportant. What is important is that you follow the precautions he advised. Your actions need not change. Ours will. For instance, I'm sure you are unaware that there are three of our men in unmarked cars who have been watching this rectory since last night. Although the shift has changed, there are three on duty right now."

Startled, Neighbors stood and peered out the window at Outer Drive. He then turned to look out the side window at Gunston. In each instance, he noted a parked car, each with a man in the driver's seat. He assumed there would be another such vehicle in back of the rectory on Rosemary.

Koznicki waited until the priest had satisfied himself that all was as stated.

"Now, Father, there will be quite a few police officers throughout the rectory and the church today. We want to secure the premises and facilities. In all cases, our people will identify themselves to you. Check their identification, then cooperate with them fully. Our people will also be inside and outside the rectory tonight.

"Tomorrow, Father, there will be many more police personnel with you through the day. None of them will be in uniform. For instance, when you hear confessions, from twelve to two, isn't it?" Neighbors nodded, wordlessly. "About every third or fourth penitent will be a police officer. We'll use both men and women. They will each enter the box, identify themselves, say nothing more, remain in the confessional from one to three minutes, then leave.

"So, you see, Father, you need do nothing different from what you and Officer Mahoney have already discussed. You will quite literally be surrounded by police. And you will be quite safe."

Some of the color had returned to Neighbors' face. But he was not feeling quite as carefree as he had been before his visitors had arrived.

"One final thing." Koznicki turned to Koesler. "You occasionally visit with Father Neighbors, don't you, Father?"

"Yes, sure . . . we're classmates."

"Well, we'd like you to do just that tomorrow after services at St. Ursula's, and we'd like you to stay through the evening. That is, if we haven't apprehended the killer by that time. Will that be satisfactory with both of you?"

The two priests grinned at each other—Neighbors nervously, Koesler reassuringly—and nodded.

Koznicki stood, as did the two priests. They exchanged farewells. At the door, Koznicki turned to Neighbors. "Most important, Father: not a word of this to anyone. It's essential that this be kept secret." Neighbors nodded numbly.

Outside the rectory, Koznicki said, "Would you like me to drop you off at the rectory or at the paper?"

"The rectory will be fine." After a pause, Koesler added, "But, why me? Why do you want me to be with Ted tomorrow?"

"Because you have a cool head. And because, after the Good Friday afternoon services, Father Neighbors would, under ordinary circumstances, be alone. In effect, it will be easier guarding two priests than one, since the killer must isolate his victim, and he would not be counting on your presence here.

"And, finally . . ." Koznicki smiled as he turned to the priest, ". . . because this whole thing is your idea. You do want to see it through to the end, don't you?"

"Indeed I do," said Koesler, who was thinking, somebody ought to write a book about this.

"It's not that I mind an all-night session like last night, Walt . . ." Sergeant Harris sank back in the chair, his hands cradling a plastic cup of hot coffee, ". . . but eventually, that sort of thing is going to affect my social life. I mean, I'm not asking for a vacation, just some sleep."

"Saturday."

"Saturday, what?"

"Saturday night you can sleep."

"That'll surprise her."

"Who?"

"My wife."

Koznicki stopped writing and looked across his desk at Harris. "What will surprise your wife?"

"That on a Saturday night, we sleep."

Koznicki shrugged and returned to writing. "How's the latest briefing going?"

"Washington's doing it now." Harris sipped his coffee. "You sure you want to maintain protection for all the priests and nuns? After all, aren't we pretty sure the target is this Father Neighbors . . . and, after him, one of the nuns?"

"Murphy's Law. Besides, what happens if some other maniac decides to get in on the action? No, with the exception of pulling the majority of our special team into the St. William's operation, and stationing the remainder with the five nuns, we go with the original plan."

"How about the guys from TSD?"

"Schommer and Brainard?" Koznicki smiled briefly. "You don't much care for them, do you?"

"They're trigger happy."

"So is the killer. If he makes his move, he'll have to do it suddenly. In such a situation, there's nobody I'd rather have on my side than somebody who's conditioned to act on split-second impulse."

Harris stood and began pacing. Koznicki continued to jot notes to various members of his task force.

After a few minutes, Koznicki looked up. "What are the names of those five nuns, again?"

"Three Bonaventures, one Agnes Goodfriend, and one Roberta Goode. But he's gonna have to get through Neighbors before he can go after any of the nuns . . . isn't he?"

"Unless he changes his mind, or his M.O. Which I don't anticipate his doing. But it never hurts to be prepared."

"Walt . . . have you considered the possibility that we might scare him off?" Harris crushed the empty plastic cup and banked it off the wall into the wastebasket. "I mean, what if he catches on? What if he figures out that the church is practically wall-to-wall police? What if he figures there's no way he can waste Neighbors and still live to get the last nun? Isn't it possible he might back off from a no-win situation like that?"

Koznicki let his pen fall across the note he was writing. "That's a distinct possibility. And we must remember that Father Neighbors and whatever nun our man has selected are no more important to him than tomorrow's date is. He has no reason to kill Neighbors and the nun except that their names fit his plan. And he has no reason to kill them tomorrow except that tomorrow's date fits into his plan. Thus, if he cannot kill them tomorrow, he will probably have no reason to kill them at all.

"Our position is to make it most difficult for him to attempt any action and impossible for him to do so without being apprehended, dead or alive. Actually, since there is one more potential victim to follow Father Neighbors, the longer Neighbors lives tomorrow, the less chance there is that he'll be attacked."

"You know, Walt, it just blows my mind that it was Koesler who figured all this out."

Koznicki smiled. "Shows you what your friendly parish priest can do—if he has an inquisitive mind and reads murder mysteries."

The two became lost in thought. After several minutes, Harris stopped pacing and faced Koznicki.

"Walt, have you given any thought to what happens if we do scare this guy off?"

"Of course. The Polish mind never rests.

"We go back to the drawing board and continue our routine investigation at the point at which it was interrupted. We have to solve the murders of eight people. But we could feel fortunate not to be investigating the deaths of ten."

If this task force's investigation were to be picked up at the point at which it had now been interrupted, the first name on one list was that of Robert Jamison.

Nelson Kane had not been as involved in or excited by a story since the '67 riots. Regularly, throughout the course of the Rosary Murders, the *Free Press* had been in the lead not only in the print media, but frequently had even beaten radio and TV. Lately, the *Free Press* was being quoted in *Time, Newsweek,* and other national journals. The copyrighting of many of the exclusive stories had forced even the *News* to attribute some of the information it carried to the *Free Press*. Kane sensed another Pulitzer in the offing.

Tomorrow would be D-Day and the '67 riots rolled into one. It had come down to one determined killer, whose luck had begun to run low, against just about every law enforcement agency in the Detroit area.

But what it really boiled down to was the killer against Koznicki's special task force.

For the past week, the *Free Press,* in almost every story on the murders, had been emphasizing the facet of the story that linked the murders with the Lenten days of special penance. That outstanding breakthrough was the *Free Press'* personal baby. It had been since the moment Joe Cox had come up with the theory.

The story had one more day to run. And nobody would've known that tomorrow was the final day, if it weren't for the *Free Press* and Joe Cox. Both the paper and the reporter had become internationally famous. The publicity did more for the paper even than being occasionally mentioned by Mary Tyler Moore's Lou Grant.

One more day to go. Kane was determined that his

paper was going to wrap up this story the way it had begun—well ahead of the competition.

Kane had just finished handing out assignments to his staff, most of whom would be hitting the bricks tomorrow in predetermined areas of the city. Cox, the one reporter who was certain to be included in this final day's operation, had received no specific assignment. Cox, himself, thought that odd. But Kane had come to respect Cox's instincts. Some reporters had the ability to be in the right place at the right time; to sense which, of a number of leads, was the most promising. Cox had that faculty, and Kane recognized that fact.

Kane noticed that Cox had just completed a phone conversation. "Cox—" he called out just loudly enough to be heard over the city room's hum.

The reporter crossed to Kane's desk and seated himself in the adjacent chair.

"Joe, you got any ideas about tomorrow?"

"You mean I get to call this shot for myself?"

"Within reason."

"Well, as a matter of fact, I do," Cox said, pulling his chair closer. "If you don't mind, I'd like to play free safety."

"Now what the hell does that mean?"

"I mean I'd like to play follow the leader."

"Goddamit, you know I hate it when people get cute! Now, what?"

"Well, I figure Koznicki is not going to ride a desk tomorrow while everything is going down. He'll be out, and he'll be where he feels the action is going to be. I don't think a weathervane could give me better directions than the head of the special task force."

"Swell idea, kid, but I'm afraid it's not unique. Don't you think somebody else might have the same game plan?"

"Probably. But how are they going to find the good lieutenant?"

"How are *you* gonna find him if he's so elusive?"

"Thereby hangs a tale, Nellie. Ever since we cooperated with the police by giving them the penance lead before we printed it, thus saving them plenty of face, there's been a subtle air of cooperation shown by at least the task force's upper echelons to *this reporter,* as some of my older colleagues prefer to express the first person."

Sensing Kane's skepticism, Cox persisted. "No, I mean it, Nellie. You know how the cops like to hold back more info than they need to. I got that treatment before we gave them the break. But since then, they've had a better attitude—at least as far as I personally am concerned. Now when I ask a question, as long as it's reasonable I get an answer.

"I think Koznicki is just a fair guy. I helped them. Koznicki, I think, sees to it they help me. They know I'm going to write what I feel needs writing. I know they're not going to let me in on anything that hinders their investigation. I trusted them not to break the penance angle before we could publish it, even to make themselves look better. I think they feel they can trust me, at least within limits.

"I think I can find Koznicki tomorrow. And I don't think anybody else can. And—one more thing, Nellie. To pull this off, I gotta go it alone."

"O.K. But keep in touch. In case something breaks, I wanta be able to move a photographer in."

As Cox headed back to his desk, Kane began a mental rundown of all the details of his preparation for tomorrow's coverage. He wanted to make certain there would be no loose ends. And, he thought, as an aid to Cox's concentration, I'll just ship Lennon off to the Soo—to do a piece on the Upper Peninsula's preparation for the tourist season.

Stan Mathis paced within the narrow confines of his paneled office in the Detroit suburb of Royal Oak. Clearly, he was very perturbed.

He sat down at his desk and, as he had many times during the week, took a newspaper clipping from his drawer and studied it.

It was the artist's composite of the Rosary Murderer.

Why did the likeness remind him so much of Bob Jamison? Could it be because Jamison was so often on his mind these days?

Mathis had carried Jamison about as far as he dared. After all, Mathis was only a district sales manager. There were plenty of superiors he had to answer to. If it had been anyone but Jamison, Mathis would have dismissed him long ago. But there was understanding, and there was pity. Before Jamison's daughter committed suicide and his wife left him, he had consistently been one of the top salespeople in the entire company.

But since those tragic events, Jamison's sales had gone slowly but steadily downhill. He hadn't been into the office at all in the past week. Called in with the flu.

Mathis looked again at the creased clipping. It was by no means identical. Some of the features certainly suggested Jamison. And the letters "R-O-B" left in the dead nun's bloody writing could have stood for "Robert."

He wondered again if he should call the police, as the caption beneath the picture asked citizens to do if they thought they could identify the man.

But, hell. He reflected on the type of crime this man was accused of. No, it was too preposterous . . . whatever else he might be capable of, Bob Jamison wasn't capable of murder—especially the premeditated murders of unsuspecting and helpless priests and nuns. Why, Jamison was a Catholic—and a damn good one. He'd even been in the seminary for a while in high school.

No. It was ridiculous even to consider Bob Jamison capable of crimes like these. But, Mathis decided, as he wadded the clipping into a small ball, he would have to have it out with Jamison the first of next week.

FRIDAY,
APRIL 8

Father Ted Neighbors opened one eye and quickly closed it. His head felt filled with cobwebs. Understandably, he'd had an unusually difficult time getting to sleep last night. So he had turned to bourbon and water to induce slumber. He regretted that now, but there was nothing he could do about the hangover.

He opened his eye once more and tried to focus on the clock on the nightstand. Nine-thirty. Any other day and this would be a disgrace. He would have missed offering the morning Mass.

But this was Good Friday; nowhere in the world would Mass be offered today. There would be communion liturgies, and most of them would be held somewhere between the hours of noon and three—the time that traditionally commemorated Christ's crucifixion. At St. William's, the communion service was scheduled for two, preceded by two hours for confessions.

Under the best of conditions, Neighbors was not a "morning person." And conditions this morning were among the worst. For many reasons, not the least of which that he might be murdered today, he did not want to get out of bed.

Eventually, a combination of habit, discipline, and boredom with bed led him to throw back the covers and swing his feet determinedly to the floor.

The hangover was not as bad as he had feared. His head was beginning to clear.

He stood and crossed the room to close the window. As he shut it, he glanced down at Gunston. A black car was pulling away from the curb. He waited. In a moment, another car, this one blue, took the black car's place at the curb. No one emerged. He had just witnessed the police surveillance team's change of shift. Security, he reflected, is having a cop around every corner.

That reminded him of something else. He opened the door of his suite and looked into the hallway. There, out of sight of the staircase but within view of his door was a man seated on a straight-back chair. He pleasantly returned the priest's stare. The chair was in the same place it had been when Neighbors had retired, but the man was unknown to him.

"Good morning, Father," the stranger said. "I'm Sergeant Ross. Nothing to worry about."

To his colleagues, Ross would have appeared strange out of uniform.

The priest nodded and withdrew into his bedroom, not wishing to chance speech until he was certain his head was totally clear.

He began preparing to shave. As his brain continued its rejuvenation, random thoughts poured in. If he hadn't been under virtual house arrest, he would've driven to the downtown YMCA, where he was a member. He would have enjoyed a game of racquetball, a swim, and the sauna. This series sprang to mind because he had a habit of shaving, latherless, in the sauna, a sight that mystified other Y members.

But the police had decided that the Y offered too many problems for security, so the trip had been vetoed. A move that was perfectly acceptable to Neighbors, since he had placed himself entirely in their hands—not, however, without the occasional reflection that so, too, had the late Father Steele—a thought that was not conducive to Neighbors' peace of mind.

The cops are going to have their hands full guarding this place, he thought, as he stepped into the shower. It's just too damn big.

The rectory had been built to house five priests, with separate quarters for the housekeeper. In its salad days, it had housed four priests, with one room left over for weekend help. Now, he was alone and lucky to be able to scrounge up weekend help.

Downstairs, the housekeeper, Mrs. Bovey, nervously served his breakfast in the dining room. She had, of course, been informed of today's precautions and the reason for them. She was responding with valor to the threat of violence, but no one could blame her for being edgy.

Breakfast was a single poached egg on toast, and coffee. In addition to all the other problems, this was a day of fast and abstinence. No meat, no solids between meals, and only one ordinary-sized meal and two small snacks. Once a quite common Church penance, now only Ash Wednesday and Good Friday called for this measure of self-denial.

Neighbors noted that Sergeant Ross had seated himself in a far corner of the living room. The policeman seemed uninterested in conversation, so the priest had brought the morning *Free Press* to the table. He wondered why his guardians always seemed to position themselves so they could see him, yet not be immediately seen by others. It was to be their M.O. for the day: in controllable situations, they were to leave enough leeway for an assailant to approach but not enough for him to succeed.

The paper's first section was filled with news stories, features, and editorial columns about the significance of this day, and the threat to the local clergy and religious, and the special measures of surveillance being provided by local law enforcement agencies. Not a word concerning the very special precautions being provided one Father Ted Neighbors. Even so, he thought, just from the general protection being given to all the priests and nuns and the broad news coverage, the guy would have to be a fool to try to get through all this.

All of which, he thought, wryly, came under the heading of whistling in the dark.

Then, as had happened so often since yesterday morning, his thoughts returned to the single most frustrating and engrossing question: why had he, Ted Neighbors, apparently been singled out as the target for today?

Why me, Lord?

Why me, Lord? Sister Roberta Goode thought.

The slim, small, red-haired, blue-eyed nun had many times thought of and prayed for the eight victims of the Rosary Murderer. Peripherally, she had been conscious of the comparative stature of the four sisters who had been killed. A hard-working religious education coordinator, an elderly nun who had won the admiration of the entire city, a dedicated hospital administrator, and a beloved member of the revered Carmelite order.

Sister Roberta regarded herself unworthy to be considered a potential member of that ill-fated group. She was merely a teacher of a first-grade class in Blessed

Trinity School. No one could possibly consider her important enough to kill.

Lieutenant Marjorie Washington, in a plain blue pants suit, perched delicately on a small desk in the rear of the first-grade classroom as she watched Sister Roberta tape cutouts of rabbits and eggs on the front wall above and at the sides of the blackboard. At either end of the corridor outside the classroom, two plainclothesmen silently surveyed the quiet hallways.

"Excuse me, Sister," Lieutenant Washington said, "but I didn't know bunnies and eggs were religious symbols. I'm a little surprised to find them in a Catholic school."

"Oh, they're not specifically religious," the nun replied, in her soft, high-pitched voice. "But they are the symbols the children are most familiar with from the commercial celebration of Easter. So I use them to show the children some of the meanings of life—beginning life and eternal life."

Most first-grade teachers, mused the policewoman, seemed to speak in singsong rhythms and had high-pitched voices. It must come from being with small children constantly.

The thought prompted her to be grateful for her police work. The business world had been an acceptable work field, but police work had always been her preference. She had never once considered teaching, particularly, now that she thought of it, the first grade.

She sensed that Sister Roberta was good at what she did. She also sensed that the nun was very frightened and was barely succeeding at covering her fear.

"How do you feel, Sister?"

The nun did not turn to face the policewoman. "Oh, I'm all right."

"I mean about today?" Washington persisted.

There was a slight hesitation. "I'm scared."

Washington wanted to hug her. She seemed so like a small frightened bird. But the officer maintained the prescribed distance. "You have nothing to be frightened of, Sister." Washington glanced at the gleaming .38 revolver barely visible in her half-opened purse. "We're not going to let anyone hurt you."

"Yes. I know," Sister Roberta Goode whispered meekly, "but why me?"

His face was a mask of pain. He wrapped the Ace bandage around his thigh as tightly as he dared while still allowing for circulation. It was the only way he could minimize the limp.

Outside of retrieving the daily paper and one excursion for food and additional medication, he had not left his house all week. With generous applications of iodine, he had managed to avoid an infection from the bullet wound.

He stood. The pain was nearly unbearable. His regular practice of trying to walk without a limp had caused a constant backache. Nothing propelled him but will power. He managed to walk with only a hint of hesitation to the small desk in the living room. He carefully checked a schedule and made several notations on it after rereading the lead story in the morning paper.

He then spent several minutes writing in a diary.

He returned to the bedroom. This time, he surrendered momentarily to the pain, stumbled, and almost fell. He stood, holding on to the dresser, sweating profusely, and shaking his head in disgust. From a dresser drawer, he took a .38-caliber revolver, a silencer, and a box of hollow-nosed bullets. He sat on the bed and began checking both gun and silencer, making certain they would not fail him.

With characteristic meticulousness, Archbishop Mark Boyle was vesting in the cathedral's rectory. He spoke to no one, and no one spoke to him. It was ten minutes before noon, the hour at which the cathedral services would begin.

As in all else, he asked no more of his clergy and religious than he himself was willing to give. And so, ever since last evening, he had had a plainclothes police bodyguard. Two guards, in fact. Koznicki had reasoned that should the killer be turned aside from his prime target due to the enormous protection given Father Neighbors, in frustration the man just might strike out at the archbishop as chief shepherd of the archdiocese.

Boyle, already clad in red cassock and zucchetto, kissed the optional and unpopular amice, rested it momentarily on the back of his head, then let it fall about his shoulders, and tied it around his waist.

He glanced to his right, where his two guards were vesting as his acolytes. Each had a revolver strapped to his belt. Each would wear a long white alb with side slits, giving ready access to a pocket, a handkerchief or, in this instance, to a pistol.

Boyle shook his head sadly. What was the world coming to? He was about to commemorate the death of Christ, the redemptive death that freed mankind from sin, while the police were trying to prevent the assassination of clergy and religious who were specially dedicated to that act of salvation.

The procession of altar boys, choir, a smattering of clergy, and the archbishop unevenly wound its way from the rectory down some thirty yards of Woodward Avenue and into the cathedral. The acolytes on either side of the archbishop had restless eyes that scanned the crowd, searching for telltale signs that would reveal a killer. In a few instances, their eyes met those of others that reflected measures of hatred or contempt, either because they perceived the archbishop as too liberal or too conservative. But most of the spectators that lined the procession's path or filled the cathedral were friendly enough. Many just wanted to see an archbishop. Archbishops, while not exactly in the category of an endangered species, were generally less accessible than politicians or even movie stars.

Inside the cathedral, several deputies from the Wayne County Sheriff's Department had been stationed at positions where, during the liturgy, the archbishop would come into close contact with members of the congregation.

The procession dispersed as it reached the cathedral's sanctuary. Boyle knelt on the readied gigantic prie-dieu.

He prayed silently for the safety of his priests and nuns, and even for the safety, if apprehended, of the killer.

Father Ted Neighbors had been all but overwhelmed by the number of people waiting for confessions when he entered St. William's church at noon. He knew there were police officers scattered among the genuine penitents, but he didn't believe the police could swell the usual numbers this significantly. Still, confessions had been unusually heavy this Lent. He didn't know why. If there were a connection between the series of murders and the increase in penitents, Father Ted Neighbors' ivory-tower mentality had kept him from seeing it.

After a brief prayer, and a reminder to himself of the routine the police had instructed him to observe, he had entered the confessional and begun a task which, if not for the threat of danger, was generally repetitive and tedious, elements that made the role of confessor a tiring one. Only one of the church's six confessionals had been converted into the new style of open room that held no dividing wall between confessor and penitent. At police insistence, Neighbors was using one of the traditional confessionals.

The church had been opened at eleven. As parishioners had begun to assemble in the pews that would form two lines of waiting penitents, the police mingled with them. Thus, every four or five persons in the line of penitents was a police officer. The parishioners, confessing and pausing to recite their penance and then leaving, made up an everchanging congregation. So, the police were able to reenter the waiting line endlessly. And endlessly, their eyes scanned the crowd.

One of the first of the officers in the waiting line was Detective Sergeant Dan Fallon. Raised a Catholic, it had been many years since he had been to a church service, and even longer since he had been to confession. It seemed to him that he was reliving a dream as he waited in the confessional line. He remembered the years the sisters at his parochial school would march whole classes over to the church for the confession routine.

It was vastly different now. This was no more than police duty.

His reverie was interrupted by the sharp sound of a metallic object falling to the church's tile floor. It had been dropped by a person two removed from him in line. Instantly, his eyes went to the object. It was a small black rosary. As quickly as he recognized the object, his hand went inside his jacket. Just as quickly, he saw that the person who had dropped the rosary was an elderly woman.

Since he was already almost on one knee, he retrieved the rosary and returned it to the woman.

They use them to pray, too, he thought.

Alone in the choir loft, Lieutenant Koznicki sat. Only his head appeared above the railing . . . like a massive "Kilroy was here" poster. He watched for anything out of the ordinary. He waited for something to happen.

Why me? Damn Nelson Kane!

So went Pat Lennon's thoughts as she sped along I-75 toward Sault Sainte Marie. Since receiving today's assignment, Pat had grown increasingly angry. Her first rhetorical question had been, why the Soo? After all, someplace like Bay City was lots closer to Detroit. However, it hadn't taken long for her to admit the problem was not the site but her reluctance to make this long drive. The Soo had two distinct and attractive seasons—one for the snow and ice fanatics and one for water, golf, and tennis nuts. It would be easy to get interviews on the changeover of tourist seaons. Probably make a good feature story.

Her second rhetorical question—why me?—had been resolved in much the same way as the first. Her objection was based on personal inconvenience. She was a good feature writer and a logical choice for this assignment. But it was impossible to complete it in one day. This would be at least a two-day assignment. She had left Detroit this morning when the city was enjoying its first near-perfect spring weather. The farther north she traveled—and she would end this trip at the northern tip of the Lower Peninsula—the more she would revisit the winter wonderland . . . one of Michigan's many mottos.

Finally, she had to admit, she did not enjoy spending a night away from Joe Cox.

Even clear-channel WJR radio began to fade as she reached the Gaylord area. Rather than suffer through the C-W music featured on stations in Michigan's boondocks, she switched off the radio and gave free rein to her mind.

She smiled ruefully as she thought of her relationship with Cox. It seemed typical of her life—going nowhere. The lyrics, "When I'm not near the girl I love, I love the girl I'm near," could have been written for Joe. Alone tonight, he probably would make sure he wasn't. That didn't much bother her; she had understood the relationship as she had entered it: no commitments.

She could have had a relationship that had "career enrichment" written all over it. Karl Lowell, the paper's executive manager, had invited her to his bed shortly after he hired her. She knew the type. Her corporate advancement would be directly correlated to her erotic availability. When she had refused him, she knew she would be offered the short end of many a stick. One of these days, she'd probably leave the *Free Press*—before she wound up on the night desk with cobwebs linking her to a chair.

This line of thought was becoming most depressing. She switched mental gears and thought of Joe. Joe with his mad scheme of following in the footsteps of Lieutenant Koznicki all this day.

This day was to be the pièce de resistance on his path to the Pulitzer. Poor guy. She envisioned him wandering all over the city of Detroit, crying plaintively, "Lieutenant Koznicki, oh, Lieutenant Koznicki . . ."

She laughed aloud.

Joe Cox's head was in constant motion. It was difficult to see much of anything with everyone standing. The crowd in St. William of Thierry's church was large, and Cox was not tall enough to see easily over those standing near him. Occasionally, he would step up on the kneeler to get a better view. This jumping-jack mannerism was extremely annoying to many of those who had come to pray, not gawk. Several of them would have told him so except that they were old-fashioned enough to consider talking in church a sin.

Cox credited his charm with having located Lieutenant Koznicki.

He had called Koznicki's office first thing in the morning, and sweet-talked Koznicki's secretary just long enough to be charming without being a nuisance. At just the right moment, he had popped the offhand question. Where might he find the lieutenant this day should the need arise? He'd caught her off-guard. She'd blurted the name of the parish. Casually, he had thanked her, hung up, and roundly congratulated himself.

What Cox didn't know was that Koznicki had given his secretary a short list of those whom she was permitted to tell of his whereabouts. Included was the name of Joe Cox, the only media person listed.

It was Koznicki's final gesture of gratitude. From here on, the reporter would receive no more favors. Koznicki had debated briefly with himself before listing Cox, but he had decided to do so because of the reporter's cooperation, because he could be trusted, and because his desire for a scoop would ensure his keeping the information to himself.

Cox's roving eyes had found Koznicki almost immediately, standing with the choir in the loft at the rear of the church. Hiding the lieutenant in the choir was like concealing an elephant in a herd of sheep.

Cox was also able to identify many other police officers sprinkled among parishioners. Each and every officer he was able to recognize was a member of the special task force. There was no doubting it. Whatever his reason, it was clear that Koznicki expected some action here.

However, all that was happening at the moment was a dramatic reading of the account of the suffering and death of Christ, from the Gospel according to St. John. Cox had to admit it was being done rather effectively.

Father Ted Neighbors had an abiding interest in the theater. Annually, he had season tickets to the Fisher. And, as the everchanging liturgy allowed, even encouraged, more drama, Neighbors had delighted in staging events such as this reading, wherein several talented parishioners had been selected and trained to deliver the various character parts in the last hours of Christ's mortal life.

Cox was more than willing to await developments. Meanwhile, he determined to absorb all that was taking place as a background for his Pulitzer-Prize finish.

St. Camillus Hospital maintained a chapel, as do most Catholic hospitals. However, on Sundays and other major feasts the hospital nuns usually attended services at St. Thomas à Becket parish church. The hospital and the church occupied the same block, and the nuns wished to identify with their ghetto community as much as possible.

Thus, Sister Bonaventure and her police bodyguards had made their way slowly to St. Thomas' for the Good Friday liturgy. The elderly nun had been deeply affected by the murder of her younger friend, Mother Marie Magdala. She had weighed their respective ages and the value of Magdala to the community, and wondered why, in God's providence, she herself had not been the victim.

There are those who say they do not fear death, but it is said in the same spirit as whistling while passing a graveyard. Not only did Sister Bonaventure not fear death; she was prepared to die. So she found it ironic when the police told her she might, indeed, be a selected target this very day. She correctly perceived her role as decoy and willingly cooperated. She was eager for the police to catch the murderer so this senseless killing would cease. She did not mind, if, in the process, she might be sacrificed.

Communion had been distributed and the sparse congregation was praying silently. On either side of the kneeling Bonaventure were policewomen. Directly behind her was a tall policeman.

Sergeant Joseph Kitch was in the church vestibule, scanning those who came and went during the service. Tall, blond and big-boned, he was dressed in a brown suit with a tan topcoat. He paced the vestibule steadily, glancing at the racks holding religious pamphlets and publications, alternately peering into the church and out the clear glass of the front door onto East Grand Boulevard.

When a child waits a very long time on Christmas Eve to see Santa Claus—so long that he begins to believe that Santa isn't coming—by the time someone dressed as Santa arrives, the child finds the thrill of recognition incredible.

That was as close as Kitch could come to describing what he now felt, as he looked out the church's front door window.

For there, standing at the foot of the front steps, looking to the left, then to the right, as if checking the premises, was the Rosary Murderer—or his twin.

White, male, about five-feet-eight, approximately in his late thirties, with an uncanny resemblance to the composite picture. When his first few steps made it quite evident that he limped, favoring his right leg, Kitch's adrenalin reached near-volcanic pressure.

A number of things happened in rapid, fluid succession. Kitch called on his walkie-talkie for back-up support, intercepted the man before he reached the front door, steered him to the side of the church, spreadeagled him against the wall and was searching him, as two black-and-whites screeched to a halt in front of the church. Four police officers joined Kitch.

"Whatcha got here?" Officer Pete Ward asked. Then, as he caught sight of the man's face and realized the resemblance to the composite, he added, "Whooie!"

"And he limps," said Kitch.

"Got a .38?" asked Ward.

"No—but it could be stashed in the church. He's got a black rosary."

Kitch had identified himself to the obviously nonplussed man, and now asked for identification. Torpidly, the captive removed a driver's license from his wallet. His name was Richard E. Jordan, his address only a couple of blocks from the church.

"Sir," Kitch said, "would you mind telling us why you limp?"

"Just going to church," said Jordan, stolidly.

"Sir," Kitch persisted, "would you tell us why you limp?"

"Good Friday," Jordan explained.

It was either a good act or a highly unlikely coincidence.

Kitch took a different tack. He asked Jordan if he had heard about the series of murders of priests and nuns. Jordan nodded. His eyes darted from one officer to another. Kitch then explained Jordan's resemblance to the composite and that the police believed that the killer would be limping. He told Jordan that if he would accompany them to the precinct house, the matter could be cleared up quickly. He advised him that he didn't have to go to the station, but that if he refused, they would have to place him under surveillance.

Jordan agreed to go. His last words, as, shaking his head, he entered one of the black-and-whites, were,

"And my wife wanted to go out for a beer . . ."

In the choir loft, Koznicki's walkie-talkie crackled. He took it into the storage room at the side of the loft. After a few moments, he resumed his seat near the railing next to Sergeant Harris.

"They had a suspect at St. Thomas'," he whispered.

"Sister Bonaventure's stakeout?" Harris returned the whisper.

Koznicki nodded. "False alarm—but almost a double for the composite. A rosary but no weapon. And he limped on his right leg."

"Bullet wound?"

"Congenitally lame. Right leg shorter than the left. Solid alibis for the crucial times."

Harris winked. "Shows we're on our toes."

"Let's stay that way," said Koznicki, as he leaned forward to look down into the crowded church.

There hadn't been this sort of subdued excitement in the city room since the '67 riots. Nelson Kane was once again directing his staff in a citywide effort to cover a story that might break anywhere. Kane was like a general plotting a campaign and dispatching troops to various sections of the battlefield.

Or like a small boy playing Joe Willie Namath playing quarterback.

Kane had been a major factor in the *Free Press*' winning its big Pulitzer for its coverage of the riots. He had sensed then that they had a Pulitzer-type story, and he sensed it again now.

Sleeves rolled up, tie pulled loose, he stood at his desk. He hung up the phone, and reinserted the ubiquitous unlit, ragged cigar in his mouth. Doug Webster, assistant city editor, approached.

"Marge Greenwood just had some excitement over at St. Thomas', the little church next to that hospital—you know, St. Camillus."

"Yeah? What?" Kane stood, feet apart, fists pressed tightly against either side of his waist. Much the way he imagined George Patton had carried it off.

"They got somebody who won the Rosary Murderer look-alike contest. Dead ringer for the composite. Carrying a rosary. Even limped."

"And?"

"The cops got him to the station house and discovered he's got no bullet wound, he's got an alibi for enough of the killings . . . and he's scared stiff."

"False arrest?"

"Nah." Webster grinned. "The guy consented to go with the cops—went along willingly. Just a dead end."

"Dead end, my ass! It'll make a damn good sidebar. Have Greenwood write it light. Lots of quotes from the guy on how it feels to end up at a police station when all you intended was to go to church."

"Right, Nellie," said a chastened Webster as he hurried back to his desk.

"Where in hell is Cox?" Kane bellowed. "Has Cox called in to anybody here?"

Several heads were raised. Each shook a negative response and returned to work.

"How in hell am I supposed to run a goddam city room when I don't know where in hell anyone is?" rhetorized Kane at no one in particular. "Webster! Is Lennon on that story up at the Soo?"

Webster covered the receiver, interrupting his conversation with Marge Greenwood. "Yeah, she left early this morning."

Thank God for small favors, Kane thought. At least he's not with her. What the hell good is a sidebar without the lead? And I don't even know the whereabouts of the guy I'm counting on for the breaking story. If I ever see that SOB again, I'll tie a line around him so I can reel him in.

"When Cox calls in," Kane announced in his edict-issuing tone, "I wanta know about it!"

There really wasn't much for a priest to do during that part of the Good Friday service called the Adoration of the Cross. Lines formed as everyone came to the altar to reverence a crucifix by kissing it.

At St. William's, a small altar boy held a comparatively large crucifix as he stood between the communion railing's center gates. Father Ted Neighbors stood next to the boy. As each person bent to kiss the rood, Neighbors would note where it had been kissed, and wipe the spot with a small linen cloth. Since the mental exercise of the proceeding was to identify the kissed spot and occasionally turn the cloth when an area became reddened with lipstick, Neighbors' mind was free to wander.

In the choir loft, Lieutenant Koznicki was intensely alert. He had calculated that this part of the ceremony held the greatest possible potential for harm to the priest, particularly with the large, pressing congregation.

Now used solely as part of the Good Friday liturgy, the Adoration of the Cross was an unfamiliar ceremony. People tended to compose their own peculiar approaches to the ritual. Some genuflected before and/or after kissing the cross, others didn't. Some made the sign of the cross, others didn't. Some parents insisted that their children, even small babies, reverence the cross. Many of these children never did understand just what it was their parents had in mind.

In short, there was a good-sized crowd mingling very close to the priest, with a good deal of confusion present.

Not a bad time for the killer to choose to strike. All officers guarding priests today had been especially alerted to this possibility.

Koznicki wished he'd been able to provide officers as acolytes for Neighbors as he had for the archbishop, but it would've been too obvious. While adults regularly served the archbishop, children were nearly always used in parish churches.

While Koznicki riveted his attention on Neighbors and his contiguous, disordered crowd, and the long lines waiting their turn, Neighbors' attention had wandered back to the first Good Friday he had experienced as a priest.

The liturgy had not been called a communion service then. And for good reason. No one but the celebrant took communion. Back then, it was called the Mass of the Presanctified. Neighbors' first Good Friday as a priest had been especially memorable, since it had been in contrast to those careful and reverential services of his seminary days. And also, because, although the ceremony was a once-annual affair, his first parochial experience had made him a victim of habit.

He had been assigned to a large, then-wealthy Detroit parish as one of three assistants to an elderly pastor. Sunday Masses were every hour on the hour. The prime responsibility had been to get one crowd out so the next could enter. Without thinking, the three assistants had applied the same philosophy to Good Friday as applied to all Sundays. Starting at noon, by racing pell-mell through complicated ceremonies, they were able to complete the entire Mass of the Presanctified by one o'clock. Breathlessly, he and his two fellow priests had tried to determine what to do next. They had a passive crowd on their hands for another two hours and nothing to fill the time. That two hours had been punctuated by such interchanges as:

"Have we tried the rosary?"

"Three times."

"How long has it been since we did the stations of the cross?"

"Forty-five minutes."

"Let's do them again."

"I just found Fulton Sheen's sermon on the 'Seven Last Words'."

"Good! Go read it."

At this point in the priest's reminiscence, the young altar boy did with the crucifix what small boys generally do when asked to hold heavy objects for interminable periods of time. He dropped it. It clattered resoundingly in what some might term a sacrilegious manner to the tile floor. A woman standing nearby did what some women do when presented with the unexpected. She shrieked.

Then several things happened in such split-second succession that they seemed simultaneous. Neighbors bent to retrieve the crucifix, thus disappearing from view. Koznicki stood and almost vaulted over the choir-loft railing. Police throughout the church converged on the sanctuary. Ross, who had been seated in the first pew on the center aisle, launched himself in a straight trajectory into the scene of action, knocking several people, including Neighbors, to the floor. Cox scrambled from his pew near the center of the church and scurried through the waiting lines toward the arena.

General commotion reigned.

Neighbors, holding the crucifix, but now flat on his back, looked uncomprehendingly at the others in a similar position. A small gentleman, who vaguely resembled a Sicilian Truman Capote, and who had been felled by Ross, looked at the sergeant and said, "Why you get so 'cited? He only drop cross!" Ross, embarrassed, rose, dusted himself off, apologized abjectly, and resumed his seat.

Cox, once he realized that nothing criminal was transpiring, returned to his pew. The young man he had jostled in his bolt toward the to-do, grumbled, "Hey, buddy, next time wait your turn! O.K.?" Cox nodded and began climbing over bodies on the way to his seat. He chanced a glance into the choir loft. Koznicki's eyes met his. Koznicki's face was expressionless. Cox had an urge to smile or wave, but the memory of the deceitful way he had tricked Koznicki's secretary kept him noncommittal.

If Koznicki had known what Cox thought he had perpetrated by dint of immense charm, it would have given him much-needed comic relief.

"Wasn't that a gas?" Brainard observed.

"What?" returned his partner.

"When Ross took that shallow dive in church and flattened all those people."

The two Tactical Services Department officers had been given a break to get some food. They picked up a couple of burgers and some coffee and were parked across from the Detroit City Airport at the side of De La Salle High School.

"He did what he had to," said Schommer.

"I wonder what the people thought." Brainard bit into his burger and frowned. He figured fast food was almost as deadly, in the long run, as the AR-15s the TSD issued.

"They probably thought this was the latest change in church liturgy."

Brainard laughed. "That's funny . . . so, every Good Friday, somebody is supposed to dive through the worshippers and knock people down!" He laughed again. "I keep forgetting you're still a churchgoing Catholic."

"Every goddam Sunday." Schommer removed the cover from his plastic coffee cup; steam poured out the open window.

"Anything personal in this detail for you, Tom? I mean, working on a case where somebody's wasting priests and nuns?"

Schommer shrugged. "No, not particularly. Just part of the job."

"Part of a damn dull job," Brainard corrected. "I can't wait to get back to TSD. How about you?"

"Yeah. But I haven't kidded myself since we got assigned to this task force. We weren't selected for our investigative ability or our love for routine work. No . . . we're the bottom line for this bunch. If it comes down to a shoot-out, they're not gonna have time to call for help. We're it. Koznicki's smart enough to know that some of his regulars might spend one too many seconds thinking before firing a fatal shot. He knows we won't."

Brainard disposed of his empty coffee container and

checked his .45 magnum. It was a much more powerful weapon than the standard police revolver. But, then, so was all the equipment used by the TSD. "Damn," he said, as he started the car, "and all this time I thought they loved us for our minds."

Bob Koesler had arrived at St. William's shortly after three. There being no further services scheduled, he had kept Ted Neighbors company through the late afternoon hours. The two were now enjoying preprandials. Koesler's was a dry martini; Neighbors', a tall, graceful glass of white Burgundy.

Koesler had long thought Ted Neighbors one of the oddest mixtures he'd ever known. Neighbors seemed, if not a man for all seasons, a person of two worlds.

He had accepted an assignment to a parish which, if not in the core city, was in a changing neighborhood. While St. William's was not what it had once been, it still was very much middle- to upper-middle-class. One day, the neighborhood would inevitably be poor. And Ted Neighbors probably would not be there then.

In nothing was the Neighbors philosophy of life more clear than in his dining habits. After receiving his appointment to St. William's and after surveying the scene of his new pastorate, his first comment had been a disgusted, "Plastic dishes!" An effrontery to his proprieties that had been quickly remedied.

Neighbors believed that gourmet dining could be as inexpensive as ordinary eating. All it took was a little extra care.

Mrs. Bovey, the housekeeper, had been a meat-and-potatoes cook until Neighbors had patiently guided her through the gourmet world.

The journey from bonne femme to cordon bleu had not been uneventful. At one point, he had recommended garlic for salad, and thence had endured biting into whole cloves of the stuff. At another point, he had suggested that a little meat would enliven the tossed salad; next time around, he had encountered huge chunks of liver sausage. These and other incidents had been learning experiences for both teacher and pupil.

Dinner tonight was typical of the Neighbors life style. Meatless it was, penitential it wasn't.

It was blue trout. Or, as Neighbors had pridefully explained, *Truite au Bleu*. It was no more expensive, he insisted, than plain pan-fried trout. It required only slightly more attention—like bringing it home live, splitting and cleaving it with a single blow, and boiling it until its eyeballs popped. It was served with parsley, boiled potatoes, hollandaise sauce, and appreciative noises made by Neighbors.

Dinner conversation was light and breezy, partly because Koesler wanted to relieve the tension, and partly because he'd never been able to take his classmate really seriously.

While they ate in the dining room, Sergeant Ross sat silently in the far corner of the living room. He had refused any food. Time enough to eat later, when off duty. Fasting was small enough a sacrifice for him in favor of vigilance and readiness.

Though the table talk mostly concerned nothing more serious than the latest clerical gossip, Koesler could not suppress concern for the safety of his confrère. Thus, when the phone rang, he jumped slightly, as he had each time anything even vaguely unexpected had happened this afternoon.

Neighbors grinned broadly. "Hey, buddy," he said with a touch of bravado, "I'm the guy he's after, not you."

Koesler returned his grin and made a saluting gesture with his fork.

Mrs. Bovey came into the dining room. "It's for you, Father," she said to Neighbors. "I told him you were eating, but he insisted."

Neighbors looked at the telephone's flashing white light indicating someone was on "hold." He looked at Ross seated near one of the extension phones. Ross nodded. Each of them picked up a receiver simultaneously, a routine they'd been following all day.

"This day you will die . . ." said a sepulchral voice. The message was followed by a few moments of silence, then a click.

Neighbors stood with the dead phone at his ear, his face rapidly losing color.

"What is it, Ted?" Koesler asked, rising from his chair. "What happened?"

Ross had Lieutenant Koznicki on his walkie-talkie, reporting.

"What did the caller say?" Koznicki asked.

Ross consulted his notes and read in a monotone that did no justice to the original dramatic communication.

"It's all right, Fred. Some nut has been making calls to rectories and convents all day, always using those identical words."

Ross approached the rigid Neighbors. "It's all right, Father," he said, in a comforting tone, "some kook's been making that same call to rectories all over the city all day. It was just a coincidence he called you. Nothing to worry about."

Neighbors dropped the receiver and retreated quickly to the toilet where he lost the *Truite au Bleu*.

The black Pymouth stopped at the corner of Gratiot and Rosemary. Sergeant Harris, who had been standing on the corner, slid in the passenger side. Lieutenant Koznicki made a right turn onto Rosemary and drove slowly down the side street.

"Anything?" Harris asked.

"Nothing. Just that incident at St. Thomas'." Koznicki checked the parking lot at the rear of St. William's. It was empty. A further glance showed that his surveillance team was in place. He drove on.

"It's getting late," Harris said. There was no reply. The two continued on the quiet residential street. "Think we scared him off?"

"It's possible. I didn't think we would. I didn't think he'd be deterred even if he discovered our presence. But, the later it gets, the less likely he'll try somthing. What time do you have?" Koznicki turned right at Dickerson.

"Seven-thirty. Three of the murders were committed later in the day than this, but he's got to allow time for a second victim, too . . . or so the theory goes."

Koznicki smiled. "Giving up on the theory already, huh?" He turned right again onto Outer Drive.

"I guess my problem is our source. I mean—a priest who reads murder mysteries? I mean, those credentials are not exactly those of somebody who graduated at the top of his class in law enforcement." Harris rolled up the window. The evening was turning chill.

"I know it's an odd source, but it's a sound theory. And even if we scare this guy off today, we'll get him. I feel it in my bones. We've got enough info to complete our investigation. We just ran out of time for now. If he doesn't act tonight, there's no impetus for him to kill again. He'll have blown his game. To paraphrase Shakespeare—" Harris raised an eyebrow, half-quizzically, half-mockingly. "—his time will be out of joint. And we'll have bought ourselves all the time we need to finish following up our leads."

After a brief silence, Harris said, "Then there's the other big, unanswered question: why? Man, I'd sure like to know why he did it—almost more than who he is."

"We may just learn all the answers if we can take him alive."

They were passing St. William's rectory. At the Gunston side, they could see light coming from the living room. The front offices were dark. A very peaceful scene.

Ted Neighbors had recovered from his earlier fright, though the blue trout was irretrievable. He and Bob Koesler had agreed that TV would not be an adequate distraction from the tension they both felt. So they had decided to solve all the problems of the Church. That pastime was even more popular among priests than the exchange of clerical gossip.

Koesler feared Neighbors was borrowing much of his courage from the wine he had sipped slowly but incessantly since dinner. It was, Neighbors had explained graciously, with just a hint of affable condescension, a Spanish red. Rioja, from the Bodegas Bilbainos winery. Spanish red or white, Koesler would have preferred they both have clear heads, at least during these last few critical hours. He started and stuck with Coke.

Between Koesler's cigarettes and Neighbors' cigars, the living room area had been converted into the proverbial smoke-filled room. Sergeant Ross, seated in the shadows at the far corner of the dining room, did not appreciate the smoke. Not only was it offensive to his lungs, but it created a layer of obscurity to a scene he wanted to see clearly. However, he said nothing. He understood the tension the two priests were under and forgave them their trespasses.

"Bishops and popes just aren't that important anymore," Neighbors said, puffing his cigar into new life. "Change is coming from the trenches."

Continuing change in the Church was a phenomenon not many had anticipated. The Second Vatican Council in the early 'sixties had been meant to effect all the change that would be necessary for several centuries. In reality, no one had been able to close the windows Pope John XXIII had opened.

"I couldn't agree with you less, Teddy. You're going by the theory that the Church is . . ." Koesler made a broad gesture, ". . . the People of God. I consider that Church propaganda at best. It's a matter of visibility."

"Visibility?" Neighbors' eyes were not as clear as they might have been.

"Visibility," insisted Koesler. The pope still makes headlines and network TV whether he's saying something significant at the UN or something silly like, women can't be priests because priests have to look like Jesus. That, in fact, is the point. The pope and most bishops, at least most U.S. bishops, seldom say anything important. Yet, they are forever getting publicity.

"For a mere priest to become important to the media, he's got to go on the record about something wildly unexpected, like—oh, like he's in favor of unrestricted abortion.

"As for the people out in the pews, forget it."

"Your problem, Robert," Neighbors slowly wagged his cigar at Koesler, "is that you think everything happens in newspapers and magazines and on TV and radio. You think if it doesn't happen in the media, it doesn't happen. But I tell you, more things happen that don't appear in the media than this world knows of."

Neighbors checked his wristwatch. It was five minutes before eleven—five minutes later than the last time he'd consulted his timepiece. He rejoiced over each passing minute, since the later it got, the less likely there would be any danger to him.

"Take marriage, for instance," Neighbors continued, as he poured himself more Spanish red. He offered the bottle in the direction of Koesler, who simply shook his head, and raised his glass still half-filled with Coke and ice. "There they are, the experts all over the world, trying to reform canon law. And when they reform it, it'll be out of date. Meanwhile," Neighbors became animated, "we in the trenches are effecting our own reform, using, for instance, the 'pastoral solution' to canonically impossible marriages. If somebody's involved in a second or third or whatever marriage and you wouldn't dare send them through the Church Tribunal process because they couldn't get a declaration of nullity in canon law—if they're satisfied that their present marriage is solid and lasting, we encourage them to begin receiving the sacraments again." Neighbors was downright triumphant.

Koesler lit another cigarette and rubbed his eyes. The smoke was getting a bit thick, even for him. "I know all about the 'pastoral solution.' I was present at the vicars' meeting when Al Thomas argued for canon law and Leo Clark argued for freedom. Clark explained that the 'pastoral' procedure was a moral response to marriage cases that were beyond the scope of present canon law. Thomas said you couldn't do that, because it was against canon law, and Clark said, yes, that's what he'd just said.

"But it gets down to this, Teddy . . ." Koesler glanced at his watch. Eleven-fifteen. Even though they were operating on a theory that was his invention, Koesler was just as happy to see it go down the drain. And the later it got, the more likely was his theory to prove false. "It gets down to this," he repeated, freshening his drink with more Coke, "all that we, in the trenches, if you will, can do with individual people, little by little, could be accomplished worldwide, overnight, if the pope signed the right document.

"Or, look at it this way: What would happen if one Catholic bishop ordained a woman?"

"She'd be a priest, I guess. Sort of a Ms. Father." Neighbors' natural ebullience was returning.

"Exactly," Koesler said. "And you don't think the official Church would have to deal with that?"

Ross' walkie-talkie emitted a crackling sound. He exchanged a few mumbled words with whomever was at the other end, then entered the living room.

"Fathers," he said, "the doorbell will ring in a few moments. It should be a police officer, but we'll observe our routine deployment."

The doorbell rang.

Koesler was glad they'd been warned. An unannounced noise might've given him—and certainly Ted Neighbors —the screaming meemies.

Koesler waited while Neighbors, and Ross, revolver drawn, exited through the door separating the living room from the office area. Just past Neighbors' office, they turned left and came to the front door. Ross peered through the small, round, one-way peephole and identified Sergeant Harris. Ross holstered his revolver, admitted Harris, and the three men joined Koesler in the living room.

"Gentleman," Harris announced, waving smoke away from his eyes, "it's eleven-thirty. It's now geographically impossible for the killer to complete his plan of attacking two victims before midnight. We've pretty much determined that if he could not attack both, he would attack neither.

"Lieutenant Koznicki is aware of the pressure you've been under, Father Neighbors. Obviously, our theory was erroneous; it was all a mistake. We're calling off the surveillance, and we want to apologize for having put you through all this."

Koesler noticed a look of surprise pass briefly across Ross' face. The priest shrugged mentally. It was *his* theory that was going down the drain, and he hoped the baby wasn't being thrown out with the bathwater. Nevertheless, he felt a wave of relief. He was almost grateful his theory had been proven inaccurate, even though he was unable to understand where he'd gone wrong.

Harris continued, speaking directly to Neighbors. "The captain didn't want you to be troubled any longer than absolutely necessary. And he wants me, on behalf of the entire department, to thank you for your cooperation."

He turned to Ross. "Let's go, Fred."

A quiet Sergeant Ross retrieved his topcoat from the hall closet and followed Harris out of the rectory, the door latch clicking behind them.

Neighbors looked at his classmate in disbelief. "This is weird," he said, finally. "It's as if I've been living with a cop all my life. First they tell me I'm gonna be murdered, now they tell me it was all a mistake. My life would've been a helluva lot less complicated if they hadn't told me anything."

For the better part of twenty-four hours, he'd felt like a hunted animal. However, the enormous amount of wine he'd consumed that evening helped Father Neighbors accept unquestioningly the surprising news that all was now well.

He shook his head. "Listen, why don't you stay the night? God knows we've got enough room. Besides, it's time to go off that Coke and had a few belts. This has been almost as bad for you as it has for me".

"I'll drink to that." Koesler finished his Coke in one long draught and set his taste buds for stronger stuff.

"Here—" Neighbors held out a small key on a string. "This opens the wine cellar in the basement. Why don't you go get us something very special, while I get a couple of our Waterford goblets. This deserves a celebration."

With that, they parted to reunite for a party. It was eleven-thirty-five.

A late-model black Chevy had been circling the neighborhood for the past half hour. The driver had noticed an unusual number of occupied cars parked near St. William's rectory. He also noticed pedestrians, at times two men, at times a man and a woman, who seemed to be slowly patrolling the area bordered by Gratiot, Outer Drive, Gunston, and Rosemary. He began to feel frustration and the beginnings of panic.

He rolled down the car window. Although the night air had a tinge of cold, he was sweating profusely. And each time he had to move his right foot from the accelerator to the brake, he winced with pain.

This is like a fortress, he thought. How could he breach their defenses? Evidently, the police had finally solved the puzzle. They couldn't possibly have provided this much protection for very many priests or nuns today. Well, it was a game with fatal consequences upon which he'd embarked when he first made his plans for revenge many months ago.

Apparently, he had lost the game. Yet he was determined to continue playing to the very end. What is it they say? The game's not over until the final out.

So far, he'd been able to carry out his plans under pretty adverse circumstances, particularly last week when the police had seemed extraordinarily prepared for him. His success had indeed bordered on the miraculous, which seemed odd, since he was killing priests and nuns. Perhaps, he thought, God favored his act of revenge even more than the lives of His priests and nuns.

As he turned once again onto Outer Drive from Gratiot, he was able to see his watch by the glow of the streetlight. Eleven-thirty-four. He had all but given up hope.

Then, as he neared the street in front of St. William's rectory, he noticed unexpected activity. He slid his car to the curb several yards past Gunston, and watched through his sideview mirror. He scarcely believed what he saw. It appeared that the police were leaving. The manned cars that had been parked in front and at the side of the rectory pulled away. The suspicious-looking pedestrians were getting into cars and driving away.

His spirits soared. Thank God, he prayed. He had his chance.

He waited several minutes. He could discern no further activity in the vicinity of the rectory. All seemed natural, calm, and as deserted as this hour of the night would call for. Slowly, he eased his car from the curb. He U-turned the nearest island on Outer Driver and headed for the rectory.

He parked in front. All was still. He left his car, pulled the collar of his topcoat up about his neck, shoved his right hand into the deep pocket of his coat, and firmly gripped the cold metal.

He started up the long walk toward the rectory. At first, all was well. Then he tripped on a pebble on the sidewalk and stumbled, limping badly for several steps. He hesitated and looked from side to side. He could see nothing but the shifting shadows cast by the thick bushes along the front of the rectory, shadows that danced in the pale glow of the street light swinging gently in the light breeze.

He gritted his teeth, but it was too late to recover his physical composure. The lonely figure limped on toward the rectory, his shadow distorted by the street light's uneven beam.

Father Neighbors, his mental processes slowed by Spanish red, had fumbled about in the closet at the end of the office hallway. He examined one type of glassware after another until he finally selected the proper pair.

Two lovely Waterford goblets in hand and a benign smile on his face, he retraced his steps toward the living room. He was just passing the front door when the doorbell rang. Instinctively, he took both glasses in his left hand and turned the knob with the other. The door was open before he recalled the routine he'd been going through all day long with Sergeant Ross.

Neighbors experienced a moment of fear that came close to terror. But, then, he remembered that the all-clear had been given and he had nothing to fear.

He didn't recognize the caller. That was strange; he knew most of his parisioners quite well. He felt slightly embarrassed that he was out of cassock and in casual attire.

"May I help you?" he asked, feeling a little vague and wishing he had not imbibed so much wine. "I'm Father Neighbors."

"I'm sorry to trouble you this late at night, Father," said

the man. "But my mother just died. She's one of your parishioners. I saw the light in the rectory and thought I could make funeral arrangements. Save me a trip tomorrow."

"Oh . . . oh, sure . . . of course. Just step into my office, and we can make the arrangements."

Neighbors led the way to his office, bumping against the door as he turned the corner. As he entered the room, he felt a chill. He noticed that the windows were ajar, and guessed he'd opened them earlier when it had been warmer outside. He'd have to remember to check all the windows later.

He sat heavily at his desk, pulled out the long, narrow funeral pad and looked up at his still-standing caller. "Now, what was your mother's—"

That was as much of the question as he completed. Afterward, he remembered two things very clearly. A pair of narrow, determined eyes looking intently at him and the open end of a revolver barrel magnified by a silencer that seemed many times larger than life.

In that instant, two voices barked simultaneously through the open windows. "Drop it!"

The man hesitated a split second that was a split second too long. A massive blast destroyed the night's silence as Schommer and Brainard fired their AR-15s.

The stranger's body slammed against the wall and ricocheted to the floor.

Blood was everywhere.

Bob Koesler had been on the basement steps, bringing up a bottle of Cutty Sark. He dropped the bottle. It smashed against the brick floor. Without thinking, he ran toward the sound of the rifle blast.

From one of the spare rooms on the second floor, Sergeant Dan Fallon emerged and came down the stairs two at a time.

From the kitchen, Sergeant Fred Ross, who had reentered the rectory from the rear, ran toward the office area, revolver drawn.

The three converged at Neighbors' office.

Koesler looked at what remained of the killer. The

priest felt desperately ill. Blood was gushing from a large hole in the man's chest, the left side of his face was missing, and there wasn't much remaining of the right side.

Koesler remembered the tortured voice he had heard in the confessional. He forced himself to kneel at the mangled body. He traced a cross in the air above the still figure, and whispered, "I absolve you from your sins in the name of the Father and of the Son and of the Holy Spirit. Amen." And then he added, "Your penance is five Our Fathers and five Hail Marys . . . I'll say them for you."

He bowed his head, and then rose. In all the confusion, he had forgotten his fellow priest.

Ted Neighbors was not at his desk. Quickly, Koesler circled the desk. Neighbors was under it. He had lost the Spanish red.

SATURDAY,
APRIL 9

Sergeants Fallon, Ross and Harris, and Lieutenants Washington and Koznicki were seated around the desk in Koznicki's office.

The Rosary Murders case was concluded, the special task force dissolved. Its members would return to their regular departments and precincts. None of them had slept. None had felt the need. One thing had led to another with such rapidity that they were consumed with desire to tie up all the loose ends. Sleep was easy to postpone.

"Well, Walt," Harris said, "Your Father Koesler turned out to be a pretty damn good detective."

"Yes," said Washington, "maybe they ought to make murder mysteries required reading in the seminary."

"—or even in the force," Harris interjected.

Koznicki laughed. "Yeah . . . Koesler was right on the

money—except for the killer's plan for the tenth murder. And there was no way Koesler could have known that was planned for tomorrow, Easter Sunday."

"It was lucky for us that guy left a diary and those detailed blueprints for the murders," said Fallon. "He called the last one his 'Resurrection' . . . a real weirdo."

"Yes," Washington agreed, "but the research and planning that went into those killings. My God! He spent months plotting, tracking the routines of those people to hit them at their most vulnerable moments."

"And," Ross addressed Washington, "your nun was, indeed, the intended tenth victim."

"Makes you wonder," Washington said, shaking her head. "I spent a lot of time with Sister Goode. She was like a little frightened sparrow. Just dedicated to helping little kids. Probably never hurt a soul. Makes you wonder how anyone could want to kill her."

"They were all in the same book," said Harris. "None of 'em were likely targets for murder. The only thing each of 'em had in common was a name that fit the killer's game.

"Which reminds me . . ." He turned toward Koznicki. ". . . d'ya think he would've tried for Neighbors last night if you hadn't pulled that reverse around left end?"

Koznicki pondered momentarily. "I don't know . . . I just don't know. we may never know. According to the timetable he left, he had scheduled the Neighbors killing for 11. Obviously, he discovered or strongly suspected our presence and held off. Whether he would've been desperate enough to try it anyway, we'll never know.

"Actually, I intended to maintain our secondary plan until 12:32 and then go to ordinary surveillance."

Ross looked puzzled. "12:32?"

"Yes." The laugh lines at the outer corners of Koznicki's eyes crinkled. "Father Koesler and I talked about that. He said from all he could gather, the killer's theology appeared to be very traditional. And he mentioned something I had forgotten: that in the old days of fairly regular abstinence laws, some Catholics in Michigan used to give themselves an extra thirty-two minutes to eat meat, because midnight 'Sun Time' didn't occur until 12:32."

"I'm getting happier by the day that I'm a Presbyterian," said Harris. "Not so many rules."

They all laughed.

"Makes you wonder about the psychopathic mind, though," said Washington. "Anybody who could be this successful at premeditated murder should've been a successful businessman and too busy to muck about in crime."

"Robert Jamison? He was very successful in his field—insurance," noted Fallon. "We talked with his manager early this morning. Jamison had been a top salesperson until recently. Funny, the guy said he almost called us because that composite reminded him of Jamison."

"By the way," Ross said, with a touch of pride, "did you all know that the next name on Brainard's check list was none other than Robert Jamison?"

"No kidding!" said Fallon. "Well, then your feeling that we were about to break this case either way was right, eh, Lieutenant?"

Koznicki's laugh lines crinkled again. He said nothing. But he was proud that his team's good hard, thorough, investigative work would've led them to the killer regardless.

"What's going to happen to Brainard and Schommer?" asked Washington.

"They're with Internal Affairs. But it should be an open and shut inquiry. Jamison wasn't playing games with that .38." Koznicki looked thoughtful.

"Actually, there are two ways of looking at what they did. The decision on what course of action to take was entirely theirs.

"One might argue that when they saw that limping figure approach the rectory, they should have apprehended him before he could possibly become a threat to Father Neighbors.

"However, one could also argue—and I'm sure they will—that evidence against the guy, at that point, might prove inconclusive. They claim that they had the suspect in view at all times in the doorway and the office—except for a second in the hallway, and they believed if he didn't

strike at the door, he didn't intend to do so in the hall."
He grimaced wryly. "I'm glad they weren't mistaken."

"On the other hand, one could claim that they wanted
the opportunity to strike on their own. Only they know.

"But I'm sure the public's relief that this murder was
stopped will not escape the attention of anyone, including
the guys in Internal Affairs. Schommer and Brainard will
probably return to TSD with commendations. And probably rightly so."

"O.K., dammit," Harris said angrily. "But wasting Jamison made it impossible to discover his motive. None of
the papers—not even his diary—held a clue as to why he
decided to kill those priests and nuns. One corner of this
case is gonna be forever open because we can't find out
from him what his motive was."

Koznicki had completed clearing out his desk. He stood
and looked at the four people with whom he had worked
most closely over the past week. He paused when he
came, finally, to Sergeant Harris.

"Well, Ned," he said, "only in fiction are you assured
of knowing everything by the end of the book. In real life,
we just have to get used to knowing that in some cases
we'll just never know."

The five officers did know that this moment marked the
end of the unique relationship of an elite group. It was
with a sense of regret that they parted and headed finally
for some much needed rest.

Mackinac Island's six square miles boasted no mecha-
nized vehicles. Mackinac's Grand Hotel boasted the
world's longest porch. On this day, it also boasted the
presence of Pat Lennon, with whom Joe Cox had been
on the phone for nearly half an hour.

Cox was almost giddy. He had told Pat of how he had
tricked Koznicki's secretary into telling him where the
lieutenant was going to be, of the humorous-in-retro-
spect incident during Good Friday services at St. William's, of the endless hours of fruitless waiting, and finally,
of the apparent cancellation of the stakeout at eleven-
thirty.

"I was sick—just sick—when I saw the cops pull away. I figured all that time had been wasted. But I had a hunch. Basically, I'd been following Koznicki all day, and I knew where his car was. When he didn't pull out, neither did I. I stayed with him like a shadow. Out of sight, but glued on.

"When the thing came down just before midnight, I was right there. Man! You wouldn't believe that scene! And I was the only newsguy there. Nobody else. I was the only one . . . Pat? Pat? Are you there?"

He'd been engaged in a dramatic monologue for so long, he began to wonder if anyone was listening.

"Yes, I'm here." Pat listened with a mixture of pride in what he'd accomplished, and amusement at his small-boy enthusiasm. So much for the clichéd cool, sophisticated, unflappable reporter.

"The cops who shot the guy," he continued, reassured that someone was listening, "were the two guys from Tactical Services. They used AR-15s with bullets that—you know . . . sort of tumble. God! You should've seen the damage. One shot got him high—practically ripped off his head. The other got him in the chest—ripped almost his entire spine out."

"You can spare me *some* of the details, if you don't mind." Pat was glad she hadn't had breakfast yet.

"I was the only one who got to talk with the TSD guys. And that's because I got to them before Internal Affairs put a muzzle on 'em.

"And the killer's name is Robert Jamison . . . remember the nun who wrote 'R-O-B' with her own blood before she died? That's it: ROB for Robert.

"The cops can't figure a motive yet. The guy's daughter committed suicide a few years back. Then his wife left him. He was doing poorly at work. Depressed. But no one's been able to figure why he did all this . . . why he took it out this way.

"Anyway, I called the story in, and guess what: they put out an extra! No one can even remember when was the last time the Freep put out an extra. Nellie decided we weren't gonna let the *News* get it in print before we did. It was OUR story. And I've got a long feature running in tomorrow's issue, too. Pat, it's a Pulitzer—everybody here just smells it.

"Pat? . . . uh, by the way, how are you doing?"

"Don't worry. I'll bring back a feature on everything you wanted to know about tourism in northern Michigan."

"There's one more thing I wanted to tell you . . ." He hesitated. "I think I'm becoming monogamous, dammit."

"Don't worry, lover; I'll be back before you can say Nelson Kane."

Father Paul Pompilio cut a small slice from his hot dog, tapped it several times in the neat glob of catsup on his plate, placed the morsel in his mouth, laid his fork down, and began masticating.

He and Father Joe Farmer were spreading lunch reading the *Free Press* account of last night's thrilling ending of the Rosary Murders case. Farmer and Father Koesler had finished eating. Farmer smoked a cigar. Koesler was "smoked out" from last night's cigar-cigarette marathon with Ted Neighbors.

"You're very prominently mentioned in this story, Bob," said Pompilio, beginning to saw off another bite of hot dog.

"Yeah," added Farmer, "your picture is even in the paper."

"The next best thing to being canonized," said Koesler. He tried to decide whether his system could stand a cigarette yet.

"It says here," said Pompilio, chewing stoically, "that you were the one who figured the whole thing out."

"Yeah," said Farmer, "I think I'll start reading murder mysteries so I can get my picture in the paper sometime."

"Well, gentlemen . . ." Koesler hazarded a cigarette. ". . . all I can tell you is that the *Detroit Catholic* is going to have just about as interesting an issue Thursday as the *Free Press* put out today."

"The inside story, eh, Bob?" Farmer winked at Koesler.

"Did you notice that the police were unable to come up with a motive for the killings?" Pompilio asked.

"Yeah," Farmer commented, "that's almost as bad as one of your whodunits without an ending."

"Or," said Koesler, *"amplexus reservatus."*

Both Farmer and Pompilio looked up from their papers inquiringly.

"Withdrawal from sexual intercourse without ejaculation," explained Koesler.

Farmer and Pompilio returned to their newspapers, each distracted by the new thought.

Koesler had resolved that it was necessary for him to continue to observe and protect the seal of confession, even now. If he were to make public what he knew, a lot of curiosity would undoubtedly be satisfied. But to what purpose? And prospective penitents, poor sinners of the future, would be uncertain that their sins would be protected from posthumous revelation. It was crucial, he decided, not to jeopardize something so historically sacred. The seal was the seal, dead or alive.

"Say, Pomps . . . Bob . . ." Farmer announced, ". . . I just heard a new one—true story—from Pete Badoglia, who just came back to Grand Rapids from being an air force chaplain."

Good Lord, not another story, Koesler groaned inwardly.

"Seems over in Vietnam, Pete was trying to get this one air force officer to go to confession, and the guy just wouldn't. Finally, it's time for the guy to be sent back to the States. So he comes to Pete and says now he's ready for confession.

"Pete asks him why now—after all, he's gone through all those dangerous missions and wouldn't go to confession, why, now that he's being sent to the safety of home, does he want to go to confession?

"The guy says he'd got it all figured out. He says he's watched the other pilots. The ones who go to confession are shot down in action. Probably, he figures, 'cause they're ready to go. So, he figures that if he's not ready to go, he won't get shot down.

"So, Pete tells him, 'Get outta here. You're . . . you're too dumb to . . .'" Farmer, as usual, was losing total control. "'. . . too dumb to . . . commit a mortal sin!'"

"Too dumb to what, Joe? Too dumb to *what?*" Pomps had lost another punch line.

My God, thought Koesler, a clean joke. What's this world coming to?

SATURDAY
APRIL 16

Monsignor William Danaher had his peculiar opinions about the Rosary Murders, and nothing that had happened or been written in the past week had made him change his mind.

Motive! he grumbled to himself, as he sat in the confessional in his otherwise empty church in an eastern suburb of Detroit. So, no one could guess at the motive, eh?

Well, he knew the motive. It was the scandalous behavior of today's priests and nuns. Priests who get into marches and boycotts instead of being on duty in their parishes, instead of ringing doorbells, bringing in the sheep. Priests who refuse to wear their clerical garb and who won't listen to the pope, who has the overall view of suffering humanity. Priests who play fast and loose and won't pray and lose the faith and leave the priesthood.

And nuns who abandon the classrooms and take jobs that any layperson could do. Nuns who shun their habits, sanctified over centuries. Nuns who can't be distinguished from laywomen. Nuns who wear miniskirts.

Where was the respect that the laity once had for their clergy and religious? That's where it was: the reverence and respect had turned into a series of murders.

Monsignor Danaher had never enjoyed many penitents.

Even in the old days when many Catholics went to Confession monthly—even weekly—there had never been much of a line waiting at Danaher's box. He was, by popular consensus, a demanding confessor who asked embarrassing questions, yelled a lot, and gave out tough penances.

Moderately tall, lean, silver-haired, he appeared to be the essence of the aescetic man of God. He was what was termed a 'one-point kneeler,' a rare breed. When he knelt, only his knees touched. He didn't rest his elbows, nor did he lean back to rest his rear on the edge of the pew.

Now nearing retirement age, Danaher welcomed the thought. These young whippersnappers had built a new Church. Not Catholic . . . more like Protestant. There were no more black and white unequivocal moral laws. Well, they could damn well live with it. He would take his modest savings and pension and retire to the home he had purchased in Sun City. He had carefully planned for that day of retirement. Putting away a little after each Christmas collection, special gifts on the occasion of being transferred from one parish to another, and skimming a bit from his regular salary.

In the beginning, he had never planned a retirement. But, as the Church changed, he longed to get away from this new monstrosity as soon as possible.

It was now nearly 9 P.M. Time to lock up. He opened his breviary. Time to say some of the Divine Office before closing shop.

Someone entered the penitent's side of the confessional. Monsignor Danaher snorted. Wouldn't you know! Wait till the last minute to come to confession! Get everything else—all the *important* things—out of the way, then come and make peace with God.

Danaher turned off the small light in his confessional, closed the door to the unoccupied confessional and waited —but not long. "All right, all right, get on with it!"

Silence.

"We haven't got all night, y'know."

Silence.

"Are you going to begin?"

"I don't know how to begin. This is the hardest confession of my life, Father."

"Very well, but, come along now."

"This has been going on for years. I've been living a lie. Going to confession and not confessing all. I was always so ashamed."

"What is it, man? Get it out!"

"It's . . . with my daughter. I don't know how it began. But I haven't been able to stop, and I haven't been able to tell anybody, an—"

"Incest!" Danaher's was the voice of the condemning angel. "Incest? No one has ever confessed such a heinous sin to me before. It is beneath a Catholic man."

"I know that, Father. Now I can see that I need help."

"How long has this been going on?"

"A . . . a few years, Father."

"God have mercy! How many times a week or month?"

"Maybe three or four times a month, I don't know. But, Father, I need help!"

"Do you have any other sins to confess besides all those bad confessions for all these years?"

"No, I don't think so, but . . ."

"Do you have a rosary?"

"Yes, but . . ."

"Say the rosary once for your penance, and CUT IT OUT!"

Danaher droned into the Latin formula for absolution. The penitent sobbed quietly.

Outside the confessional, the man listlessly ran the beads through his fingers for several minutes. Suddenly, he stood, and shouted, "I need help . . . I don't need the goddam rosary!"

He flung the beads in the direction of the sanctuary, and ran out into the night.

ABOUT THE AUTHOR

WILLIAM X. KIENZLE was born in the Detroit
hospital where one of the rosary murders is committed. A former priest, he was ordained in 1954
and spent twenty years as a parish priest, including
over fourteen as editor-in-chief of the *Michigan
Catholic*. He is presently the director of the Center
for Contemplative Studies at the University of
Dallas. Kienzle has written editorials, articles,
reviews, interviews, columns, etc., which have
been published in the *Michigan Catholic, MPLS*
Magazine, *Ave Maria* Magazine and the *Liguori-
an*. In 1963, he won the Michigan Knights of
Columbus Journalism Award. Kienzle has had
an abiding interest in police work throughout his
adult life. *The Rosary Murders* is his first novel.

WHODUNIT?

Bantam did! By bringing you these masterful tales of murder, suspense and mystery!

☐	10706	**SLEEPING MURDER** by Agatha Christie	$2.25
☐	13774	**THE MYSTERIOUS AFFAIR AT STYLES** by Agatha Christie	$2.25
☐	13777	**THE SECRET ADVERSARY** by Agatha Christie	$2.25
☐	12838	**POIROT INVESTIGATES** by Agatha Christie	$2.25
☐	12458	**PLEASE PASS THE GUILT** by Rex Stout	$1.75
☐	12073	**THE DEADLY PIECE** by Pete Hamill	$2.25
☐	11415	**DIRTY LAUNDRY** by Pete Hamill	$2.25
☐	12408	**LONG TIME NO SEE** by Ed McBain	$1.95
☐	12310	**THE SPY WHO CAME IN FROM THE COLD** by John LeCarre	$2.50
☐	12443	**THE DROWNING POOL** by Ross Macdonald	$1.95
☐	12544	**THE UNDERGROUND MAN** by Ross Macdonald	$1.95
☐	12172	**A JUDGEMENT IN STONE** by Ruth Rendell	$1.95
☐	12114	**IN A LONELY PLACE** by Dorothy Hughes	$1.95

Buy them at your local bookstore or use this handy coupon for ordering:

Bantam Books, Inc., Dept. BD, 414 East Golf Road, Des Plaines, Ill. 60016

Please send me the books I have checked above. I am enclosing $_____ (please add $1.00 to cover postage and handling). Send check or money order —no cash or C.O.D.'s please.

Mr/Mrs/Miss_____

Address_____

City_____ State/Zip_____

BD—2/80

Please allow four to six weeks for delivery. This offer expires 8/80.

THE MYSTERIOUS WORLD OF AGATHA CHRISTIE

Acknowledged as the world's most popular mystery writer of all time, Dame Agatha Christie's books have thrilled millions of readers for generations. With her care and attention to characters, the intriguing situations and the breathtaking final deduction, it's no wonder that Agatha Christie is the world's best selling mystery writer.

☐	10706	SLEEPING MURDER	$2.25
☐	13262	THE SEVEN DIALS MYSTERY	$2.25
☐	13690	A HOLIDAY FOR MURDER	$2.25
☐	12838	POIROT INVESTIGATES	$2.25
☐	13777	THE SECRET ADVERSARY	$2.25
☐	12539	DEATH ON THE NILE	$2.25
☐	13774	THE MYSTERIOUS AFFAIR AT STYLES	$2.25
☐	13775	THE POSTERN OF FATE	$2.25

Buy them at your local bookstore or use this handy coupon:

Bantam Books, Inc., Dept. AC, 414 East Golf Road, Des Plaines, Ill. 60016

Please send me the books I have checked above. I am enclosing $_____ (please add $1.00 to cover postage and handling). Send check or money order —no cash or C.O.D.'s please.

Mr/Mrs/Miss_____

Address_____

City_____State/Zip_____

AC—2/80

Please allow four to six weeks for delivery. This offer expires 8/80.